THE CASSAFORTE CHRONICLES, VOLUME II

The

Buccaneer's

Apprentice

V. Briceland

flux™
Woodbury, Minnesota

First Edition
First Printing, 2010

Book design by Steffani Sawyer
Cover design by Kevin R. Brown
Illustration on cover and on page i by Blake Morrow/Shannon Associates
Map on pages viii–ix by Jared Blando

Flux, an imprint of Llewellyn Publications

Library of Congress Cataloging-in-Publication Data
Briceland, V. (Vance)
  The buccaneer's apprentice / V. Briceland.—1st ed.
    p. cm.—(The Cassaforte chronicles; v. 2)
  Summary: On his first sea voyage, seventeen-year-old Nic Dattore faces vicious pirates then, with a motley crew of castaways, decides to commandeer the pirate ship to return home, racing against time to save the magical city of Cassaforte from a diabolical plot.
  ISBN 978-0-7387-1895-8
  [1. Seafaring life—Fiction. 2. Blessing and cursing—Fiction. 3. Pirates—Fiction. 4. Fantasy.] I. Title.
  PZ7.B75888Buc 2010
  [Fic]—dc22
                              2009030497

Flux
Llewellyn Publications
A Division of Llewellyn Worldwide, Ltd.
2143 Wooddale Drive
Woodbury, Minnesota 55125-2989, U.S.A.
www.fluxnow.com

Printed in the United States of America

Acknowledgments

Writing a novel may be the most isolated of pursuits, but happily I have been surrounded by many people who have lent their expertise and opinions in the shaping of this book. I owe much gratitude to my friend Patty Woodwell, for her helpful reading of an early draft. My editor Brian Farrey offered many helpful suggestions for which I'm also thankful. I also must thank Craig Scott Symons for his unflagging support.

As a young man, my father was fond of C. S. Forester's series of seafaring novels following the career of the young, seasick midshipman Horatio Hornblower. With his appreciation for a nautical tale of derring-do in mind, it is to him that I dedicate *The Buccaneer's Apprentice*.

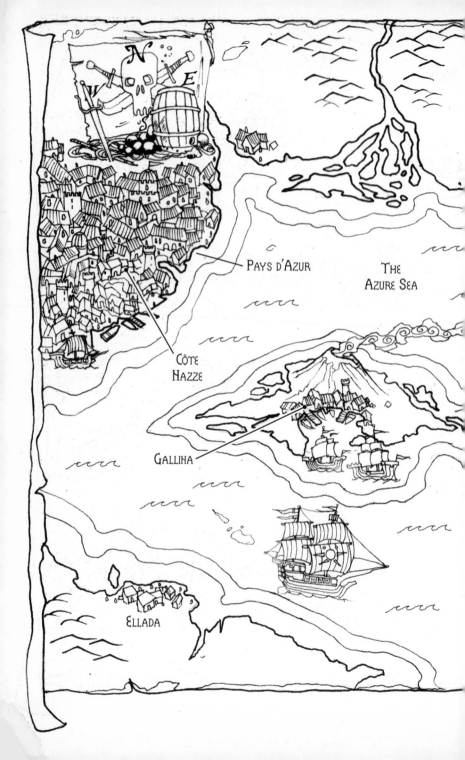

PAYS D'AZUR

THE
AZURE SEA

CÔTE
HAZZE

GALLINA

ELLADA

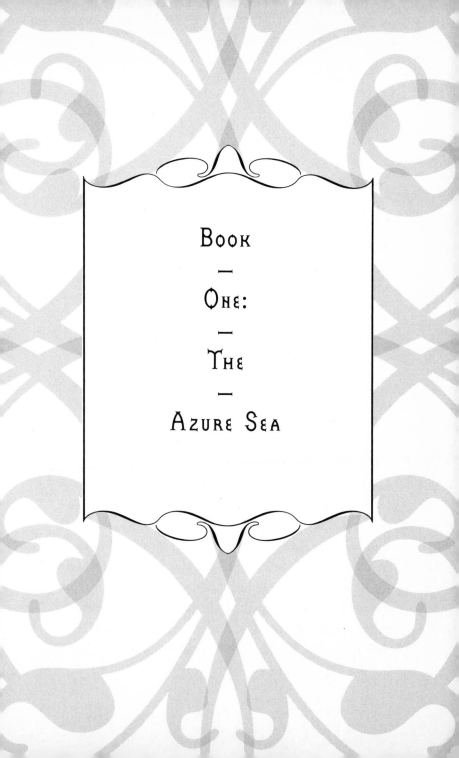

Book
—
One:
—
The
—
Azure Sea

1

Old sailors tell tales of a passage in the Azure Sea where the most seasoned of captains fears to plot his course. The Dead Strait, as it is called, lies far from the warm climes of Cassaforte and Pays d'Azur, close to the tiny Azure Isles, where wild savages live. Only a captain who is a fool—or worse, a villain—would dare venture into its treacherous waters.

—CELESTINE DU BARBARAY, TRADITIONS & VAGARIES OF THE
AZURE COAST: A GUIDE FOR THE HARDY TRAVELER

The little theater on the Via Buonochio known as the Larkspur was built to hold only two hundred patrons. On a good evening, though, when twin full moons hung low in the midnight sky and the streets of Cassaforte were full of people enjoying the prolonged twilight, the Larkspur's owners packed their stalls to capacity and beyond. In the wings, seventeen-year-old Niccolo Dattore could smell the crowd's sweat and their perfumes mingling with the peppery aromas of the clove balls the more sensitive sniffed to keep their noses clear. The collective heat from their bodies was more oppressive than that from the blazing footlights nearby. Nic sweltered from them both. Behind the tall velvet curtains, he waited with outstretched arms holding a costume change for his mistress—a robe liberally splattered with red, to simulate gore.

"Lad." The voice whispering in his ear was his master's. Armand Arturo himself, of Armand Arturo's Theatre of Marvels, and author of *Infernal Mysteries of the Bloody Banquet: A Tale of Blood and Woe,* which played now before the fascinated crowd. "You've got to go on."

"What?" Nic could barely turn his eyes from the gruesome sights unfolding before him. The actor known as Knave was center stage, wearing a massive false mustache and long wig of raven deeper than even Nic's dark locks. Knave brandished a stage sword with a secret reservoir of carmine stain and roared and declaimed his lines as he chased a screaming Ingenue about the stage. Signora Arturo and Infant Prodigy, in blond headpieces as Ingenue's older and younger sisters, cowered beneath a table. Soon Knave would turn his attention to Signora Arturo, who would dash offstage for her quick change, and then stagger back on for her exaggerated, and overacted, death. Knave took a mighty leap forward, and landed with both feet before the table with a mighty *thump* that startled the audience into gasping. "I have to go on where?"

"You've got to go on," Signor Arturo repeated in a weak voice. Nic turned, but couldn't find his master in the darkness of the wings. "I'm taken, lad. It's up to you."

Thump. Another of Knave's mighty leaps seemed to shake every one of the Larkspur's timbers. "Taken? Taken ill?" Nic whirled around to find the actor, but his green eyes were still too dazzled by the footlights to see. "Are you sick, Signor? I can't go on in your place, if that's what you mean." *Thump.* Onstage, the women screamed, and many in the audience screamed with them. "Signor, I'm no actor. I'm a servant. I don't know the lines." The heat was oppressive. Nic dabbed his wet forehead onto his shoulder.

Thump. "You will know what to do." Signor Arturo's voice was now but a whisper that grew fainter with every syllable. "Go on. The lines will come." Kind as ever, that advice.

Another thud, the mightiest of all, seemed to splinter the Larkspur apart. It was then that the theater faded away, and Nic Dattore woke from his deep dream. Though the heat and humidity were still oppressive, he was no longer in the comforting familiarity of the theater, or even in Cassaforte. He was far from home in the middle of the Azure Sea, on the stern deck of the *Pride of Muro* where he had crawled earlier that night, hoping for a breath of air. He bolted upright.

His ears rang and his head buzzed from the shrieks and cries, and the mighty thumping noises. When Nic blinked the gritty crust from his eyes, he first focused upon the stars overhead. The moon Muro, large and bright, hovered over the western horizon. His sister, Lena, reigned with him to the north. Their glow illuminated the sea around him, catching ripples upon the inky void. Yet Nic paid no mind to the arms of light extended in his direction. All his attention was upon the all-too-real sword at his throat, and the man brandishing it.

It was said only a fool or a villain navigated into the treacherous waters of the Dead Strait, and yet Captain Vittorio Delguardino of the *Pride of Muro* had done just that, earlier in the afternoon. Even a short-sighted man should have noticed the expanse of seaweed floating upon the Dead Strait's waters. Sea Dog's Deceit was its name. It blanketed what appeared to be the calmest part of the sea, where all winds ceased. Yet beneath the seemingly placid surface ran a deadly undercurrent south. A man fallen overboard might become entangled in its heavy tendrils and find himself unable to fight the current to save his own life. Even a ship as seasoned as the *Pride of Muro* could not resist the inexorable pull of the undertow. It had taken only an afternoon for the captain to completely lose his bearings.

"*An gellion beau ze bond!*" At the base of the ladder leading up to the tiny stern deck stood a man. His dirty hair was restrained by a kerchief stiff with grime and dried blood. His snarl revealed stretches of brown gum where his teeth should have been. "*Beau ze bond!*" he repeated, brandishing a torch in his left hand. The right clutched a blade, the likes of which Nic had never before seen. Longer than a knife, yet shorter than any sword, its tip sported vicious teeth. The hilt, under the man's thick fist, had been carved from bone. From it hung wisps of something like straw. "*Beau ze bond!*" he bellowed.

"I am! I am!" One of Nic's former masters had been

accustomed to rousing him in the stables some mornings by throwing pitchers of ice water over his head. That awakening now seemed infinitely kinder than this. "I'm coming!" he added. Though his arms shook, he held them above his head. His heart seemed to hammer a dozen times for every step he took. "See? I'm coming. It's all right. It's all right."

The last words might have been more for himself than for the stranger. Nic willed himself to put a foot onto the first of the ladder's six rungs. He kept one hand in the air to indicate his surrender but used the other to keep himself from falling as he descended from the quarterdeck. All the time, his eyes darted across the tiny merchant ship's deck, searching for clues. How this situation had come to pass while he slept, he couldn't imagine. "*Kalla!*" yelled the man, gesturing with the sword.

"I am. Just … stay calm," he replied. Talking to the man felt like trying to soothe an angry hound. It might not understand the exact words, but it might pick up on the tone. Once both Nic's feet were firmly on the deck, he turned and held up both hands. "Calm yourself." He was astonished to hear the words come out more as a command.

The pale-skinned man seemed equally surprised. His eyes opened wide; his nostrils flared with rage. From his nearly toothless mouth came that word again. "*Kalla!*" Nic shook his head. There was one terrifying moment when the man raised his short sword into the air, making Nic shake on unsteady legs. "*Kalla,*" the man said once again in an almost smug voice. He gently lowered the blade until its

6

lethal point rested on Nic's left shoulder. The weight of the blade pierced through his woolen shirt and into his skin. Tears sprung to Nic's eyes. He'd been a servant all his life. If there had been anything he'd learned from a long string of bad-tempered masters, it was the importance of masking suffering. Letting it show only invited worse. The pain of the blade, though, was too intense to ignore. The sword's sharp barb seemed to dig into the bone.

Nic obeyed the command, lowering himself until he was kneeling on the deck planks. In the distance, he heard the sound of raised voices, muffled and indistinct. The hold's hatch was open, but the voices could have come from any-where. Had they been the shouts and thuds of his dream? "I'm nobody," he said, trying to buy time. "I'm just a servant. I was sleeping up there." The man's blade forbade him from turning to point. "You have no quarrel with me."

The voices were louder now, filling the night with unfamiliar words in a foreign tongue. From the hatch below emerged a man—a gentleman by any standard, but especially compared to the ruffian keeping Nic cornered. His coat was cut of fine blue fabric and had been richly embroidered with braid over the shoulders and around the wrists. A tricornered hat trimmed with gold sat atop a white periwig set with a perfect curl in his forehead's center. "Please, sir," Nic called out, trying to make himself heard above the panicked drumbeat of his heart. "Help me!"

The gentleman turned. "Cassaforte?" he asked. All four of the syllables sounded foreign, the way he pronounced them. He raised a pencil-thin eyebrow. Two other men, dressed similarly though less richly, climbed the ladder from the hold to join him.

"Yes!" Surely the fine nobleman would be able to explain the confusion. Nic noticed that the rogue holding him at sword point bowed his head to the fellow in the tricorne. "I am from Cassaforte. Tell this man …"

Nic had scarcely begun to speak than the gentleman strode over, grabbed him by the hair, and looked into his face. The toothless villain dug the sword's tip deeper into Nic's flesh, bringing even more tears to his eyes. "Have you anyone hidden on this vessel?"

"You're from Pays d'Azur," Nic said, placing the nasal accent at last. "Please, help me. There's no one hidden on here. But we're—"

One of the attendants cut him off with a word. "Comte Dumond," he said, in an Azurite accent as well. "These are not the dogs from Cassaforte. You are wasting your time."

The comte smelled of cologne and of spicy breath-paste. Now that he was bathed in torchlight, Nic noticed that he sported an enormous mole at the crest of his cheekbone. His eyes were cold and hard as he studied Nic's face. "*Non*. They are not. You are of no consequence to me, boy," he leered. It almost seemed as if he enjoyed the pain written plain on Nic's face. When he let go of Nic's hair, Nic reeled backward in shock. To his underlings, the comte commanded, "Tell them they may do what they will with the boat and its survivors. If the dogs have left any, that is."

"What kind of man are you?" Nic spat, hating him.

The comte turned and sneered. "The kind you wish

you were." With a whirl, the comte strode away on heavy heels, where his men waited to help him into a small craft bobbing in the water at the boat's edge.

He had never intended to help. Comte Dumond was the devil himself. Nic would remember his name, he vowed. Gods help the man if he were ever within Nic's reach. At his back, he yelled, "Scum! I'll track you to Côte Nazze if I must, to make you pay!"

"*Kalla*," growled the toothless man, reminding Nic who was in charge.

He would have to forget the comte now. Once again, Nic only had himself. "Listen," he pleaded, ignoring the fact that tears were running down his face and stinging his cracked lips. "We can work this out. You don't have to hurt anyone. I'm sure if you talked to Captain Delguardino..."

The mangy swordsman seemed to recognize one of Nic's words. "*Kap-i-tan?*" he repeated, laughing. "*Kap-i-tan!*" A flood of unrecognizable syllables followed, but when he was done, the man moved the torch with a swoop. Its flame nearly roasted Nic's face as it passed a few mere inches away. "*Vomo sor vu Kap-i-tan*," said the man, inviting Nic to look at the spot illuminated by his torch.

On the day that Nic and the rest of the troupe that comprised Armand Arturo's Theatre of Marvels had boarded the *Pride of Muro*, Captain Delguardino had met them on the docks. He had seen their performance of *The Infernal Mysteries* in Massina the night before. So humbled was he to be the man commanding the vessel that would transport the troupe to the coastal city of Orsina that he shook all their hands individually, from Armand Arturo and his company of regulars, down to Nic himself. However, no one had impressed the captain more than Signora Valine Arturo, Armand's wife and mistress of the troupe. When she stepped forward and curtseyed her rotund figure so deeply that Nic had been able to hear the creaking of the bone stays that created her hourglass shape, the captain had immediately swept off his hat and bowed even lower, until it seemed his forehead might scrape the gangplank.

He had worn a sharply blocked tricorne, decorated with carved jet and stuck with a black plume. Now, the very same hat lay just outside the door to the captain's quarters below the stern deck. The jet was broken and scattered on the wood, the plume mashed.

Nic stared at the open door and what the torch's light illuminated beyond it. At first all he could see was a hand, curled into a claw and covered with some dark smudges. Blood, Nic realized with certainty. It was the same blood that puddled beneath the unmoving head on the deck, staring sightlessly into the darkness. Captain Delguardino had taken his final bow.

"Oh, gods," Nic murmured. When he returned his gaze to the murderer above him, the man let loose with a feral smile and tightened his grip on the blade. The razor point reminded Nic to remain as docile as possible.

For the first time, he realized that the wisp of yellow hanging from the blade's bone handle wasn't straw at all. It was human hair, still clinging to a strip of scalp that had dried to leather.

2

No wind in the sails, a seaman's in need.
Blood in the waters, sailors, take heed.

—A COMMON CASSAFORTEAN SAYING

A piercing feminine cry ripped through the dark, obscuring even Nic's own thudding heartbeats. Almost immediately a man's voice silenced the scream, snarling in the same unfamiliar language as Nic's assailant. *"Kama asay var,"* shouted a man coming up from the hatch. Like his comrade, he carried a flaming torch in one hand. The man's face had been tattooed with black ink in a sinister design. His free hand dragged something up the hatch ladder. He shook it like a sack. *"A var asay var,"* he said, over the screaming.

"Kama quan?" asked Nic's attacker. *"Sa kapitan sera vana morto."*

Nic realized where he'd heard that sound before. "Infant?" he called out, trying to ignore the insistence of the blade in his shoulder. "Infant Prodigy!"

The screaming stopped, or at least assumed words he could understand. "Niccolo?" he heard. The sack unfolded into the girl who'd been the company's Infant Prodigy. Between acts, she danced the hornpipe, sang ballads, and brought tears to the eye of the most hardened laborer with her recitation of any one of the top dozen sentimental broadsides of the day—and all at the tender age of eleven. Or so she was billed. Though dressed in a child's clothes, she was in reality four years older than Nic. At the moment, her screams were ten times louder than anything she'd ever produced on stage. "Nic!" she repeated, scrambling to her feet and lunging toward the stern. Scarcely had she made it to her feet than she was diving face-forward for the deck. She did not make impact. Her captor had too firm a hold on the sash around her waist. Her eyes lolled around until they rested on Nic once more. "The crew is gone."

"Dead?"

"Some jumped overboard!" Infant Prodigy continued trying to squirm away. "These awful pirates killed any who fought back."

"What of the Arturos?" Nic's assailant was still talking to his comrade. If these were pirates, they were far grimier and smellier than the ones he'd seen in his master's dramatic presentations.

"Gone!" The lump that had been growing in Nic's throat since his rude awakening seemed to swell to the size of a lime at Prodigy's wailed news. "Taken into the night. Abducted! Vanished!"

Somewhat absurdly, it occurred to Nic that Infant Prodigy might have been fed too steady a diet of melodramas. Other than an actor upon the stage, who talked like that? "Who's left, Prodigy?" he dared call out. "Are any of the company still below?"

"Only I remain!" The other pirate's torch dipped low enough for Nic to see Prodigy's face. Despite the histrionic way the young woman spoke, she looked truly miserable. Her long blond hair hung limp. A runnel of blood trickled from her forehead down the cheek of her heart-shaped face until it was washed into nothingness from tears. "When I heard noises, I hid in the stores. So did the Signora, but she's so big that they saw her right off. I was behind a barrel of *yemeni alum* but they heard me crying after I thought they'd left … ow!" Prodigy's attacker gave her sash a savage yank and began to move to the deck rails. He was taking her off the ship onto a rowboat. Just before she vanished, she pleaded, "Nic. Do something!"

"Prodigy!" he called in the darkness. It was too late. Her pirate had thrown her like a bundle of dirty linens over the railing and into some small boat out of sight. Her cry of astonishment was cut short when she landed below with a thud. The thug called out as he leapt over and followed.

The protagonist of one of Armand Arturo's potboilers would have known the exact necessary course of action to retrieve Prodigy. Hero was always nimble on his toes, whether he was rescuing Ingenue from a certain death at the hands of Knave's henchmen or wooing her with poetry. Hero, as played by Armand Arturo himself, could fend off a dozen swords with nothing more at hand than a broken walking stick. He could untie Ingenue from a sacrificial altar with his teeth while simultaneously fighting off two priests of the dark gods. If this were one of the Arturos' plays, Hero would already have swung from a rope around the mainsail to take on both the pirates, thrilling the audience with a carefully choreographed dance through the air that would knock them both flat.

However, Nic was not in a theatrical hall, with its colorful costumes. He was far away from its scents of oranges and perfumes, its crowds, and its bright footlights. Nic was stranded in the middle of the Azure Sea, as distant from land as he had ever been in his life. He had no knowledge of which way lay his home—whatever that was. The body four feet away was not an actor lying motionless with red silks spilling from his coat to imitate blood. It was real, and Nic could only imagine how many more might be littering the boat. There was no way for mighty Hero to save the captain now, much less Nic, the troupe's lowest drudge.

Yet if he did nothing, Nic realized through the fear and pain, he soon would be lying as lifeless as Captain Delguardino and his men. A casualty, his name quickly forgotten by anyone who had ever known or cared about him. The realization ignited a heat deep within. Not that anyone had ever cared, other than the Arturos. Most of his other masters had never bothered to learn even so much as his name. *Boy* or *mangy cur* had been good enough for the likes of him, all his seventeen years. Only the Arturos and their company had ever done him the favor of treating him as human. No matter what it took, he was going to repay the favor, here and now.

Perhaps the twin gods of the moons indeed stretched their arms over the waters toward Nic that night. Or perhaps the blood rushing through his every vein stirred his mind into motion and prompted his eyes to seek out opportunity. Whatever the cause, the pressure on Nic's shoulder suddenly ceased. The pirate lifted his weapon hand—very carefully, Nic noticed—up to his turned head. He was scratching his nose, still watching the rowboat speeding away from the *Pride*. The time for action, if Nic intended to take it at all, had to be at that moment.

He lunged. Up from his aching knees he rushed until the top of his head connected with the pirate's midsection. The crunch that followed resounded from his neck to the base of his spine, leaving the top of his skull feeling flattened and throbbing. The stratagem worked, however. With a whuff, the brigand fell back, stumbling for several feet and carrying Nic with him, until the pair collided into the iron hand pumps used to evacuate water from the hold. Something heavy fell from the pirate's hand, thudding across the deck. Only once the man was sliding down onto the boards did Nic roll off. With his heart thudding faster than a tambour at a festival jig, and his breath heaving in rasps that pained his lungs, he scrambled backward. The seat of his pants protested at being scraped across the wood, but Nic would have frayed the fabric to shreds if it helped him gain his feet any faster.

"*Ungh ... kascado ...*" The pirate, still groggy, tried to focus on Nic's face. Apparently the impact had knocked the man's skull against the pump handle. A cut ran across his forehead, oozing from his temple to his right eyebrow. The pirate noticed the flow of blood at the same time. Too perplexed for anger, he raised his hand to his brow and pulled it away, staring at the glistening red mark it left.

What was this? The pirate had a free hand? Though Nic's head still ached unlike anything he'd ever before felt, he pulled together his wits and looked around. The pirate hadn't dropped his spiked blade. That would have been too undeserved a stroke of good luck. The torch he'd been carrying, however, lay burning on the deck not two arm-spans away. Its flames flicked into the night sky and left the faintest of black scars on the wood beneath. *Tuck and fold*, Nic thought to himself, remembering the choreographed tumble with which Signor Arturo's Hero had thrilled many an audience during staged sword fights. While in his sitting position, he pulled his legs in close, then rolled twice in the torch's direction. He landed on his toes and knees, and in one swift motion, grabbed the stock in his hand and sprang to his feet. His lip tickled from something warm. When he lifted the side of his free hand to his mouth, it came away red with blood. Nic ignored it. The torch roasted the right side of his face. "Get off this ship." His voice sounded cracked and frightened, he realized. He took a deep breath and tried to sound more authoritative. "Leave this vessel at once!"

The man's eyes traveled up and down his body. Nic could only imagine how he looked in the brigand's eyes. Very probably he recognized him for the boy he really was. They were quite the contrast: man and boy, pirate and servant, leathery-skinned skeleton and spare youth. Nic might have been the better-fed, but the pirate was an experienced fighter—and certainly killer. That, surely, had to be what the man was thinking as he wiped blood and snot from his nose onto his forearm, spat, then used the pump for support as he stood. He shook his head. Nic took it as the warning it was. "*Vi tolo anscolado.*"

"No." Nic didn't know what he was refusing, but digging in his heels against the man's demands felt right. He took the torch with both hands and brandished it as he shook his head. "Get off this boat." When the pirate didn't move, Nic gestured with the torch. "Go!"

In the torchlight, shadows pooled in the man's sunken cheeks and eyes. Emaciated as he seemed, he was wary and hunched over as well. If he was anything like Nic at that moment, every nerve in his body must have been on edge, prepared to leap into action. Which is why it was a surprise that, rather than lunge at Nic, he raised his free hand, cupped it to his mouth, and let out a whoop—the fiercest howl Nic had ever heard in his life. Deeper and wilder it seemed than the combined howls of outrage an audience might muster at one of Knave's onstage atrocities. Louder it was than any of the half-wolf hounds one of his masters had kept, even when they bayed during a double full moon. After a few seconds of that ear-splitting shriek, Nic suspected that he now knew how curdled blood felt, as it pumped through his veins.

Still, he didn't flinch. He'd had men yell at him before. Save for Signor Arturo, all his masters had been screamers of insults. They all had puffed out reddened cheeks, summoned up their worst curses, and let loose. Nic had taken enough of the abuse not to let it rattle his determination. This man was not his master. He would not bow down to him. It was sheer stubborn determination that made Nic answer, with simmering anger, "You do not scare me!" The words were a bald lie, of course. He'd never been so frightened for his life. Yelling back, however, bolstered his spirits. The words and the torch in his hands felt like the only light he had to cast back against the darkness. "You don't!" he growled, as the man continued the ululation. "And you can quit your damned noise!"

As if understanding, the man's shrill cry ceased. He bared his gums in a smile. His eyes shone with triumph as he paced to the side. Together, he and Nic trod a slow, wary circle, never taking their eyes off each other or closing their distance. Around his fingers, the pirate twirled his short sword as easily as a juggler at a city fair. Nic's torch caused arcs of light to dance across the shining blade. The pirate made a feint, suddenly thrusting in Nic's direction. "*Valla!*" he said nastily, when Nic responded with a leap back.

"*Valla* yourself!" Nic was annoyed with his clumsy and instinctive reaction to the man's ploy. He was being tested, he realized. Well, he had a weapon too. The torch in his hand might not be as sharp as a sword, but with his loose, dry clothing, the pirate seemed wary of coming anywhere near its tongues of flame. Nic thrust it forward, feeling pleased when the pirate dodged the jabs. "That's right. Boo!" He jutted out his lower jaw and snarled like a dog.

The pirate's smile faded. His attention raced between Nic and the torch he carried, keeping a careful watch on both. "*To mallo nasquinta*," he growled, making the words sound like an oath. "*Ved si?*"

This time, when he jabbed forward with his blade, Nic was alert and ready to counter. The pirate leapt back when Nic's torch swung out. Sparks from its blaze flew into the air and flared into nothingness under the pirate's nose. With his free hand, the pirate rubbed his face, making sure his short whiskers weren't alight. "Oh, you're afraid of the fire, are you?" Nic jeered, taking another broad swipe with the torch. He was pleased to see how wide a berth the pirate gave his makeshift weapon. "That's right. You keep away from me. Got it?"

Whatever triumph Nic might have felt for having the upper hand quickly evaporated, for in the distance came a wail from the still waters of the Dead Strait. It sounded so much like the pirate's shrill vocalization of moments before that for a fraction of a second Nic wondered if some vast sea monster had surfaced from beneath the masses of Sea Dog's Deceit, managed to swallow whole the terrible sound, and then, a minute later, belch back its echo. But no. Another high-pitched, piercing cry joined the first. Then another. Soon the night was filled with the sound of screeching voices. The pirate, Nic now understood, hadn't been trying to frighten him. He'd been summoning his comrades with some pre-arranged signal. Now they were on their way back. How close were they, and how soon might they arrive?

In the brief moment Nic took to look back over his shoulder into the darkness, the pirate made his move. From the corner of his eye Nic caught sight of a flash of metal and heard the man's premature chuckle of triumph. It was pure instinct, and no small amount of luck, that sent Nic whirling back around. The blade came crashing down onto the center of the torch's stock with such force that, in the seconds that followed, Nic was certain the bones of both his arms had been shattered. The pain of it caused moisture to spring to his eyes. He blinked it away and looked down. Somehow he still managed to clutch the torch with both hands—and the short sword was buried tightly in its hilt.

The pirate seemed just as surprised as he. With a twist that made Nic feel like his palms were being skinned, the man savagely tried to wrench the blade from the wood. Nic's arms flew into the air at the motion, but still he held on, stubbornly refusing to relinquish his one weapon. Again the pirate gave another savage yank. "I don't *think* so," Nic growled. This time, in the moment after the man's brute force failed again, he yanked back. To his surprise, the pirate released his grasp; Nic almost lost his balance as both the torch and the sword embedded in its length came away in his hands.

A snarl crossed the pirate's lips. He seemed as startled at losing the upper hand as Nic. His fingers curled into fists, and a wild gleam appeared in his narrowing eyes. This, Nic realized, was the look of a man with nothing to lose, and such men were the most dangerous of all. Nic knew what was coming next.

When the man lunged into the air, Nic knew he had only one chance left. A silent prayer to the gods on his lips, he raised his torch high into the air, stepped to the side, and with as much strength as he could summon into his numb and bleeding body, he used the torch as a club. It swung and struck his attacker's skull in mid-air, connecting with a sickening thud that once again nearly jarred the torch from Nic's sore hands. Nic heard, rather than saw, the man's body collapse onto the deck. It spun back over front until at last the pirate rested with his face to the planks, motionless. Nic lurched forward, feeling as unsteady as when he'd first stepped onto the *Pride of Muro* for the first time. When he held up the torch, he saw that the pirate's eyes were wide open and lifeless. A trickle of blood oozed from his nose and was coagulating on the wood beneath him.

The pirate was dead.

There was no time for self-congratulation or relief. Scarcely had Nic time to absorb what he'd done when a face appeared over the railings. Like the man he'd just killed, this pirate had the same sunken cheeks and withered appearance, though he only sported one eye. The space where the other should have been was a mere concavity with a half-smile where his lids had been sewn together. He had more teeth than his comrade, though, and he bared them in a hiss as he sprang, pantherlike, onto the deck.

"I killed your friend," Nic announced, brandishing the

torch. Ridiculously, it still sported the short sword. Staring down the new arrival, Nic reached up, grasped the handle, and tilted the blade back and forth until it worked free. He felt more confident with the torch in one hand and the sword in the other. "I'll kill you too."

The new pirate might not have understood Nic's words, but his tone was clear. The man's tiny, black eyes glittered in the torchlight as he studied his fallen comrade and then the boy who'd brought him down. At last he did the unexpected. He laughed. Then he turned and said something into the darkness at his feet. Nic heard more laughter in reply, from the man's unseen allies. One, two, and then three pairs of hands appeared over the railing.

Nic was outnumbered. He'd barely been able to fend off one man. He knew he was no match for four. Though the man who had first boarded the boat was weaponless, two of his cronies carried blades—one short like Nic's own, the other curved and cruel-looking. The third fellow, taller and broader than any, carried both a torch and a whip of some sort. Its ends glittered with tiny pieces of metal embedded into the leather. As Nic stared at it, the man smirked and fondled its folded length.

There was no help for him. Nic did the first thing that came to mind. He ran.

Across the deck his feet carried him, around the pumps and over a coil of rope that had unspooled from the mast. The torch singed his hair as he looked behind to see if the men were following. They were, shouting at each other to coordinate every move as they pounded after him. Nic took the ladder to the hold in very nearly a single leap, unable as he was to grip its sides with his hands full. The area below deck was a shambles. The pirates had ransacked the galley for its food, taking the caskets of dried meats and flour for themselves. A glass container of wine-purple olives lay shattered on the floor, and tin plates and utensils were strewn all over. Two bodies lay huddled on the ship's port side as Nic pushed his way deeper into the boat's recesses. Though he didn't stop to look, he was certain they were both of the *Pride*'s crew.

When Nic threw himself down a short flight of steps into the lowest section of the ship's hold, it was no less ravaged than the deck above. The troupe had been quartered here for their voyage. Though it was by no means spacious, the tiny space had been the troupe's own, shared only with the ship's emergency supplies. If it had been less dark and airless, Nic might not have been sleeping above that night. Unlike the rest of the troupe, who were used to close accommodations, he had spent most of his life sleeping outdoors. Every container, every trunk, every private reticule that any member of the troupe had possessed seemed to have been ripped open and dumped onto the floor during the pirates' search for valuables. Baskets of props had been upended. One of the troupe's painstakingly painted backdrops had been slashed into ribbons. It lay unfurled and trampled in the floor's center.

During the sea voyage, the shuttered portholes along the hull had been nailed shut. Two of them had been forced open during the earlier assault, creating a cross-draft that caused Nic's torch to flicker wildly. Clearance was low in this section of the ship, and Nic was tall and lanky enough that the top of his head would hit the ceiling above if he stood upright. He kept his neck bent and blade at the ready as he watched the men stalk down the stairs toward him. They weren't in any hurry, either. They actually seemed to enjoy playing this cat-and-mouse game.

Nic backed through the clutter and mess, stumbling over little trinkets and fake weapons from the Arturos' prop boxes, until at last his back was against something hard and wooden. One of a collection of barrels, it felt like, near the ship's prow. It had been pulled away from the others, as if the pirates had attempted to move it but found it too heavy. Nic realized that it was back here, more than likely, that Infant Prodigy had attempted to hide when the ship had been boarded.

"*Valla te que,*" said the large man with the whip. Its length lay uncurled at his side now, and the little pieces of metal embedded in the ends scraped across the floor boards whenever the man twitched his wrist. Another man gestured, pointing for Nic to come to them.

He shook his head. He wouldn't go willingly. Especially not as the last person left alive on the ship. "I won't."

"*Valla te que,*" said the first man. Nic knew the man's icy tone meant business.

Desperately Nic looked around, hoping to find some way out. He brandished the torch in his left hand, twirling it as if hoping it might give him inspiration. To his surprise, the four men's eyes collectively widened at the motion. One of them, the smallest, held up his hand and gasped. "What?" asked Nic, not really expecting an intelligible answer. "What did I…?"

He looked to the side, following the men's glances. On the thickest part of the barrel, in script traced in black and painted in with gold, were the words *Yemeni Alum*. Suddenly Nic understood. *Yemeni alum* was a fine, gray powder, imported from the far east, that could be used for any number of explosive purposes. Festival celebrants used it to create katarin wheels, fiery circular display pieces that shot sparks into the air as they propelled themselves around and around. Warships used it for their cannonados, packing the powder tightly behind heavy stone balls. Even the Arturos used small amounts of *yemeni alum* for small explosive effects that left their audiences speechless and mystified. Four pirates collectively six times his size were frightened of him—and all because he stood near a barrel of powder with an open torch. Of all the absurdities!

"I see," he said, almost enjoying the moment. "You probably don't want me to do this, then." Nic knelt down slightly to place his blade on the floor. It was the less important of his two weapons, now. With his newly free hand, he yanked off the barrel's top and discarded it with a clatter. Again, the smallest of the pirates recoiled, almost seeming to want to flee. The man with the whip stepped forward and blocked his access to the stair, however. Nic nodded at their reaction. "And very likely you wouldn't want me to do this, either."

All four of the pirates leapt back slightly when Nic

suddenly switched the torch from his left hand to his right, moving it a finger-width above the barrel's lip. The smallest began to babble excitedly. He was immediately shushed by the others. "*Valle te quantro oso yemeni*," said the first man who'd boarded the *Pride*, flicking his fingers at Nic. He spoke in the quiet, soothing voice of a man trying to address a mad dog.

Nic shook his head. Of one thing he was certain: this would be his only chance for escape. His right arm outstretched so that the torch still hovered over the open barrel, he edged his feet toward the open starboard porthole. The men kept their eyes on his trembling hand, not on his footsteps, just as he'd intended. Nic had no idea how quickly the *alum* would catch alight, but he had no other choice. He was now the one with nothing to lose in this mad enterprise, and one thing to gain: his freedom. "May the gods help me," he murmured.

By the time he had willed himself to let go of the torch, he knew exactly how far to stoop in order to thrust his head and shoulders through the portal. One desperate scramble later and he was plunging out into the darkness, tumbling head over heel until he struck the water with his back. Something wet and scratchy clung to his face—tangles of the seaweed that covered the stilled waters.

He heard the first explosion seconds later, followed very quickly by a second, and then a third. His ears were filled with water and the Sea Dog's Deceit, but even with that buffer, the noise was deafening. Behind him he felt heat and flame, and heard screams of agony. By the time he had managed to turn himself over in the strands of thick growth and to clear his eyes, the ship had already begun to burn. Nic began to kick his feet, hoping to float on his back away from the increasingly furious blaze.

He'd done it again—ruined everything, that is. Perhaps the particulars had changed, because it was true that never before had he been stranded alone, in the dark, in the middle of the Azure Sea next to the burning hulk of a ship. Yet once more, however, he'd lost another master and mistress—and these had been the kindest he'd ever been fortunate to find. "It's the curse," he mourned aloud in the direction of the western moon. "It's my bloody curse, haunting me to the end."

Scarcely had he said the words when there was a final explosion, the largest of all. To Nic, it thundered loud enough to crack the ship in two. For a moment he had a confused impression of motion and speed as small objects and pieces of burning wreckage flew around him and into the water. At the last, something heavy hit his head, and he knew nothing more.

3

In my travels I have seen how the poor and indigent of other so-called civilized nations are all but invisible to those fortunate to have the advantages we share. How much I hope that our future society of artisans and craftsmen will recall their duties to those without our privileges.

—ALLYRIA CASSAMAGI, TO KING NIVOLO OF CASSAFORTE,
IN A PRIVATE LETTER IN THE CASSAMAGI ARCHIVES

Long before even his blurriest, earliest memory, Nic had been orphaned in an inn near the river gates in the northernmost neighborhoods of Cassaforte. The inn's mistress, saddled with the expense and inconvenience both of having to dispose of a lifeless woman and feed her squalling child, promptly had a student clerk draw up papers of work debt for the as-yet-unnamed infant. They obligated Nic to remain in her service until he had paid off not only the cost of the physician who had been summoned to attend his mother during his birth, but the cost of her funeral, the cost of his wet-nurse, and any expenses incurred thereafter.

When the inn's mistress died from choking on an olive pit, Nic's indentures went up for sale. At the age of four, he had served a master who daily tied a rope around his middle and sent him into sewer pipes too small for any but the youngest of boys, with instructions to retrieve any lundri or small valuables that might have washed there. When that master fell into the canals and drowned, clutching a bottle of plum wine that could not be pried from his fingers even after death, Nic's papers were sold to a hoodlum who trained dogs to fight each other. The man had his throat ripped out by one of his prize mongrels in less than three months.

By the time Nic had reached his tenth year, he had been through as many masters. By the age of sixteen, he had swept out stables, spent months gutting fish, and learned to remove semiprecious gems from their settings and replace them with less valuable glass imitations. He had collected rags from the households of the Thirty, and cleaned the cages of a small traveling menagerie that had spent a summer touring around the towns of the Northern Wilds. He had diced pork for mincemeat, tended the hooves of cart mules, and collected ribbons from dustbins to be trimmed, ironed, and sold again to the unsuspecting.

There were only two constants in Nic's life. The first was that sooner or later—though usually sooner—his new master or mistress was sure to pass away from some violent means. They didn't die in their sleep, or of old age, or from quiet illnesses that made themselves known only at the last. No, Nic's masters met their makers in the most gruesome means possible. Poisoning, garroting, stabbing, drowning in a bowl of chicken and fig soup … after a procession of masters who'd met their ends in untimely ways, nothing seemed too absurd.

When Nic was sixteen, he had discovered the reason for this strange series of events. It occurred shortly after the ascension of King Alessandro to the throne after the attempted coup led by Prince Berto. To celebrate the victory of Risa Divetri (or as she was universally hailed, Risa the Enchantress) over Prince Berto, small fairs had sprung up all over the city in the days following. The only one Nic had been permitted to see by his master at that time had been the massive festival outside the city's temple. Though the Temple Piazza was usually a wide-open space where vendors congregated to sell snow-white doves and garlands of moonflowers only on high holy days, for three solid weeks after Prince Berto was delivered to justice, the broad tiled expanse housed the largest bazaar that anyone in Cassaforte had ever seen.

As Nic followed his master, known as the Drake, he had stared at a quartet of savages from the Azure Isles, with their ritual face scars and almost indecent lack of clothing, as they carved sharp spears and clever flutes from shoots of hollow bambua. He had blinked and gawked at the rich carpets from the far east. His nose had twitched with longing in the direction of the open-air spits and ovens from which one could buy all manner of food—meat pies, roasted fish on skewers, hot potatoes caked in rock salt, and even dainty pies bubbling with fruit juices. He must have visibly licked his lips, or let the hollow rumbling of his stomach become audible, because when they had passed a cheerful, plump woman selling handfuls of roasted sweet nuts, the Drake had reached out and given a mighty cuff to the side of Nic's head. "Eyes in front, dunce," his master had snarled.

"Yes, signor." Following years of custom with other, similar masters, Nic had managed to learn the type of servility required of lowly domestics like himself. His masters liked it when he hunched over to hide his height, or pulled his cap low over his chopped black hair. He peered out at the world with quiet and unobservant green eyes, and rarely spoke, unless spoken to. He was a shadow, a nobody.

"Gentlemen." The Drake inclined his head in the direction of two members of the Thirty, of the house of di Angeli. It was they who removed their red caps to him; the Drake's own liripipe hat remained artfully draped and untouched. "Ladies," he'd intoned to their richly dressed wives, as their hands flew to fuss with the gaudy ribbons lacing their bodices. Nic had seen others pay deference to his master before, but never on such a large scale. The demand for stolen fine goods must have been more popular than Nic had ever imagined.

One of the di Angelis had finally summoned the nerve to step forward. "Pray, Signor Drake, forgive my interruption of your enjoyment." Nic had always assumed that the members of the Seven and Thirty groveled to no one, but here was a di Angeli truckling to the Drake. "It occurred to me to inquire, however ... ?"

The Drake had nodded to Nic. It was his signal for Nic

to step forward and gesture for the di Angeli to approach. Once the man had come closer, grateful, Nic held out his arms to keep anyone else from intruding, so the two could have a private conversation. "Speak," said the Drake.

"It's only that I was wondering…" Signor di Angeli's voice had seemed higher than a young boy's, so excited and nervous was he. "They say," he'd murmured in a low voice, "that the painting of Crespina Portello executed by Parmina Buonochio was recovered from the wreckage of Caza Portello and has made its way into your most esteemed hands…" By the end of the speech, his voice was scarcely more than a whisper.

"I am fortunate to have in my inventory a fine *reproduction* of the Parmina Buonochio painting," the Drake had announced, his dark eyes narrowing to a slit. "Of much the same proportions and qualities as the original, intact and in mint condition save for…" The Drake let his words trail into nothingness, and sniffed. With meaning, he'd concluded, "…a small amount of dust."

"A reproduction. Ah yes. Of course. It is this *reproduction* in which I am interested." Signor di Angeli had bowed in apology, buying into the Drake's fiction. Nic knew the painting had been looted from the wreckage of Caza Portello not three days prior, in the dead of night. He had been the one running the stolen loot to the Drake's waiting gondola, from where the Drake's diggers had recovered it from underneath fallen roofs and bridges.

The Drake had barely seemed to notice that the man was present. "I take it you are interested?"

"I am indeed. Highly interested. Crespina Portello was an ancestress of my house."

The man should have revealed less of a stake in the painting, Nic realized. His greed for the stolen merchandise was so obvious that now the Drake could squeeze an extra few hundred lundri out of him. "I like you," said the Drake. His voice was devoid of anything approaching actual appreciation. "You appear to be a man who knows on which side his bread is buttered. Come talk to me during business hours. I'm certain we can come to a ... reasonable agreement. That is, if there are no other bidders."

"Ah yes. No other bidders. Of course. If I might ..."

The Drake had raised a hand. Nic bowed low and indicated that Signor di Angeli should step back. His kinsman and their ladies all bowed and curtsied, and they were on their way again. From his position a few steps behind, Nic had witnessed the crowds part before the Drake as he strode, giving him his due. Even the merchants behind their stalls bowed or tipped their hats as he passed, pausing their conversations until they could see his back. And how did the Drake respond to those who paid deference? He'd ignored them in much the same way he'd ignored Nic, taking it all in, but not acknowledging a thing.

Through the festival they had marched, past booths and open spaces where dancers performed and jongleurs frolicked, past orators denouncing the evils of greed and benches where people washed themselves with lilac-scented water so they could enter the temple cleansed. Perhaps sensing the wall of aloofness the Drake had projected wherever he went, no one spoke a word to them.

That is, until they had reached a section of the festival less opulent than the rest. It was on the northern edge of the fair, close to the Temple Bridge, where the crowds were less thick and the attractions less vivid, that a woman had stepped out and directly into the Drake's path. "Your fortune for a lundri, signor," she said. The woman appeared old behind her actual years. Her face was lined and pockmarked, her lips thin, and her dark, curly hair streaked with gray. A black-and-white dog limped beside her. It took Nic a moment to realize that the poor hound was missing one of its hind legs. The Drake had done nothing save stop in his tracks, recoil, and raise an eyebrow. It was enough to make the woman drop her price to ten percent of that she had previously named. "Ten luni, then," she said, her long hoop earrings dangling as she spoke. "A bargain for a gentleman such as yourself." Her accent was not of Cassaforte, Nic had realized. Perhaps she was one of the *zingari* who roamed the continent in small bands—or a charlatan who wished to give that impression.

"Woman, I make my own fortune." The Drake's tone was dangerous. Nic wanted to warn her to avoid angering his master, but could not.

"I see great riches, signor," she'd wheedled. Her fingers played with her hair, and then danced across the space between them until they landed on his chest. Stroking the Drake like a cat, she had purred, "Don't you want to hear about the future I see for so great and mighty a man?"

"I do not." The Drake hated to be touched. When the *zingara* had dared lay hands on him, he had flinched back. His right hand curled into a fist and rose into the air, ready to strike down the woman with a mighty clout. Though she did not see, her dog most certainly did. The lame hound let loose with a howl that was nearly deafening.

It was nothing, however, compared to the screech the woman had let out. She was not wailing over the Drake's upraised hand, which had been arrested in mid-swing, but at Nic himself. She had pointed at him with a shaking finger. "The boy!" she'd cried.

Nic had looked behind himself. But no, he was the only boy in the immediate area. Surely the *zingara* couldn't be talking about him, however. He was only the Drake's dogsbody, the lowest and most disposable of his many servants. He wasn't supposed to be noticed. Nobody in the entire festival had paid him the slightest attention, skittering behind as the Drake cut his way through the crowd. Drawing the Drake's displeasure might have meant a beating, or a whipping, or worse, and there was no guarantee the man would wait until they were back in his home.

"My boy?" asked the Drake, merely turning to look at Nic, as if for the first time.

Relieved that she'd arrested the Drake's temper, the woman began to babble. "He is surrounded by the black humor, signor. He is cursed!" The Drake studied his servant while Nic tried to seem as quiet and inconspicuous as possible. "No good will come to him, nor to any master he might have!"

"Really." The Drake was fully focused on Nic now. Though his right fist had remained frozen in the air above his shoulder, the fingers of his left hand searched for the coin bag that hung at his side. From within he fetched a ten-luni piece, shining and new, which he held up as bait. "Tell me more."

The woman's eyes never left the coin. "Cursed he is and cursed he will remain until he encounters one even more cursed than he," she'd crooned as her fingers twitched. "The curse is in his very blood. Beware, kind signor. Beware of him!"

Nonsensical as the woman's words should have been, Nic almost believed it. A curse would explain the unfortunate path his life had taken, not to mention the unusually early demises to which his previous masters had succumbed. He had been keeping his head hung low, but he couldn't resist looking up to see what the Drake thought of the woman's proclamation. When he saw displeasure making the man's eyes even darker, he immediately wished he hadn't.

"Interesting." Tired of listening to the *zingara*, the Drake flung the ten-luni piece into the mud. Immediately the woman dove into the grime to find it, while her dog barked and limped to assist. The Drake's head cocked. "What's your name again, boy?" Nic had to wet his lips and clear his throat before he could tell him. "And your surname?"

"None, sir." It was true. No one had ever known the identity of the woman who had given birth to him.

"And would you hurt me, your master, Niccolo?"

"Never, sir."

"I'm glad to hear it." The Drake had paused. The slightest of smiles crossed his lips. Nic could have predicted that any one of the Drake's smiles was twenty times more dangerous than a frown. "Let me ensure that you don't."

That was the day Nic had learned that the Drake disliked wasting a readied fist.

"I'm cursed," Nic had said that night to his fellow servants, the Dattores, while warming himself by their small fireplace. Tiny squares of paper saved from his day's errands lay at his feet. "It's not fair. Aren't you supposed to *do* something to be cursed, like displease the gods or ... I don't know. Steal something?" Nic picked up the topmost square of paper, which had been used to wrap some fish. It still smelled, but not badly. With nimble fingers, he began folding it into triangles.

"The gods forbid." Renaldo Dattore had removed his metal skullcap from which hung framed optic lenses. He had been peering through them at one of the paintings recovered from the Portello ruins earlier that week. It was not the portrait of Crespina Portello after which Signor di Angeli had been inquiring. That lay against the wall on the other side of the tiny hut the Dattores shared, along with an identical copy that was still drying. "If all it took to be cursed was to steal something, we should all of us in this household be under a black cloud."

"Renaldo," chided Michaelo, his partner, as he had crossed the room with a wooden bowl full of soup, hot from the fire. "You and I do not steal."

"We assist the man who does." Renaldo shook his head. "Which is worse?"

Michaelo was a small man with a trim red beard, who typically wore a broad smile. From appearances, one might have supposed him a tumbler or some sort of street entertainer. No one save his masters would have guessed he was one of the most accomplished forgers in all of Cassaforte, capable of mimicking a painting so finely and with such patient detail that it was indistinguishable from the original. It was even rumored among the Drake's other servants that Michaelo's original surname had been Buonochio, before he had changed it for Renaldo's. "We do not choose our indentures," he'd replied, winking at Nic as he brought him some of the same stew. The Dattores did not have to share their meager rations with him at all, so Nic did not complain in the least that his bowl had contained a smaller portion. "Our masters select us. We have no choice. Niccolo, let me look at that cut."

While Michaelo had used a wet cloth to clean the jagged welt across Nic's cheekbone, Renaldo slid his chair back a respectful distance from the painting he had been examining. He blew onto a spoonful of his dinner. Like Michaelo, he also sported a short beard, but his hair was dark and his features thick and coarse where Michaelo's were fair. "Do we really have no choice?" he'd wondered aloud. "Does having no choice make us less culpable, when a master turns to thievery? Perhaps we are the ones who are cursed."

"Nonsense. Both of you." Michaelo had finished with the cloth, and pulled a little stool up to the fire, where he huddled over it with his own bowl. They had shared the warmth of their hut and their company most evenings with Nic since the third week after his work-debt had been transferred to the Drake. They had felt sorry for him, Nic supposed, having to burrow into the stable straw with the other work beasts at night. While it was true that, once the temple bell tolled for the last time each day, Nic would have to return to the stables lest he get the couple into trouble, at least there were a handful of hours every day in which he felt almost human. "No one is cursed. Especially you," he added for Nic's benefit. "Your masters' unfortunate demises have to do with probability."

Nic shook his head. He had finished folding the paper. It had taken the recognizable shape of a boat which, when set upon the water, would actually float for a while until completely soaked through. Somewhere in his distant childhood he'd picked up the hobby of folding paper into various shapes. It kept his hands busy and his mind occupied in the evenings. He liked making boats the most. "What do you mean?" he asked as he set down the little boat to eat his stew.

"Probability. The odds. As in, when the Master plays taroccho and places a high wager on a good hand, he thinks the probability of anyone having an even better hand extremely low. Of course, because a probability is low doesn't mean it can't occur."

"What my dear Michaelo is trying to say, I believe, is that when any man indulges in a life of crime, he can expect his life to be nasty, brutish, and short. When one has a string of villains for one's master, and yes, Michaelo, I do include our own esteemed master in that category," he'd said in response to Michaelo's disapproving cluck. Neither of the Dattores had ever referred to the man in question as anything but "The Master," just as none of them ever called him "The Drake" to his face. "When one's indentures fall into the hands of villain after villain, it's a small wonder that they end up meeting the ends they richly deserve." Renaldo had put down his bowl on the table with a clatter, then stared at the painting he'd been busily repairing. Other artifacts from the wreckage of Portello lay in boxes around the hut as well, vases, paintings, trinkets, and valuable knick-knacks alike. All of them waited for Renaldo's craftsman hands to fix, or for Michaelo to copy so they could be sold to multiple purchasers, while the Drake kept the originals. "If only your curse would work now," he muttered.

"Tush!" Michaelo had crossed his index and middle fingers, kissed the tips, and held them up to the heavens to ward off bad luck. Nic didn't miss the look of longing in his eyes, however. The Dattores had been with the Drake for years, and it was rumored that they had done such good work for him that he had stipulated in his will that upon his passing, their work debts were to be erased.

"Every time I lose a master, though," said Nic, thinking about the second constant in his life, "the costs a new master pays to buy out my papers are added to my indentures. If I kept one master for years, instead of months, I might be able to work off the debt. Eventually. But if my masters keep dying, I'll never be able to work off the total."

"It does seem a pity," clucked Michaelo.

"That's the way the world works, son." Renaldo had sighed. "At least for those of us with nothing."

"How old were you when you went into your indentures?" Nic had asked them. The cut on his cheek hurt when he changed expression, so he had attempted to hide the wretchedness he felt.

"Seventeen, after my father died and I had no money to pay his debts." Renaldo spoke as if it were a very long time ago.

Michaelo had leaned forward. "Niccolo, son, surely it's not all bad, being in service to the Master? You're fed, you're clothed. You're not out on the street, or spending nights beneath the Temple Bridge."

Nic knew the man's words were kindly meant, yet he couldn't help but feel bitter. "My food and clothing are added onto my work debt. I sleep in the stable. I'm fortunate if I don't wake up covered with mule manure." He'd stared at Michaelo. "You didn't tell me how old you were when you went into service."

Michaelo sighed and had looked to Renaldo for aid. Renaldo simply shook his head and motioned for him to speak. "It was twenty-two years ago, out of necessity," he'd said at last, in a voice so quiet that it was barely audible over the crackling branches in the hearth. "I was not as sensible in my youth as I am now. But Niccolo, your luck will change. You'll be a free man one day."

"When I'm old and past caring," Nic had growled, staring at the floor. "I'm sorry, I know you both mean well, but if I had any luck, it ran out long ago." He stood up. "I'd best go."

"No, stay until the bell," urged Michaelo. "We'll go over your letters together."

"I'll have no use for reading, when I'll be a dogsbody for the rest of my life." Nic would rather have stayed in the warmth of that fire, with the only two friends he'd ever had in his entire life, but on this particular evening he'd wanted to be by himself for a while. Huddling in the stable with a mule blanket around his shoulders might have been a poor second to his present company, but looking at the Dattores only reminded him of the long years of service he had ahead.

"Lad." Renaldo held open his arms as Nic crossed the hut to go. From his chair, he gave Nic a gruff, fatherly hug, then held both sides of his head and said, with meaning, "Your luck will change. You'll be your own master soon."

Outside the sun was setting. In the distance, the horns-man for the palace let loose a peal. The replies from the seven cazas surrounding Cassaforte's coast would soon follow. The temple bell would toll within the hour. "Thank you," said Nic. He stood, slipping the unfolded squares of paper into his pocket. He had no use for the finished paper boat. "It's nice to dream about." Without a word more, he slipped out of the hut.

From outside, he couldn't help but take one last and envious look through the open window at the couple within. From the shadows he watched as Michaelo sighed and picked up one of his folded paper sculptures. The man examined it a moment before letting it drop from his fingers into the fire. "He'll never get out from under, will he?"

Renaldo shook his head. He picked up his metal skull-cap and donned it, then swung down two of the optic lenses so he could resume his close examination of the painting he had been studying. "I pray that the gods will have mercy on him," he announced. "For none of his masters ever have."

ᛟ

Cazarro, I regret to hear of the disappearance of your daughter.
Surely the youngest girl is always a father's jewel, and I pray the
gods speed her restoration. If she has vanished into the underbelly
of the city, however, there is no guarantee she will ever return. It
is a sordid place of disease, filth, and despair, where the weak are
preyed upon by creatures whose villainy you can scarce imagine.

—DISTRICT OFFICER PERLA VENUCCI,
IN A LETTER TO CAZARRO IANNO PIRATIMARE

ᛟ

Perhaps the gods heard Renaldo's prayers that night, or perhaps he had been right about the odds finally catching up with Nic, because it was a mere two months later that the young man's luck changed for the better. It happened on a rare moonless night, a time when men seemed more restless and the public houses and gambling dens of Cassaforte could be relied upon to fill to capacity. Long after the temple bell had pealed its last for the day, Nic had found himself rousted from slumber and pressed into accompanying the Drake to the Viper's Sting, an inn in Cassaforte's port district. Nic had punted the gondola from one end of the city to the other, trying hard not to let the Drake witness his yawns along the way. It wasn't easy. No matter how late his duties had kept him up that night, he'd still have to wake by sunrise to begin his morning chores.

The canals on two sides of the Viper's Sting were both cluttered with gondola when Nic finally punted close, but one of the inn's servants, seeing their illustrious guest, had motioned for Nic to take an empty and choice spot near the landing. "A pleasure to have you, signor." The servant scraped and bowed to Nic's master while Nic assisted him from the craft. Indoors, their reception was no less fulsome. Scarcely had the Drake stepped inside and glanced around at the crowded quarters with an impassive and supercilious air, than the inn's owner himself had appeared. Bobbing and offering the inn's fullest hospitality, he escorted them to a room in the back. On either side of their path, various people had bowed or curtsied or removed their caps and placed them over their hearts. Of Nic they noticed nothing. All attention was on his master.

Though there were fewer people in the back, it was no less smoky or quiet. Several tables had been set up for taroccho, and at the head of the largest and most illustrious was a chair, taller-backed and more elaborately carved than the others. It was here that the innkeeper had paused, hastily motioning for the Drake kindly to wait a moment. The man occupying the chair had cupped his cards to his chest when the innkeeper leaned down to whisper in his ear. From his dress and bearing, Nic could tell that he was of the Thirty, and the look he gave the Drake had been almost hostile. Still, when the innkeeper was done whispering, the man rose. His back stiff, he had bowed with formality, but without respect, and took another place at the table. The Drake had immediately stepped forward to take the ceded position.

At a snap of his master's fingers, Nic had scurried to remove the precious occupant's markers, snuff box, and flagon. When he had delivered them to their owner, now several seats down, he had heard the man muttering to his neighbor. "Damned officious, if you ask me."

A few of the table's occupants had appeared to recognize the Drake, and greeted him with tips of their caps. A few others were more reserved in their manner, seeming to side with the slighted member of the Thirty. One man in particular, however, seemed neither intimidated nor offended by the Drake's presence. He was a round-faced man drinking wine nearly as red as his cheeks, who had leaned over his neighbor and held out a hand in the Drake's direction. "A pleasure to have a new player to fleece, a pleasure indeed," he said, chuckling. "Armand Arturo. Perhaps you've heard of me? Armand Arturo's Theatre of Marvels?"

The Drake had regarded the man's hand in much the same way as if someone had proffered him an obviously bad oyster. "No, signor," he replied coldly. "I have not."

"Ah well. Ah, well." After an awkward moment, the red-faced man withdrew his hand. While the member of the Thirty shook his head and hissed insults into the ears of his neighbors, the Drake took up the deck of cards, and began to deal. "And you, lad? What's your name?"

Nic looked up in surprise. The man was addressing him. His eyes studied the boy, seeming to take in the details of his face, the cap pushed low over his forehead, the dark, bedraggled clothing he wore that was dirty from the stables and still damp from punting. They were kind eyes, Nic decided. Still, no one had ever spoken to him when he was with the Drake. His lips worked uncertainly, but no sound came out. "Boy." The Drake snapped his fingers. "These cards are sticky. Get another deck from the innkeeper." His fingers dug into Nic's collarbone as he drew him close to murmur into his ear. "Make sure they're not marked, as I've taught you."

It was difficult for Nic not to wince at the bruise the Drake was no doubt leaving, but he was used to how his masters did things. He was no more than property. The Drake no more expected Nic to respond to the polite inquiries of strangers than he would expect one of his walking sticks to start announcing the time of day. In truth, Nic felt uncomfortable with the scrutiny that particular night, for the day before the Drake had been in a temper, and left a visible bruise to show it. Nic had pulled his cap lower over his face and went to do as he'd been bid. He had made certain to inspect the card backs in private, however, so as not to offend the innkeeper.

The Drake played taroccho, Nic knew, not only because it allowed him the leisure to drink heavily between deals, but because he had a talent for reading the intentions of the other betters around him. It was obvious from the way the youngest man at the table fondled his chips and stared nervously at the table's center, for example, that he had wished the two upturned cards there would turn into something better for his concealed hand. From the smug way the man of the Thirty smiled as he had regarded his own hand and tossed more money into the porcelain teapot that had held the round's winnings, it was easy to deduce that he was confident of holding three identical kings or queens. The Drake, meanwhile, remained impassive and impossible to read. His face could have been cold as the marble statues in the city's temple, and his tactic worked. Over the course of the next hour, while Nic stood behind his chair and suppressed yawns, the Drake repeatedly pulled the teapot over in order to empty out its contents before him, at the conclusion of each round.

Only one other man had won nearly as much as the Drake, and that was the red-faced man. Signor Arturo continued to exchange pleasantries and jokes with his neighbors as he played. The man barely looked at his cards before tossing in wagers. When he won, it was with apologies and thank yous alike to all as he raked in the markers. When he lost, he laughed heartily at his mistakes. It was as far distant from the Drake's own clench-lipped, stony silence as a soul could get. It was obvious that the other players—even the man of the Thirty—minded losing to Armand Arturo far less than they did to Nic's master.

The commotion of the Viper's Sting had done nothing to help Nic keep awake. On the contrary, the constant buzz of noise made him wearier and less able to keep his eyes open. To prevent himself from falling asleep, he invented small tasks to perform, to keep active. He had adjusted the screens by the fire to keep the Drake's temperature warm, but not too hot. He had fetched spiced wine when the inn-keeper or one of his wenches was elsewhere, and plates of dried fruits from the kitchen to keep the Drake full.

It was during a trip to the kitchens for a packet of *tabbaco di foglia* before the Drake's pipe got low that Nic had turned away from the kitchen mistress and found the red-faced man hovering in the door, staring at him. Oh, he had a handful of forest nuts that he was busily cracking open so he could feast on the meat within, but Nic was obviously the object of his scrutiny. "You're an interesting one," he had announced.

Nic was so unused to anyone addressing him with anything other than an order that he found himself tongue-tied. Instinct made him bow, however. "Now, now," said Signor Arturo, cracking open another shell. "Nut?" Nic's stomach had growled at the offer. It was torture to be surrounded by so many people eating when his last meal had been hours before and meager in scope, but he shook his head. "Oh, come boy. I've plenty. How old are you? Fifteen?"

Before he could stop the man, Nic found his hands being stuffed with forest nuts, their shells roasted and split to reveal the red husk and green meat within. Hastily he thrust them into his pockets before anyone else saw. "Thank you, signor. I am sixteen. Seventeen in a few months."

"You're older than I thought. What's your name, then?"

"Nic, signor. No surname." Nic's voice had remained quiet. His eyes darted in the direction of the main room, looking for some avenue of escape.

"You'd best not let the Drake find you talking to his boy like that, signor," called out a passing serving wench as she waltzed by, two flagons in her hands.

"And why not?" said the man, still sounding cheerful. "Are we not all free men—and women—of Cassaforte, able to speak with whom we please?"

"You and I, maybe," said the wench. She gestured with a flagon at Nic before disappearing into the public room. "The boy? No."

"Saucy girl," said Signor Arturo, watching her flounce off. Then, in a more confidential voice he added to Nic, "And pretty, eh? But don't tell the wife I said so," he added with a wink, once he caught Nic's involuntary grin. He had pointed to his finger, around which lay a gold marriage band. "So, lad, what is it you want to do with the rest of your life?"

It was impossible to resist the man's infectious good spirits. "I—I don't know, signor." He shook his head. "I do what my master bids."

The expression with which the signor regarded him was kindly, yet his eyes narrowed. "You're indentured, no? But that won't last forever. Don't you have a dream, lad?" he had asked, crossing his arms and regarding him curiously. "Something you'd like to do once you've worked out your debt? Nothing to make your soul sing as you get through the dark days? Hmm?" No one had ever asked Nic about his wants before. They weren't discussed in the servant's quarters of any of the houses where he'd worked. Wishing was something other people did. For a moment he gawped at the man, trying to think. "What has that master of yours done to you?" asked Signor Arturo. His hand reached out. Before Nic could stop him, he had removed Nic's cap, exposing a purple knot the Drake had left with a well-aimed blow. The man also took in Nic's blackened left eye, which he'd been attempting to conceal. "It should be a crime, beating the dreams out of a boy before he's dared to dream them."

Gruffly, Nic snatched his cap back and shoved it back onto his head. "Sorry," he said, knowing the man hadn't meant any harm.

"It's me who should be apologizing, boy. It's just that when I saw that bruise—"

"Oy." The serving wench entered through the kitchen door and gave a whistle to Nic. "He's on the move, looking for you."

Every nerve that had relaxed around Signor Arturo jangled with alarm. Nic adjusted his cap, made sure he had the packet of *tabbaco di foglia* in his hands, and turned to apologize. Signor Arturo, however, had vanished without a word. His disappearance turned out to be well-timed, for mere seconds later, the Drake met Nic at the closer of the two kitchen doors. His eyes had darted around the premises, searching for something. "Where the devil have you been?" When Nic had held up the packet of dried pipe weed, the Drake had snatched it away and peered into the busy kitchen. "Tell me, boy, and be truthful, or I'll snatch your tongue by its roots." Nic swallowed hard and held his breath when the Drake's face loomed close, smelling of sweet wine and decay. "Was anyone in here asking you to help him cheat at cards?"

The question was so far removed from what Nic feared that all he could do was shake his head. "Who would ever ask me that?" he finally said, when the Drake stared him down.

"Yes," said the Drake, grabbing his collar and pulling him out into the public room. "Who would ask such a thing indeed?"

It had occurred to Nic at that moment, dragged into the smoke and commotion of the noisy room, how silly he'd been, frightened to admit even to himself that he'd indulged in a harmless bit of dreaming. Not even that—a scrap of fantasy about whether or not he should be permitted to dream. Of all the ridiculous things to worry about! If Nic had been sleepy before, he felt wide awake now. "Ho, my friend!" a hearty voice called out, cutting through the room's din with practiced ease. Both Nic and the Drake turned to see Armand Arturo standing in the doorway of the private room. "You're missed at the table."

Nic knew that Signor Arturo had to have exited through the kitchen's far door, then circled around to the private gaming room. The Drake obviously didn't. He kept blinking at the space between themselves and the still-swinging kitchen door they'd just exited, as if it were impossible to conceive of any other route.

"Come, man," called out Signor Arturo. "I'm sure you've more lundri for me to take."

"Oh, will you now," breathed the Drake, so softly that

only Nic could hear. In a loud, challenging voice he replied, "I believe you must be mistaken, my friend. 'Tis you who could stand to lose a few more pounds... of coin."

The crowd laughed. "Oh, I see, I see," said Signor Arturo. He patted his waist. "A jibe about my weight. I see. Very good. Very good, sir. Well then." He cleared his throat loudly. "Perhaps the Drake would care to open his coin purse as boldly as he does his mouth and join me in a special two-man hand of taroccho. Unless, that is, the esteemed signor is too busy beating his servants to beat such a one as me."

The Drake's fingers had dug into Nic's collarbone. With a roomful of witnesses, however, anything more violent would only justify Signor Arturo's taunt. It took a great deal of deliberation for the Drake to loosen his grasp and make his tone pleasant and conversational. "Oh, I believe I could best you, signor," he'd sneered, eyes pulled into slits. "In one of any number of things. Cards included."

"Very well then. I've a wager you'll not be able to resist, then," said the other man, beckoning with an open arm. "Particularly if you aren't afraid to play for stakes higher than mere markers."

"I fear nothing. What are we to speculate?"

"Privately, if you will." Signor Arturo had nodded in Nic's direction.

After a moment's consideration, the Drake pushed back his servant, so roughly that Nic gasped when he hit the wall. "Stay until you're called," growled the Drake.

Nic slid down to the floor to wait, legs curled. He'd

watched as Signor Arturo talked in the doorway, and as the Drake listened and at last nodded. Neither of them looked in his direction as they disappeared into the gaming room.

For long minutes he marked time. He'd watched as the innkeeper ordered more trays of dried fruits and sweet wines be taken in to the gamblers, and kept out of the way of the inn's mistress and her ever-busy broom. He counted the logs waiting to be thrown into the blazing fire, and the jars of pickled limes sitting on a shelf. All that long while, while he waited and waited for the evening to be over and for his master to emerge from that back room, pockets bulging with coin, he wondered to himself. What exactly would he do with himself, if one day he were to escape from his indentures? What made his soul sing? To some-one who'd never really considered the matter before, it was a daunting question. Nothing stirred him—and yet, given the opportunity, anything might.

In the end, it was not the Drake who returned from the back. Signor Arturo emerged after a half-hour's play, his face sober. Hands on his hips, he looked around the public room until at last he spotted Nic in his position against the wall. "All right, lad," he said, striding over and offering the boy a hand up. "It's time we're on our way."

"But my master ..."

"Is me. No," Signor Arturo said, in response to Nic's look of incomprehension, "it's true. I've won your inden-tures from that vile, loathsome ... well, that's neither here nor there. You're stuck with me, now. And the rest of the Theatre of Marvels, of course."

"Wait." Nic stood stock still. "You've *won* me?"

"And it wasn't easy!" said the man. "I had to put up the deed of my theater against your indentures. Still. Two knaves and two kings beats a handful of triumphs every time. Let that be a lesson to you, lad. Think big and wager large!"

Nic still refused to believe what the man was telling him. He was free from the Drake, and the Drake hadn't even expired? Perhaps all that talk about his curse had been utter nonsense, after all. "You wagered your theater for me?"

Right then, the friendly serving wench stepped out of the back room and grinned broadly in Nic's direction. "Congratulations, love," she said with a wink. "And good night, Signor Arturo." She blew a kiss in his direction.

It had to be true, then. Nic had a new master—and one who was infinitely more congenial than any he'd had before. "Well." Signor Arturo coughed into his hand. "Indeed. Shall we, ah, yes? Go?"

With a hand on Nic's shoulder, he gently escorted the boy in the direction of the exit. "You really won me?" Nic asked, incredulous still.

"Yes, and I'll keep you on, on three conditions." Nic nodded, but not until they were outside in the night air made cooler by the deep canals did Signor Arturo speak again. "One. Dream a little for yourself."

Nic nodded and, for the first time in ages, allowed a grin to cross his lips. It felt unfamiliar to smile, but now that it had started, he didn't want to stop. "All right, sir."

"Two," said the man, counting off his fingers. "You'll have to have a surname. Pick one you like, if you haven't one to call your own. How many can say they've had that chance?"

What other name could he pick than the one belonging to the only friends he had? "Dattore," he had announced, without hesitation. "I'd like to be known as Niccolo Dattore, sir."

"And so you shall. Done. Now let's get back home, Niccolo Dattore. Come on." The man's voice was gruff as he thrust his hands deep into his waistcoat. "We've a bit of a walk ahead of us."

Nic's step had turned into a scamper as he kept up with his new master. "But what's the third condition, signor?"

"Oh! That." The man had laughed. "The Signora might not take it well if she found out I'd been gambling the deed to a theater that..." He coughed again. "Well. Doesn't technically exist. So. Word to the wise, eh? Just between us men." What Signor Arturo didn't know, though he might have suspected from the sheer width of the smile crossing Nic's face, is that he would have kept any secret of his new master to the very grave.

Another thing that neither Signor Arturo nor Nic knew was that even as they walked down the canal path in the direction of the city's center, two men were waiting in the shadows for the Drake to emerge from the Viper's Sting. They were servants of the member of the Thirty whom the Drake had so rudely unseated not two hours before, and in their hands were daggers.

When the Drake's body was found three days later, floating on the shore, his face was so unrecognizable that his corpse was never identified. It eventually was buried in a pauper's grave. When the master failed to come home for some time, the Drake's disreputable creditors assumed the worst and quietly dissolved the household. To the servants they gave their due, then claimed the rest for themselves. Although it was to be a long time before Michaelo and Renaldo Dattore ever saw Nic again, they remembered him fondly, and often wondered what had become of the lad whose curse had made their freedom possible.

5

The Cassafortean Theater is quite unlike what civilized patrons of the arts encounter in other countries. The actors play the same roles from play to play—broad archetypes such as the Old Man or the Ingenue—though of course the plots vary. And my dear, most scandalous of all is that they allow actual women to perform female roles upon the stage!

—Dama Carolynn de Vere,
in a letter to her sister, the Honorable Grubb

When Nic awoke after the destruction of the Pride of Muro—and he did awaken, though with a head that seemed three times its normal size and the sunlight forcing tears from his eyes—it was with a mouthful of sand and an overwhelming certainty that he was dead. He was not, of course. He had been kept afloat during the night, saved by the buoyancy of Sea Dog's Deceit, which accumulated clusters of air bubbles within its dense tendrils. Entangled in the weeds and unconscious, Nic simply had drifted to the shore of one of the Azure Isles, that archipelago of small islands avoided by sea vessels and civilized men. On the sands he had lain, lapped at by the tides, until at last he had forced open his crust-covered eyes and stared with disbelief around him.

Nic spent a moment staring at the bushels of soggy seaweed he'd dragged ashore with him, and then at the carrion bird circling hopefully overhead. His head hanging, he studied the flotsam on the beach, and watched an unafraid crab skitter sideways across the sands. His eyes took in the horizon before him. It was vast and beautiful, true, but also endless and empty... and likely to remain so.

"Well then," he said at last. With a great deal of stiffness, he pulled himself to his feet and began to take stock of his new situation.

Away from the beach, a wall of stone rose a dozen armspans in the air. Its crumbling face was visible only when Nic stumbled closer to it, for tree trunks were growing between the strata of rock, digging in and clinging on to the cliff as if for sheer life. Their trunks grew out and down, covered with oval leaves and heavy with a scarlet, shiny fruit that looked almost tomato-like, but which lay easily in the flat of his hand when he plucked one from a low-hanging branch. He sniffed at it cautiously, then broke through the skin with his nails and tasted the juice. When it didn't cause his throat to swell or his tongue to go numb, he took an experimental bite. The fruit's sweet flesh and astringent juice would have been refreshing under any circumstances, but to his starving stomach it was a gift from the gods.

There was enough fruit here to keep him fed for weeks, he noted with some satisfaction. As he ate, he walked along the sand in front of the stony outcropping. The dense foliage might protect him slightly in a storm. Three fruits later, when his face was sticky and his belly sated for the moment, Nic came across a dark opening in the rock—a low entrance leading into a hollow within which he could almost stand up. It was deep enough that he could crawl to the back and be completely sheltered by the overhang. Yes, he decided, the little cave could easily be his home for now.

With his legs a little stronger, he ventured back to the beach. Nowhere on the horizon could he see the blackened outline of the *Pride of Muro*. In truth, he had no idea in which direction it might lie. The restless sea, however, bore the evidence of its destruction. Scattered along the beach was wood from the ship's wreckage, some of it charred from the explosion he had caused, the rest broken and splintered. At first he thought only splintered remnants of hull had washed ashore. Then as his eyes became more accustomed to the sun's glare from the sands, he noticed something gleaming from atop a section of hull slightly over an armspan round.

Racing as fast as his unsteady limbs could carry him, he found the short sword he'd wrested away from the pirate the night before. "You again!" he said, laughing. Its blade was half buried in the wood. Only by planting his feet on the planks and tugging with all his might did he eventually loosen the weapon. The human hair hanging from its handle was stiff from salt water and sun, but once it was his again, Nic tossed the weapon around in his hand. It was a horror, lovingly made as it was. The hilt of polished bone sported a leering skull at its end. Still, a blade could be useful for cutting firewood, or gutting fish, no matter how hideous. As for the section of hull it had been buried in—well, Nic had some definite ideas of how it might be useful.

Ignoring for the moment the other little trinkets and commonplace treasures he was beginning to spy among the flotsam, Nic salvaged a length of rope floating in the shallow waters. Within minutes he had fastened the rope to the circular section of hull and turned it into a sled that he could drag along, very similar to one he had used when he had been apprenticed to a farrier. That sled, however, he had used to transport horse droppings from stable to dung heap. On this one he piled wood and boxes and whatever scraps of sail or rigging he could find, before dragging it up to his cave in the rock cropping. It was dirty work, but hard labor was exactly what he was used to. What was more, it kept him from having to think overmuch on his situation, which was exactly the last thing he cared to do.

The sun moved from the east to overhead, and then from its noontime height to a lower position in the west. It was not until it was round, red, and swollen over the horizon that Nic stopped to take stock. He had covered the cave's front with planks of wood and sections of hull to protect it from the elements. He'd then draped it with armfuls of the dried seaweed that littered the beach, and finally covered them with a layer of brush from the trees hanging overhead. The effect was not unlike the game-hunting blinds he had constructed for the master he'd had not four years before, who had supplemented his income as a fence of stolen goods by poaching in the royal wilds north of the river gates. Using a tinder box he had found entangled in Sea Dog's Deceit, he created a small fire outside the cave to keep him warm after dark. He'd considered building a larger bonfire on the beach in order to attract the attention of a larger boat and perhaps rescue. However, instinct told him that the pirates might still be in the area—or worse, the pompadoured noblemen of Pays d'Azur. Theirs was not the attention he wished to draw.

Every muscle ached, strained more than ever before in a single day. Though he intended to gather fruit and fill his stomach again before resting for the night, through the overhanging branches of the fruit trees he spied something of size bobbing on the waters. Strangely familiar it seemed, too. Though it was too small to be a ship, it was larger than anything he'd dragged to safety through that long day. With the thought in mind that it might be something of use, or even rations to vary his diet of fruit, he unfolded his weary arms and legs and tramped down to the sea's edge once more.

There was just enough light for him to swim out to the object and push it to shore. He recognized its domed lid before he set foot in the water. It was the Arturos' costume trunk, an ancient carved hulk of wood rumored to have been fashioned by Caza Legnoli before its demise. Like any of the objects blessed by the cazas of the Seven, its primary purpose of containing many objects had been enhanced by the prayers of the craftsmen who had carved it out of a single massive trunk from the royal forests. Its interior could be packed more densely than the average container, and once its rounded lid was closed and fastened, the trunk was far lighter to carry than it appeared. So light and buoyant was it, in fact, that less than half of it was submerged beneath the water.

As he had with so much other junk that day, Nic hauled the trunk to shore and then onto his makeshift sled. The other bits of wreckage hadn't meant anything to him beyond mere survival. They hadn't belonged to the people he'd cared about. He knew that if he wrenched open that air-tight lid, the sights of those dazzling costumes and the lingering scents of the actors' perfumes and grease paints would flood over him. He would relive that entire glorious year he had spent, out from under the Drake's thumb, watching the actors play their familiar roles in a dozen different plays. He would remember how, line by line, he had come to learn those plays so well, standing in the wings of every makeshift stage. If he opened that trunk, he'd have to remember the happiness of the Arturos on the day they had received the invitation to go on this sea voyage—and worse, he would have to relive the terror of the night before, and of losing them.

Only when he had finally reached his camp and pushed his cargo off the sled and into the cave did Nic fall to the sand. On his knees, he leaned forward and rested his arms and head atop the trunk, not caring that its carved curlicues dug into his cheekbone. All day, by the brunt of sheer labor, had he managed not to mourn the loss of his master—his friend, really. All of his friends, gone. Dead, or worse. Gone, without a chance for him to say farewell. "Oh, Signor Arturo," he said aloud. His choked voice echoed in the hollow of rock. "Signora Arturo! Infant Prodigy. Knave. Ingenue. Pulcinella!" Over and over he repeated the list of players until his voice was ragged and hoarse and he could continue no more. "I'm sorry," he whispered at the end. "I'm so sorry."

He curled his body to the side of the trunk and lay there in the cave's chill, away from the small fire he'd earlier built, murmuring his sorrow, until at last he slept.

Nic's second day on the island began with the sounds of gulls shrilling on the cliffs above. When he opened his eyes, it seemed as if the sun streaming through the barricade of wood and brush was even brighter than it had been the day before. The light was very different here, in the middle of the Azure Sea. In Cassaforte, the sunlight was almost golden. Sunrises and sunsets glowed. Here, in warmer climes, it was yellow-white, blazing, relentless. The temperature made Nic shed the vest he was accustomed to wearing. After a moment's thought, he loosened the ties of his shirt, but kept it on to protect his skin from burning.

The tasks he performed afterward were so practical that he could see them becoming his routine. He waded in the warm waters of the Azure Sea and picked small shellfish from the sand. Their meat he placed into the smaller of the *Pride of Muro*'s fishing traps, salvaged the day before. Once he had set the traps in the water and, using several knotted ropes, tied it to the trunk of a tree growing on the beach, he gathered tinder for a fire, then helped himself to several of the sweet fruit hanging just within reach overhead. He even found an old broadside swept ashore by the tide and dried by the sun. Deftly his fingers began to fold it into triangles, and then swept down the corners, over and under until moments later he had a dish centered with a sail-like pyramid in the center. He set the paper boat afloat in the sea waters lapping the beach, and watched it sail back and forth in the shallows.

By the light of day, his prospects seemed sunnier. He was alive and in one piece. He had shelter and the means for fire. He had food aplenty. Save for the issue of water, Nic had in possession more worldly goods than ever before all at once. He knew that he could survive. Yet for how long would he want to?

The lack of water worried him. He'd passed the day before with only a few swigs of weak wine at the bottom of a flask. Though the fruit's juice had slaked his thirst somewhat, Nic knew that under the relentless island sun, he couldn't continue to live on the squeezings of fruit alone. With the abundance of plant life growing on the cliff's face, as well as the visible growth waving atop it and far in the distance, there either had to be a source of water to keep it green, or else rain fell in abundance. With that in mind, Nic fashioned a length of net into a harness. Once slung over his shoulder, it carried one of the emptied flasks as well as a wrapped portion of hardtack salvaged the day before. His short sword in hand, he was ready to explore.

Once Nic had walked a goodly distance toward the island's interior, the rock wall began to decline in height until at last it was only three times his height, then two, and finally low enough that by standing on tiptoe, he could see a gentle incline rising from its top. "Well then," he said aloud, entangling his sword's hilt into the netting, so he could use both hands to climb. "Let's see what's up there."

What was up there was more island than Nic had suspected from his limited view on the beach. Nothing in all his ventures with the poacher into the royal forest had prepared him for the panorama before him. Wild and utterly untamed, it was. A vast sweep of waist-high grasses ran down to the island's other edge, perhaps a half-hour's walk away. Nic's own encampment appeared to be at one end of the long and narrow strip of land, while the other lay out of sight, hidden from view by the sun's dazzling reflection upon the sea.

Curiosity prompted him to investigate the rest of the island, but something else made him hold still. The solitude and the quiet made him realize something that filled him equally with as much excitement as it did fear. He was his own master here. In this place, on this island, he had no indentures. While he remained, he was no man's servant, no dogsbody to be ordered about. He had no schedule to keep. No chores to perform, save those he chose. Much as he had loved working for the Arturos—and that had scarcely seemed like work at all—he was now at no one's mercy, or pity. "I'm king here," he murmured aloud as he gazed across the horizon. For the first time, he was the only person in control of his life.

It was with a buoyed sense of purpose that Nic looked

thoughtfully at a clump of trees toward the island's center. Trees needed fresh water to survive, he reasoned. They might be clustered around a spring or some kind of hollow that collected the rain. Sword once more in hand, Nic took a deep breath, decided to make the best of his situation, and set off on the hike.

His short time serving the fence with a taste for poaching was proving more valuable than Nic would ever have suspected. One of the tasks for which Nic had been responsible during those ventures into the royal forests had been to cover the tracks of both his master and himself, ensuring that none of the king's rangers might suspect their illegal treks to capture game from the sacred lands. He had used fallen tree branches to rearrange the grasses they had trampled, cleared and buried all traces of their camps and blinds, and made very certain to fix anything that a sharp-eyed ranger might spot.

However, someone else had taken no such precautions.

There was another person on the island. Of that Nic was suddenly certain. His eyes could trace an irregular path in the field that wended from the shore inland, tromped down as if not only by heavy steps, but by something heavy dragged all the way from the beach, up the slope, and through the tall grasses. The deep trail ended at the edge of the wooded area. Sword at the ready, Nic dropped his sling on the ground and followed.

The trail was definitely not his imagination. Whoever had traipsed through here had made no effort to cover his tracks. Low-level twigs lay on the ground, broken from the surrounding trees. Their leaves were still green, indicating that the stranger's passage had been not long ago. Nic's hand shot out to touch two of the fresh wounds on the bark. "Dry," he murmured, sniffing his fingers. The trespasser had not been too recent. Perhaps two or three hours at least.

Nic's eyes remained alert as he followed the path into the glade. His ears prickled for the slightest noise, but all he could hear was the pounding of his own heart and the sudden rasp of his lungs as they tried to draw in air. He took a moment before every step, edging into the shaded woods sideways, sword ready to strike out. It was obvious where the path was leading him. As he'd suspected, deep within the overhanging trees lay a small pond. Beyond it, a stream flowed in the direction of the island's far end, splashing along mossy banks with a playful sound. A lone bird dove through the enclosure. Its cry cut through the silence, setting Nic on edge. Of another person, there was no trace.

A series of upturned stones and trampled grass betrayed the path's end at the edge of the nearly still pond. After gazing carefully to all sides, Nic knelt down by the pool's edge and helped himself to a handful of the water. It was sweet and cool to the taste, and fresh in his mouth, free of any stagnation. That was a relief, then. But about the stranger somewhere in the vicinity … could he have been in search of water as well, dived into the pool, and emerged on the other side? Possibly. Nic was no expert in tracking, though, and picking up a cold trail might take him hours.

"*Vyash tar!*" The sound of a human voice made Nic

nearly jump out of his skin. Sword ready, he spun around, only to see no one behind him. "*Allo!*" said the voice again, sounding like iron pincers scraping against blocks of ice. "*Allo! Tuppinze yere!*" Nic's head spun in every direction except for the one from which finally he realized the noise was coming—up.

A man hung above him, his fingers grasping in Nic's direction. One of his legs was tied with rope that suspended him upside down, so that his long black hair spilled toward the ground. The man's face had been painted blue, though much of the dye had flaked off or had been sweated into his hair since his capture. He was from Charlemance, Nic suddenly realized—or at least had adopted that far-flung country's habits of bluing one's skin. His garb was more tattered and begrimed than Nic's own. Nic judged him to be a pirate, rather than a fine ritter or even a commoner of Charlemance.

The man seemed to be trying to communicate, begging Nic with gesture and strangled sounds to release him. He made sure the man saw his sword before speaking. "What are you doing up there?" Though the stranger was twice his age, Nic spoke with authority. Then he remembered that the pirate more than likely wouldn't understand a word he said.

To his surprise, however, the man did seem to comprehend. His lips worked a moment before replying. "Cassafort?" he asked, and then at Nic's expression of amazement, "You are from Cassafort City?"

"I am from Cassaforte," Nic replied, suspicious. The

stranger had been caught in some sort of trap. The rope suspending him had been tied to the top of a young but sturdy tree that even now bobbed and flexed as the man struggled. He took a step forward, so he could see better. "What are you—?"

Too late did Nic hear the warning crack beneath his feet. He did not see the stones fly that he had disturbed with his step. Had he noticed the lithe tree bent almost double among the other tree trunks, he might have been more wary, but the second trap caught him completely off-guard. In mere seconds, all the blood in his body seemed to be rushing to his head. His world was upside down. He watched, dizzy, as his sword fell from his hands and onto the ground, six feet below.

Worse than being tricked in such a way was the man's reaction. "Ah-hah-hah-hah!" he howled, his laughter echoing throughout the wooded area. For a long minute he laughed and laughed. Tears ran from his eyes onto his forehead and into his hair, carrying more of the blue dye with it. So hard did the man shake and guffaw that he began to spin at the end of his rope. Slapping his knees with mirth didn't help to slow him down.

"Oh, shut your mouth." Now that he was face-to-face with the man, although upside down, Nic was certain he was a pirate, probably escaped from the conflagration two nights before. Nic was trapped, and it was his own fault. The rope that had captured his leg was knotted in a complicated pattern that clutched his ankle like a vise. He couldn't even find the beginning or end of it. "What do you know about Cassaforte, anyway?"

"Cassafort City," the man said again, almost as if correcting him. "She too is from Cassafort City."

"Who?" Nic might have understood the man's words, but he made no sense. "Who is from Cassaforte Cit … Cassaforte?"

"She." When Nic shook his head, the man pointed down. "She."

A girl stood on the ground below Nic, her eyes blue and her hair long and golden. In her hands she carried a long club, heavy and blunt. She swung it hard at Nic's head before he could think to dodge. He had only one coherent thought as he sank once more into unconsciousness: that the girl was the loveliest pirate he was ever likely to see.

6

It was due to a tiresome error on the part of a housemaid that we received tickets to see not the Marvelous Theatre playing near the city's center, but to see some third-rate, attenuated troupe called the Theatre of Marvels appearing in the southwest. My ears are still ringing from the two hours of mugging we had to endure, and I have taken steps to dismiss the housemaid.

—PALMYRIA FALO, OF THE THIRTY, IN A LETTER TO HER MOTHER

When Nic's eyesight had begun to focus on the rocks above his head a few hours before, he first wondered if he'd been dragged back to his own shelter. He was in another cavern of sorts, but its craggy ceiling was higher and the sand rockier beneath his feet. Not that he could move his feet. They had been bound fast with rope and tied to his similarly restrained wrists, so that he was curled into an uncomfortable ball, only able to lie on either side, or to pull himself up and sit on his behind. He'd had a brief notion of rolling himself around the crates and sacks and out from the cave mouth to escape, but a mouthful of sand and an uncertainty of who might be out there had so far prevented him. The back of his head throbbed. He wished he had a little more freedom with his hands.

What he wished had been tied—gagged thoroughly, in fact—was his companion's mouth. The blue-faced pirate with whom he'd been captured hadn't stopped talking since Nic had woken. "When you making the pirate? Eh? Eh?" he was asking now. His attempts to speak in Nic's tongue were heavily accented. Nic knew nothing about the language of Charlemance, but apparently the inhabitants of the city of Longdoun all spoke as if they had mush in their mouths. When Nic didn't reply, the pirate prompted him once more. "Eh?"

"I didn't make the pirate," Nic growled back, pulling himself from his near-fetal position until he was sitting upright, with his back against a barrel marked *possoins salés*. "I mean, I'm not a pirate." He tried to peer at the cavern's other occupant, who had been unconscious since Nic had come to. All he could tell was that the unknown man was very old and frail. Like a bundle of broken sticks, he lay atop a pile of burlap sacks stuffed, by the smell of it, with dried grasses. His mouth was open, and his jaw limp. He breathed shallowly, like a sleeping baby. Unlike either of the conscious prisoners, the old man's hands were not bound. "Signor," he hissed, trying to awaken the man. "Are you awake?"

"Maxl, he making the pirate when he less than you." The pirate thumped his chest with his chin, to show that he was the Maxl in question. Not even his loud voice awakened the sleeping captive. "How many years you having?"

Nic had learned that not responding didn't shut the man up. It merely made him inquire more aggressively. "Seventeen," he said, trying to sound as uninterested as possible. To the old man he called out once more, "Signor!" He still received no response. Perhaps the girl had done a sight more harm to his skull than she'd managed on Nic's own.

"A-ha! Maxl have four and ten years when he go to sea first time. Less than you!" The pirate's blue face twisted with gleeful triumph. If this were a competition, Nic thought, it was one of a highly unusual nature. "Maxl live in…"

"Maxl live in Longdoun then," Nic said along with him. He'd heard several stories so far of Maxl's upbringing in Longdoun city. Between the descriptions of the riverside town's docks, Maxl's humble beginnings as a pickpocket, and the allegedly rollicking tales of his drunken aunt known far and wide as "Fat Sue," he didn't think much of it.

"Yes!" said Maxl, his face sunny. "Maxl live in Longdoun then. Fat Sue tell Maxl no go out after dark, bad men be around. But I go out, and am taken up by, what you call, uh, uh?" Nic shook his head and stared out into the darkness beyond the cave mouth. He could see sparks from a small fire flying into the air, but nothing of whoever might be warming themselves at it. Maxl made herky-jerky motions with his shoulders. "Gang. It kind of gang. They walk night streets, kidnap men, make men into sailor. If they not wanting to be sailor, too bad! Hah! Hah!"

"Press gang?" Nic said. He'd heard of such things before, these illegal gangs that delivered unwilling yet able bodies to captains, depriving them of their freedom and families. One of Nic's own masters had made idle threats to sell Nic to a press gang, but Nic had always hoped they were fictional conceits, made up to scare the young.

"Press gang! Yes! Is thing. Smart boy." The pirate grinned at him. Unlike the man who had held him captive on the *Pride of Muro*, at least Maxl's teeth were all intact. They might not have been pretty, but they were all accounted for. "You being like Maxl, yes? Both very smart."

Nic thought of the Arturos then, and of Captain Delguardino and all the men of the *Pride* lost at sea, and felt an angry fire burn within. "No," he retorted, staring the man square in the eye. "We are not alike." Even as he said the words, though, he couldn't help but wonder. Maxl might have been twice Nic's age, but no matter how different his long black hair was from Nic's dark, short crop, and no matter how encrusted with blue dye his face was compared to Nic's sunburnt cheeks, it sounded as if they'd both had less-than-ideal childhoods. Not to mention the fact that they both had been pressed into labor against their wills. Deny it as Nic might, they were somewhat alike. "And I'm not a pirate."

"No?" Maxl's eyebrow shot up.

"No!"

As if sensing Nic's outrage at the accusation, Maxl cocked his head. For the first time, Nic noticed that both of his earlobes sported small loops of gold. "You carry *shivarsta*." Nic shook his head. "*Shivarsta*," repeated the pirate. "To stick. Big cutting…" Maxl made gnashing motions with his teeth.

"Sword," Nic said. For the first time he remembered the

short sword he'd been carrying before his capture. Where was it? After looking frantically around the cave, he finally saw it plunged into the sand, close to the mouth. Its blade glowed, reflecting the fire just beyond the cave's entrance. "Pirate sword."

"Pirate sword, yes, but special," Maxl agreed. "You kill big, uh, importance man. Take hair. Make pirate sword."

"No," Nic said, stiff. "I kill pirate. I mean, I killed the pirate. I took his *shivarsta*."

Maxl swallowed and seemed to understand. "You kill pirate?" he asked. "Ugly pirate? Holes in mouth, yes? Much thin?"

"That's the one."

"That is Xi! I know him. Terrible man. And you kill him?"

"All by myself." When Nic shrugged, Maxl seemed to shrink back a little. Fine. If fear inspired the man to shut his mouth for a few minutes, he'd make him scared. "I killed many pirates last night," he hissed through clenched teeth. "You boarded my ship. You took my friends."

"Not Maxl! Maxl not part of Xi and them. I leave crew before that. Men you kill, bad men. Maxl not bad!"

"Well, I killed every single bad man I could. I made the ship go boom!" he said, mimicking the noise of the *yemeni alum* exploding. "So my advice, signor, would be not to anger me too greatly. Understood?"

Whether or not Maxl grasped everything completely, he at least nodded, his eyes wide. He seemed to regard Nic with a newfound respect. "You take hair?" he asked, his voice quiet. "You take dead man hair, pirate-killer? After boom? For Xi's *shivarsta?* Make it yours?"

"Maybe later I'll have yours," said Nic, growling slightly. That seemed to quiet the man completely.

Once Nic was certain Maxl had snuffed his curiosity to ask any more, he spent a few moments inching forward across the sand until he was at the side of the old man lying on the sacks. He still breathed—there had been a few moments when Nic had worried they were sharing their space with a dead man. The man's face wore the lines of sixty or more years of everyday living. What was left of his hair was thin and dry, and his long beard was uncombed. His long robes had once perhaps been fine, but sun and sea had reduced them to a bleached mass. A track of dried blood streaked his forehead. "Are you awake?" Nic felt foolish for even asking, when it was perfectly obvious the man was dead to the world.

Or perhaps he wasn't. At Nic's question, the man stirred. His hand reached for his face, landing uncertainly on the prominent nose in its center, then batting away something imaginary. His mouth worked. "You're really awake?" Nic asked, suddenly excited.

The old man sighed. Slowly and with great deliberation, his eyelids flickered open. "Mmm?" he asked, through cracked lips.

"*Hallo?*" Nic spoke no language other than his own, but he'd heard the merchants calling out to their customers in other tongues before. "*Ola?*"

"*Oi!*" Maxl spoke up. When Nic turned, startled, he

found the pirate watching with interest. "That how we do in Longdoun," he volunteered.

The old man must have heard Maxl's outburst. The tip of his tongue shot out to wet his lips. He murmured a few syllables, none of which were recognizable to Nic's ears.

"He talk in Pays tongue," Maxl announced with authority. Nic's mouth twitched. How was he supposed to talk to someone in Azurite? Luckily, Maxl offered a solution. "I talk to him for you. Maxl talk good Pays tongue, just like they talk in Côte Nazze."

"Is it as good as your Cassafortean?" Nic said with a grimace.

Maxl seemed to take it as a compliment. "Yes! Thank you! Watch." He cleared his throat, and then in an extremely loud voice, "Allo! *Bongzur! Voo avec* big pirate killer, *comprendvu?*"

"Even I," Nic turned to announce, unimpressed, "can tell that was not a proper sentence."

"Do I know you?" The words had sounded like the rustle of autumn leaves across an empty piazza, but they were distinct enough. Nic shifted on his knees to face the old man again. His eyes were focused now, though they blinked with confusion. "You look like someone I know."

"We're like you," Nic told him, inching forward until he was kneeling directly beside the old man. "Prisoners. Wait," he said, suddenly realizing something. The man had spoken without accent or flaw. "Are you from Cassaforte?"

"Yes, I am."

"Cassafort City!" exclaimed Maxl, seeming to follow

the conversation. "Yes, beautiful! Many beautiful women! All love Maxl. Hah! Hah!"

The pirate barked out his laughter so loudly that it echoed throughout the cavern. It must have been audible from without, for a shadow crossed the sands in front of the entrance. Long and dark it loomed, though its owner did not materialize.

"Is everything all right in there?" It was the girl, Nic knew. She spoke with a strange accent, almost like the languid tones of Pays d'Azur, but yet not quite. "Sssh," he warned the others. Maxl immediately stifled his amusement.

"Old man?" the girl called, a touch of warning in her voice.

It seemed to take the elderly gentleman an eternity to struggle to a half-sitting position. He was indeed a gentleman, Nic could now tell. The aristocratic nose, the former formality of his beard and robes, the gentility of his words, all bespoke a certain class. If he was not of the Seven and Thirty, he was at least very well connected among their society. "All is well," he called out. His voice did not sound strong, but it carried like an actor's. "No need for alarm."

The three men waited while the shadow seemed to waver with indecision. After a moment, however, it receded. They all seemed to relax. Nic had only caught a glimpse of the girl, shortly before she'd banged the back of his head and rendered him unconscious. "She's dangerous," he whispered to the old man. "The girl. She took out both of us on her own."

"She-tiger," said Maxl. "Killer of pirate-killers. Almost!" Nic shot him a dirty look.

"Yes, she's dangerous indeed," the gentleman agreed. By his sober nod, Nic understood that she had overcome him as well. "I would fear crossing her."

"What do you know of her?" While the old man thought, Nic rapidly began to theorize. "She's not part of Maxl's group of pirates."

"Maxl pirating no more," he reminded them. "Never see girl, ever, before here."

"She must be part of another group of buccaneers," Nic said. The idea sounded more persuasive as he spoke it. Wasn't the cavern filled with supplies plundered from cargo ships? "But is she the leader? Or just one of them?"

The expression on the old man's face was difficult to pin down. "Surely the girl is too young to lead her own merry pirate band?"

"And that accent," Nic said. "What is she?"

"Half of her is of Cassaforte," said the old man, turning his head to look at the cave entrance. He was sitting up straighter now. Though he did not appear to be a strong man at all, his posture had dignity and bearing. "Half of Pays d'Azur."

Nic nodded. That made sense. In the short time he'd heard her speak, she'd managed to combine the lilt of his own language with the nasality of Azurite. Exotic, it sounded, but familiar. "Why in the world would she attack a half-countryman?"

"Well…"

Nic thought he saw the direction in which his elder's doubt was heading. "True. She might not have known I was a countryman. Perhaps if I just talk to her..."

Maxl had a definite opinion on that suggestion. "Pirate not care. You say Maxl should not attack Charlemance boat, because he is from Charlemance? Pirate say pooh that." He struggled forward, jerking back and forth to scoot across the cave floor regardless of his bonds. "When man become pirate, he is becoming free man, man without country." He wrinkled his nose and tossed back the hair that was tickling it. "Or sometimes woman," he admitted.

"But that's insane," Nic told him. "You don't lose your heritage because you become a pirate."

"A pirate is an outlaw. I'm afraid no country is going to set their banners flying with joy at the sight of a pirate frigate. They disrupt the flow of goods and make the seas a place of terror." Nic nodded at the old man's words, thinking of the dread he'd felt upon wakening at the mercy of a pirate's blade, two nights before. Any man who'd say such a thing had to be trustworthy. "No offense, my piratical friend, but that is the way of the world."

"Maxl no...offense." The pirate mouthed the word carefully, as though it were the first time he was using it. Cheerfully, he added, "Is true. Pirate answer to no country. Is why Maxl not pirate no more."

"Signor. What is your name?" Nic asked, on sudden impulse.

"My name?" The man hesitated before answering. "Jacopo. Jacopo Colombo."

"Signor Colombo, listen to me. My name is Niccolo Dattore. I have lived in Cassaforte all my life. I was on a ship, the *Pride of Muro*, sailing from Massina to Orsina with my master and his troupe of actors. My master was asked to bring his Theatre of Marvels on tour, in honor of King Alessandro naming Milo Sorranto as heir to the throne," Nic explained to the old man. He spoke hastily, as if expecting the girl to step in and separate them at any moment. "Maxl's men boarded our ship. They killed the captain and most of the crew."

"I am not being in that," Maxl protested, scraping forward a few more inches. "I am off boat before orders made. Why you make noise?"

"I'm making noise," Nic said, furiously moderating his tone because he was, indeed, making too much of it, "because you—they—took my master and his lady, and all the troupe! I'm making noise because I'm gods-know-where in the middle of the sea without a chance of getting back home. If I had a home to go back to. Which I no longer do." He turned to the old man. "For the first time I had a master I was proud to serve."

"You do revenge on him." Maxl pointed out. "You kill the pirate killing him. That is honor. Be happy!"

"Stop making it sound like something to be proud of!" If Maxl didn't pick up on Nic's every word, his tone got through. The pirate shrank back. "If that's honor, I want none of it. It didn't make me happy. One man is dead at my hand. Probably four others as well." Thinking about the enormity of what he'd done caused a point at the front of his skull to ache. "I had to, though. I *had* to."

One of Jacopo's hands reached out to steady Nic. "It sounds like it was self-defense."

Nic nodded. "Honor won't bring back the captain or his men. Honor won't bring back the Arturos, and now they've been sold for … for … for soup! Or for their gold teeth."

"Sell chicken for soup," Maxl said, almost attempting to be comforting. "Live folk make better slaves."

"That's superb news, Maxl," Nic snapped. "I thank you for that. Slavery is so much better." It wasn't, of course. Nic added it to the list of things he couldn't bear to think about. "What did I expect, coming from the man who thought stringing a bit of hair from my sword would make everything right?" The old man didn't seem to understand, but Nic realized that now was not the time for any further explanation. "Listen," he told Jacopo, trying to turn in place. "She didn't tie you up. Undo my knots. Let me free. I'll take care of the girl." It was a grim thought, attacking someone again, but for the last two days he'd done what he'd had to do to survive, and he was prepared to keep at it for as long as necessary. "Then by the gods, I swear I'll find a way for the two of us to return to Cassaforte."

"That would be most gratifying, my friend." It occurred to Nic then that perhaps Signor Colombo might be thankful enough to offer him a position in his household, if he were to find them a way home. "But as for the girl, I don't think…"

"Undo Maxl too?" The pirate's teeth were white in the gloom as he tried to smile at and charm the old man.

"No. He's one of them. We don't know what he'll do." Nic had never sounded more firm in his life.

"I not know girl!"

"He's a pirate."

"How many times am I telling you. I am being...eh...I not have word. Old man, foots up, smoking pipe and whittle on wood, working no more."

"I believe," said the old man, his fingers fumbling with the rope around Nic's wrists, "our friend is saying he has retired from his former profession."

"Retiring, yes!" Maxl seemed pleased to be understood. "Undo Maxl now?"

"Pirates don't retire," Nic growled. Now that the restraints around his wrists were loosened, the blood flowed back to his fingertips with a vengeance. For a moment they felt like fat, prickling sausages, but the pain had subsided by the time the last of the hemp fell from his hands. He attempted to reach back and assist as Jacopo turned his attention to the knots around his feet. "He's the enemy."

"Undo Maxl!" the pirate demanded.

"I am releasing Niccolo here," the man explained. "He appears to be the victim of circumstance. Possibly he may be of aid."

"Maxl can aid!" The pirate shook his wrists.

One of the clumps of rope next to Nic's left ankle was proving particularly tricky. Both the old man and Nic picked at it blindly with their fingertips. "Just be quiet," Nic urged the pirate.

"Undo me. Or Maxl yell for girl."

It was blackmail, plain and simple. Nic gawped at him. "No!"

"Girl!" Maxl bawled at the top of his lungs, before either Nic or the old man could hush him. "*Girl!* Allo! Halp! Fire! Murder!"

Nic felt the knot spring free as the mouth of the cave darkened. Against the shadows from the fire and the dark twilight horizon loomed the girl's shadowy form. The outline of her long, flowing hair was edged with gold, and she appeared to be wearing some kind of boy's billowing breeches. "What's going on in here?"

"My dear—" the old man began.

Nic, however, had no time for the man's diplomacies. It was time for action. The last of the ropes coiled from his ankles as he sprang toward the girl. He was aware of Jacopo's dismayed cry and of Maxl's howl behind him, but they were drowned out by the deep, guttural grunt he let out as he lunged at her figure. Only at the last moment did he think of his sword, stuck into the sand.

The girl couldn't have known that he was free and lunging at her, but some instinct made her leap sideways. Instead of connecting with her midsection as he'd planned, Nic nearly missed her altogether. At the last moment, though, his arm shot out and grabbed the girl, tackling her to the ground. Over and over each other they tumbled until they landed outside the cave on the sand. The girl spat out a mouthful of grit, leapt to her bare feet, and crouched into a fighting posture. Azurite curse words tumbled from her lips.

Nic had landed on his face, his nostrils full of sand. He snorted it out and blinked to clear his eyes, only to see the girl looming above. By the light of the fire, he could see her thick, curly hair hanging around her face, making her look like she wore a head of snakes. "*Bâtard!*" she bellowed, and then pounced.

This time it was Nic who propelled himself away, rolling to one side before she could land atop him. He'd underestimated her. Though she was no older than him, and a girl, she was an equal if not more dangerous opponent. Still, Nic hadn't grown up in the back warrens of Cassaforte among thieves and worse without learning a few tricks of his own. Before he swung his legs into the air and pulled himself to his feet, in his right hand he grabbed a handful of sand. He kept it clenched tight into a fist. "Shame on you!" he growled at the girl. "Your captive is old enough to your grandfather. What honor is there in that?"

"What would you know about honor?" she snarled back. Her curious accent only made the words sound more full of disdain. "Working for *them*."

Nic's temper flared even more hotly. "The Arturos are honorable folk," he retorted without thinking. "They have always been good to me! I would give my life to save them from someone like you." His sword was directly behind her, just within the cave's mouth. If he could edge around her to it, he could get the advantage.

"What?" she asked, not seeming to understand. Then suddenly it didn't matter. "Stop! Don't move a hand's span more," she warned, arresting Nic in mid-step.

"I'm not," he assured her, holding out both his free left hand and the clenched right fist.

"What are you up to, spy?" she asked, suspicious.

"Spy?" Nic asked. Where in the world had she gotten that idea? If only he could get to his sword.

Perhaps some flicker of his glance or inclination of his body gave away his intentions, because the girl risked a look over her shoulder. She spied the sword buried in the sand, and a smile of triumph crossed her lips. Nic's heart sunk. She was going to get it for herself. "That's mine," he warned her. His mind began working quickly. "It's cursed, like me. Woe to you if you touch it."

She seemed to eye the carved bone handle and its trophy of human scalp. "Liar," she finally announced.

"Find out if I am," he warned. Every muscle in his body tensed as he readied himself to make his move. "Have you heard of Prince Berto and the accursed withering of his arm?"

"Prince Berto was cursed by the Scepter of Thorn and the Olive Crown," she said. She eyed the weapon once more. "Not by a killer's sword."

"The curse is the same," Nic said, sounding more confident at her hesitation. "Care to discover for yourself?"

Apparently the girl did not. She stepped away from the cave. Nic saw her fist draw back. It was time to make his move. He forgot about his throbbing head. With a cry of triumph, Nic let loose the handful of sand he'd been saving for exactly this moment, letting it fly in the girl's face. She would be blinded by the dirt and rock, allowing him to grab his sword and gain the upper hand. Jacopo would help him bind her as she had him, and he could use her as a hostage to barter his freedom with her comrades.

At least, that was the theory. For at the very same moment that Nic loosed his handful of sand, the girl sent a similar hidden volley in his direction. His eyes watered and stung, abraded by the sharp grains that flew into his face. For a moment, the air hung heavy with dust, and both Nic and the girl coughed and spat and fell to their knees, trying to clear their eyes.

It was into this pitiful display that Jacopo Colombo stepped. He came to a stop between them. "Niccolo Dattore," he asked, in the mildest of tones. "Would it be too much of an inconvenience were I to ask that you not kill my daughter?"

7

*The natives of the Azure Isles are a savage race, with teeth like
vipers and a ruthless thirst for blood that would give pause even
to the mighty armies of the Yemeni. Or so it is rumored, for no
sophisticated soul has seen them and lived to tell the tale.*

—CELESTINE DU BARBARAY, TRADITIONS & VAGARIES OF THE
AZURE COAST: A GUIDE FOR THE HARDY TRAVELER

It had not taken Nic very long to figure out something
after he began his service to the Arturos. No matter
how many broadsides printed with rapturous reviews they
pinned to the boards outside their theaters, and regardless
of the way they referred to the Theatre of Marvels as the
finest performing artists in the countryside, they were not
one of Cassaforte's major dramatic troupes. The dockside
stages on which they appeared were rowdy wrestling rings
compared to the opulence of the city's finest theaters—particularly those near the mouth of the Via Dioro, in the palace square. The Arturos' homegrown scripts, well-received

though they might have been, were not penned by the foremost dramatists of the lands. Ingenue, though pretty, was not as lovely as the famous actress Tania Rossi, who was not only featured in many a Buonochio painting and honored by no less an august personage as King Alessandro himself, but was courted by many elder sons among the Thirty.

No, the Arturos were definitely a second-rate theatrical troupe. During most seasons they provided a cheap evening's entertainment to workers and everyday merchants. In the summers, when the city's theaters were too warm and close to encourage attendance, the Arturos took to the road to entertain the smaller towns deep in the *pasecollina*, the stretch of farmlands and vineyards that ran for a hundred leagues to the mountainous foothills that marked the Vereinigtelände border. They had played in the famous open amphitheater of Nascenza, true. More likely they were to be found in a converted barn in the cow town of Turran, or playing to the entertainment-hungry craftsman in one of the several insula outposts.

Nic had been with the Arturos for perhaps two months when they had visited Fero, a small crafting colony of the Insula of the Children of Muro. The drama they had performed that night was typical fare—Hero was being called upon to save Ingenue from being forced into marriage with the conniving Knave, with Pulcinella acting as Ingenue's maid and Infant Prodigy providing songs between scenes—and Nic had been standing off in the darkness, ready to help Ingenue with her costume change. He had seen this particular drama perhaps a dozen times by that point and knew many of the lines as well as the actors, but as always, he was caught up in the melodrama. A big grin on his face, he watched as Ingenue gasped and tossed her hair while the Signora, playing her disapproving older sister, begged her not to leave home.

So caught up in the action was he that he nearly jumped out of his skin when he heard the voice of his master in his ear. "The purest of ham acting, isn't it? You know, I intended that part to be Ingenue's mother, not sister. The Signora claims she's not old enough for that sort of role, of course." Armand's hand restrained Nic from leaping to attention. "No, enjoy it, lad. It's all part of the magic. The magic of theater." Seeing Nic's expression, his master smiled as well. "You like it here with us, do you?"

"Oh, yes sir," Nic had replied with all the fervor he knew. "More than I can say."

"Good lad. Good lad," said Armand Arturo. He crossed his arms. "Have you ever thought about it?" At Nic's quizzical expression, he added, "The stage, my boy. Taking a turn on it."

"You mean acting?" Nic nearly laughed. "I couldn't do that."

"You couldn't? No, of course you couldn't, no, of course." The man had scratched his chin and studied Nic for a moment. "So you've never, say, been polite to one of your former masters on a day he's treated you badly? Or smiled and pretended you weren't in pain when every bone and bump ached?"

Nic's hand automatically flew to the place on his forehead. The knot the Drake had left there had vanished by then, but a half-moon scar the shape of his cane handle would remain there for years to come. "That's not the same."

"It's acting, Niccolo." Signor Arturo had leaned in close, because Ingenue and Knave were then speaking in quieter voices. "It's remembering what normal and happy are like when you feel anything but, and saying lines you must instead of the words you want. We do it in the flames of footlights. You've done it by the light of day, every day of your life. Some have a better knack of it than others. Trust me, Nic, lad, you could do it. I have an eye for talent." He laid a finger aside his nose and winked. "I have the eye."

Though he understood what Armand meant, Nic was still dubious. "I still think it's different," he said. It was still a novelty to be able to disagree with one of his masters. "On the stage, you have to know where to enter and exit. There's props. There's business."

"My poor lady," said his master, pointing at the stage. Ingenue and the Signora were carrying out a complicated bit of business in which the Signora was supposed to be concealing a love letter to Ingenue from Hero, so that Ingenue would assume that Hero was no longer faithful and true. Only tonight, the Signora had forgotten the letter. Her hands dug into her bosom where it should have been, and kept coming up empty. She continued to say her lines as she dug more deeply. When it became obvious that she would have to do without the folded paper, she continued on as smoothly as if she'd had it. Did the craftsman and apprentices in the audience notice? If so, they didn't show a trace of distraction, as absorbed as they were in the summer night's proceedings.

"She's improvising, though," Nic said. It had been a neat piece of business.

"And getting away with it. She's a professional, that woman. Better than Knave." Signor Arturo whistled. "You should see how very bad he is without a script. Oh, the stories I could tell, lad. Why do you think she's getting away with it, though?"

Nic thought for a moment. "Because she didn't falter," he had said at last.

"She looks like she knows what she's doing. She appears to be in authority," said Armand.

"People believe that?" Nic wanted to know.

Signor Arturo laid his finger alongside his nose once more, and then pointed at Nic. "That's all acting is. You take a deep breath. You stand straight. You become the person that you want them to believe in. And then you go on."

It was a night that Nic had reason to recall, stranded in the Dead Strait. The fire warming them was much smaller than the one that had been blazing before the makeshift stage in Fero. But it was just as dark beyond the edges of its flickering light, and the stars were in nearly the same position as the summer before. While he wasn't exactly treading the boards among the footlights, he was having to act—specifically, act like the man that Jacopo Colombo treated him as, instead of a lost servant adrift in the most remote reaches of the Azure Sea. "What I'm about to share with you, Niccolo, is confidential," the old man was saying. By the crackling fire, the man sat with a posture that would not have seemed amiss at the dinners of the Thirty. Still, for all his

93

dignity, he still appeared to be immensely frail. "Have you heard my name before?"

Jacopo's daughter watched Nic's every reaction. Her eyes reflected the flames of the small fire—or else they blazed on their own while she studied his every slightest movement. Self-conscious of her appraisal, yet still attentive, Nic shook his head. "No, signor."

"The name I gave you is my own, but it is not my title." Jacopo's daughter shot him a warning look. He quelled her with an upraised hand. "Among some circles, I am addressed as Nuncio. No," he added quickly, after noticing Nic's reaction of surprise. "This is not the place for bowing or whatever you've been taught to do."

"If," said the girl suddenly, her Azurite accent strong, "he has been taught to do anything."

"Darcy." Jacopo's brow furrowed. Nic was offended, but not very deeply. People of privilege thought the worst of him constantly.

"Papa, we don't know a thing about him."

"I listened to them talking in the cave, my dear."

"You fell asleep," she pointed out. Nic noticed for the first time how heavy her eyebrows were, as they crumpled in on themselves. They were almost a man's brows, though on the girl they somehow seemed appropriate. "You weren't supposed to fall asleep."

"Nonetheless," replied Jacopo, sounding slightly abashed, "I heard enough to know that the boy is a victim, not a villain."

"A victim of the same pirates who have brought you to

these dire circumstances!" Whether Nic was appealing to the father or daughter, he was uncertain, but he managed to modulate his voice so that he sounded as if he knew what he was talking about.

"No." Jacopo ignored a warning glance from his daughter, who announced her frustration by taking what looked like a long pair of tongs the length of her arm and jabbing with them at the fire's hot coals. "Though Darcy and I have been stranded on this isle for nearly a week, it was not brigands who forced us to become castaways."

"Then who, signor?" Nic felt ill-equipped to deal with the confidentialities of a nuncio. Kings and courtiers were more Jacopo Colombo's usual set ... not a dogsbody like himself.

Jacopo sighed. "I was not always Nuncio to Pays d'Azur. My father had been a hero of the Azurite Invasion, and after Pays d'Azur withdrew its forces from the siege, he used his honor fee to establish a mercantile concern." Nic nodded with the respect the information was due. Heroes of the invasion were those who had lost a limb or more during Cassaforte's most bloody battle. "It was a business I handled myself from the time I was a young man. I have lived most of my life in Pays d'Azur, in the capital of Côte Nazze. I married there. My daughter was raised there. I buried her mother there, long ago." Darcy turned her head then until her face was concealed by her thick mane of hair. "It was my home, and I counted the people as my friends. When King Alessandro re-ascended the throne after the coup, not long ago, he requested I become his ambassador. He appointed me Nuncio of Pays d'Azur, and my life changed."

"How?" Nic asked, both baffled and intrigued. He would think the elevation in status—acting as the king's messenger to the court in Côte Nazze—would be dizzying in its scope. "Surely not for the worse."

The father and daughter looked at each other. Nic's eyes darted between them as he strained to make out the mute conversation they seemed to be having. "Much for the worse," Jacopo said at last. His shoulders sagged. "Not long after I took the appointment, I was approached by people in the know who suggested ... nothing concrete, mind you ... that my predecessor's demise might not have been as accidental as it was said."

"Accidental?" Nic shook his head. "You mean he was ... ?"

"Murdered." Darcy's light voice should have been too sweet for such a harsh word. She sent shivers up Nic's spine, though. "Pushed down a flight of marble stairs in the nuncio's residence."

"By whom?" Nic wanted to know. "Surely not anyone in the court?"

"Oh no. No, no, no." Jacopo laughed uneasily. "He had made enemies, we were told. Debt collectors." Jacopo reached out a hand to settle his daughter, who was stoking the fire with the tongs again. "Afterward, we began to notice certain things. A great deal of floor wax on the marble, for example. A bottle of wine that had been unstoppered and discolored."

"A poisonous snake in my father's chambers. And a fire in the nuncial house."

Nic looked aghast. "All that?"

"Yes," agreed Jacopo. To Nic, he said, "And then there was another incident that put all others to shame."

"Why not come out and say it, old man? There was an assassin." Darcy's voice was flat.

"Our lives have been lived on edge for many months. Then yes, there was an assassination attempt. My daughter did not take it well." Nic felt a sudden stab of sympathy for the girl. He'd thought her cold and hard. Perhaps she had to be, with her father's life in constant danger. "So we left," Jacopo continued. "I told our household that my daughter and I were taking a month in the countryside, to settle our nerves. A trusted servant helped us gain passage on a craft from Côte Nazze sailing for Cassaforte. A mere sailboat, really—a pleasure craft that had belonged to one of the Azurite aristocracy. My plan was to report back to King Alessandro and beg him to relieve me of my duties, so that my daughter would be assured her father might live for a little while more, at least." He reached out and stroked his daughter's hair. She, in turn, returned his affectionate gesture with a sunny beam that exposed all her teeth. After a moment in which they basked in each other's smiles, they both turned to Nic.

"Of course, signor," said Nic, inclining his head to them both. Inwardly, however, his heart thudded. For a little over a year now, he had been spectator to many a drama on the stage. He could tell when someone was acting. "Yet how came you to this island?"

"Oh." Jacopo seemed surprised he'd skipped over that part of the narrative. "Of course. There was a storm..."

"We lost the wind..." Darcy began to say at the same time as her father. Panic-stricken, she stopped talking.

"There was a storm and you lost the wind?" Nic asked, cocking his head. He felt even more uneasy.

"There was a storm," Jacopo said, slowly and carefully, as he watched his daughter's reaction. "We lost the *good* wind, then found ourselves stranded."

"And your boat?"

Darcy looked stricken, somehow. She turned her head to conceal her emotions. "Gone," said Jacopo. It was obvious he wished to bring the story to a hasty close. "But surely I've convinced you that returning to Cassaforte as quickly as possible is in all of our best interests."

Nic nodded gravely. Jacopo and Darcy Colombo had convinced him indeed—convinced him that they were lying, at any rate. Little of their story added up. Their conflicting tales about how they'd come to be stranded were only part of it. Why, for example, would a debt collector carry on a vendetta against an ambassador, much less murder him? And why would the same debt collector attempt the same with a man of no blood relation to his predecessor? Perhaps parts of the story had been cobbled together from half-truths. It was obvious that Darcy was highly protective of her father. Something must have happened to frighten them both.

"Of course," Nic murmured, trying to seem understanding. In the near-darkness, his face gave away none of his misgivings. "But perhaps rescue might be closer at hand than we thought," he said, suddenly inspired. Once convinced he had the Colombos' full attention, he explained. "There was a man from Pays d'Azur who boarded the *Pride of Muro* at Massina. His name was..." Nic pretended to think. "Dumond?"

Oh, yes. The white lie had the exact effect as he'd thought it might. Darcy ceased her restless fidgeting and sat still. If it had not been so dark, Nic might have been able to see how white her skin had gone. Jacopo, too, froze. He drew in one very long and raspy breath. "Dumond?" he finally asked. "It's a common enough name in that country."

"He was quite tall," Nic said. "He wore a blue military coat with gold braid, insignia upon his shoulders, and sported a mole upon his cheekbone. He was looking for someone. Cassaforteans, he said. Perhaps the court at Côte Nazze was worried at your disappearance and dispatched him to assure your safety?"

Nic was not mistaken in his suspicions. Jacopo quelled whatever his daughter was about to say with one raised finger. "Oh," he said, weighing his words carefully. "That sounds very much like the Comte Dumond. I wouldn't say he was concerned about us, though. I doubt he's even heard of our departure. No," he continued, his voice gaining in strength as he spun the tale, "the Comte Dumond is a high officer in the navy of Pays d'Azur. An ambitious man. But no, he wouldn't be interested in the pair of us, not at all."

Nic couldn't help but push a little. "But if he knew the Nuncio to Pays d'Azur was in distress, surely..."

"No." Jacopo was firm. "Besides, his business is in clearing the waters of pirates, not small affairs like ours." Clearing the waters of pirates? Or colluding with them? No honorable officer would ever have pirates do his dirty work, of that Nic was certain. "But Niccolo, it is late, and we have all had long days. May I suggest that you make camp here near the fire and sleep? We can speak in the morning of our next actions."

Nic agreed to the suggestion. Now that the excitement of the fight had faded, his every muscle ached. The back of his head began to throb again. "We will speak in the morning," he assured them both.

Once they had left the fireside, however, Nic could hear the father and daughter arguing in hushed whispers, beneath the hanging fruit trees further down the rock face. The Colombos had lied to him. For whatever reason, they didn't trust him with their story. Nic was not surprised at the discovery, exactly. In his experience, everyone had an agenda tailored to their own desires. The only truly altruistic man he'd ever met had been his last master, and even his kindness had not broken Nic's curse. Knowing that the Colombos kept a secret did not make him dislike them—he would merely have to be careful until he knew exactly what they wanted.

Nic curled into a ball atop a pile of empty burlap sacks, and let the fire warm him. The whispering continued for some time, then faded into the rustling of the tree branches and the constant rush of water upon the sands. Though his future was as uncertain as ever it had been, he slept soundly for the first time in days.

8

Landlocked though Vereinigtelände may be, at least we are not prey to the whims and money-lusts of pirates, like those of Cassaforte. Their navy is constantly having to battle pirates determined to lay ruin to traders entering and exiting their ports.

—THE SPY GUSTOPHE WERNER,
IN A SECRET MISSIVE TO BARON FRIEDRICH VAN WIESTEL

Fog the color of lamb's wool had settled on the beach overnight. When Nic opened his eyes, he couldn't see past the edge of the branches hanging over the area in front of the Colombos' shelter. Something had awoken him. When he tried to sit up and take stock, he realized that somebody was behind him. Her hand was on his mouth.

"Sssh," Darcy warned him, in his ear.

Nic rolled out from under the girl and sat up on his knees. His heart pounded and his chest began to heave, as if his body were readying for another tussle with the girl.

"What are you doing?" he gasped out. "By the gods, you're a lunatic!"

"Sssh!" The girl's scowl grew more furious at the sound of his voice. "My father is sleeping."

"Fine. Just don't … don't wake me like that *ever* again!" Honestly. The girl had been raised with every advantage, yet she was more of a savage than Nic ever had been. The look she threw his way was pure scorn. She rose from the pile of sacks where he'd slept, brushed off her knees, and retrieved a spade from beside a log near the dead fire. Or the almost-dead fire, that was. While Nic righted himself and rubbed his face to convince himself that this was not a dream, Darcy stooped to dig through the layer of gray ashes to the embers underneath. The buried nuggets glowed a bright red when she blew on them. Into the curved bottom of a pottery shard, she scooped a spadeful of the embers, then set it aside. She threw some tinder atop the stirred campfire, stood, and grabbed from the sand the tongs she had used the night before to poke the fire.

"Follow," she said.

"I'm not your servant!"

Darcy shushed him with a finger to her lips. Fine. Nic would come, but he wouldn't have to like it. Carrying the ruined pot by the edge, Darcy began scurrying down the tide line, in the direction of the island's other end. Nic's boots spat up sand as he followed. He marveled at how the girl somehow managed, in her breeches and bare feet, to outpace him to an extent that she was almost invisible in the fog. Only once did she look back to see if he was still following. When her eyes met his across the mist, they seemed to measure him. She looked Nic up and down, taking in his height and breadth, the cut of his hair and the hang of his shirt, and summing it all up as she might a column in a ledger. It was only for a moment, but Nic found himself curious what she saw in that time.

By the time they reached their destination, Nic was slightly out of breath from trying to keep pace. They were in a small grove of trees heavy with long, glossy fronds. The growth was not as dense as the small forest where the pool of water lay, but its branches hung nearly to the ground, providing them a sense of privacy. She ignored him completely as she set down the pot. "We had to come all the way out here to talk?" Nic said. His voice sounded almost angry. The girl spoke the same language as he, but at no time in the last day had she given him any indication that she actually listened. "I mean no disrespect, signorina, but while you and I are on this island, I think we should set a number of things straight."

"Oh?" Darcy turned, her eyebrows raised. Really, she looked like a Buonochio painting, with her fair hair falling around her pale skin. "What things are those, boy?"

A Buonochio painting would not have captured the utter scorn she managed to pour into that single last word. "For one thing, do not address me as *boy*. I am not your servant." He'd said the words a few minutes before, but now they sounded confident. "I'm happy to be consulted. I want to help. But I refuse to be ordered. I think your father would agree with me on ..." Nic's words trailed off into silence. Something had moved, within the cluster of trees.

He thought it was a trick of the fog, but no, something living was stirring restlessly beside one of the trees. Not merely animal, either—it was a man, slumped and sitting, his arms wrapped behind him around the tree's trunk. "By the gods," Nic murmured, closing the distance between them. "Maxl?"

The pirate's lower lip was split and caked with dried blood. His eyelids seemed heavy, as if he could barely open them. A dark bruise was beginning to form over his left cheekbone. Groggily, he looked up at Nic. His mouth struggled to form a single word. "Help?"

"What have you been doing?" Nic demanded, whirling around. Darcy had brought the bowl closer to the tree. Black smoke rose from the cinders within. Again, the girl made no sign of having heard. "I said ..."

Darcy whirled around. "I'm not your servant either," she said. The intensity of her voice startled Nic. "And anyway, it's not what I'm doing. It's what you're going to do."

Nic didn't understand. He shook his head. "I'm going to let him go."

"No, you're not." Darcy flipped up the metal tongs so that they swung through the air and landed in the palm of her right hand. Again, she seemed to measure him with her eyes. "Why should we?"

"Because you can't—he's injured!" When he'd observed Darcy summing him up before, Nic had wondered what total she might have reached. Judging by the scorn upon her face, she obviously found him wanting. "By the gods. You've been beating him!"

"He has information," she replied, marching over to the bowl.

"What information?"

Her head tilted. Her eyelids lowered. The sigh she let out was pure contempt. "This dog wasn't aboard your ship. The one you 'destroyed.'" She said the last word as if she didn't quite believe his story. "He didn't float to the island, like you. He says he left his crew before they invaded your craft. How did he get here?" Nic thought about it for a moment. She was right. There hadn't been any large sections of destroyed ship for Maxl to cling to. "His ship must have been close enough for him to swim from—which it wasn't. My father and I have both been watching these waters. Or else he had a boat."

Of course. Nic remembered seeing the trail on the grassy slope, the day before. Maxl had some kind of raft or small rowboat that he had dragged from the beach through the field, leaving the deep trail he'd followed into the woods. It made total sense. What didn't add up, however, was why Darcy was now using the tongs to clutch one of the embers from the pot. When she pulled it up, its surface had cooled and formed a black crust. The moment she blew on it, though, the ash flew away and sparks followed, exposing the hot, burning core. "Fine. He had a boat," Nic said, trying to sound reasonable. "Ask him where it is."

"I have." Darcy took the ember and thrust it against a tree trunk across from Maxl. The bark beneath it began to smoke, slowly at first, then with increasing vigor. When Darcy pulled away the tongs, the heat left a black scar. "He wouldn't tell me."

"No boat," said Maxl. He looked exhausted. Nic couldn't look at the cut on his lip without wincing. "Maxl is having no boat."

"There *is* a boat," she snapped. "And you're going to tell us where it is." She began to advance.

"What are you planning to do?" Nic asked. His heart almost skipped a beat. "Torture him?" She was, he realized. She intended to harm the pirate in order to find out how he'd gotten to the island on his own. He waved his hands. "What's wrong with you? You can't do that!"

"I could," she announced. Without warning she thrust the tongs forward, so that his fingers wrapped instinctively around the long handles. "But I'm not. You are."

"What?" The biting ends of the tongs were close enough to his own face that he could feel the heat from the nugget of burning wood it held. "I'm not."

"Oh, but you will." Nic was so wary of dropping the ember onto himself that even as she grasped him from behind and pushed him across the sand to the tree where Maxl was tied, he kept squeezing the handles. "You're going to demand he tell you everything. And if he doesn't …" She pointed to the black scar on the tree trunk nearby.

"You've gone mad!" Nic tried to resist. He didn't want to have anything to do with this nonsense. Still, he was wary of letting loose his grip of the hot coal. "You can't expect to me to … I won't!"

Darcy's accent might have been an exotic tickle in his ears, but her words were corrosive. "You said you'd help us in any way you could."

When Nic looked over at Maxl, he could see the pirate's eyes had grown as large as the twin moons themselves. Perspiration beaded on his forehead, running along the worry lines there and catching at the brows. All of his wiry muscles struggled to loosen himself from the bonds that restrained him to the tree, but Darcy had tied the knots too tightly. Whether or not Maxl understood every word of their conversation, he certainly understood Darcy's intent, and it frightened him so much that he was squirming like a trapped animal. "I'm not going to help you like this!" Nic snapped back.

They were standing in front of Maxl now. The hot ember was only a handspan from the pirate's face. It cast an orange glow that cut through the mist. "You've killed men before," Darcy growled through her teeth. "This should be nothing to you."

She picked the wrong thing to say. "I didn't have a choice." Still squeezing the tongs, Nic wrenched himself out of the girl's grasp. He turned around to face her. "It was either him or me. This situation is entirely different. If you want information from Maxl, I'm sure there are other ways to get it than *torturing* him."

"Yes!" said the pirate, nodding fervently. "Other ways!"

"He's one of *them*." Darcy still looked at the tongs as if she intended to grab them from Nic and burn her captive herself. "He's like an animal. They don't have feelings."

"I am having feelings!" cried Maxl. "Many feelings. Many many feelings!"

"Does your father know you're doing this?" Nic demanded.

The girl shook her head. "He doesn't have to know everything."

Nic was outraged, now. "I don't know what you're up to. Perhaps living on this island has given you moon-fever. Maybe you were crazy before you left Pays d'Azur. But let me make one thing perfectly clear: I am not your servant, and I *certainly* am not your executioner." Nic looked over to Maxl, who was regarding him with hope. "Until he does something to merit it, I won't lay a hand to this man."

Darcy's lip curled. "Is that so?" The three words, combined with the girl's obvious contempt, fanned even higher the flames of Nic's indignation. She followed them up with another observation. "Perhaps it's because you're not man enough?"

"You are insane." Nic turned. The fog was just as thick as it had been all morning, but he could see far enough through it to discern a gap in the nearest outermost trees. He flung the burning coal through it like a javelin, then marched over to the spot in the sand where it had landed. His boot kicked some sand over its top to starve it of the air it needed to burn. "Absolutely insane," he said, walking back with the tongs hanging from one hand.

"What are you going to do?" Darcy taunted him. "Tell my papa?"

"If I have to!" Nic threw the tongs down onto the

ground, then let out a sound of utter exasperation. It was a purely animal cry, half grunt and half attempt to rid himself of the anger that roiled within. "Of all the bloody luck. I could have lived here quite nicely on my own. By myself. I could have lived on fruit and roots and small animals and been master of my own island. But no. I have to share it with . . . with a pirate . . ."

The pirate in question, still looking apprehensive though not as panicked now that he was no longer in imminent danger of being burned, said, "I like fruits!"

". . . An old man, and a girl who clearly is worse than any savage. You're scarcely civilized!"

"We have no other options, boy." Darcy's words were blunt. "If you're too soft for the grown-up world, then fine. Leave. Go back to your roots and fruit. I don't want to see your ugly face again."

Nic was all astonishment. On top of his immense irritation with the lass, he now had to deal with the stinging notion that she thought he had an ugly face. Before he could react, though, the pirate spoke up. "Take Maxl," he begged Nic. "Maxl good servant. Take me."

"You're staying here." Darcy spoke directly to him. "You and I still have business." She moved for the tongs that Nic had thrown down.

"No." Nic grabbed the girl by the wrist. "I won't let you."

Maxl had relaxed some in the previous moments, but now that his safety was once more in danger, he began babbling in a cracked and hoarse voice. "Listen to him. Listen to nice boy! I show you everything. Boat, everything. Is not needing to hurt me! Please!"

Darcy arrested her struggle with Nic and turned to the pirate. "Everything?"

Maxl nodded. "Not you. Him. Nice Niccolo."

"You'll show him?" At Darcy's question, the pirate nodded his head with vigor. "Fine," she finally snarled, reclaiming her wrist from Nic's grasp. To Nic, she added, "He's all yours, then. I hope you don't come to regret it."

That was all? She simply was intending to walk off and leave them? Nic couldn't believe it at first, but Darcy crossed the little grove of trees to its other side. "I'll be fine," he told her. "I can handle myself."

She turned and snorted. "You might need this," she said, holding up something that had been leaning against a tree trunk.

It was his sword. The *shivarsta*. She hadn't carried it when they'd walked here together, so she must have brought it earlier. Maybe, if the embers hadn't worked, she'd intended a worse form of torture. The idea made him shiver as he closed the distance between them. "Thank you," he said with the greatest formality as he took his weapon from her.

"Good luck," she said with the utmost of coldness. Nic was about to return to Maxl's side without a word more when to Nic's surprise she caught him by the wrist. Holding him as tightly as he had held her a minute before, she pulled him close and stood on tiptoe so she could whisper into his ear. He expected another barb from her tongue— an insult, a poison-laden comment about his manhood, perhaps. Instead, though, she merely muttered, "Very good work."

"What?"

His ears hadn't deceived him. "Excellent performance," she said, in a soft voice that Maxl wouldn't be able to overhear at his distance. "It was almost as if you knew what you were doing." To his slack-faced reaction, she cocked her head. "It's one of the easiest ways to extract information," she explained. "Two guards enter a room with a prisoner. One is awful and promises to do all kinds of terrible things. The other is nice and tries to talk the awful guard out of it. The prisoner almost always is grateful to the nice guard and agrees to cooperate." Nic found it difficult to say anything, so astonished was he. "What? It worked."

"You used me," he gasped, almost breathless.

"Well, yes," she said, releasing her grip on his wrist. "I had to. I didn't think you'd do it willingly."

"I thought you were actually going to torture Maxl," he hissed, becoming angry once more. "I thought you were out of your mind. You were play-acting."

"Of course I was," she said, offended that he might think otherwise.

"But his bruises!" Nic had to struggle to speak quietly. "His lip!"

"What kind of monster do you think I am?" she asked. "He couldn't see in the fog and ran face-first into a tree when I was dragging him here. He was so dazed after that I doubt he remembers it."

"Oh gods," said Nic, deflating. "You duped me."

"It worked, didn't it?" Darcy raised an eyebrow. Nic thought he saw a flash of a smile play across her lips, but he couldn't be sure. "Now, listen," she added, all business once more. "Go find that boat. I know he has one."

"Wait. You listen." Nic leaned in close. He wanted the girl to hear loudly and clearly what he had to say. "Don't ever do anything like that to me again." When she didn't respond, he wanted to shake her. Instead, he decided to unsettle her with words. "I know you and your father lied to me last night. I don't know who the Comte Dumond is, or what relation he has to you both, but I know there is one. I don't care if you don't trust me. You don't know me from the King of Indee. That's fine. Keep your secrets for now." Nic looked the girl square in the eye.

"Yes. We lied." Darcy's blue eyes had turned cold and hard during his speech. Nic was surprised that she admitted the deceit without shame. "I suppose you think you're clever to have noticed." Nic shrugged. That hadn't been what he'd thought at all. "Let me tell you this, though. My father and I are on a mission of extreme urgency. It's vital to Cassaforte. The faster we all return home, the better." She paused to let that sink in. "If you aid us, I'll see that you're rewarded."

Nic couldn't help but think of enough of a reward to cover the work debt of his indentures. And just as quickly, he tried to forget it. They were all stuck here, and needed each other. He would have lent his aid without reward. "Fine," he said, resolving to inquire no more. "But if you want my help, you'd by the gods better be honest with me in the future. Both you and your father." He waited a moment for it to sink in. "Understood?"

She nodded. "I understand." For a moment, Nic thought she would have some retort to make, but instead she merely bit her lip, trying to decide something. "Just get the boat," she said at last. Then she raised herself on tiptoes once again and did something unexpected. Nic felt her lips first on one cheek, and then on the other, as soft and delicate as the brush of butterfly wings.

Then she was gone, sprinting off into the fog. It was just as he'd observed, the first time he'd seen the mild-mannered, quiet man who had taught him to play draughts transform into broad, villainous Knave once he stepped into the footlights. Sometimes the biggest performances came from the most unexpected sources.

9

Yes, but if pitiful Cassaforte were ours, no pirates would dare come near the might of Vereinigtelände nor its armies.

—Baron Friedrich van Wiestel,
in a secret missive to the spy Gustophe Werner

🍂

M axl's eyes were still big when Nic returned. "Where is girl?" he wanted to know.

"Gone." Nic's voice was gruff as he walked around the tree. Darcy had restrained the pirate there with a single rope, looped into a number of complicated and not-at-all-professional knots. For Nic, who had learned proper knot-tying under a number of his masters, it was a relief to know the girl wasn't super-competent at everything.

"You save me." Maxl strained to turn his head to look at Nic. "I thank you hundred by hundred times."

Nic couldn't help but notice the gratitude in Maxl's

eyes, which were as big and brown and liquid as any hungry puppy's. "You're welcome," Nic said. "We had a talk. She won't do it again." He felt confused about what had just transpired. If the man hadn't been in any real danger, had Nic really saved Maxl at all? It certainly didn't feel like it. But then again, no matter how feigned Darcy's intimidation might have been, at least Nic's reactions were real. That had to count for something.

With a single strike of his sword, Nic chopped the rope in half. Maxl grunted in surprise at the sound of the impact the blade made as it dug into the tree trunk, but once his hands were free, he fell forward, scrabbled in the grass and sand until he regained some control over his muscles, and then rose to his feet. Nic was still trying to work his blade from the tree when he saw Maxl charging at him. Had it been an attack, there would have been nothing he could have done to defend himself—but the pirate was merely enveloping him in a tearful bear hug. "I thank you thousand by thousand times," he snuffled into Nic's shoulder. "You are true friend!"

"Ah. Everything's ... all right." Nic was unused to giving anyone comfort. Awkwardly, he patted the pirate on the back. For the first time he noticed what a bundle of bones Maxl really was. Though he gave the impression of being wiry and strong, it seemed as if Nic could feel every ridge on the man's spine. "You're okay," Nic said, trying to put some conviction behind it. "She won't hurt you now. So long," he added, trying to sound firm, "as you show us where that boat is."

Maxl not only believed Nic's words, but he seemed to be accepting his authority. "Yes, yes, show you everything," he agreed, nodding fervently. "You trust me now, yes?"

He looked so pitiful that Nic couldn't help but agree. "Yes, I will trust you." Maxl's eyes lit up. "But only," Nic added, impressed with his performance enough to push it a little further, "if you swear that you're no longer with your crew. That is, swear you're not a pirate any longer, and that you won't betray me. The man who saved your life."

Would Maxl agree? After a flicker of hesitation in what surely had to be the time it took for the words to translate into his native language, the pirate opened his mouth. "I serve you now," he said. Nic's mouth parted with surprise. "Maxl call you master."

"No!" Nic's reaction arose from genuine shock. He hadn't at all wanted to be anyone's master. It was the one role for which he was thoroughly unprepared. "Not your master. Not that. We... we work together. You and me. Friends. Yes?"

Maxl stared at him for a moment. He stood taller. The expression around his eyes seemed to change into something new. Nic hoped it was respect. "Friends," he agreed. Without warning, he cupped his right hand to his mouth and spit on his palm, then held it out to Nic.

Nic balked. When he held out his own hand, Maxl shook his head, and then pantomimed spitting. It took an act of will not to wince as Nic dribbled into his own hand. The pair shook heartily. Only when Maxl embraced Nic in another hug did Nic dare to wipe off his hand on his pants, where the pirate couldn't see. "And now I show you, my friend, yes?" Maxl said, once the ritual was over.

"Let's go!" said Nic, gesturing for Maxl to lead the way. Nic kept a firm grip on his sword, though, just in case.

The sun was beginning to rise, and its brilliance was already burning away the fog. Enough of the dense mists remained to confuse both Maxl and Nic when they emerged from the low-hanging fronds. It took several moments for them to orient themselves. The Colombos' camp was to the south, and the rest of the island stretched ahead to the north. Along the beaches they traveled, walking on the firmer land where the sands ended and the grasses began. Nic let Maxl lead the way. Despite their sworn declaration of friendship, he felt better knowing the pirate was not at his back. Maxl scarcely noticed. He was too busy working free the sundered ropes hanging from his wrists, and reveling in his new freedom.

Maxl slowed down his pace when the woods at the island's center became visible through the last of the mists. Like a hound sniffing the trail of its fox, he looked over the grasses until he saw something. Nic followed when he sprinted forward. He too could see the trail Maxl had left over the fields. Though the winds had revived the bent grasses nearly to their natural, upright shape, enough of the stalks were broken that anyone looking for the serpentine path up the slopes might see it. "Is this way!" Maxl called back, his voice excited.

Nic was slightly out of breath before they were halfway

across the field. "Why in the world did you drag it all the way inland?" he wanted to know.

Maxl had managed to free both his hands, by that point. The remnants of the rope twisted around his neck. "Grass too short in hiding," he said, as if the answer were obvious. "I cannot leave on beach. Float away." His hand curved through the air, imitating a bobbing boat, Nic supposed.

Fine. That made sense, but the longer Nic traipsed along the path Maxl had left the day before, the crazier it seemed for a single man to drag a boat. Nic had in his mind a vision of this miraculous craft. It would have at least a sail that would allow them to catch a breeze and navigate back to civilization. While it might be a little cramped for four people, at least with enough provisions for a few days, they might leave behind this isolation and uncertainty. If they had to push all afternoon to get the sailboat back to the shore, he'd do it, just for the hope of escape.

Maxl hummed to himself once they reached the forest's edge. He pointed to one of the trees. "Trail." He pointed to his temple. "Smart, yes?"

Nic peered where the pirate had pointed. The tree's bark had been carved away in a fashion that was invisible to the casual eye, but readily apparent to anyone who might be looking. Other trees on either side of the path they made through the woods had been similarly marked. Though the trunks here were fairly far apart, they were close enough that Nic found himself revising mentally the size of this wondrous sailboat that would be taking them away from this place. Surely it was narrower than he'd imagined. Perhaps it was an exotic build of craft he'd never before seen.

He wouldn't have long to wait, however. Shortly after the last of the marked trees, Maxl gave a cry of triumph and lunged forward to a mass of greenery. Sharpening his eyes, Nic saw that the pirate had used some of the large-leafed fronds growing at the forest's edge in order to cover up what he'd wished to hide, and then stacked it with brush. Babbling in his own tongue, Maxl pulled off some of the debris from one end of the camouflaged lump, revealing the boat's pointed bow. Over the edge he dove, his rump high in the air as he searched for something. Moments later he emerged, triumphantly brandishing a small bag.

"What's that?" Nic asked, running over to begin removing brush from the boat. The elephantine fronds Maxl had draped over it were still supple, even damp from the morning's fog.

"My things," Maxl said, still excited. He immediately sat cross-legged on the ground and opened his cache, pulling out a small mirror with which he examined his face. Nic watched with curiosity as Maxl touched his cracked lip, and then grunted with dismay at the sight of his bruised face. Instead of complaining, though, he reached into the bag and produced a small jar. After unstopping its cork, he dipped two fingers into the paste within. He smeared it on his right cheek, leaving behind a trail of deep blue.

Nic stopped working as he watched the pirate rub the goo around one side of his face with practiced efficiency.

"Why are you doing that?" he asked. It seemed curious to him that of all the things Maxl might choose to do with his newfound freedom, bluing his skin would take first priority.

"Is what we do in Charlemance," Maxl explained as he dipped out more of the mixture for his forehead and other cheek. "Custom. Even the damas and ritters, they blue in my homeland." He traced over his eyes, then his forehead, to show where they applied the paint. "We are warriors. This is what we do to show."

"I know," said Nic, confused. "But pirates—you said a pirate was a man without a country. Don't you leave all those customs behind when you join a crew?"

He'd touched a nerve, he could tell. "I am not pirate no more," Maxl said for what felt like the hundredth time.

Nic cocked his head. "I think you never were a pirate," he said. "Not deep down inside. You talk about Longdoun like it was still your home. I've heard you reminisce about Fat Sue." The pirate's reaction, almost guilty, convinced him he was right. "You still blue your face. You consider yourself of Charlemance. You probably wish you were back there. You're not a man of no country."

"Is not crime," Maxl muttered, quirking his lips as he checked out his results in the mirror. Nic couldn't say that the bluing had really done the man's looks any good, but at least it had concealed the bruising. "Especially not being pirate no more."

"How long were you a pirate, Maxl?" Nic asked. He began removing brush once more, excavating the boat beneath the debris.

"One year," said Maxl, putting the cork back in his precious jar of dye. "Subtracting two moon-months. Before, Maxl was slave. Dive off coasts, deep waters. Wrecked ships. Not coming up for hours, looking for the what's-it. Cargot?"

"Cargo," Nic corrected. Some of the brush was unexpectedly thorny, which made grappling with it slow going. "Hours? How could you breathe underwater for hours?"

"Dome of air," Maxl explained, making a cupped shape with his hands. "In water. I am breathing from it."

"A diving bell?" Nic had heard of such things, but had never seen one.

"Many men die from the deeps, if they come up too fast from them. I pretend I am very sick once, being sold to pirates on *Tears of Korfu*. I do what they say. But never really pirate. You are right, Niccolo. Smart boy."

Just as Signor Arturo used to, Maxl put his finger alongside his nose. The gesture made Nic curiously homesick. Much as he'd relished the sense of dominion he'd experienced upon landing on this island, he missed the sights of home—the way the palace dome glowed come sunset as Cassaforte's horns began sounding through the dusk. The crowded waters afloat with gondolas, the busy market squares. He missed the scents of roasting fowl and spiced wines, and even of the musty waters of the back canals. He choked down the lump rising in his throat. "And why did you leave?" he asked, changing the topic.

"Because of man from Pays d'Azur," Maxl said. He regained his feet, tucked away his jar in the tattered sack that had carried it, and began to help Nic. "Bad man."

"Bad man?" Nic asked, his attention arrested. "Do you mean the Comte Dumond? Tall man? Ah, spot here?" He pointed to his cheek, indicating where the comte's mole had been.

"Yes! Bad man!" Maxl agreed. "He say to Captain, 'If you attack this ship, this one, and that one, I give you gold. More gold for finding special cargot...cargo.' Captain say, 'Yes, is more easy to take money from you than be real pirates. We do what you say, grow fat, hah-hah!'" He sneered, then turned his head so that he could spit on the ground. "That is when Maxl say, these men, they not real pirates. Real pirates are men without country, answering to no one except captain. These men with their greedy fingers, they are little thugs."

Nic's mind was working a mile a minute. He had witnessed Comte Dumond ordering about the pirates who'd boarded the *Pride*. What Maxl said made sense, in a twisted sort of way. A crew acting on its own whims had its own, well, romantic independence. It was the type of thing that Signor Arturo had written plays about. A criminal-for-hire, though, was someone that no one respected. "And you didn't want to be a thug."

"I am not being a little thug!" Maxl sounded indignant at the idea. "There were handful on *Tears of Korfu* who are agreeing, but only I am brave enough to say no. When night is coming, I take boat and leave, come to island to decide what next. Who is knowing where I end? Not Maxl. Could be slave again. Could be stranded. Could be dead." He shrugged. Enough of the boat was clear that the pirate could climb in. He sat down inside. "Better than being thug."

Nic was fascinated. "So this *Tears of Korfu*, it was nearby?"

From his gunny sack, Maxl produced a handful of some kind of nuts. He hungrily feasted on them and said, through a mouthful, "There is a good chance it is still."

"Why?"

"No captain."

"No captain?" Nic repeated. "What does that mean, no captain?"

"When there is no captain, crew decide who new captain is being. Can take days. There is lots of pounding of chests, big talking." Maxl sighed and let the last of the handful of nuts trickle from his hands into his mouth. "Fighting. Long. Puts me to sleep."

The information interested Nic no small amount. Was it beyond sense to hope that aboard the *Tears of Korfu* there might be some trace of information of what happened to his master and the rest of the Arturos' company? Perhaps he might find where they were taken, so that once they had returned to Cassaforte, he could notify the authorities. Perhaps even Signor Colombo, with all his connections, might be able to help trace and rescue them from slavery. If they were even still alive. The faint spark of hope made Nic almost giddy. "Why is there no captain?"

Maxl regarded him as if he were daft. "He is dead."

"How do you know? You left the ship before they

began..." Maxl was nodding with his head at Nic's side, causing him to break off his sentence and look down. "What?" he asked. All he had in his hand was the sword. "The *shivarsta?*"

Maxl's head nodded up and down, as if the answer were obvious. "You have the *shivarsta*. This is meaning one thing. You kill Xi. Xi was captain. If you was pirate, you would be captain now."

"Oh." Nic took a deep breath, and looked at the sword, then back at Maxl. For the first time, he actually noticed the vessel in which the man was sitting. It was scarcely longer than a grown man's height. Though it had two planks set across its width to accommodate passengers, the fit for four people, he realized, would be cramped. "Maxl," he said, trying to temper the disappointment he was suddenly feeling. "This isn't a sailboat. It's a rowboat."

The man erupted into laughter. "Very funny! Of course is not sailboat."

Any visions Nic had of speeding across the sea with the wind at his back vanished in the face of reality. "But we can't get back to Cassaforte in a rowboat!"

In one fluid motion, Maxl leapt to his feet and planted his hands on his hips. A ferocious grin almost split his blue face in two. "No," he agreed. "But in *Tears of Korfu*, we travel in style. Yes?"

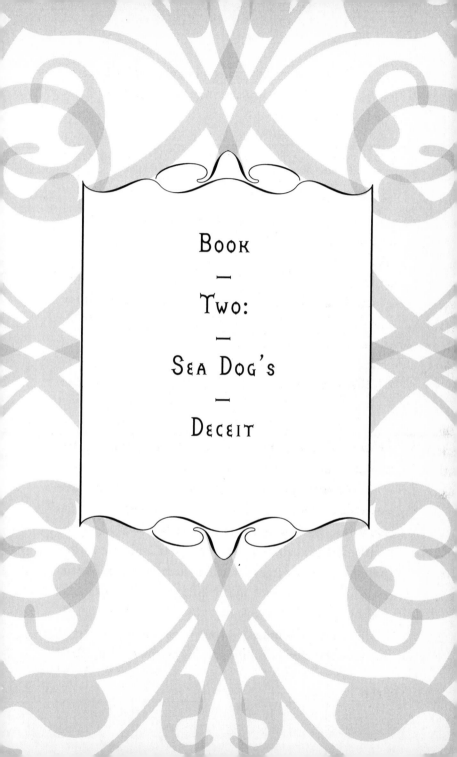

BOOK

—

TWO:

—

SEA DOG'S

—

DECEIT

10

*Ingenue: My life is naught! Who is to save me
now from the clutches of this vile wrongdoer?
Knave (fastening her wrists): Shush. Your doom approaches.
Ingenue: Hist! Is that the tread of Hero on the stair?
No, it is not! I faint! I wither! I weep!
Knave: You know, if you spent a quarter of the
time struggling that you waste talking, my dear,
you might have saved yourself three times by now.*

—FROM THE GLASS BLOWER'S OTHER DAUGHTER: A PERILOUS &
THRILLING TALE OF HAZARD & DECEIT, PENNED BY ARMAND ARTURO

For many years after, a popular play graced the stages of Cassaforte. Entitled *The Buccaneer's Apprentice, or, A Dread Tale of Adventure Upon the Bonnie Blue Seas*, it played to houses all around the Via Dioro. Acting companies fought for the rights to perform the piece. It was so popular that it could fill a house to capacity, and still have patrons paying for the privilege of watching from the aisles. The finest actors of a generation squabbled openly for the chance of playing any of the lead roles.

The most rapturous applause of all the drama's scenes, however, was reserved for the opening of its second act. Backstage, two boys hidden at opposite ends of the stage would sit upon the floor with their feet firmly planted, pumping furiously at handles attached to machinery that would rotate broad, low flats painted in blues and greens, moving them from side to side and up and down so that they resembled sea waves. Two flat discs hanging from the battens, both painted with treated bone ash so that they seemed to glow in the dark, represented the moons. Onto this picturesque tableau would roll a set piece painted to resemble a rowboat. It would contain four players.

The first, usually a junior of the company, would typically be sporting a scarf tied around his head. From beneath would protrude dark hair the color of Nic's, though much longer and fashionably twisted into beribboned plaits hanging halfway down his back. "Ar!" he would cry in a thrilling baritone, as he pointed to the horizon. "Thar be the scurvy ship."

"Indeed it be," would say the handsomest of the foursome. He was always played by the troupe's Hero. Even the famed Donatello Raello, born into one of the houses of the Thirty before rising to fame as the leader of his own company in the Via Dioro's jewel of theaters, played the role to great acclaim. At the advanced age of forty-five, however, most of his critics had to admit that he had far too much girth to pass as a seventeen-year-old servant boy. "And a wicked vengeance shall we rain down upon them all. By the very grace of Lena, I swear it!"

"And I," would say the troupe's Ingenue, who though typically attired in a boy's shirt, breeches, and boots, as well as a piratical cap perched at an angle atop her blond curls, would display enough of her womanly curves so that there was no confusion in the audience as to her true gender. "I shall taste blood for breakfast!"

"Vengeance shall be ours!" would intone the oldest of the foursome, usually a gray-haired member of the troupe who specialized in aged character roles like Philosopher or Vecchio. Despite his years, he would also be clad in the clothing of a pirate.

"No," would say Hero, lowering his spyglass. "Vengeance will be *mine*. Row on!" he would command the long-haired pirate. From a pocket he would produce a rounded triangle of cloth affixed with a narrow ribbon. Once slipped over his head, it would be revealed as an eyepatch, making him even more fearsome to behold. "Row on, and let us feast like starving men upon their misery!"

At this juncture in the production, two more boys would man the counterweighted ropes in the wings. Hand over hand they would pull as fast as they could. The battens would rise, taking with them the painted clouds that covered the backdrop. The audience, hitherto quiet and attentive, would gasp, because looming over more layers of the bobbing waves, surrounded by thousands of points of phosphorized light representing the stars, would loom the giant hulk of a pirate ship. More shadow than reality, its silhouette would seem an almost-impossible construct of ropes and riggings, of vast, complicated sails and black, inscrutable flags flying from masts that extended into the flies. More often than not, the first sight of that vast pirate ship, produced by the illusions of stagecraft, would send audiences into an impromptu flurry of applause.

Even Nic, who watched the show's very first production from the upper balcony of The Beryl, standing at the back, a cap pulled low over his eyes, was impressed by the sight of that ink-black ship blotting out the stars of the heaven as it seemed to bob upon the waters. Like the rest of the audience, he applauded with enthusiasm.

But it was nothing like the present reality—though the costumes were similar. It was true that Maxl sported a kerchief tied around his head to keep his long hair from blowing into his face, and that he had changed his grime-ground tatters for a billowing white shirt and tight black breeches. Jacopo was outfitted similarly. Hunched over on the rowboat bench, he seemed both chilly and more than a little bit embarrassed to be out of his formal robes of state.

Both moons were high in the sky and waxing to fullness. Bathed in their twin glow, Darcy's expression was not difficult to read. In fact, Nic had been avoiding it since they had eased away from shore. "I am quite capable of rowing, you know," she asserted, not for the first time.

"Maxl and I are fine," Nic assured her, trying to sound as if he meant it. They had been rowing since dusk, and had left behind their own camp long ago. It had taken almost an hour to reach the next islet in the chain, which had been smaller than their own and seemingly just as deserted (or as Nic hoped, much more so than his island had turned out to be). He was, in fact, knackered. His shoulders felt as if they were on fire. His forearms had progressed from hurt to numb to heavy, and now felt as if made from stone. He paused in his exertions to wipe his brow before the perspiration could run into his eyes. "Thank you."

Darcy had taken for herself a man's red shirt, leather breeches, and a pair of leather boots too big for her feet. Any womanly curves she might have possessed were fairly well disguised beneath the oversized garments. "A cold sweat is a certain sign of imminent exhaustion," she commented, her arms crossed. "Excessive panting, paleness, and a short temper follow, topped off by nausea." She cocked her head in challenge. "Soon you'll be tasting your breakfast."

"Darcy." Jacopo's voice carried reproof. "The boy is helping us."

"Yes, of course he is. Therefore he's beyond reproach. How unseemly of me."

Nic ignored the brush-off, and hoped that it arose simply from an illusion Darcy hoped to preserve for Maxl of contention between them. He was feeling a little sick to his stomach, but not all of it was from the rowing. Knowing the challenge that lay ahead was enough. "I'm fine," he replied, trying not to seem snappish.

"This is what I am not understanding." Beneath his new finery, Maxl was little more than the sparest of muscle stretched over a narrow framework of bones, Nic knew. It was difficult to understand how the man could keep rowing without seeming to tire. "The women of the two sex, she is handed everything. The man gives her the clothes, the flowers, the books, the jewelry. He opens the doors for her. When they walk down the street, he is on the outside so the pig dung is not tossed on her skirts so much."

"Longdoun sounds like a charming city," murmured Jacopo.

Maxl's teeth gleamed in the moonlight. "Yes! Thank you!" He continued with his thought. "The women of the two sex only have to smell nice, look nice. Yet you carry the wood. You fight like man. You want rowing. Why do extra, yes?" He swatted Nic, who nodded. "See? Master Nic, he is agreeing."

"He *is*?" asked Darcy, her tone dangerous.

"Yes. I mean, no." Nic was confused. On a certain level he knew that Maxl was speaking nonsense. At the same time, though, Nic had been forced to carry out the most menial of tasks every day, all his life. If he were given the option to sit back and watch, and not have to act upon a dictate, wouldn't he take it? Wouldn't anyone? "I'm not agreeing all the way."

"You are not satisfied with being girl?"

Darcy's voice remained a growl. "No, I am not satisfied. The ladies of Charlemance may cultivate a life convincing others that they are debilitated simpletons, but the women of Pays d'Azur and of Cassaforte, I assure you, are no mere lapdogs."

Something about the way Darcy spoke caused Nic great confusion. While he couldn't help but admire her sentiments, he was a little frightened of the way she pounded out her words, like a workman driving home nails. Ever since the day she had kissed his cheeks, he'd hoped to maintain a good standing in Darcy's eyes. Yet he felt embarrassed to admit how much her esteem meant to him. He cleared his throat and tried to side with her argument. "In Cassaforte, women hold as many positions of power as men," he explained to Maxl. "We have women nuncias and artisans, female guards…"

"Truly Cassafort City is a city of savages," clucked Maxl. "When the men are so weak they make their women to fight. It is from having enchantments no other country has, yes? Everyone lazy from not working. Poof! Magic is doing it all."

"Enchantments aren't like that. Craftsman enchantments on an object only enhance its primary purpose. Like the Arturos' trunk. It's enchanted, but it simply holds more than it seems it ought. Furthermore, we don't *make* our women do anything," Nic argued.

"Why? You are not know how?" asked Maxl.

"Shall I tell you what I know?" asked Darcy, her irritation flaring once more. "I know that if I pushed a certain blue-faced savage out into the middle of the ocean, none of us would give two lundri were he to drown there."

"You are pulling the bluff," Maxl retorted.

"Am I? Test me, buffoon."

"You are mean girl, very tough yes, but you need me."

"Perhaps we do need you." Darcy's voice cut through the night like a blade through a crisp apple. "Yet I'm willing to test the theory and cut you loose."

"Daughter." Jacopo reached out and settled his hands on Darcy's back, as if sensing she might spring at Maxl and carry out her threat.

"You need to stop," Nic told Maxl, thoroughly annoyed with him.

"Niccolo." Jacopo used the same tone. "Our friend is merely trying to arouse your ire." When Maxl began snickering to himself, Nic knew the old man had hit the nail on the head. "It would behoove us all to keep our tempers even during this stressful venture, if we are to succeed. Including you, sir," he added to Maxl.

"Hush," said Maxl, holding out a hand.

"I will not be silenced on this matter. The coup of a ship by a mere four people, three of whom have no experience with piracy whatsoever, is a matter of utmost gravity, and it falls upon us…"

"No, hush," said Niccolo. In the distance, two golden lights burned on the horizon, larger than any of the stars in the heavens. The waters reflected their wavering glow. "Row on," he whispered at last, signaling for Maxl to draw them closer.

The moment, as it appeared on the stage much later, resembled what Nic remembered of that night, but only in its superficials. The moons did make the waters of the Azure Sea shine like a mirror as their small boat cut through it on its journey to the slumbering ship. The clouds did part. Most importantly, the silhouette of the *Tears of Korfu* did loom against the night sky, blocking out the stars behind it. But its black form was not as large nor as impressive as it grew upon the stage; it did not have as many sails or as much rigging, nor did it have a single flag flying from its one mast. In fact, the *Tears of Korfu* was a mere sloop, the tiniest of boats that could carry a crew. The two lights that Nic and Maxl had spied from afar turned out, at a closer distance, to come from portholes set into the ship's aft, likely marking the captain's quarters. No shadows moved within.

The sea lapped gently at the boat's hull as they quietly rowed near. The cargo they had been towing behind the rowboat drifted with the pull of the tide. So they would not drift, Darcy used a rope to fasten their craft to a hook sunk deep into the hull. Both Maxl and Nic set their oars into the boat's bottom as quietly as possible. To produce little to no noise seemed to be everyone's goal.

Maxl put a finger to his lips. It was an unnecessary gesture. "Stay here, until I say so." Careful not to rock the rowboat, he slipped over the side and into the water with barely a splash. His form disappeared into the depths. Before it seemed humanly possible, he surfaced a dozen feet away near the ship's bow, snorting water from his nostrils. Liquid ran down his long mane and his back as he pulled himself up. After letting the reflected moonlight bounce for a few moments from the waters, Nic realized that Maxl was climbing up a chain—probably for the anchor. Like some sort of monkey he ascended, scampering from the water's surface into the air, then lunging up onto the deck as if he'd done it a hundred times before. Of course, knowing Maxl's history, Nic suspected he probably had.

After his disappearance, they had to wait in the shadows, on the side of the boat away from the moons. They could all be killed at any moment, Nic knew. Vengeance hadn't been at the forefront of his mind when he'd formulated this plan.

No, he'd come up with it out of necessity. He and the Colombos had to return home with as much speed as possible. Earlier that day, when Maxl had uncovered the rowboat and mentioned that the *Tears of Korfu* was anchored so close to their own island and unlikely to move until a new captain has been settled upon, Nic had instantly dreamt up the most unlikely of plans. It was so outrageous that the scheme might have been ripped from the pages of one of the Arturos' potboilers. Yet it was improbable enough to work. His mind had raced as he'd asked, "Maxl, exactly how many of you pirates were aboard the *Tears of Korfu?*"

"Perhaps making ten and two?"

There in the woods, by the little rowboat, Nic had performed some rapid subtraction in his head. Twelve pirates, and Nic had already taken out the captain and three more. Maxl had defected. So there were seven, more or less, and four on Nic's side. True, one of Nic's proposed invasion force was an old man, but not all problems had to be solved with brute force. He had the advantage of two strong young people and an inside informant. Hopefully, the sheer surprise of it might catch the remaining mates off-guard. "Maxl," he said, knowing he was making more work for them both. "We need to take the long way 'round the island to where I came ashore, on the trip back."

When Nic and the former pirate had finally paddled their way across the outgoing tide to the Colombos' camp,

Darcy and Jacopo had waded out into the waters to help them draw in the rowboat. Darcy had scowled at the sight of the Arturos' costume trunk, bobbing along on the water on a rope tied to the boat's end. "I hope those are more provisions," she had commented. When Maxl had then produced the fish caught in the traps Nic had laid out his first day, she and her father had been mollified.

"I can't believe you were actually supporting his ridiculous argument," Darcy now said, bringing Nic back to the dark and the present.

"I wasn't!" Nic replied, keeping his voice low. "I agreed with you."

"You agreed with *him*." Though he could not see Darcy's face, Nic certainly could imagine the storm clouds gracing it.

"The only part I agreed with was that if you had two men to row for you, why would you want to take an oar?"

"Because I can. And because I might want to. Isn't that enough?"

"Sssh." Jacopo reminded them of the danger nearby.

"Fine, you can row next time," Nic told her, returning his voice to a whisper. "I would love the opportunity to relax."

"Because it's so relaxing to sit about helplessly while everyone else does the important work for you."

"It might be," Nic said, trying to ignore the irony in her voice. "I wouldn't mind, once in a while. If you knew what real work was..."

"Oh, very well. I see. You think of me as a pampered lapdog as well, do you?"

"Darcy, my dear..."

Yet Jacopo's daughter was too heated to silence herself. "I thought we were allies," she scolded Nic. "I thought we were working well together."

"At times. When I know what you're doing," he agreed.

"Didn't I agree that we would go along with your plan? Didn't I agree to play ... dress-up?" Yes, indeed she had. Nic had been able to tell, however, once he'd opened that Legnoli-crafted trunk how very unlikely she thought the plan to succeed. She had curled her aristocratic lip at the sight of those much-used costumes as though he'd presented her with a chest full of bull droppings. "Then the least you could do would be to agree with me when I require it."

"Humbly do I beg your pardon," Nic retorted, at his most formal. "Though to me, it seems a bit funny for someone who dislikes being treated like a lapdog, to treat others that way."

He felt a stab of satisfaction when she couldn't reply. It took a moment before Darcy opened her mouth again, and when she did, her father intervened to stop her. "I think silence," he suggested in a tone that was not to be challenged, "may be advisable in this situation."

"Fine," Darcy replied. Nic sensed, rather than saw, her crossing her arms.

"Perfectly fine," he said, keeping his hands in his lap.

"Shush," said Jacopo. Not eight feet overhead, at the edge of the sloop's railing, they heard the sounds of footsteps. For a split-second, Nic hoped it was Maxl, ready to help them up. When the footsteps continued, he merely hoped that whoever it was had not heard their petty squabbling. Whoever was above them began to whistle. Imperceptibly, all three in the boat below relaxed. Nic realized he'd been holding his breath.

It was ironic that at that moment, a fish leapt from the water high into the air, falling back with more of a splash than Maxl had made either leaving their rowboat or boarding the *Tears*. The whistling ceased. Nic sensed all three of them stilling themselves and leaning even further into the shadows. "*Oi?*" said a voice from above. "*Kella stas veni?*"

Nobody, Nic thought to himself, hoping the answer might somehow transmit to the man. *Nobody but us pirates.*

Perhaps it worked, for after a moment they heard a chuckle, as if the patrol realized he'd become alarmed at nothing. He began whistling again, but only for a moment. What quickly followed was the sound of an impact, followed by grunting. Moments later, something dark and heavy fell from the deck into the water, resounding with a mighty splash as the body hit the sea sideways. Nic recoiled, not from the water splattering his face, or from knowing what had caused the sound, but from something unexpected striking his face. Instinctively his hands reached out, only to find themselves grasping some kind of hemp surface—a rope net stretching from the deck down to their boat. "Master Nic! Come!" he heard Maxl whisper. "Missy Colombo! Old man! Now is time!"

Nic's heart began to pound at a reinvigorated rate, once he had scaled up the net that left his hands scratched and punctured. Maxl had assisted him over the railing, and then turned to help Jacopo while Nic leaned over to pull up Darcy. "I'm fine," she snarled, as she neared the summit. Nic noticed, however, that she clung to his forearm when he offered it, and grunted a brusque thank-you once she'd regained her feet on the deck. "What's the status of the crew?" she asked in a whisper.

"Three are in captain's cabin." Maxl's arm was still damp, when he set it on Nic's shoulder. "They are still waking. One is swimming with fishies. He a bad man. You are not wanting business with him. Others are below deck, but you wish I am locking hatch in case they are waking?"

It took Nic a moment to realize that Maxl was addressing him. He was so used to having someone else give the orders that it seemed unnatural to be deferred to. "Oh," he said, remembering he was supposed to be in charge. Enough light spilled from both the moons and the deckside porthole to the captain's quarters that he could plainly see Darcy's raised eyebrows. Gods, he must look like such a bumbling fool to her. "Yes. Locking the hatch, please. I mean, er, lock it." Maxl leapt to follow the order.

"And now?" Darcy asked.

He didn't know what he was doing. This plan, while all his, needed someone who was actually *able* to execute it. Nic wasn't a pirate. He had none of the know-how. Even with Maxl's coaching, he wasn't going to be able to follow through. They were doomed. "I think it's time we addressed those who are awake," said Jacopo. One of his hands went to Nic's damp shoulder. In a soft voice, he said to the boy, "You know, my friend, often in my line of work, the only thing necessary for me to do is let the nuncio's robes of state do the talking. Dirty they might have been when you met me, but they were designed to impress."

"They were a costume," Nic said, understanding. That had been the reason he'd wanted to board the *Tears* dressed as buccaneers, rather than in the rags they'd been sporting. "I know."

"Exactly." Jacopo took the liberty of removing Nic's tricorne, then fishing something from Nic's shirt pocket. It was a small patch of fabric affixed to a dark ribbon pulled from one of Signora Arturo's fine dresses. "I could remain silent and not have to say a word, and by the virtue of my robes alone, be called a philosopher, a wise man, a judge, or a saint." His fingers trembled slightly as he laid the patch over Nic's left eye, then pulled the ribbon around the back of his head. "And you, by virtue of a few leftover scraps and a little bit of inexpert basting..."

Once Jacopo had tied the ribbon with a knot, Nic turned around to face him. He retrieved his tricorne—once Captain Delguardino's, washed up with so much flotsam onto the shore—and put it on his head again. "I am a dread pirate, come to wreak vengeance."

"A dread pirate indeed." Jacopo smiled. "As for the vengeance...well, try to leave a few of the crew alive. I think only Maxl has any idea of how to sail a ship, and he can't do it all by himself."

This was it, then. Of all the trials Nic had faced in the last few days, in many ways this was the most frightening; it was a path he had chosen, rather than one he had been herded down. The balance of their combined futures lay on his shoulders, and it was all he could do to force himself to take a step forward. Then he saw Darcy, standing to the side, watching him. He half-expected a sneer from her, or some kind of sharp jibe. Instead, all she did was stare. Was she nervous, too? Perhaps on his account?

He didn't have a chance to ask. Maxl returned from battening down the hatch. "We are going now," he said, striding forward and pulling Nic behind him. "Is better we surprise them, than other way around."

"All right," said Nic, before he could think. "Wait. My name. I don't have a name."

"Why, you are being Master Nic!"

"No, my pirate name." He hadn't thought far enough ahead. He didn't have a character. At the moment he was just Niccolo Dattore, playing dress-up, like Darcy had said. He hadn't transformed himself into anyone else.

Worse, it might be too late. They were standing outside the captain's quarters, and Maxl had his hand on the latch that would open the door. There was a sense of urgency in his voice as the former pirate urged, "Are you ready?"

"He's ready," said Jacopo.

Nic wanted to disagree. Whatever Jacopo said, a flowing shirt, a tricorne, and a patch over one eye did not a pirate king make. In fact, he couldn't cope with the patch at all. Hastily he grabbed it and stuffed it into his pocket, just as Maxl flung back the door.

They all were nearly overcome by the scents of pipe tobacco and the smoke from burning coals, and the dark, sweet aroma of rum. The men within were crowded around a table covered with coins and cards. At first they didn't turn or even notice that strangers and not comrades had entered their space. With startled shouts, though, they suddenly dropped their cards and leapt to their feet. Nic's hand instinctively reached for his *shivarsta*. It sliced through the air as he pulled it from his belt. To his side, Maxl sported a dagger, and Darcy a stage sword that looked impressive enough, though it would retract into its hilt with the slightest pressure upon its tip.

The largest of the three pirates began to curse in a foreign tongue. "Maxl!" he cried, and then followed it up with a few choice swear words. As he withdrew, hands raised, Nic caught sight of himself and his friends in a looking-glass that hung over the tiny grate opposite the door. Perhaps they were more fearsome than he imagined. Maxl was a sight as he leered through his blued face and gestured with his dagger for the pirates to keep away. The Colombos, likewise, looked suitably sinister in their costumes—especially Darcy, who scowled convincingly as her eyes darted around the tiny cabin.

And as for Nic... well, he scarcely recognized himself. The last few days had completely transformed him. His black crop was wilder and fuller as it spilled from beneath Captain Delguardino's tricorne. His thick eyebrows seemed determined. A few days in the sun had rendered him less pale and sheltered. He'd left Massina a boy, and now in his costume looked every inch a man. "Macaque," Maxl was saying to the large man who seemed to be leading the trio. His face was ruddy and full, and his eyes seemed sunk deep into his skull, as if he peered out at the world from a distance. "Is nice to see you again."

"You're back, are you?" The man known as Macaque spoke in Cassafortean, following Maxl's lead. It was obviously not his first language, but his words carried only the slightest of accents. "Thinking you can best me?" For someone seeming confident, his looks at Nic and the Colombos were nervous enough.

"Would not be difficult," said Maxl, sniffing.

"Well, you're too late. We're setting sail in the morning—with me as captain. Isn't that right, boys?" The other two pirates nodded with less enthusiasm, though they made sure to stand well behind Macaque.

"We are setting the sail in the morning, yes," Maxl said agreeably enough. "But with *new* new captain."

"You?" Macaque spat on the floor of his cabin. "A scrawny skeleton? Not bloody likely." Maxl shook his head. For answer, he merely bent at the waist, inclining toward Nic.

Nic hesitated as all attention turned in his direction. "This *boy*?" asked Macaque. He laughed, and dropped his hands. "That's a good one, Maxl. I'd soon as put a kerchief on a sheep and let it take the wheel as pay attention to any boy like that."

Before anyone knew what was happening, Darcy strode forward. "Mind your manners, signor!" She planted her feet in front of Macaque, then hauled off and slapped his face, hard as she could.

The round-faced man recoiled in shock. His mouth dropped, and then his hand rubbed his jaw. "Bloody hell! I'll have your skin for that, you little bitch."

"Lay one hand on her and you'll pay for it." Nic was surprised at the voice that came slithering from his lips. It was quiet, yet firm. Its syllables were almost sinister in their intent. He'd heard that voice before, from someone else. Darcy, too, seemed surprised. She resumed her place beside him.

"Says who?" asked Macaque, his face reddening with anger.

Nic took a step forward and thrust his fist in the man's face—not to strike him, but to bring the hilt of his short sword within Macaque's vision. He saw all three pirates noticing, for the first time, the carved bone and the tuft of human hair hanging from the end. At that moment, he knew he had their attention. The slightest of smiles spread across his lips. He remembered where he'd heard the voice that had come from his lips once before.

Recalling Signor Arturo's advice, he stood tall. He drew a deep breath. And he became the person he wanted them to believe. "My name is not important," he reassured them with oily smoothness. "You may address me as the Drake...or Captain, if you prefer."

11

Speak the words given to you by the playwright, and those words only. Do not improvise. Do not interpret. Do not allow stage business to interfere with the text. Stand erect and declaim them loudly, suffering not that any of the words the playwright has taken so much toil to produce be lost upon the audience.

—ADVICE TO THE ACTORS,
BY THE FORGOTTEN PLAYWRIGHT CARMINA SPALDI

During his inglorious reign as Western Cassaforte's most prolific trafficker of stolen goods, the Drake had cultivated a number of mannerisms that told the world at large that he was not to be trifled with. Though he was not of the Seven or even the Thirty, the Drake had adopted their posture—shoulders back, head high, right leg extended slightly forward as if perpetually posing for a Buonochio portrait. Though he had not been born into riches, he knew the secret language of the wealthy, and knew how to shine among those who prized gold and possessions above all else. It was amazing how readily Nic recalled those idiosyncrasies for himself, as he stretched and adopted the postures and traits of the cruelest of his former masters. Without fear of being attacked, he strode around the cabin and inspected its meager charms, regarding it as though he might a rival's pigsty. "Disgusting," he pronounced at last. "But it will do, for my purposes."

"For your purposes, eh?" Macaque's sneering tone, Nic noticed, was not as confident as before. He'd been taken down a peg or two.

"Indeed." Nic tilted his nose and stared at the man, then used the tip of his *shivarsta* on the substantial seat of Macaque's pants, turning him around as if inspecting the cut of the man.

"And what purposes might those be?" asked Macaque.

He was obviously resentful of being handled like cattle, and knowing it amused Nic. Had the Drake felt so smug and glad of it when he treated those around him like dirt? "My purposes?" Nic spun Macaque back around, and began pacing across the room once more, this time to take in Macaque's companions. One of them was a dark-skinned man with fine features, probably hailing from the Distant East. The other, though no longer young, stood a full head above anyone else in the room. His mass and muscles made him seem almost sculpted from clay and brought to life solely for destruction, like a golem from a child's story. "Glory," he said, not bothering to raise his voice. Let the pirates strain to hear him. "Riches. Infamy." The dark-skinned man licked his lips, and almost seemed to nod. "The same things as you."

Maxl had been quiet for several moments, seeming as stunned as anybody at Nic's transformation into a creature he'd never before seen. Now he found his voice. "Listen to this man, this Grake," he agreed. "You are fools if you not."

"Drake," Darcy corrected through clenched teeth.

"That is what I am saying," Maxl assured everyone. "Drake."

"Drake as in mallard?" Macaque was not the sort of man who took humiliation lightly, Nic could tell. "A duck? Quack, quack?"

With a graceful move, Nic let his *shivarsta* slice through the air in an arc, and then slipped it through the notch in his belt. "Drake as in dragon," he explained, again softly, this time circling Macaque with the slow pace of a panther. "A fire-breathing…deadly…ravenous creature that few have actually seen, but which all fear." He saw Jacopo raise his eyebrows and blink. Even Darcy, though she was keeping a stern look upon her face, seemed startled at the transformation.

The only important reactions, though, were from Macaque and his men. Macaque had almost audibly gulped during Nic's speech. Now he seemed fixated on the short sword hanging at his side. "You and your men. You killed Captain Xi?"

"I alone killed Xi. We fought man to man, and I bested him," said Nic. He let his fingers play over the *shivarsta's* bone handle. "My crew and I—" He nodded at Darcy, to let her know he acknowledged her gender. "My crew and I have come to claim our due."

Macaque spread his lips into something that resembled a smile, though it was not in the least friendly. "Have you, now? And what's to say my other men aren't without, ready to slit your lily-white throats?"

"What's to say we haven't already taken care of these other men?" Nic asked, maintaining the Drake's maddening calm. "The handful you have left, that is. My understanding, Signor Macaque, is that you're at least five men down. Is that even enough to run such a concern?"

Macaque's flinty eyes darted in Maxl's direction. "Traitor," he growled. "You've told them all you know, haven't you?"

When Maxl shrugged, Nic cocked his head. "Don't blame the man for knowing on which side his bread is buttered," he assured the pirate leader. "He's only acting in his own best interests. As should you."

The tension in the room was palpable. Maxl was still crouched and ready to spring if necessary, as were both of Macaque's flunkies. The Colombos both had their stage weapons drawn and at the ready. Only Macaque and Nic stood in any posture that resembled relaxation, and Macaque seemed decidedly ill at ease. Smoothly as the Drake's personality came oozing out of him, Nic wouldn't have been at all surprised had Macaque suddenly ordered his men to attack. After a long pause, however, he crossed his arms. "What are you proposing? Because if you think…"

As had the Drake so many times before, Nic raised a hand to silence the man. "I am proposing that, for the sake of your life and the lives of your crew, you accept me as your captain." Macaque's lips pursed at that demand, as if he tasted sour lemon. "I also propose that we rendezvous with the rest of my fleet. Once united, you will see what true piracy is—and true riches."

"And where is this fleet?"

"Docked at Cassaforte," Nic replied smoothly. He only had to carry the charade that far. If Macaque were to find no pirate fleet once they were all safely home... well, the city guards could take over the problem at that point.

"Cassafort City, eh?" Macaque raised his eyebrows. "We'd have to pick up provisions in Gallina to make it that far."

"Well then. What say you?" There was a tense moment as all three of the pirates looked over the impostors. Macaque took in the fashions that Nic and the others had created using the Arturos' costume chest. His eyes lingered over the clean whites of the men's shirts, the carved jet black and newly replaced feather of Nic's tricorne, and the rich red of Darcy's blouse. He seemed to compare Jacopo's and Darcy's shiny, elaborate blades with his own battered sword, and to study the costume jewelry they sported on their fingers and necks. "I ask you this, Macaque," said Nic in the Drake's sinuous tones. "Which is better? To be the captain of a rag-tag ship so poor that it has to accept bits and bobs of work from Pays d'Azur, or to serve under another and know riches enough to buy a lifetime of pleasure?"

Nic suspected he'd had Macaque the moment the man had asked his proposition. When the man licked his lips at the mention of riches, he knew it for certain. "If you are as powerful as you claim, then you know there are customs," he at last said, after clearing his throat.

"Nothing worthwhile is ever gained without struggle," Nic replied with a smile.

"You're old enough to know that, then. How shall we do it? By the blade?" Macaque's voice grew louder and more intimidating.

Nic suspected the fool was trying to work up the courage to fight, face-to-face, with the youth who had somehow bested his captain. Only Nic knew that it had been a combination of sheer luck and opportunity working in his favor. "No."

Macaque cracked his beefy hands together. His knuckles cracked like kernels of corn over a hot fire. "Bare hands? Revolvers? How would you like to meet your maker, boy?"

Nic's eyes flickered in Darcy's direction, meeting her glance. She shook her head with so slight a motion that even anyone studying her closely might have missed it. Was she warning him? Or did she not want him to take the risk? Nic couldn't help but wonder. His voice was barely a murmur as he wandered over to the table where the coins and cards still lay, abandoned mid-game. "Signor Macaque. Your sloop is already many hands down. Surely we both realize that your loss would be much grieved?" With a smile, Nic added before the man could protest, "What I had in mind would result in a casualty less. How good a player of taroccho are you, sir?"

Ah, yes. He had appealed to the man's greed as well as his vanity. "None better," Macaque assured him. He strode around to the other side of the table and swept the cards together. "Are you suggesting we settle our differences through a game of chance?"

"Three games," Nic replied. Macaque seemed to be confident of victory. Nic, however, had month upon month of the Drake's victories at cards in mind. His former master would have eaten the would-be captain as an appetizer for his dinner. "When I win two of them, you'll cede the title of captain to me."

"Three games," agreed Macaque. "And when you lose two of them, boy, I'll put you and your comrades to work like you've never been worked before."

Nic's only reply was an icy smile meant to imply that the like would never come to pass. "Master Drake," said Maxl. Nic noticed that his voice was more strained than usual. "Having word with you, please?"

"Of course. Excuse me," he said to Macaque, and began to stride over to the room's far side.

The man nodded, then handed off the collected cards to the brawnier of his men. "Urso." He rattled off a series of instructions in a foreign tongue, sending the man lumbering in the direction of a desk in the cabin's corner.

"What did he say?" Nic murmured in Maxl's ear, once they had a small amount of privacy.

"He is asking him to get the more fresh cards," Maxl replied. His hands dug into Nic's shoulder. "Are you knowing what you are doing? This man, he loves his taroccho. He always is winning."

"Is this wise?" Jacopo asked. He, too, seemed concerned.

"I appreciate the vigor with which you have invested yourself in this endeavor, but it seems a dangerous caprice."

"You are gambling with our freedom," Darcy growled, more to the point. "Not just yours. Mine and my father's as well."

Nic dropped the character of the Drake to speak to his friends, but some semblance of the man remained in his tone. Perhaps it was the testiness of his voice that came through most strongly when Nic said, "I know what I'm doing."

"How can you?" Darcy demanded. "What has made you such an expert on games of chance?"

"You will have to trust me," Nic replied, his words low and even. "I wouldn't have wagered our futures if I wasn't confident I might win."

"Might? What if you don't win? What if we're worse off than we were on the island?"

Darcy was angrier than she'd ever before been. Her eyes flashed with fire, and though she modulated her volume so that she couldn't be heard beyond their little circle, Nic could tell she meant business. "How could you be worse off?" he asked, sounding a bit impatient himself. "Were you really enjoying your diet of fruit and sea-soaked biscuits that much? Do you want to hop back onto Maxl's rowboat and head back to that oh-so-comfortable cave where you were living?" From her stubborn expression, Nic knew he was getting through. "Then trust me to win this bet."

"What if you lose?" Darcy wanted to know. Her father placed a hand on her shoulder, still looking worried himself.

"Macaque is very, very good with the cards," Maxl repeated, seeming almost as worried as she.

"If I lose," Nic answered, watching Urso return to the table with a cleaner deck than the grimy set Macaque had given him, "then we're still off the island. We can try to sweet-talk Macaque into thinking he can take over the rest of my fleet." Darcy snorted, though Nic could tell she was weakening. "If he won't take us to Cassaforte, then we'll wait until we dock at a major port. We'll escape. The point is that we'll be on the move, which is more than when we were holed up on that island."

"Yes," nodded Maxl. "I agree. Is much better."

"Are we ready?" asked Macaque, interrupting their chat.

"Are we?" Nic asked Darcy.

She hesitated a moment with a mouthful of doubts. Then she swallowed them all. "Aye, Captain," she finally agreed.

12

Now Pelly is the girl that I love dearly
With her lips of coral and her eyes of foam.
But Pelly is the girl who warned most clearly
That when I set sail, I sailed to my doom.

—From a traditional sea shanty

ld man. Maxl." Nic had assumed the Drake's cool
exterior once more. He snapped his fingers to attract
the attention of the men. It seemed wiser not to use Jacopo's
name before the pirates. "Secure the deck and make sure no
one disturbs us."

"Qiandro, join them." With a nod of his head, Macaque
dispatched the scrawnier of his two comrades out the door
as well. "Urso. Remain with me."

"Thorntongue," Nic said, with a snap of his fingers
in Darcy's direction. "You'll be staying here as well." He
walked back over to the table and slid into the chair with

a view of the cabin door, forcing Macaque to sit with his back to the entrance. It was the type of ploy of which the Drake had been fond—a silent chess move designed to put the other player at a disadvantage no matter how insignificant.

Darcy seemed about to open her mouth to protest her new nickname, but in the end she kept quiet. "Thorn-tongue, eh?" said Macaque, rubbing his jaw where Darcy had struck it a few moments before. He settled down in his chair with his legs spread wide apart, and wiped his hands on his belly before shuffling the fresh cards. "Apt name for a spirited wench."

Darcy smiled back sweetly. "The last man who addressed me as *wench* returned to his wife minus two of his precious baubles."

"There, there, Thorntongue," Nic warned. "Play nice with our new friend. She can't help it," he assured Macaque with a lazy drawl. "Raised by wolves. None of the social niceties."

"I imagine not." The pirate seemed a little put out by the girl's barbed retort. If he was the sort of man who expected all women to simper and giggle at his remarks, no matter how boorish, Nic thought to himself that he was in for quite a shock when it came to Darcy Colombo. Macaque evened out the edge of the deck onto the wood with a sharp crack, and then set it in the table's center. Once Nic had cut, as was the custom, Macaque dealt out seven cards for each of them, played the head and the foot cards in the table's center, and then set the remainder of the deck between them. "Your move, fancy-pants," he announced, almost insolently.

Taroccho was a simple and fast-paced game in which players had multiple draws from the deck to form the best collection of runs within the deck's suits, or matches across them. The twenty-two arcane cards, favored by fortune-tellers for their soothsaying, acted as stoppers; they could neither be used nor discarded, and a handful of them could ruin a player's chances of forming anything useful. The head and foot card Macaque had just dealt, which both players could use for their runs and matches, were from the arcane suit—The Fool and Fortune's Wheel. So they were no help at all. "I'll have a pair," announced Nic, discarding the three and knave of cups and drawing two cards to replace them.

From the Drake, Nic had learned that most card players often gave away the quality of their hands with subtle, unspoken cues. The man holding four kings and a trio of queens might lean forward and smile, or tap his foot in nervous excitement as he waited to collect his winnings. The unlucky fellow with little but arcane cards trying to bluff his way into a pot of winnings might bite his lip, or slump almost imperceptibly. Macaque sweated. Perspiration rolled from his brow, making runnels down his red cheeks when he was not mopping at them with his kerchief. Whether or not this was an indication of what he held was difficult to tell, for it was warm in the captain's cabin. "I'll be taking three," he announced, after staring in Nic's direction for a moment.

Nic already held a pair of sevens. During the second round, Nic found himself favoring the pentacles for the rest of his combination. He very nearly had a run of three or four. "Two more," Nic announced, swapping out the cards. Both were pentacles, but neither of them completed the run. He waited for Macaque, watching as the man mopped his brow some more. "Your turn, friend," he said at last.

"I know," muttered the pirate. For so long and so hard did he stare at Nic's fan of cards that for a moment Nic wondered if he was willing himself to see through the thick paper to the card's faces themselves. It seemed an eternity before Macaque opened his mouth. "I knock," he announced, reaching out to rap on the table three times.

Nic's lips parted in astonishment. Knocking brought a round of taroccho to an end. It was an imperative that any player could make before he took his turn, forcing everyone to lay down their hands and compare who had the winning combination. In games with multiple players it was often put off for as long as possible so that the amount of money in the pot might grow, but this game was for higher stakes than a few coins. Nic spread out his cards upon the table, with the pair to the left and the non-connecting pentacles to the right. "Sevens."

"Eights," replied Macaque, dropping his cards unceremoniously to show several arcane cards, and the eights of cups and swords. Urso clapped slowly with his enormous hands.

Nic's eyebrows rose in surprise. Only a fool or a genius would have knocked a round so quickly with that hand. "You must have been very sure of those eights."

"Strike while the iron is hot," Macaque said, clearing his throat. "That's my motto. One game is mine, Drake. Good luck on the next." He pulled together the cards, arranged them into a single deck, and pushed it over to Nic for shuffling.

Why was he so hoarse, if he spoke so confidently? Nic didn't know. The only thing of which he was certain was that his own self-assurance was shaken. He'd thought that besting Macaque would be easy. But then again, the Drake hadn't won every hand he'd ever played. He certainly had lost the all-important one that had set Nic free. "The iron must be very hot indeed," he remarked, as he riffled the cards in his hands, with a pointed look at Macaque as he blotted his forehead again. The pirate ignored his jibe. It was most curious, though, that the man was so tense and nervous, and so intent upon Nic's hand when he should have been paying attention to his own...

Oh. Of course. The answer came to Nic instantly. It was small wonder that Macaque had been staring at the backs of his cards. They were marked. The Drake had always kept a sharp eye out for cheaters. Woe betide the man who dared attempt to fleece him, for it would not be long before the canal tides were stained with the offender's blood. Perhaps one of the very few things that might be said in the Drake's favor was that he never stooped to use a marked deck himself—and it was indeed fortunate that he was so wary of cheaters that he had taught all his servants how to spot cards that had been altered to favor their owner. Macaque's special taroccho deck was marked in a common enough pattern.

Certain small dots had been filled in among the embellished floral corners of each card to give away its suit and the rank. Only the arcane cards had been left untouched, as they did nothing but block a player from collecting anything more useful.

Nic reached the end of his shuffling and set the deck on the table. "Cut," he commanded. Fine. If Macaque wanted to cheat, let him. What he wouldn't know was that Nic would be onto his every move.

"Sir." As the pirate took the bottom half of the deck and placed it on the top, Darcy attempted to get Nic's attention. "A word?"

"What is it, Thorntongue?"

Only Darcy's fingernails digging into the back of his shoulder betrayed how very much she disliked that impromptu nickname. "You are going to lose us our freedom, fool," she growled into his ear. "Let me kill him now."

"No. No killing." Nic kept his response to a whisper. They were overmatched, with enormous Urso glowering at them both.

"Fine. You do it, then. Obviously you've gotten in over your head. Don't ignore me!"

"A good round," Nic commented in a public voice, beginning to deal the cards. He pulled his shoulder out of Darcy's grasp. "May my luck be as good this deal."

"Indeed," rasped out Macaque.

Nic smiled. Instead of fanning out the cards this time, or arranging them by suit and rank, he kept them in a tight bundle in his hand, peeking to see what he had very quickly. Three of his cards were arcane, of all the luck, but of the remaining four were the two and the four of staves. The three of staves lay upon the table as the foot card. It was the lowest of all possible runs and, in a normal game, nothing more than a beginning of a good set of combinations, yet the stakes of this match were different. Macaque's lips pursed and worked as he tried to make out what Nic held, but Nic merely kept his hand cupped and lolled back in his chair. "Are you planning to draw?" he asked at last.

"Yes. Yes!" Macaque slapped down a pair of cards and replaced them. Cheat that he was, he apparently never thought to suspect his opponent of the same tactics. His own cards were fanned out so plainly that Nic could easily tell that in addition to the four arcane cards he'd managed to pick up, his hand held nothing of worth. "Very well. Your play."

The look upon Macaque's face when Nic reached out to knock upon the table was priceless. The perspiration beading his forehead seemed to double in volume. "Are you certain, boy?" he asked, mopping away, though by now the kerchief was so soaked with moisture that it was nigh useless. "You haven't even taken any cards yet. I'll let you take it back if you've misplayed."

"Quite certain." Nic dropped his hand on the table, exposing the run.

It was with a number of choice expletives—none of which brought so much as the faintest of blushes to Darcy's cheek, Nic noticed—that Macaque reluctantly displayed his own lack of a hand. "You were lucky," he commented, casting dark looks at both Nic and at Darcy, as if he suspected her of reporting to Nic what was in Macaque's hand.

"Very," murmured Darcy, who had been standing behind Nic the entire time.

"We'll let the last game decide it, then?" Inwardly, Nic was trembling, though he refused to let it show. He'd managed to find a way to turn Macaque's cheating to his own advantage, though, and that was something. Perhaps he did stand a chance in the end.

Macaque had only just finished dealing the last of the fourteen cards and setting out the head and foot when the door from outside burst open, revealing Maxl. "Master Drake," he said, out of breath.

"Later," said Nic, picking up his cards. He was wary that Macaque might have been looking at the marks as he dealt, but the man didn't seem particularly adept at recognizing the symbols very quickly. Certainly, though, he seemed to have seen that the last card was nothing but an arcane. The three of pentacles and the three of swords lay on the table.

"But Master Drake..."

"Are either you or the old man injured?" Nic asked, keeping his voice disinterested and cold.

"No, but..."

"Am I in immediate danger?"

"No. But Master Dra—"

"Then it can wait," Nic pronounced, pretending to glare at Maxl. "You know better than to interrupt my pleasures."

"I do?" Maxl immediately seemed to recall himself. "I do. Yes, I do. But—"

Darcy let out an enormous *sssh!* that not only quieted Maxl, but silenced everyone else in the room as well. Nic looked at his cards. The only ones matching were a pair that he brought to the front, concealing their backs from view. Four of the cards were from the arcane suit, leaving him only a single card with which to play. "One," he announced, exchanging it. The look upon his own face was grim, he knew.

Macaque held a good hand, free of any of the arcane, Nic could tell. He concealed a pair of queens, and when he exchanged three of his hand, managed to pick up a pair of aces as well. "One," Nic repeated, exchanging his sole free card. Into his hand came another arcane—The Lovers, whose entwined arms and glances seemed to mock Nic in their very happiness. Unless he was to discard his pair, he had no further plays. He fanned out the five arcane cards as if examining his options, though he kept the pair obscured behind them, and set his hand face-down upon the table. "I'm blocked," he announced. Behind him, Darcy softly swore.

A look of triumph crossed Macaque's face. He knew he had Nic. Already he held two pairs, and with Nic blocked, he had three exchanges to make his hand even better. "Looks like your luck has run out, Drake," he crowed, while he made the first exchange of three. Apparently he found nothing of use among the cards, because he exchanged three more almost immediately. "Indeed," he said, riffling through the new cards. "I'll enjoy having you swabbing my decks. Knock you down a peg or two, it will."

"Will it, now." Nic managed to sound disdainful, despite his nerves.

"Oh yes." Macaque slapped down the three cards that he'd just drawn, and took their final replacements. "There's something particularly satisfying about bringing a tilt-nose down to the level of real men. You think with all your high-and-mighty ways you're better than the rest of us, but you've never done a lick of work in your life, mate." He licked his fingers in order to better grab the cards as he rearranged them. He immediately laid down the three trash cards in his hand. The queens and aces he laid down side by side. He grinned wildly. "Well get ready, boy. You'll be working harder than you ever have in your short and lazy life, once you're under my command."

Nic looked first at the two pairs, and then at the man who had slapped them down. Ice seemed to chill his stare. "The news may come as a surprise to you, Macaque," he announced, picking up his hand. He lay down the first of his arcane cards, The Lovers. "But I am no stranger to hard labor." Slowly and deliberately, he laid down the The Ruined Tower and The Moons as he spoke. "In my career I've gutted and skinned animals. I've scrubbed floors. I've emptied chimneys and tanned hides and pressed grapes and cleaned up after chickens." He laid down The Chariot. "I've shoveled more shit than you've ever produced in your life. Which, judging solely by your appearance, has been no inconsiderable amount." Macaque bristled at the insult, sitting up in his chair and reaching for the knife at his side. Darcy, in turn, brandished her sword as if she'd forgotten it couldn't cut so much as a lump of butter. Nic tossed down the last of the arcane cards, The Hanged Man. "Hard work doesn't scare me," said Nic. He set down the pair he'd held down from the beginning. "And neither do you."

Macaque crowed at the sight of the two cards Nic had managed to hide the entire time. "A low pair!" When he realized what the pair was, however, he froze. Behind Nic, Darcy gasped.

"A pair of threes—staves and cups," said Nic, allowing the slightest of smiles to cross his lips. "I believe they match the threes upon the table, making four of a kind." Nic rose from his seat, letting his chair scrape back. "My two pairs beat yours, Macaque. Am I right?"

Macaque's ruddy complexion turned pale. With his tiny eyes he stared at the cards as if he couldn't believe what he saw. He mumbled something indistinct.

"I beg your pardon?" asked Nic, tilting his head as if he hadn't been able to hear.

Through clenched teeth, Macaque growled, "Yes."

"Yes, what?'

"Yes, you're right." Macaque's lips curved into a snarl. When he looked at Nic and saw his raised eyebrows, though, he realized what Nic was demanding. "Yes... *Captain*," he finally spat.

When Nic turned to Urso, the giant nodded. "*Si. Kapitan.*"

"See to it that you clear the cabin of your ... things," Nic told Macaque, leaving the vivid impression that any such things Macaque might have would surely be reeking and ridden with lice. "I'll tell my crew to move in." And with that, Nic ducked under the cabin door and back out into the relatively cool night air.

Maxl couldn't wait to speak. "Master Nic—I mean, Master Drake," he said, anxious as any puppy whose owner had just come home.

Beside him, Jacopo looked worn with worry. "What happened?" he asked his daughter.

"We won," she said simply. "Nic won."

It was difficult to tell, but Nic thought she sounded glad about it. "Maxl," said Nic, addressing him with a clap on his shoulder. "You know the men here. Tell them I have defeated Macaque in fair combat and that they answer to me now. Furthermore, in secret, tell them Macaque attempted to best me using a deck of marked cards. If any would like to see the cards in question, I will show them how they were marked." The man looked shocked at that information. It even quieted him for a moment. "That should keep him from making any claims that I was the one who cheated." When Maxl opened his mouth again to speak, Nic interrupted him. "That should be your first priority."

"But Master Drake," Maxl repeated, grabbing Nic's arm. "Down below. There is something you must see." He began tugging him in the direction of the hatch, which lay open. Maxl scampered down the ladder with grace, still pulling Nic after.

"Yes, we won," Nic assured Jacopo, as he descended the ladder. "We'll set course for Gallina as soon as we can, and then home to Cassaforte after."

"Good gods," said the old man. Tears were in his eyes. "I can't believe you've done it."

The hold below was smellier than that of the average small ship. The scents of mold, dry rot, and the stink of unwashed skin were strong, and almost overwhelming. The pirates appeared to live in squalor, however, with bundles of clothing and weapons strewn everywhere. Crusts of bread littered the galley table, where a bold rat perched to fill its belly. It was obvious that nothing had been washed, cleaned, or cleared, for days. "Have the crew attend to this mess first thing," he told Maxl, who rapidly seemed to be assuming the role of first mate.

"Yes, yes, of course," said Maxl, still tugging him in the direction of the aft. "But you must come to see."

"What in the world is so important that you have to show me immediately?" Nic asked him. "Is it some kind of stolen goods?"

"Stolen in a way, yes," Maxl agreed.

"Unless it aids us in returning to Cassaforte, I don't really care what it is," Nic sighed as Maxl opened a door far back beyond the crew's sleeping area. Buoyed as he was by his recent victory, the lateness of the hour and the sheer weariness of his body were beginning to take their toll. All he wanted to do was sit down, and perhaps have a bite to eat.

"You will care." Maxl propelled him through the open

door, holding his new captain's head down so that it wouldn't collide with the low opening.

When Nic stood up on the other side, he found himself confronted not by gold galleons or piles of pirate booty, but by six bodies, all packed into an impossibly tight space. Their hands had been tied behind their backs, though the kerchiefs that had been gagging their mouths had been loosened and hung around their necks. Startled at the sight of the captives, Nic instinctively drew his blade, letting it slice through the air as he leapt back.

The oldest woman among the captives let loose with a shriek. It was operatic in scope and volume, almost forcing Nic to cover his ears. And yet, it was familiar enough to arrest any movement. His jaw dropped with astonishment. "Signora Arturo?" he asked.

"Niccolo?" answered the Signora. She seemed as equally astounded to see him. "Our little Niccolo?"

"Oh gods," said Nic. From somewhere, Maxl had produced a lantern and joined him. Nic looked from face to face. All his weariness was forgotten once more. "Infant Prodigy. Knave. Pulcinella! Ingenue! Signor Arturo! You're all alive!"

"Nic? By the gods, is it really our Nic?" The theatrical troupe's leader appeared to be stricken with utter disbelief. Whether it was at his liberation, or the costume in which his rescuer appeared, Nic couldn't tell.

It was difficult for Nic to breathe. He felt as if his throat were closing, from the emotion of it. "Untie them," he commanded Maxl. "Untie them all. But keep them away from me. Far, far away."

And, to the astonishment of all, he stumbled out of the tiny enclosure and escaped as quickly as he could back to the main deck and the privacy of the captain's quarters, so he could be alone.

13

Just between you and me, I find the little comical theatrical troupes so much more entertaining than their stuffy counterparts. Leave the Via Dioro theaters to the Thirty and their snobbery. Let us take our clove balls and candied ginger and have a few laughs from the dockside players!

—ANGELINA BUONOCHIO,
IN A NOTE TO HER SISTER GIULIA, CAZARRA OF DIVETRI

"N ic! Lad!" Signor Arturo had beaten at the cabin door so many times now that Nic was surprised it hadn't been battered down. "You're being silly. I'm fine. We're perfectly all right."

"That's why you've got to go away," Nic called. It was surprising, how hollow and full of echoes the captain's quarters sounded once he'd all but barricaded himself in. He'd entered seeking some kind of comfort through solitude. Although the space offered enough of the latter, of the former it afforded very little. After seeing the captain's stained mattress, he'd discarded any notion of curling up

169

on it until it had been washed and fumigated. "If you don't, bad things will happen," he called from where he'd sat down on the floor, under a map of the Azure Sea.

"That's nonsense."

"That's my curse," Nic told him through the closed door. "I should have told you when you took me on, and I didn't. I hoped it would go away. And look what happened."

"Nothing happened!" The exasperation in his master's voice wasn't the result of his stage training. It was perfectly real.

"Nothing happened? You were all kidnapped by pirates and nearly sold into slavery!"

"Well, yes." Armand's gift for extemporaneous speech failed him, as he tried to bluster his way through that one. "But..."

"But it didn't happen." Signora Arturo's voice replaced her husband. She used the soothing tones for which she imagined she was famous. "Niccolo. Little love. Have your man open the door for us. Let us show you our gratitude."

"Don't you do it, Maxl," Nic rasped out. He'd entrusted his friend with the key that Macaque had left for him on the captain's table. "Just leave me alone, all of you. We'll be leaving for Gallina at dawn, and you can buy passage back to Cassaforte from there." He tried to ignore the squawks of outrage and surprise audible through the door's heavy planks. "I've told you, it's not safe for you to be near me, with my curse."

"What can I say to make you change your mind, my boy? There's no such thing as curses. Everyone knows that."

To his master's pleas, Nic had to turn a cold heart. "You believe in curses. It's true. Isn't there a curse in *The Infernal Mysteries of the Bloody Banquet*, which you wrote yourself?"

"The *Bloody Banquet* is a work of theatrical fiction! There's also a demon who tries to marry Ingenue in it, but that doesn't mean I believe the denizens of the underworld are truly on a matrimonial spree."

"I've seen you murmur a prayer to the gods whenever you spill the table salt," Nic supplied as further evidence. "Why would you do that if you didn't believe?"

"Good gods. This is ridiculous." A disgusted voice from outside the door cut through the babble. "Maxl, give me that key."

Nic heard a muted protest, followed by the sounds of a brief scuffle. Moments later, the mechanism of the door was turning as Darcy Colombo admitted herself to the room. Maxl followed, rubbing his hand on the back of his head as he shut the door behind him. "She is bonking me on head," he complained, perplexed at how to handle the girl.

She tossed the key back to him as she made her way across the room, then came to a stop in front of Nic. Arms crossed, she announced, "Are we done with our little tantrum?"

Nic didn't appreciate the scorn in her tone. "I endangered myself for you and for your father," he announced. "I deserve a little more respect than that."

"The fig doesn't fall very far from the tree." Darcy stared down at where Nic was folded upon himself by the wall. "I meant, I was wondering how much of 'the Drake' was put on, and how much of it was you. Apparently he's more like you than I thought." When Nic glared at her, hurt, she nodded. "There he is again."

His retort was short and simple. "That's unfair."

"What's unfair is how you pretend it was only your own self you endangered over that card game. You endangered all of us. Yes, I know," she interrupted when he began to protest. "We would have found a way out of it. Fine. You're clever enough to have figured something out."

Nic couldn't help but be surprised how her scolding had turned, no matter how begrudgingly, into a compliment. "You—you think I'm clever?"

Her lips worked without words for a moment before she explained. "You've lived such a curious life that it's left you, I think, with a talent for thinking on your feet. And for self-preservation." Without warning, she sank down to the ground and joined him on the floor. Nic had a mental image of her doing just that in the gowns she likely wore in her everyday life, and had no doubt that it would be a ravishing sight, with her skirts richly arrayed around her and her golden hair tumbling down her back. Now, though, in her makeshift pirate outfit and with her hair tucked beneath her cap, she looked like any other boy—or more honestly, like Ingenue dressed as a boy in one of Signor Arturo's outlandish dramas. "I suppose I should learn to trust your instincts more."

It was as handsome an apology as he was likely ever to receive from her lips. He nodded. "Thank you."

"I thought you cared about these people," she said. "It's obvious they adore you."

"I do care." His protest was soft, as suited the mood. "I'm just worried—I'm worried that because of me, no good will come to them. I couldn't live with that."

A moment of silence passed in which she said nothing. "My mother went to the gods nine years ago, when I was eight. She started to appear in my dreams after that. Sometimes she still does. There's nothing mystical about it. I'll dream that I've gone down to breakfast and there she is, sitting at the table, eating fish and olives as if it were the most ordinary thing in the world. In my dream I'll tell her that I had another dream she died, and she'll laugh and pat my head." Darcy sighed. Her blue eyes looked into some far-off, imaginary distance. "When I wake up and find she's gone again, never to come back, it makes for the worst morning in the world."

The sadness in her voice made Nic want to reach out and take her hand, but he refrained, not certain how welcome she'd find the gesture. "I'm sorry."

Perhaps he had betrayed himself with the slightest of motions, however, or perhaps she sensed his kindness and wished to reciprocate, because without any hesitation she reached out and put her own fingers around his. "You, Niccolo, are living the dream. You've found your friends alive and largely unharmed. Though," she admitted, "the one dressed like a baby seems to have cried herself hoarse." She squeezed. "Lena and Muro have given you a gift. To turn away your friends would be dishonoring the gods."

The warmth of her hand alone almost made him give in. He was so unused to this kind side of Darcy that witnessing it made him feel as if he'd done something truly awful to bring it about. "I am so worried, though," he said slowly, trying to measure out every word, "that my curse may cause something worse to happen to them."

Darcy shrugged. "So what?" That was more like what Nic was used to from her. Then suddenly, she smiled again. "You'll think of a way out of it, for all of us. Right?" She withdrew her hand and pulled in her feet. "So shall I let them in, or do you want to continue your tantrum?"

"I'm not having a tantrum!" he protested, laughing weakly. "A tantrum is not something any of my masters would have tolerated, so I've never thrown one."

"It shows," Darcy commented. With a brisk motion, she pulled herself to her knees, and then her feet, so that she could brush dust from her breeches. "When you want a *real* lesson in tantrum-throwing, come to me. I'll show you how to stomp and pout and shrill like a professional. Don't laugh. My servants could tell you stories that would make your hair stand on end. Oh, come here, you." As Nic finally stood on his feet, she moved in close so that she could reach out toward his head.

"I…um…" Nic dodged, much embarrassed.

"Your hair is a little…on the sides," she explained, awkwardly trying to smooth down some fly-away locks before thinking the better of it and retracting her hands. Finally she let him attempt to fix it himself. "There," she said, once he was more presentable. "You look handsome."

They stood close, face-to-face, at a proximity Nic had never before been with a girl, much less a young lady of means. He couldn't have moved if he'd wanted to, so fraught with tension was the moment. Was he supposed to say something? Do something? If so, it lay beyond his realm of experience. She, too, seemed transfixed, unwilling to look directly into his eyes, but unable to look away from them. For the longest time they seemed to stand there, motionless.

Then Maxl let out a cough to remind them that he was still there, and the tension diffused. They stood away from each other, relaxing. "Handsome for your ugly face, anyway," Darcy said. Immediately after the words came out, she colored.

"Ah...you can open the door, Maxl," Nic said, coughing furiously as his friend obeyed. Darcy retreated, vanishing among the bodies that, without invitation, began to invade the captain's quarters. But even with all the noise and the talk and the boisterous cheers that soon began to fill the tiny quarters, she wasn't in the least forgotten. Not by Nic.

The reunion produced more weeping among the troupe than Nic ever would have imagined possible. Of course, any actor worth his salt could cry at the drop of a cap, as the Arturos were fond of saying. But Nic was almost convinced there was enough salt water coursing from tear ducts to form a sea rivaling the one upon which they sailed. Signor Arturo had ruffled his hair and called him a good lad for saving them, while the Signora had enveloped him in her massive bosom and hugged him as if she might never let go. Pulcinella sat at his feet and immediately set to re-sewing the broken jet in his cap, while Knave inspected the cupboards for wine and called for a celebration to end all celebrations. Ingenue, while hanging on to every word of Nic's abbreviated tale, managed both to wring her handkerchief with anxiety and flutter her eyelashes prettily in Maxl's direction, though twice he mistook her flirtation and offered to fetch spoonfuls of mint vinegar for her stomach pains. Infant Prodigy, while all the talking was going on, tumbled prettily and entertained them all with her splits. As Darcy had pointed out, Infant Prodigy had lost her voice from crying, and thus (perhaps not sadly) was unable to sing.

Second only in enthusiasm to Nic's own reception was the troupe's reaction to learning that the chest containing most of their costumes and many props had escaped unscathed from the disaster. They had lost all their scenery rolls, most of the paint they used on their faces, and any personal effects they might have carried in their own valises. However, the notion that something as venerable as the Legnoli chest might have survived only served to cheer them all.

Gradually Nic was able to make out that they all had thought him long dead, the only member of the traveling troupe to meet a dire fate at the pirates' hands. They had all been herded by the crew onto boats taking them to the *Tears of Korfu* while Nic slept aboveboard and unnoticed. All, of course, save Infant Prodigy, who had seen Nic being held at sword's point by Captain Xi, and assumed the worst when he had not joined the rest. Of the *Pride*'s explosive end they did not know, for they had spent all their time since in the small, dark quarters with little air, less food, and only one chamber pot to share between them. "I've known theatrical lodgings with fewer amenities, but not by much," joked Armand. The others laughed heartily at the joke, though Signora Arturo only wept a little more.

By the time dawn's edge had begun to redden the horizon, Knave was snoring heartily in one of the chairs around the table, while Infant Prodigy had tumbled to a stop atop the dirty mattress. Signora Arturo had fallen asleep, exhausted, in an upholstered armchair near the captain's desk, with Pulcinella snoozing at her feet. Ingenue had long ago given up on Maxl, after he failed to notice her many comments about his muscles during the retrieval of the costume chest from the waters, and had chosen to take a nap in a corner. Only Signor Arturo and Nic were still awake, and they had chosen to exit the cabin and confer at the ship's prow. Behind them, Maxl barked out orders to those remaining of Macaque's crew, preparing them to set sail. They bustled around without question. One of them even whistled as he set to his job, providing a cheerful counterpoint to the silent majesty of the sunrise.

"We'll all pitch in, you know," Armand assured. He thumped the boy on his back. "You won't be short-handed on our account."

"I couldn't ask that."

"Why not?" asked the actor. "None of us are afraid of hard work, lad. You know that."

"I know. I don't want any of you to..." Nic shook his head. He didn't want to have to complete his sentence. He didn't want any of the troupe to have to labor unduly because of the trouble he'd gotten them into. No matter how many times he heard it, no matter how many people said the words, Nic simply couldn't shake the conviction that his curse had caused it all. "I know you don't believe me," he started again. "There's something about me that causes trouble for people. Some flaw in my nature. I don't know whether it's because of my birth or..." Nic sighed with the deepest of frustration. "I'm afraid even to stand close to you, Signor! A roc might fly down and swoop away with you. A leviathan might swallow the ship whole."

"Unlikely," commented Armand. "Besides, lad...ah, I shouldn't be calling you that. You're more of a man than I, with all the combat you've seen in the last week."

The sun's leading edge made the sea's waters glow as the light rippled its way in their direction. "None of which I wanted."

"You'd be a fool if you did crave such ugliness. A damned fool. And I'm glad you aren't." Signor Arturo stared out to sea for a moment, then regarded Nic with kindly eyes. "But it's happened, and it's part of you now."

"Like the Drake." The words tasted bitter in Nic's mouth. At his master's upturned eyebrows, he explained. "I never thought I'd be anything like him. He's so much a part of me, though, that when I opened my mouth in front of Macaque, he came bounding out."

"That's acting, son."

"No, you don't understand." The man whistling as he swabbed the deck turned his head at Nic's raised voice, though apparently he didn't speak enough of the language to understand. He smiled slightly and nodded with respect at his new captain before returning to work. "I wasn't pretending. I *was* him. I talked like him. I thought like him. I even moved like him and not like myself at all."

"That's acting," repeated the expert in the field. Armand stood back and leaned against the railing as he regarded Nic. "When you took to our little company so readily, standing in the wings and memorizing every line of every one of my plays, I wondered if you might have the gift. It would make sense. All your life you've had to stand to the side and observe, haven't you? You'd be a very dull lad indeed if you hadn't picked up on what made your masters unique. Why, I'd be surprised if you couldn't do a very good Armand Arturo, king of actors and actor to kings!" When Nic started to think about the various tics that he associated with his master, Armand seemed to notice. "Though don't, lad. The mirror of truth can be disconcerting for as vain a soul as I."

"I never wanted to be an actor," said Nic, slowly.

"Didn't you? Pity. I thought you'd be a good addition to the troupe."

"As what?" Nic shook his head. "A replacement for Knave? That's what I seem to be suited for."

"I rather thought you'd make a good Hero. Eventually." When Nic lifted his head in surprise, Signor Arturo smiled. "Don't embarrass me, lad. I can only stuff myself into Hero's tights for so long. Vain I might be, but even I can look into the glass and realize that audiences will accept me as the dashing young lad for only so long. Besides, if I had a new Hero, we could at last produce some plays with Vecchio in them."

"You're not old enough for Vecchio," Nic protested. "And I could never play Hero. I'm not … like that." Emotion prevented him from saying anything else. Surely Signor Arturo was the kindest man ever to be born.

"You're loyal to say so, lad. Many thanks to you."

"No, I mean it. The audiences love you as Hero."

"That they do. Indeed they do, lad," sighed the Signor, though with enough of a touch of whimsy that Nic knew he was joking.

The humor grounded Nic somewhat. Although he was leagues from any place he'd ever known and never really had a place to call his own, the chuckle welling inside him made him feel a little like he'd come home. "Besides," he said. "You don't want one of your servants up there on the boards."

"Oh, Nic." Any amusement in the man's voice had vanished. "You don't imagine that I still wish to be your master, do you?" Nic blinked, not certain what the man was saying. Did he mean he intended to sell his work debt once more, when they returned to Cassaforte? Armand must have seen traces of fear in Nic's eyes, because he put his hand on the boy's shoulder. "How can you think that I ever intended to be anything other than your *last* master?"

Nic swallowed, hoping that he understood aright. "Truly?"

"Truly. The moment we're back home, you and I will darken the doors of the debt registry, haunting the foul place until the denizens within take my ill-gotten coin and erase your indentures. You shall be a free man at last. Did you ever think I intended otherwise?"

Nic felt nearly choked with gratitude, but he knew he had to refuse. "I couldn't ask you to do that. Not after you've lost everything because of me."

"Niccolo Dattore." The actor crossed his arms and leaned against the rail. "Neither I nor my good lady would have anything at the moment, were it not for you. When I write my memoirs, our little adventure will make a pretty chapter. Most importantly, it will not be my last chapter, which is the most important thing. Eh?" Before Nic could blush any more deeply from the sheer pleasure of the news, Armand changed topic. "Now, tell me about the girl."

"The girl?" Nic asked, not comprehending at first. Then, on seeing Armand's knowing, raised eyebrows, he managed to redden even more. "What about her?"

"That's what I'm asking you," said Armand in the confidential tone of two friends talking about the fairer sex. "What about her?"

"I…I haven't seen her in a while," Nic sputtered. He was so confused of his own feelings about Darcy that he thought it impossible anyone else had noticed them. He was surprised to see Armand raise his hand and point.

Up against the a blue sky streaked with pink, where the stars still held forth against the encroaching daylight, Darcy stood in the crow's nest in her breeches and boy's shirt. Her blond curls had come loose from her kerchief, and hung loosely down her back. One of her hands clutched the top of the mast while the other worked a rope through some sort of pulley. Once it had been threaded through, she called down in Azurite to Urso below, who sent up enough slack so that the rope could feed through back down to the ground. With Darcy's help, Urso managed to catch the tip and tie it down again. Darcy, in the meantime, turned round and, upon seeing the pair looking at her, waved to them both. The smile that made her face captivating, however, was only for Nic.

"You've seen her now," Armand commented knowingly. "And she's seen you."

Nic's feet struggled to keep himself in place. He wanted to run and tell Darcy his good news. "It's not like that," he explained, trying to believe it himself. "This isn't one of your stories, Signor. Life's not always about a boy and a girl." In the end, he lost the battle against his feet. As Darcy lowered herself from the last rungs of the rope ladder down and jumped down to the deck, he first shuffled, and then took quick steps, to meet her.

Armand Arturo watched him go. At the last, he laid a finger aside his nose. "Oh, yes," he said to himself with no little degree of amusement. "Indeed it is." Still laughing to himself, the actor shook his head and strode back to the captain's quarters, so that he might awaken his wife with a kiss.

14

*The dread pyrate MacKeephir, known far and wide as the Blighte
of the Seas, was not hung for his crymes when the monarche of
Ellada captured his foul vessel. Instead, he was most thoroughly
gutted, then while still crying out for mercy, had each of his limbs
tied to chains which were dragged in the four directions of the
compass by quarter-horses set to full gallope. His head was decapi-
tated by a silver blade and the entiretie buried beneath a crosse-
roads by the light of a double fulle moon.*

—From Tall Tales of the Wide Sea: A Nursery Primer

O f all the strokes of good luck granted Nic during his
ill-starred time upon the Azure Sea, surely the most
fortunate had been in meeting Maxl. Through observation
and experience, his blue-faced friend had been involved at
some point in his life with every aspect of a sloop's day-to-
day operation. He knew how to set a course using both a
compass and a sextant. He knew the intricacies of the rigging, and the correct ways to repair a sail. He knew which
parts of the *Tears of Korfu* needed to be kept clean, and on
what schedules. He managed to talk Ingenue into making an inventory of the poor stores in the ship's galley, in

order that Nic could make a list of what was to be prepared for various meals as they sailed to the port city of Gallina—and more importantly, so they would know what to purchase upon docking, so they could make the rest of the trip to Cassaforte.

In fact, so marvelously organized was Maxl that Nic had little to do in his role as ship's captain. The pair of them would retire to the captain's quarters after each meal so that Maxl could inform Nic what had to be done in the next few hours. Nic, in turn, would memorize the assignments and make an appearance to give out orders, while Maxl trailed along behind to give translations when necessary. "But what do I do?" Nic had asked, the first day.

"You are giving the orders," Maxl had told him, shrugging.

"But I can't do that and not do any of the work."

Maxl didn't seem to understand Nic's protest. "But that is what masters do," he said, puzzled. "Is what they are good at. Is why they are the master, no? You do everyday work, they think you one of them. You work beside them in emergency, then they respect you." The more Nic thought about it, the more right it seemed. The Drake gave out orders enough, but would never have been caught dead doing any of the actual labor. He wouldn't have muddied his hands extracting valuables from the wreckage of Caza Portello, after its fall. In fact, he would have been as far from the scene as possible, letting his servants muddy themselves. Training himself to think like the Drake instead of being helpful, like Nic himself, was going to be the most difficult aspect of this entire job.

Particularly so when the Arturos' troupe had thrown themselves so whole-heartedly into the endeavor. Not a single one of them had disagreed with Signor Arturo's plea that they treat Nic as their captain and address him as the Drake in front of the *Tears of Korfu*'s original crew. None had turned up their noses at the tasks Nic and Maxl had assigned. Ingenue and Pulcinella had taken to galley cooking duties with great enthusiasm, rendering the salted fish and meats tastier than anyone would have believed possible given the scarcity of ingredients left in the pirates' cupboards. Infant Prodigy, once freed of her skirts and little girl's attire, scampered up and down the ropes as swiftly as any boy, and developed an acrobatic knack for swinging between them to attend to any duties that involved climbing the rigging. Signora Arturo cleaned and scrubbed every surface without complaint, while the men attacked the hard labor as if they'd been born to it, thanks to a little instruction from Maxl and a little coaching from Signor Arturo telling them they were all performing the roles of their life.

In fact, the first two days at sea went so smoothly and without incident that Nic found himself breathing more and holding his breath less. When at first the *Tears of Korfu*'s sails had been hoisted and they'd begun skimming across the sea in the direction of Gallina, Nic had been convinced that between what he pretended to be and what he actually was lay a gulf so wide that no bridge could ever span the two. After two days of salutes and nods and deferential inquiries into his health and desires, even from among Macaque's men, he was beginning to wonder if it even mattered. Seeming was just as good as being, to them.

Then there was Macaque himself. Nic had developed a tendency of avoiding the man when he could. There was something about the way Macaque would stare at him with baleful eyes whenever the two were in the same vicinity of the tiny ship. It was unpleasant enough that, when Nic realized he'd have to encounter the man, Nic would keep moving in order not to have to exchange more words than a few pleasantries. This morning, for example, Nic could see Macaque staring at him as he worked upon the foredeck with Urso and Qiandro, repairing a net riddled with tears. It was too late to return to his cabin, and besides, the day was fine and he had no desire to cramp himself up indoors. He nodded at the trio as he sauntered by, hands behind his back.

"Morning, Drake," said Macaque, regarding him with his tiny, black eyes. Somehow he made the words sound mocking.

"*Kapitan*," murmured Urso and Qiandro in a more subdued tone. Urso even nudged Macaque with an elbow, reproachful of his lack of respect.

The Drake would not have spent time educating Macaque, and neither did Nic. Instead, he merely kept his eyes cold as his left hand casually tickled the hilt of the *shivarsta*, and raised his eyebrows. He stared long and hard until Macaque cracked under the pressure. "I mean, good morning, Captain," he muttered.

Nic relaxed his stance somewhat, without actually becoming friendly. "Good day."

Before Nic could move past, Macaque looked up from his coiling to remark, "We'll be in Gallina before the afternoon, most like." Nic nodded, agreeing with what Maxl had told him the night before. "I was wondering if me and the boys might have a little shore leave," Macaque winked. "A little drink of the good stuff, a little gambling, a little wenching. You know."

"Do I?" asked Nic. Several days of pretense had helped him hone the Drake's frosty language to a fine edge. "Do the tavern keepers of Gallina have a higher tolerance for cheaters than I, then?"

Macaque colored, then translated quickly for his comrades' benefit. Both of them snickered at Macaque, a reaction he clearly hadn't expected. He reddened even more. Nic knew that having Maxl spread the word that Macaque had been cheating at cards had done a world of damage to the man, as every remaining member of the crew had lost at taroccho to him at one time or another. "Is that a yes, then, Captain?"

"We are setting in to Gallina for provisions only," Nic responded. "Not... *wenching.*" Nic managed to pronounce the word with the utmost distaste. "I've given my first mate onshore duty assignments," he said, realizing even as he spoke that he'd have to inform Maxl that he'd made such a claim. "If he feels that they are done in a timely and efficient fashion, and there are hours enough left in the evening for recreational purposes, then I care not what you do with them. So long, that is," he added, staring Macaque up and down, "as my crew is back in plenty of time to set sail on the morrow. And free of love bites, if there's a wench on land who'll have the likes of you."

Macaque had, out of habit, been translating for his companions as Nic spoke. His friends laughed outright at the conclusion, probably at the sight of a boy laying out so plainly a man many years his elder. Urso punched Macaque in the arm, a gesture that Macaque shrugged off with a scowl. Nic thought the matter closed, but Macaque barked out, before he could continue his stroll, "So, Captain, tell me about this fleet of yours. The one up north," he added, at Nic's upraised eyebrows. "The mighty fleet of pirates we're supposed to be joining."

"Macaque." From the hatch below, where he'd been breakfasting later than the rest of the crew, Maxl had appeared. He vaulted up the ladder and walked over. "Why are you bothering our captain with your questioning?"

The implied threat in his voice didn't put on ice any of Macaque's insolent tone. "I don't believe our captain said it was a bother, Maxl," he replied, all innocence. "It's not, is it, Captain? I was simply curious about this mighty pirate fleet that we'll be joining. And while we're at it, Captain, what were you doing in the Dead Man's Strait? There's little enough treasure to be plundered there. Why so far from your mighty armada, if there is one?"

It was obvious that Macaque intended to sow dissension among the ranks, however he could. Though he hadn't translated for Urso and Qiandro, the two pirates obviously were over-familiar with Macaque's grating tone, because they simply gave each other a certain look of suffering, then lowered their heads to continue with the mending. "Tell me, Macaque. Do you care?" Nic asked. With Maxl at his side, his confidence always bolstered.

Macaque sniffed. "Of course I care. I want to know what kind of concern I'm joining, don't I?"

"I'm surprised to hear that, frankly." Nic widened his stance, and kept his hands behind his back when he talked. The Drake never moved without purpose, never fidgeted, and never let himself appear ill at ease—no matter how much the boy inside him might have quailed at Macaque's questions. "Because from what my first mate tells me, Macaque, *concern* is one of the things you rarely show. Hmm? Concern in your duties. Concern in your manners. Concern in your mode of…" Nic sniffed before concluding the thought, as if catching a whiff of offal, "…your mode of dress. If you showed more concern in any of those areas, or in all three, I might have witnessed the kind of improvement I expect from my crewmen."

"Straighten up," barked Maxl, punching Macaque to correct his posture. He added a further cuff to the head to knock the pirate's grimy, wide-brimmed hat to the deck. "Be showing a little respect!"

"Sorry," mumbled Macaque, sounding genuinely contrite, or at least sorry for having opened his mouth unwisely.

His eyes, though, told another story. Nic feared the lingering hatred behind them. "Sorry, Captain."

Nic took a step forward. "You know, Macaque," he murmured in a low voice, "if you don't desire to continue with your mates, you can feel free to make your stop in Gallina more permanent. You don't have to say a word. Just pack what belongings you have and disappear. "

"Captain!" From above, in the crow's nest, a cry from Infant Prodigy pierced the air, shrill and clear. She had recuperated most of her voice, though it still sounded raspy at some pitches.

"I hear you," Macaque replied to Nic.

He still appeared sullen, but at least Nic wanted to make sure he got his message across. "I won't mind in the least, if you disappear, you know."

"He is understanding, Captain."

Maxl placed a hand on his arm and tried to tug Nic back, but he was too far gone as the Drake to stop. "In fact," he hissed in the man's ear, "it would be so pleasant for me to see the last of you, Macaque."

"Captain!" It was not Maxl's intervention that caused Nic to turn, but Infant Prodigy. Like the acrobat she was, she skimmed down the ladder on fleet feet, spun around the mast, then did a triple-somersault until she landed directly at Nic's feet. In older days, it was the sort of performance that might have garnered a hefty round of applause from an appreciative audience. As it was, only Urso clapped, his stone face momentarily lit up with delight until he caught Macaque's glare and went back to his mending. Infant

Prodigy proffered the spyglass she'd been using. "I believe you'll want to see this."

Nic hesitated. Whatever it was didn't sound good. "Will I?" When Infant Prodigy pointed to the north-northeast, the direction in which they were headed, Nic took several broad steps to the ship's rail. Through the spyglass he peered, squeezing one eye closed so he could see through the scratched and dirty lenses. Across the horizon he scanned, looking for whatever it was the actress had spied. "Gods," he sighed, when he caught the first glimpse of what he was meant to see.

"What?" asked Maxl, trying to peer in the same direction. Without any aid, he wouldn't be able to see anything at this distance, Nic knew. He thrust the viewing device into Maxl's hands, waited until he was looking through it, and then pointed. "We have company," he whispered.

Maxl's hands scrabbled for the glass. It took him several adjustments before he could see what Nic had just spied. He swore under his breath, and then handed back the instrument. "Blockade," he said with unusual terseness.

"Are we near land?" Signora Arturo had appeared from down below as well, huffing and puffing up the galley ladder. Of the women, only she and Pulcinella had declined the switch to men's breeches, and she had to gather her skirts with one hand and hold them tight in order not to fall. With a judicious use of her needle, however, her new costume somehow managed to convey a nautical jauntiness. "I do hope so. Tell me we are, dear boy."

"Blockade?" Jacopo Colombo had been attending to

his duties at the aft, and at all the bustle, came down to see what all the fuss had been about.

"Blockade!" Signora Arturo clutched her chest, shrieked, and looked to the heavens with a silent prayer.

The noise brought out several more of the crew, including Darcy. Whatever she'd been doing below deck had left her face blackened with soot. She emerged up the ladder, blinking with wonderment, looking first at her father and then at Nic for some kind of explanation. Nic placed the spyglass to his eye once again. When first he had looked, he'd seen only two ships in the far distance. Now that he swung the glass around, he could see more—four, six, eight, perhaps twelve in total, all spaced across the horizon. What Nic knew of shipbuilding could probably have been written on a packet of tea, but to his eye they all seemed identical in their bulk, their three-masted majesty, and in the ominous import of the cannonados darkening their hulls. "They're ships of war," Nic announced.

"Are you witnessing their sails?" Maxl inquired, his own fingers obviously itching to clutch the far-seeing device again. "What is being on them?"

Nic had to squint to make it out. "A flower," he said at last, seeing the outline on a smaller ship's sail. Unlike the others, it seemed to be traveling back and forth along the long row of ships, perhaps patrolling the waters. "An iris."

"The iris crest," Jacopo said, without emotion, "is the national symbol of Pays d'Azur." Darcy, without realizing it, let out a hiss.

During the relative calm of the last day and a half, Nic

had almost forgotten the now-familiar sensations accompanying a rush of fear—the prickling of the back, the shivers along the spine, a heat beneath his arms accompanied by a thudding of his heart and a sudden need for air, as if he'd forgotten how to breathe. It all came back to him in a rush. He did not welcome it. Still, he had a crew looking to him for some kind of response. "Well," he said, curling his lips into what he hoped was an ironic smile. "My old friends from Pays d'Azur. What a pleasure."

He handed the glass over to Maxl, who once again turned it across the skyline. "This is what I am seeing," he announced, sounding excited. He lowered the spyglass and grabbed Darcy's hands, bringing them together at face level until her fingers touched. Like an artist, he sculpted the shape they made into an inverted half-circle. "This is being the Gallina harbor, yes?" In the air, he made stabbing motions in the air, creating an invisible downward arc between Darcy's wrists. "Pays d'Azur is posting warships across, so they control city. But," he added, after a moment's hesitation, "is not looking like a siege. Other ships, they are coming out."

"So they're controlling the port, not impeding it," Nic said. He thought over the meaning of that information.

"Perhaps they're searching for stolen goods," said Signor Arturo, sounding worried. The *Tears of Korfu* had held precious little in the way of goods of any sort when Nic had taken over. A lead casket containing a moderate amount of gold was all Nic and Maxl had been able to find of the pirates' spoils. Very likely, they had intended to make more from the sale of the Arturos to slavers. "Searching for something at some rate."

"Or someone." Darcy pronounced the words flatly, but when Nic looked around, her eyes were wide as saucers.

"Yes. Well." In the Drake's bored voice, Nic spoke loudly enough to be heard by all. "It is fortunate we have nothing to hide, is it not?" He turned to Maxl, and asked more quietly, "Is there somewhere else we could find provisions?" The man lowered the spyglass and shook his head. "And we absolutely must stop?"

"If we are seeing them," Maxl breathed into his ear, so close that Nic could almost feel his whiskers, "they are seeing us."

"Back to work," Nic announced to everyone. Darcy still looked at him with unanswered questions in her eyes, but in front of anyone else she would never say anything. "Pretty lady of the galley, if you would accompany me for a moment." Nic immediately took Signora Arturo by the arm and escorted her away from Macaque and his crew. She responded to the courtesy with a little coo of pleasure, then leaned in with avid interest when Nic bent in close, once they were out of everyone else's earshot. He spoke as Nic, and not as the Drake. "I need you, without asking any questions, to conceal the old man and the girl as best you can. They must be completely hidden."

"But why?" The Signora clapped her hands over her mouth, aware that she had completely ignored his request for no questions.

It was difficult to be curt with the woman. "Mistress,"

he said, imploring her. "Pretend that this is one of your husband's plays, and that Darcy and Jacopo are Ingenue and Vecchio, father and daughter, pursued unjustly for a crime they did not commit." Nic had not given the Arturos any information about the Colombos' background. To them, the pair had been simply two more refugees Nic had managed to rescue in his battle to return to their sides. Perhaps he was gilding the lily a bit, but the Signora was listening with an eager expression, taken in by the skeleton of a good story. "You are Zanna, daughter of Muro, Mistress of the Hunt, come upon them in their time of need. What do you do?"

"Oh, naturally I conceal them, by the rules of the hunt!" Already the Signora was throwing herself into the role, Nic could tell. "I would be costumed in something beautiful and white, of course, with a high neck that would frame my face in the footlights. She's the star of the show, Zanna is, isn't she? And of course, I would be so beautiful that their foul pursuer would forget his chase, whilst I seduce him with my feminine wiles. Little will he suspect, though, that I and the forest animals under my command have concealed the pair beneath twigs and leaves, and lulled them into a quiet sleep with my beautiful song." So clear was the vision in her head that she sighed, enchanted.

"Ye-es." Nic felt he had to intervene before she completely lost herself. "Except that you're going to be wearing your pirate lass costume, and you're on a strange boat, and there are no twigs and leaves or forest creatures about. And please don't sing. Can you do it?"

Signora Arturo scoffed. "Can I do it! Of course I can do it. Although it takes an actress with the proper *seasoning*, shall we say, in order to get the true complexity of a character such as Zanna across. She is dispassionate, you know, of the world of man and yet not quite human. A heart of trembling feeling concealed in the unemotional form of a demi-god…" While his mistress rattled on about her role, Nic turned. Jacopo and Darcy were still looking out to sea in the direction of the unseen blockade. He motioned them over, while steering the Signora in the direction of the main hatch. "What a delightful plot. I really must get Armand started on a new production the moment we are back home," she was still saying, by the time the Colombos joined them. "*Zanna's Wiles: A Pastoral Tragedy in Three Acts*. No, five acts. Three is scarcely enough." A smile crossed her face as she took Jacopo by the hand. "Come, my squirrel," she told him, before addressing Darcy. "And you, my little nutkin. Zanna will take care of you."

The expression Darcy cast him as she was hustled below deck was of sheer confusion mingled with terror. He stepped over to the hatch opening and knelt down before she disappeared. "It will be all right," he told her and Jacopo both. "Just listen to the Signora. Will you trust me?"

"Of course," said Jacopo.

Darcy, on the other hand, didn't seem as convinced. Last down the ladder, she bit her lip and nodded, however. "Do what you must," she whispered when she reached the bottom.

"Come now. Hurry. We haven't much time," said the

Signora, scurrying them beyond Nic's sight. Nic straightened himself and sighed, feeling decidedly not at all like the man of scorn and contempt that he was supposed to be. Perhaps the Drake had been right to disdain the world. Caring for the people within it only led to anxiety and vexation.

Then again, he realized with a smile that he quickly concealed, perhaps it was a good thing to know that he was not as much the Drake as he had feared. Nic straightened his neck, elongated his posture, cleared his throat, and readied himself for what came next. He was certain that it would take the performance of a lifetime. Two people's lives depended upon it.

15

Do not say of your poor cousin that he is gone to Gallina. Rather, say nothing at all, or if you must, say merely he is at sea. Even saying that he is dead would be preferable than to let anyone know that one of our blood has given himself over to the wildest and most uncivilized of lands.

—From a communication between Amilitta Mancinni, of the Thirty, and her four children

It was said that the coastal island of Gallina had been founded when refugees from the country of Ellada, anxious to find a less stringent place to practice their diverse religious practices, wrecked their ship on the island's rocky shores. They settled in the one tiny area that was habitable, nestled in the isle's natural harbor, and prospered. Had the island been closer to Ellada, that kingdom surely would have annexed it at some point during the previous few hundred years. If it possessed more arable land (or indeed, any arable land at all), it might have grown to be more of a force among other countries. If it had been larger, or positioned anywhere at all of strategic import, some other nation with an eye to controlling the Azure Sea might have conquered its people long ago.

But the city of Gallina perched precariously on the beaches of a wall of rock jutting up from the sea floor. A volcano kept the city in shadow for all but the earliest daylight hours, cooling it during the warmest months. The shadow also produced an air of perpetual gloom exacerbated by long weeks in which clouds of ash shrouded the isle. Gallina attracted as residents misfits and merchants who were not particularly picky about their clients, as well as exiles and those of a more criminal bent. Visited as it was by merchants and freebooters alike, it was not a city one visited for its fine temples, or its cultured manners. Yet at least the view of Mount Gallina was fine from the water on this particular day, Nic thought as he regarded ships sailing in and out of the low clouds obscuring the harbor.

He'd had long enough to observe it. As the *Tears of Korfu* had sailed close within sight of the giant warships blockading the harbor, a contingent of smaller patrol boats had ventured over the waters in their direction. At their prows were strung bundles of triangular flags that, as Maxl had explained in the privacy of the captain's quarters, signified various maritime messages. This particular combination of red and white meant to drop anchor and proceed no further until further instructions.

And await they had. For two hours now, they'd sat motionless in the water, doing nothing and saying little. The old members of the crew were positioned on barrels by the rail's edge, watching the harbor and the boats that appeared to be protecting it. The members of the Arturos' troupe milled about, gossiping among themselves as they attempted to figure out exactly what this meant for their own immediate futures. As for Nic, he kept an eye out, trying to discern some pattern. It was no coincidence that warships from Pays d'Azur were here. They were searching for the Colombos. What was interesting, however, was that none of the boats leaving Gallina for the high seas were stopped at all. Whatever the Azurites expected to find, they were not worried about it being smuggled out of the city.

At long last, from the largest and most preeminent of the warships ventured another patrol boat, set in a course designed to intercept them. Nic watched its progress as impassively as possible, waiting without a word as it lowered its sails several dozen spans from their own boat. On its deck the men scurried like the ants of a colony, working as one to winch down into the water an even smaller craft roughly twice the size of Maxl's rowboat. Several other men boarded it when it reached deck level. As sailors in bright blue rowed the passengers closer and closer, Nic knew with certainty that the man in the small craft's center was none other than the Comte Dumond. There was something in the bearing of the man's posture and in the tilt of his head that bespoke of an arrogant nobility. Nic remembered hating it the night the man refused to come to his aid, aboard the *Pride of Muro,* and he bristled to see him even now.

The three officers accompanying the comte may have been those who had been aboard the *Pride* as well, but Nic did not remember them as clearly. One of them called out in his own language. While Nic stood near the deck's railing, motionless, matching the comte in the rigidness of his posture, he allowed Maxl to reply in broken Azurite. Finally, as the small boat bobbed right next to the *Tears*, the officer spoke in words Nic could understand. "What is your business in Gallina?"

"We are coming to pick up the supplies," Maxl called down. "The hardtack, the water, the wine, the meats."

"And who are you?"

"We are being the crew of the *Tears of Korfu*," Maxl replied, trying to sound as polite as possible. "Please be letting us pass. We are peaceful."

Comte Dumond, when he spoke, had a voice that could cut through any conversation with ease. Nic could see the mole on his cheek's crest clearly from this distance. "The *Tears of Korfu*," he said, his eyes moving over the line of crew at the rail's edge with loathing. "I know this craft, of course. It is why I insisted on coming myself. They are pirates."

With a hand, Nic restrained Maxl from replying. "I disagree with your choice of words. We are adventurers," he announced, breathing deeply and supporting the words with some hitherto-unknown strength from within.

"Pirates," replied the comte. Like a hawk choosing its prey, his eyes focused on Nic for the first time. He took in the boy's youth and the tricorne atop his head, and seemed to judge him. "And partaking of my coin, if I recall."

As always, the moment Nic had summoned the character of the Drake, all his stage fright vanished as the role took over. He could now match the comte arrogance for arrogance. The way the man had rubbed his thumb across his first two fingers as he spoke of coin made Nic feel dirty—just as the comte intended. "Perhaps under the previous management," Nic drawled as the Drake. "But it is something of which I, as current captain, know nothing."

"Is it, now." The comte did not seem at all amused. "Where is Captain Xi?"

"It is," replied Nic. He was aware that all aboard the *Tears* hung on to his every word. It seemed as if they collectively held their breaths, afraid to disturb the conversation with so much as a stirring of air. "It further distresses me to be the bearer of bad tidings: Captain Xi is no longer with us." He made the traditional bowing of the head that the polite performed when speaking of the deceased, but barely enough to pay the man respect. "A pity he could not be here to answer any questions you may have."

"Do I know you?" the comte asked suddenly. He twisted to get a better glimpse of Nic. "I know you somehow. What is your name?"

"I am called the Drake by those I command." Beneath his character's reserve, Nic began to feel a prickle of alarm. What if the comte connected a frightened boy lying on the aft deck of the *Pride of Muro* with the self-assured commander he was trying to portray?

"Drake?" The comte turned over the word in his mouth as if it were something dirty and unfamiliar. "As in, a type of duck?"

"As in the *dragon*. Rawr!" Nic had parted his lips to say

much the same thing, minus the *rawr*, but his first mate had beaten him to it. Nic lay a hand on Maxl's shoulder to restrain his obvious anger.

The comte barely seemed to notice. He had managed to toss his poisoned barb, saw that it landed, and didn't seem to care where. "I suppose I can hardly enforce an agreement made with a previous captain," he said, ignoring Maxl altogether. "A lawless crew of pirates, by definition, have no honor."

Nic seethed. The man spoke of honor, but what honor was there in hiring freebooters to attack and kill the crew of ships like *The Pride of Muro*? What honor was there in allowing innocents like the Arturos and their company to be sold into slavery, or in letting a servant boy fend for himself at the mercy of a man little more than a savage? "I suppose you are an expert on honorable behavior, then?"

"I honor my king and country," the comte replied. He seemed taken aback that Nic would address him so familiarly. The three officers accompanying him began murmuring among themselves. "He would not question my loyalties."

"Nor do I," Nic assured, smoothly. "I, too, have my own loyalties. To my own people." Though he raised his hands to indicate his crew, Nic had a city full of individuals in mind. "I must do what is best for them. Which, for the moment, means sailing past your little...military exercise...and buying provisions where we may. Do we have your permission?"

One of Nic's masters once had a mastiff trained to growl at the slightest threat, real or imagined. It seemed to Nic that the comte bristled at his words in much the same way as that hound. "It is a pity you do not care to prolong such a pleasant conversation," said the comte, oozing false regret.

"My stay outside this harbor has been prolonged enough," Nic said. "Three hours or more by my reckoning, and we have a good deal to do in port before setting sail on the morrow."

"Such a short stay."

"I hope it is. Unless you have more business with us?"

The face-off between the two personalities seemed destined never to end. Neither the Drake nor the comte seemed likely to stand down. Comte Dumond regarded Nic with derision for a long moment. At last he adjusted his exquisitely-coiffed periwig and replied. "We are seeking two fugitives," he said, eyes once again scanning the line of crewmen at the railing. "Criminals. Jacopo Miandro Colombo and Darcy Fontaine Colombo are their names." During the stab of fear that followed the comte's distinct enunciation, Nic thought for a moment that the Drake might vanish completely and leave standing only the cowering boy within. Yet despite the shock, Nic's facade held. "Your previous captain had accepted an incentive to locate them, with a further bounty if he was successful."

Now, more than ever, Nic was grateful that he'd always referred to the Colombos as Thorntongue and Old Man whenever the ship's original crew was about. "Captain Xi," Nic hastened to correct, "was never my captain. Merely my opponent." He smiled with what he hoped was a world of meaning.

"I see. And you know nothing of the two outlaws?" Nic pulled his lips into a line and shrugged with indifference. "A pity."

"What did these ruffians do to merit your country's displeasure?" Nic asked. He smiled. "Did they eat their garlic snails with the wrong fork?"

"For that offense my king does not order death upon sight," riposted the comte, unamused. The news made Nic shiver, inwardly. The words that followed did not ease his heart. "They are wanted for murder—the murder of the Vicomte San Marquis, in cold blood. All you need know is that the reward for their capture would set a man up for life. Or a woman," he added, with a nod at Ingenue, in her breeches. For once, she did not respond with a batting of her eyelashes or coquettish curtsey, but merely a blank and slightly hostile stare.

"Naturally I should be glad to inform you should I hear of the miscreants." To his left, Nic heard motion and a cleared throat. Both he and Maxl turned slightly. Nic was certain the sound had come from Macaque. The notion disturbed him that the sailor might be aware of more than Nic realized. Macaque, however, merely spat over the railing and resumed the leaning pose he had adopted there, his face unreadable.

"My officers have been boarding many craft entering Gallina harbor to ensure that the two are not smuggled aboard," the comte declared, with a speculative look to observe how Nic reacted.

Though his heart jumped, Nic refused to let fear show

upon his face. "Were I a guilty man, I might inquire by what authority you do so, as Gallina is neither a principality of Pays d'Azur, nor does it answer to any authority but its own."

"We have every authority—!" squawked one of the officers, with a heavy accent.

"But I am not a guilty man," Nic had continued smoothly, as if he hadn't heard, "and therefore my ship is yours to inspect. Come aboard if you wish. Rummage through my hold, though you'll find it sadly empty, thanks to Captain Xi's mismanagement. There may even be a few spare strips of dried fish for us all to enjoy."

By the look on Comte Dumond's face, Nic feared that he had erred on the side of arrogance. He had pushed too far with that comment about Azurite authority, he knew. Yet the Drake had felt it right to make that comment, and what the Drake wanted to do, Nic had so far allowed. The very last thing that Nic wanted was for the comte or any of his men to set foot on the *Tears of Korfu*.

The comte struggled to make a decision. Nic knew everything hinged upon this very moment—his freedom, his future, and the future of everyone aboard the ship. If caught harboring the Colombos, they could all be impounded in dungeons in Côte Nazze for the rest of their lives. They would be separated and tortured, never again to see their homeland. Jacopo would disappear for whatever he'd done. And as for Darcy... Nic had to swallow hard and try not to think about it. He needed to do something. "Maxl," he said, forcing himself to speak. "Lower the ladders so that we might receive visitors."

The boatmen prepared their oars, ready to row closer. The three officers nodded, convinced that Nic had responded correctly. "Yes sir," said Maxl, turning so that he could order the crew.

"No." Suddenly the comte held up his hand. "Such a thing won't be necessary." Nic and Maxl both faced him again. Nic raised his eyebrows, seeming bemused. "We are done here. Take us back to the *Faucon*. I trust you and your crew will enjoy your brief stay in Gallina, Drake," said Comte Dumond, inclining his head ever so slightly. His oarsmen began slowly turning his small craft around. "But may I advise, as someone who despises dealing with the likes of pirates such as yourselves..."

"Ah. Adventurers, I believe you mean," Nic smiled slightly.

The comte's tone grew so steely that Nic almost worried he might change his mind about inspecting the holds. Now that his boat had reversed direction, he had to stand, turn, and raise his voice to make a final address. "Let me advise that in the future you take your *adventures* elsewhere. There are too many lawless outfits in these waters. One never knows when one might have to begin to purge the sea of its impurities. No?"

Nic let him have the last word. He raised a hand in farewell, and then waited until the comte and his men were a respectable distance away before moving again. When he nodded at Maxl, his first mate barked out, "Back to work, all of you!"

"Maxl? Signor Arturo?" Nic said their names low. "Please follow me below."

207

Nic's heart was beating fast as he lowered himself down the hatch ladder and sprinted through the enclosures of the lower hold. No one was in the galley, or in the crew's sleeping quarters, or in the forward storage rooms. But when Nic heard noises in the smaller area that the women had been using for their own quarters, he burst through the door.

"Lah!" A high soprano assaulted his eardrums. "What brute has invaded this sanctity of maidenhood, this temple of femininity? Can I not rest in repose to cleanse my skin and soul?"

Nic blinked. Somewhere Signora Arturo had found an enormous iron hip-bath and filled it with foamy bubbles. She reclined within, visible only by her fluttering long lashes and her wig of red curls floating above the foam. Her face was fully painted. She had even applied several beauty spots in strategic places. "It is the Captain, madam!" Pulcinella stood beside the bath holding one of the Signora's large costumes, a flowing shepherdess gown with an enormous cone-shaped farthingale that covered most of the floor. It appeared as if she were waiting for her mistress to leave her bath and climb into the outfit.

"Come to ravish me again, have you, blackguard? You *men*!" shrieked the Signora. "And you have brought others to witness my degradations! You vile, brutish—!"

"No-oo," said Nic, once he overcame his surprise enough to speak. "It's just Nic. I've brought Maxl. And your husband." When he looked over his shoulder, he discovered both men had caught up in time to witness the scene. Maxl looked particularly wide-eyed.

"Oh," said the Signora in her normal voice. She peeked up over the masses of bubbles. "Hello. Are we out of danger, then?"

"Yes, my dear," said Armand, shaking his head. "We are, for the moment. Though you may not be."

"Where are Darcy and Jacopo?" Nic asked.

Nic heard a splashing sound as the Signora poked at something within the water. The bubbles heaved up into the air. From out of the depths of the hip-bath stood Darcy. She was wet from head to toe, her hair and clothing both soaked and clinging as the bath-water streamed down into the tub. In one hand she clutched a breathing tube. At the same time, Jacopo poked his head out from beneath one side of the billowing farthingale, the lace of the skirt hanging like a bonnet to his head.

"My dear," said Armand Arturo. He wrung his hands as if squeezing oranges for a bowl of wine punch. "Out of curiosity for how much you throw yourself into a role, are you entirely disrobed under there?"

"Armand!" gasped the Signora, aghast. "I am wearing a bathing shift!"

Darcy sputtered moisture from her lips and spoke. "Not much of one."

Nic shook his head at them both. "The first thing we're going to do," he announced, "is to shut the door. And get you something to dry off with," he added to Darcy. She tried to clear the wet hair from around her eyes. Sternly, he added, "and then it's time you told me everything. And I mean *everything*."

16
—

Of all the countries upon this continent, Pays d'Azur is perhaps the most civilized, and certainly the most sophisticated. No one would ever question that it is the most charming. The people of its capital, Côte Nazze, are well-mannered to a fault, and fall over themselves to offer every courtesy imaginable to the weary traveler.

—CELESTINE DU BARBARAY, TRADITIONS & VAGARIES OF THE
AZURE COAST: A GUIDE FOR THE HARDY TRAVELER

Hic had been busy. By the time all of Darcy was dry save for her hair, he had, much to the distress of the Signora, folded what few hair-curling papers the women were able to salvage from the bottom of the costume trunk. From the yellowing squares he'd fashioned a swan, a pair of paper boxes, and an entire fleet of angular miniature boats. It was one of these that Darcy picked up from the wooden bench where she slid next to her father. The expression upon her face was contrite. "We didn't lie to you completely."

She had told him that before, on the beach of their deserted island. "Are you really Nuncio to Pays d'Azur?"

Nic asked Jacopo, wanting to hear it from his lips. From the Arturos, Nic heard a gasp. He thought it only fair to let them sit in on this session, given that their troupe was sacrificing so much for the pair.

"I assure you I am," said the old man. In his oversized shirt and breeches from the costume vaults of the Arturos, Jacopo looked vaguely ridiculous as a would-be pirate. He still retained some of the pomp and posture of a statesman.

Nic nodded, not doubting him at all. It was obviously the role to which the elder Colombo had been bred. "And she's your daughter?"

Darcy sighed. "Of course I'm his daughter, fool." At Nic's impassive expression, she sighed, and ran her fingers through her damp curls. She turned the paper boat over in her hands, examining it half-heartedly. "I'm sorry. I'm an ungrateful brat for speaking so, after all you've done."

"You can hardly blame me for asking," said Nic, crossing his arms. "In the first version of your story, you told me you left Pays d'Azur because of a debt collector, collecting a debt with which you had nothing to do. You told me that Comte Dumond was no one you knew. Yet from his lips, I hear that he is your sworn enemy and that you are both criminals in the eyes of Pays d'Azur—murderers, no less—to be executed on sight. In other words," he continued, staring at them both, "there's a bit of a discrepancy."

Perhaps there was enough of the Drake in Nic's voice to make both the father and daughter stare guiltily at the floor. "I told you that there were incidents after I assumed the position of nuncio," Jacopo said, measuring every word.

"A waxed stair, a snake. An assassin."

"Yes. All of that was true. They were sent by the court of Pays d'Azur."

The Signora, though she had promised to keep quiet, could not hold her tongue. "How horrid."

Jacopo inclined his head in her direction. "Why?" Nic asked.

"Because it would have been convenient for Pays d'Azur to have no ambassador from Cassaforte," said Darcy.

Jacopo agreed. "The first two times they cared not whether I lived or died. Scaring us home with our tails between our legs would have been enough. But then I discovered what they hoped I wouldn't, and the third time…"

"The Vicomte San Marquis," Nic guessed.

"He was sent to kill me." Jacopo's voice had grown very soft as he spoke, so soft that he could scarcely be heard above the sounds of the ship's passage through the waters and the cawing of the harbor gulls. "They thought an elderly gentleman would be no match against a young, strong courtier anxious to prove his worth to a corrupt king. And they were right, except…"

Darcy laid her hands atop her father's, stilling him. She made a soothing, shushing noise. He nodded gratefully. Nic watched the two for a moment and finally caught Darcy's glance. "You," he said. He should have seen it before. She bore that look in her eyes of haunted reserve he imagined he now wore in his own. "You killed him."

"I took no pleasure in it," she snarled. Nic recognized the reaction. It was his very own, to having to kill Captain

Xi and his men. "I don't even remember much about it. It simply happened. I had to protect my father."

Nic wished he could comfort her in turn, but father and daughter seemed to seek solace from each other. He remained motionless, merely saying, "I cannot blame you for that."

"Those days before were terrible." Darcy's voice was barely a whisper itself, but the ferocity of it cut through the quiet like a blade. She looked from Nic to the Arturos to Maxl. "We knew we had to leave for Cassaforte as soon as possible, but we couldn't give any indication of our plans. We had to pretend that everything was normal, to make it seem as if nothing was amiss. Yet every moment of the day we had to keep watch for false servants, for threats in every shadow. You cannot imagine it."

"I believe that Niccolo can imagine it, my dear." Jacopo had composed himself somewhat. Enough, anyway, to cut into his daughter's narrative. "One night, the Vicomte San Marquis bribed his way into the household and concealed himself behind a tapestry in my chambers. If my daughter had not accompanied me after dinner that night...if she hadn't seen..."

"We'd both be dead," Darcy said flatly. The paper boat in her lap had grown slightly damp from handling, but she picked it up by the ends and studied it.

"Of course, we knew we couldn't stay," Jacopo said, easing past the difficult memories. "It was imperative that we made as speedy an escape as possible. Luckily, with the help of friends, we managed it that very night."

"Not all of Pays d'Azur is corrupt." Darcy's defensive

words, and the lilting accent in which she spoke them, reminded Nic that she was half of that country.

"No," agreed Jacopo. "There are still many who do not support the current court. But they have no voice as strong as the Comte Dumond."

"Who has the king's ear in all matters," Darcy finished. She stared at Nic and at the others as if she dared any of them to judge her. "The rest of what we told you is the truth. A member of the court whom we trusted offered us a very small craft and a man to sail us from Côte Nazze to Gallina. We escaped by dead of night with nothing to our name, and only the provisions already laden on the small boat, only to be met by more treachery."

"The servant who was to guide us to Gallina demanded payment to keep us out of the hands of the Comte Dumond." Darcy sounded bitter again. "Payment to follow his master's wishes." Nic began to feel vaguely uncomfortable. He remembered the conversation he'd had with Darcy on the beach, in which she'd offered him a reward in exchange for helping them and he'd accepted. Did she think the less of him for that?

"And you killed him?" Nic asked.

"Are you getting all this, my dear?" the Signora murmured to her husband. "It's good stuff." He nodded with vigor.

From above deck, someone called down the hatch. Maxl rose. "We are arriving in Gallina. I need to be above."

"Go do what you must," said Nic, motioning him away. He intended to stay until all his questions were answered.

Darcy did not reply until Maxl had left the tiny room. "I did not kill him. Nor did my father," she said. "Though we should have."

"Darcy showed the man mercy and forced him off the boat, allowing him a small crate of biscuits for flotation," said Jacopo.

"It was a cork float," Darcy corrected. "I thought we might need the biscuits."

"You had a sailboat?" Nic asked, muscles still aching as he thought back to that long night in which they had rowed for hours to reach the *Tears of Korfu*.

"Had, in the sense that we lost it. Neither of us could sail, you see," said Jacopo. He was beginning to sound evasive again. On the main deck, sounds of heavy footsteps and shifting crates began to creak the wood above their head. Nic heard a cry as Maxl ordered the anchor lowered.

His daughter was more blunt. "I wrecked us, after we came too close to a reef, off of the island." Apology was in her eyes when she looked at her father. "By the time you came, it was beneath twenty feet of water, in two pieces."

Nic had distrusted the pair's tale before, and he'd been correct to do so. Though the skeleton of their story had been factual enough in spots, the fleshing out had been too sketchily done, too hasty to swallow. Now that there were more details, he believed them. One essential element still hadn't been explained, however.

Nic opened his mouth to ask a final question, but Armand Arturo beat him to it. "But what's the *motivation*?" he exploded. Heretofore he'd done an admirable job of remaining in the background during the interview, but the actor could contain himself no longer. "I'm sorry, lad, but while it's a gripping tale of skullduggery and treachery and all the elements that sell out the upper stalls, it's lacking that *thing*, that essential element that ties it all together."

Nic nodded, agreeing with the man. He returned his attention to the Colombos. "What was it you found out that made you such a threat?"

Here again the pair began to look uneasy. "The court of Pays d'Azur has always regarded Cassaforte in the way an older brother might regard a sister ten years his junior. That is, pretty enough and sometimes an asset, but never an equal. They think of Cassaforte as a tiny principality worth acknowledging. However, our independence and general unwillingness to do the things Pays d'Azur wishes, simply because Pays d'Azur wishes them, has long irritated them. If they seized Cassaforte, they would be one step closer to controlling all the nations bordering the Azure Sea."

Again, Darcy cut to the point. "They intend to invade Cassaforte. The Comte Dumond is to lead a fleet of warships upon the city and lay siege to it, as Pays d'Azur did during the Azurite Invasion."

Behind Nic, the Arturos gasped. Neither were old enough to have lived through the Azurite Invasion, but the collective memory of it had lain like a shadow across the interceding decades. Half a generation of young men had been lost during the two years when Cassaforte had been cut off from the rest of the world. "I'm afraid my daughter is correct," said Jacopo. A thud from the deck above caused them all to jump, so great was the tension in the room. He settled himself again. "I fear the results would be worse, this time. Pays d'Azur has learned from its prime tactical mistake of beginning the invasion when Cassaforte was at its strongest. Our people were unified then, and we had a strong monarch and military force. Now, we have a king they regard as enfeebled."

"Ridiculous!"

When Nic and the Arturos began to protest, he held up a hand. "I know. King Alessandro has been much improved by the Olive Crown and the Scepter of Thorn. Even an old man such as I regard him as a very old man indeed. Cassaforte's guards were weakened after many of its ranks were expelled for following Prince Berto during his coup. When Pays d'Azur heard that Alessandro had named Milo Sorranto, a commoner, as his heir, they assumed he was mad. That he was weak."

"But it was thanks to Milo Sorranto and Risa the Enchantress that Cassaforte stands," said Nic.

"Yes, but there are whispers that many among the Thirty would rather see a bastard child son of Prince Berto assume the throne than a mere commoner. Please, take no offense," said Jacopo, looking at his audience. They all murmured politely. "Pays d'Azur sees Cassaforte as a weak country made even weaker by internal dissent, and ripe for the plucking. And believe you me, they intend to pluck it and make it their own. Which is why, Niccolo, we still need to return home with all possible speed. The warships are still here, as is the Comte Dumond. If we arrive in Cassaforte before them, perhaps we will have enough time to summon the good will of Vereinigtelände to aid us in the resistance."

"How would we live during an invasion, Armand?" The Signora was almost in tears. She daubed at her eyes with a handkerchief and leaned into her husband for comfort. "The theaters would be closed. I can't be a tavern maid again. It's been too long, and I'm too fa-aa-aaat!"

"Sssh, sssh," the actor replied, comforting her as he rubbed her back. In his eyes, though, Nic could read concern.

"You must aid us," said Jacopo to Nic. "The need is as urgent as ever. Maybe even more so."

"Help them, Niccolo," implored the Signora, sniffling.

"Please help." Darcy added her appeal to the others. Nic looked around the group, astonished. They seemed to be confusing the Drake that he'd been portraying with his actual capabilities. His mouth worked impotently for a moment, before Darcy added, "We'll see to it that you're rewarded well."

Those words alone decided him. "Is that really what you think of me?" he asked, rising from the chair where he sat. Little boats fell from his lap and scattered. The contempt in his voice was, for once, not an imitation of a voice he'd heard before. It was his own. It flowed from some angry place within, in abundance. To be so judged, after so much! "Do you really suppose I would put my life in danger—put all of our lives at danger—for a bit of gold in my pocket? What sort of person must you be, to conceive that only people like you—people of means and power—have a sense of…of duty? Of decency? *Oh, Nic's only a bit of a scrub. We have to give him luni to make him do the right thing.* It doesn't work that way."

The girl's blue eyes flew open. Perhaps she was ashamed of what she'd said. Perhaps she was merely taken aback. "Niccolo. I didn't mean…"

"We have not known each other for long, Darcy Colombo, but I pretended to myself that after these experiences we at least knew each other well." He studied her up and down, and tried to harden his heart. "I see I was wrong."

He wheeled around and opened the cabin's door. "Niccolo?" he heard Jacopo call out.

"I've got to see to the provisions," Nic growled. "If we're to set sail as soon as possible, there's much to be done. Don't worry. I'll be getting us all back to Cassaforte." He stopped in the doorway for a moment. "It's my country, too," he added, and then slammed the door behind him.

Through the galley he marched, stomping so hard that several of the tin plates on the dining table rattled. Never before had he been so angry that it actually seemed to impede his vision, but at that moment every blood vessel in his eyes seemed ready to pop. Was this what throwing a tantrum was like? Because if so, Nic required lessons from no one.

He was about to step onto the bottom rung of the ladder above when a noise caught his attention. Someone was standing in the entryway leading to the male crew's sleeping quarters. "Macaque," said Nic, freezing in place.

Everything about this situation was wrong. Macaque's bunk in the cabin had been stripped. His few personal belongings had been stuffed into a gunny sack slung over his shoulder. As Nic stared at him, waiting for an explanation, Macaque's lips pulled into a sour expression. "I'll be going, if you please," he said.

Nic didn't move from the ladder. The man would have to push past him. The timing of Macaque's defection made him uneasy. "Why?"

Macaque struggled for a moment. At the last, he seemed to make the decision to come clean. "You know why," he said, grinning. He strode around Nic and into the galley. On the table lay several mugs that he examined until he found the one that was his. Into the gunny sack it went, and along with it, his personal plate. "I know what you're hiding."

"What am I hiding?" The voice that came out was more Nic than the Drake. He attempted to correct the oversight by drawing up his posture and sneering.

"I know what your game is, Drake." While Nic began to sweat, Macaque hauled the sack over his shoulder again, and stood in the galley entryway. He was an imposing man, larger than Nic by far. "Keep the girl and her father for yourself. Collect the reward. Abandon your crew and sail off, happy as a duck."

That hadn't been his game at all, Nic knew, but he played along. "What reward?"

The laugh that Macaque let out was nasty. "I bain't stupid, and you bain't as fine a card player as you pretend.

Maybe I didn't see it when you stepped on board with your precious cargo in tow, but when you were talking to that fancy-pants, the comte, and invited him aboard, I recognized a bluff when I saw it. Even if he didn't." He spat on the floor. "Move."

"Where do you think you're going?" Nic asked, refusing.

"To collect the reward myself. You might have him and her for now, but I'll be damned if I let you collect the gold. Move out of my way."

"Listen to me, Macaque." Nic was fully the Drake now. He tried to sound reassuring. "We can work this out between us, man to man. Perhaps we can come to a gentleman's agreement."

Nic's brain raced as he tried to come up with some kind of way to stall. Unfortunately, Macaque didn't seem to be about to give him the chance. "We won't be making one of those."

"Then I'll stop you," Nic said, aware that he was dangerously close to babbling.

"With what? Your mighty muscles?" Macaque laughed.

"I'll have Maxl stop you. Maxl and the rest."

Macaque shook his head. "They won't stop me. Not if you're down here dead."

Nic felt a meaty hand on his shoulder, seeming to crush the bones within. He looked up, and saw Macaque's tiny eyes diminishing to slits. His other hand drew back into a fist that aimed for his face. Nic winced, knowing what was next to come.

A hollow sound of metal reverberated throughout the

hold. Like a small gong, it rang. Nic opened his eyes, surprised and relieved to find his head still connected to the rest of his body. Macaque still stood before him, but his neck was twisted to the side at a curious angle. His grip on Nic's shoulder lessened, then vanished completely. His body fell to the ground in one massive, graceless, crash that made Nic leap back to avoid being knocked over.

Darcy stood in the spot behind him. In both her hands she held one of the galley's massive iron frying pans, which still vibrated from the impact it had made against Macaque's skull. The Arturos and Jacopo were behind her, looking shocked.

Darcy and Nic stared at each other for a moment over the pirate's unconscious form, until at last Nic summoned enough breath to wheeze out, "Thank you."

"You're welcome," she replied, sounding equally surprised and exhausted. They regarded each other with a mixture of emotions—appreciation mingled with wariness.

Finally Nic wiped his face on his sleeve and began to compose himself. "I now think," he said, looking around their little group, "that we could use a slight change of plan."

BOOK
—
THREE:
—
MAARTEN'S
—
FOLLY

17

The plans are complete. I have sent guards to deliver them to the cazarro, but I know, as I have known with so many other of our pet projects, that I will never live to see this one come to fruition. My dear, it is pitiful that I must ask this question—but when did you and I become so old?

—ALLYRIA CASSAMAGI, TO KING NIVOLO OF CASSAFORTE,
IN A PRIVATE LETTER IN THE CASSAMAGI ARCHIVES

Had Gallina several hundred years to establish itself, it might have been deeper than three or four dirt streets spread wide across the beachfront. Had it attracted more permanent residents, or a less shady population, its architecture might have rivaled Cassaforte's graceful bridges, spacious temples, and deep canals. Had it fewer donkeys and more sewers, it might have smelled a good deal better.

Yet it hadn't. Once Nic was ashore, he found himself disappointed with the city. From the deck of the *Tears of Korfu*, Gallina had given the impression of being a bustling metropolis. Its ports had been alive with flurries of craft smaller than their sloop moving in and out of the complex rows of docks that surrounded Gallina on every side. Back and forth they shuttled from the larger ships belonging to merchants and adventurers alike, anchored further out in the harbor, their colorful flags flapping sharply in the breeze. Shrouded in the mystery afforded by a layer of the white ash-cloud befogging its streets, the city had almost appeared beautiful—just as the thinnest layer of snow could render picturesque the most rank pile of stable dung.

"Pfaugh!" Nic's face momentarily twisted with distaste as, for the second time since he had set foot on shore, he narrowly escaped a cascade of slops descending from a second-story balcony. Behind him, Ingenue shrieked and leapt back several feet. The sensation of firm land underfoot after days aboard the sloop were disorienting enough as it was. All of his party walked as if they were slightly inebriated.

As it turned out, the air of intoxication made them fit in quite well among the populace of Gallina. Of all the stucco-covered buildings lining both sides of the muddy street, every other one seemed to be a tavern of some sort. Grimy men and squalling women reeled in and out from the entryways, laughing and yelling in dozens of different tongues. Some of them still clutched their tin mugs of ale as they sallied to the next public house. Only Maxl, among their group, seemed unaffected by his sea legs. One hand on Nic's shoulder, he pointed at the archways of the taverns. "No doors, see?" he said. "There is no shutting down here. Everything is open all hours of the day and night. They call Gallina the city that is never sleeping."

"Well, if this is what a city that isn't sleeping looks like, I would advise a good forty winks!" When she had been told she would have to carry all her possessions from now on, including her own clothing, the Signora had at last abandoned her skirts for a more practical pair of breeches and a wide leather belt. Without her wide farthingale, she looked considerably slimmer, yet somehow in her fluttering she managed to convey an imminent and most feminine case of the vapors.

"It's very small," complained Knave as he peered about. "Do they even have any theatrical establishments?"

"Is the docks," Maxl said. "They are being larger than city itself. They are having warehouses and merchants there, as well, yes."

"You know," said Pulcinella. Like her lady, she had also consented to don boys' breeches, though she was more used to them from her clownlike roles on the stage. "If we were ever to strike out on our own, this might be the very place. New audiences every night."

"But they wouldn't speak the language," Knave pointed out. He turned to wink at a bawd flaunting her wares from a high window. Thoughtfully, he added, "Though they might not necessarily have to."

"We'll have no talk about disbanding the company." Armand Arturo comforted his wife with a pat on her arm. "We may be small, but Armand Arturo's Theatre of Marvels has not seen its last performance."

The section of Gallina through which they moved would have been any other municipality's shadiest area, bustling with the poor and the pock-marked and echoing with the raucous sounds of laughter, shrieks, slaps, and crude language. Drunkards lay on the wooden porches of the taverns, passed out in their tracks. Cassaforte had its own similar neighborhoods—though perhaps not quite as extreme or as rancid—near its docks and river gate. However, the problem with Gallina, as far as Nic could see, was that the seedier areas weren't confined to any specific sector. They were the entire town. Through the street Maxl drew them onward, pausing every now and again to recite from memory the instructions given to him. At last, at an intersection where a group of small children ran up to them, begging in a foreign tongue for coin or food, he halted. "This is it," he said, nodding at an open archway to the northeast.

Nic felt uncomfortable with the little ones crowding around him, hands outstretched and eyes wide. Though he couldn't understand a word they said, he saw the need plain upon their faces. To them, he was a gentleman in fine dress. How could they know that he was as poor as they? "Are you certain?" All the stucco facades looked the same to him.

At that moment, from the upper story window directly over the archway, a woman eased out her torso. Stays from her waist to bosom accented her buxomness; she was all but falling out of her corset as she leaned out the window. Spying Maxl's painted face, she gave him a wink. "*Oola*," she called, waggling fingertips that had been dipped into something sticky and then inserted into powdered mica, so that they seemed to sparkle. "*Benado qui?*"

Nic could have sworn that beneath the deep blue, the man blushed. After he stopped laughing, Maxl called out something in the woman's tongue. She replied in kind, and he nodded to the group. "This is the place." To Nic, he added in a confidential tone, "You are being young, so be taking it from Maxl, do not kiss any of the women here. Especially if they are having sores." He touched the area around his lips.

"I'm not kissing any of the women whatsoever!" Nic said, perhaps a little too loudly.

The Arturos looked surprised at the outburst, but concealed their amusement behind barely suppressed smiles. Darcy's face colored, but before she could respond, Maxl turned to her. "And you," he said, shaking his finger as if scolding a naughty child, "if you can refrain, do not be bonking people on the head."

"I don't hit *everyone* on the head," she replied, sounding a little sullen.

"Oh yes. You angry, *bonk*. You worried, *bonk*. It is always with the *bonk, bonk, bonk*. I am thinking, and you may be correcting me if I am wrong, that the bonking on the noggin is not the best way to solve every problem," Maxl responded. Nic found himself nodding, and he felt sure that Macaque might agree, were the man with them and not tied up and gagged and stuffed in the Legnoli trunk, back aboard the *Tears of Korfu*. The Signora had insisted that they leave the lid cracked for air. Nic, even with that small mercy, shuddered at the thought of that tight, dark space.

"It's not completely my fault that we have to do this." Darcy wouldn't stand to take any of the blame. "I've never heard of trading in a boat. Horse carts, perhaps. But entire ships? Who has ships to trade?"

"On Gallina everything is traded." As if to prove Maxl's words, a blind youth shuffled through the muck of the streets past their group, calling out for people to buy the necklaces that hung in ropes from his arms. "Even the large ships. People are coming here, they gamble, they bet what they have, including deed to ship. Yes? Sometimes they are betting things they don't even have, yes? Am I right?"

Maxl's appeal to Signor Arturo caused the gentleman to cough into the crook of his elbow. "I wouldn't know anything about that," he mumbled, his hasty words drawing a look of inquiry from his wife.

Nic turned to Knave, who had been adjusting his costume. Of all the troupe, he alone had traded in his piratical uniform for something different—a subdued ensemble they all hoped made him look more like a merchant passing through Gallina on his way to somewhere better. "You know what you're supposed to do?"

"Of course," said the man. He cleared his throat. "I'm to find Signor Trond Maarten somewhere within the lounges of this … establishment." The expression he gave the ladies of the group was of apology. "I'm to appear as if I were merely another customer. And then, when you begin negotiations, I'm to reveal myself as another merchant of stray sea craft and outbid him."

"But not by much," said both Maxl and Nic at the same time. Nic continued, "Just enough to make him match your price. We haven't much in the way of funds."

Knave looked offended that they had to remind him. "I'm a professional." He adjusted the fabric around his throat, and then the cap upon his head. "Trust me." Without another word, he strode into the building.

Signor Arturo sighed. "He's off script," he sighed. "There's no telling what will happen."

"There, there," said the Signora, patting his hand. "It won't be as bad as in Nascenza, when he forgot and thought he was in a different play altogether."

Jacopo watched Knave enter the establishment. "I wish we didn't have to do this," he sighed. "It seems so much wiser simply to load provisions and go."

Nic explained the rationale behind his decision once more. "Enough blood has been shed, Signor. I won't stand for Macaque's soul to meet its makers simply because it's more convenient for us." Jacopo seemed inclined to agree with him, but Nic felt the need to hammer the point home. "We cannot sail to Cassaforte with him as our bound prisoner. The *Tears* is too small for that type of concealment. If he is allowed to roam freely among the crew, he will cause as much dissent as possible. That we also cannot afford."

Darcy, when she spoke, seemed apologetic for her part in the affair. "Father, what Nic has proposed is best. We should simply abandon the *Tears* and leave Gallina for Cassaforte in a completely different ship. My mother's countrymen are not inspecting outgoing craft. When Macaque is found aboard the *Tears* by its new owner, neither he nor they will have any idea how we left Gallina."

"Until they track down and speak to this Trond Maarten

fellow." Jacopo did not sound convinced. "Then they'll have a clear idea."

"By which time we'll be well upon our way and out of their reach." Nic spoke with such authority that everyone save Jacopo seemed convinced. "The Comte Dumond is not an unintelligent man. What if, between our last encounter and now, he has remembered where he has seen me before? What if his patrol boats are watching for our return to the *Tears* even now? We are in too precarious a position to allow overconfidence to lay us low."

Amidst the street's dinnertime cacophony—the cries, the shouts, the laughter and the drunken chorus from a nearby tavern—Jacopo's only focus was upon Nic's words. At long last, he nodded. "You are much changed," he said to the boy.

The observation rattled Nic. It was one of the few things Signor Colombo could have said to him to rattle his nerve. "I—I don't think I am," he stammered. Darcy was staring at him. Her scrutiny made him even more nervous. "I don't feel different. I'm still who I was before, only ..."

"Lad." Armand Arturo shook his head. "Don't apologize. Not for being our savior." Before Nic could rebut the charge, the actor announced to the group, "I think we've given Knave plenty of time to infiltrate. What say you we begin the latest in our series of clever deceits, eh?" He waggled his eyebrows. "However, I suggest the ladies of our group may wish to excuse themselves from this particular exercise."

Ingenue and Infant Prodigy both let out sharp cries

of disappointment. Signora Arturo, for her part, let out a laugh. "And let you boys in that place by yourselves? I think not, husband, and if you think about it closely, you'll agree to let us in there to keep an eye on you."

No husband could deny a wife so fervid in her expression. In fact, the actor was taken a little aback at how strongly his lady felt about the matter. "Of course, of course," he reassured her. "I was only thinking of the more delicate sensibilities among our group."

"Armand." The Signora crossed her arms. "I worked as a tavern wench. Pulcinella has been married three times. Ingenue and Infant Prodigy have seen more male backsides changing costumes in the wings than has the seat of a public privy. And as for this one…" she indicated Darcy. "She's basically a boy in a girl's costume, and a savage one, at that." Darcy blinked, and seemed startled. "There is scarcely going to be anything within those doors that will shock any of us." Point made, she raised her eyebrows in triumph.

The actor assented. With Nic as their leader, they made their way to the darkened arch on the corner. The moment they crossed the threshold and into the warm, close room just within, the atmosphere changed. Gone were the dismal sights and smells of Gallina's streets, replaced by the scents and dressings of a woman's boudoir. Everything within had been decorated in pale corals, or delicate pinks. The staircase was painted a blue the color of the Azure Sea on its sunniest days, while a rug underfoot seemed to be woven from threads dyed in the colors of the world's most valuable jewels.

"*Oola?*" The hostess who stepped into the room to greet them was perhaps the same age and build as the Signora, yet her matronly figure had somehow been contained in a much smaller corset with a cincher that reduced her waist to miniscule proportions.

So much of her ample favors were on display that Nic nearly averted his eyes, but at the last moment he recalled himself and stepped forward. "Ah, madam," he said, as the Drake took over. "A hundred good days to you."

The hostess smiled broadly at his bow. "Such fine manners!" she replied. The language of Cassaforte was obviously not her first tongue, but in her line of work she had picked up enough of it to make herself easily understood. "Deevine! Outstanding! Oh, signor, 'ow long it 'as been since we 'ave 'ad a real gentleman in Solange's!" She reached out and caressed Nic's cheek in a way that quite embarrassed him, in front of the others. "And so many of you! Do they all want girls? Solange can provide! I 'ave all kinds of girls. Fat girls for you, yes?" she said, pointing to Maxl. While Ingenue steamed, Solange puffed out her cheeks and looked stern. "Fat and a little mean is what you like, yes? Skeeny girls for you," she said to Signor Arturo with a sunny expression. The Signora's jaw began working in outrage. "Yes, I know your type!"

Nic firmly removed the woman's hand from his cheek, before it wandered to any more intimate areas. He held it in his fist for a moment, then gently kissed the knuckles. They smelled of the same perfume that hung so heavy in the air. "Gentle madam, fascinating and no doubt diverting as it would be for me, or indeed, any of my party, to partake in the graces and conversation of the charming damsels under your, ah, tutelage, it is not their company we seek."

The woman known as Solange may not have followed the nuance of Nic's speech, but she seemed to understand the general import. "No?"

"No," he said, clasping her hand with both of his before at last releasing it. "I am a man of business who has been told that a colleague I seek spends his dinnertimes within your delightful establishment." For a moment the woman looked crestfallen at the news that not one of the more than half-dozen potential patrons in her lobby seemed interested in giving her any actual trade. Nic, however, plucked from his pocket one of the gold pieces from Captain Xi's money box, and held it up. "Trond Maarten is his name."

"Oh! But of course!" Solange nearly snatched away the coin before it was even proffered. "Signor Maarten, 'e is in the pink dining 'all. I will show you, yes? Come, come." The woman gestured to Nic. "I show you."

Before Solange could get very far, Nic turned to his party. "Maxl and I will go. The rest of you, stay here."

"May I come?"

Darcy's request was so solemn that Nic had to hesitate. "Yes," he said. "But quickly."

The first floor of Solange's establishment seemed composed almost entirely of parlor after parlor, all of them painted in various shades of pastel and furnished with silk-covered sofas trimmed with fringe. On the walls hung tapestries of topics that to Nic's eye appeared quite rude.

Candelabras of ormolu sat on every small table, illuminating the rooms with a warm glow. They were not brightly lit, however, and judging by many of the intimate conversations Solange's customers were having with the women of her staff, most of them preferred it that way. At long last, after Nic had become convinced that Solange had to have bought all the stucco buildings around her own and knocked down the walls to create her feminine sanctuary, they came to the pink dining hall.

Pink it certainly was, from the flocked paper covering the ceiling and walls to the eye-popping salmon of the sofas. Even the great wooden table that took up most of the room's space had once been painted pink, though wear and tear had chipped its surface. Laden with food it had been, too. An enormous roast fowl of some sort glistened with a dark brown skin in its center. Only one of its breasts had been cut into and eaten. Smaller plates lay around with delicious-looking viands that Nic had not seen since serving the Drake's table—dishes of candied carrots, of braised mushrooms, a bowl of game stew, spiced mutton and creamed rutabagas, as well as many foods Nic had never before tasted or smelled. Nic was glad to see that Knave had found his way back here. He and several other gentlemen were busily helping themselves to the provender. Some of Solange's girls entered with full dishes and left with the empty plates, occasionally tarrying to tease the customers.

"'Ere 'e is, yes?" Solange smiled and pointed.

"Thank you, my dear." Nic once again reached for the woman's hand and brought it to his lips. "I will have to show you my appreciation more fully…later." The proprietress, apparently not immune to the blandishments of young men such as Nic, simpered like a girl, curtseyed, and then excused herself.

The customer at the table's end was perhaps the most teased. On his bench, to either side, sat two of Solange's prettiest young women. One of them lifted a fork laden with food to the gentleman's mouth. The other waited for him to chew and swallow, then dabbed at the corners of his mouth with a napkin. "Are you Trond Maarten?" Nic asked.

"And who is asking?" The gentleman seized a chunk of turkey from his plate, stuffed it into his mouth, and then cleaned off his fingers with his lips as he studied Nic. He was astonishingly bald and did not even wear a periwig to hide his lack of hair, as was the fashion. His eyes were green and piercing, and his skin was as pale as the snows of his northern homeland, judging by his accent. "Yes?"

"I am known as the Drake," Nic said smoothly, striding across the room so he could address the man directly, without having to speak over the other diners. "I am a man of business. I was told that you are the man to talk to about trading one boat for another. You are a dealer in these matters?"

One of the fillies at Maarten's side whispered something in his ear that made him grin. He looked at Nic and said, "Trading a boat, eh?"

"Indeed." Smoothly, Nic proceeded. "You see, in my tradings, I find it necessary—"

"Mynheer Drake. I have no need to know the whys and wherefores of your business. In fact, for my safety, it is much better that I do not know. So please." Trond Maarten rose from his bench to reveal that he was a very tall man indeed. The two pretties beside him cooed with displeasure. "Spare me any fictions you may have composed about your so-called tradings. They would only bore me." He turned to the casement behind the head of the table, and opened the doorlike windows onto the very smallest of balconies. Then he leaned down to whisper something into the ears of the beautiful dark-skinned woman who had been holding his napkin. She rose, and with lowered eyes, excused herself from the room. "Instead, tell me of this ship you need to unload."

Nic nodded at Maxl, who stepped forward to explain. "It is a one-masted sloop, being build fifty years before."

"Ship maker?"

"I am not knowing this," said Maxl, bowing. "But I am believing it is originally of my own country of Charlemance, probably Dubris, where ships are being made."

"Mmm." At that moment, the dark-skinned beauty returned. In one hand she carried the largest spyglass Nic had ever before seen; it dwarfed the one he'd used aboard the *Tears of Korfu* by at least three times. Its bronze shaft was elaborately carved, though slightly worn. She handed it to the trader and began to pull down the three legs of the bundle she'd been carrying in her other hand. Once assembled, it provided a sturdy base for the spyglass, which Maarten set into the cupped receptacle waiting for it. He moved the entire device next to the window, and motioned Nic over. "What is the name of the little lady?"

"They call me Thorntongue. Why?" Darcy said, alarmed to be addressed.

"He means the sloop, Thorntongue," Nic said.

"Oh." Darcy looked as if she wished she could vanish into the rose-colored rug underfoot.

Nic could hardly blame her for sounding so defensive. She was, after all, treading on enemy ground on this island. "She's known as the *Tears of Korfu.*"

Because the city was built on a steep slope along the base of Mount Gallina, and because Solange's establishment was located at the highest of the three long east-to-west thoroughfares running parallel to the water, Nic found that the dining room at the building's back had an elevated and admirable view of the bay. Looking down, he could see the rooftops of the building lining the next street over. "And where did you set anchor?" asked Maarten. When Maxl told him, the man swiveled the glass to the north-west. "Show me," he told Nic.

It took Nic a self-conscious moment to find the ship, unaccustomed as he was to seeing it from shore. Eventually, however, after trial and error, he managed to find the ship's flag. "There," he said to the man, careful to back away from the spyglass so that it didn't shift.

"*Tears of Korfu,*" read Maarten. "Aye, she's a little beauty. Not as much wear on her as I expected, either. The type of craft sought after by those in the speedy shipping business. Or piracy." He stood away from the glass and studied

Nic and Maxl up and down, taking in the details of their costumes. "I take it you're into speedy shipping, then," he added blandly.

"What can we get for her?" Nic asked, jumping right into the heart of the matter. He didn't dare risk a look over at Knave, who he hoped was listening. "I have no wish to appear over-eager, but time is of the essence in this matter."

"If we were dealing in cash, I would give you four hundred and fifty kronen for her, no questions asked. That would be roughly twelve hundred oboloi. Or seven hundred Cassafortean lundri. Four hundred and fifty kronen is more than fair. You won't have seller's regret at that price."

"Four hundred and fifty, eh?" asked Nic. Knave was supposed to pipe up at this point. Perhaps he was waiting for a more strategic moment. It was difficult to know, with actors.

"Though of course, you can take in trade any craft in my shipyards of that worth or less, if you prefer."

"I'm just not certain..." Why wasn't Knave speaking up? Nic pretended to be thinking about it, and looked around the room. Knave had a drumstick in one hand and the other around the shoulders of one of Solange's pretty lasses.

"Four hundred and seven-five, then. That's... almost seven hundred and forty lundri. You can appreciate that's a bargain. Yes?"

The man seemed fairly firm on the new price. So firm, in fact, that Nic rather doubted anything would make him change it. He looked helplessly in Knave's direction, willing him to speak. Then, from Darcy came a loud expostulation. "Four hundred and seventy-five kronen!" she said, slamming her stage sword onto the table. All the other diners, as well as the women flirting with them, jumped at the impact. "That's an outrage."

"Thorntongue." Nic shook his head.

"An absolute outrage!" she declared, still at the top of her lungs. "I'm sure that a *reputable* tradesman would give even more for such a *fine, neat craft.*"

Such an outcry could have woken the dead. It was more than enough to bring Knave to his senses. Slightly groggy from the wine that was flowing freely at the table, he rose to his feet. "Ah. Yes," he said. "I am a reputable tradesman. I find the price you named an outrage," he announced. His voice was absolutely flat and expressionless, and when he glanced around the room, he did so with a nervous clearing of his throat. "An absolute outrage. I will give you more than that." He nodded at Nic as if to say, *this is going well, isn't it?*

"How much more, kind stranger?" asked Thorntongue, when for a long moment the actor said nothing else.

"Um." His fists clenched and unclenched into balls as he thought. Finally, inspired, he raised a finger in triumph. "Four hundred! And seventy-*six*! Kronen!"

Nic wanted to groan. Maarten pulled his face into an unreadable mask as he thought about the counter-offer. "Take it," he said at last.

"What?" Nic and Maxl and Darcy all spat the word at

once. Darcy looked with disgust at Knave. In turn, he looked terrified.

"Take it!" Maarten sat back down on his bench and helped himself to a mouthful of meat pie. "You won't get a better offer than that. The man's obviously a trading genius!"

"I … I …" Maxl, for once, was speechless.

"Take it!" said Maarten once more. "It's a much better deal."

Nic tried to smooth the matter over. "I don't know that man," he assured the trader. "It's only a single kronen. And it was your custom I sought. Not his."

For a long, long moment, Maarten stared at him. Nic held both his breath and his cool, hoping against hope that Knave hadn't ruined the scene. After what seemed like an eternity, Maarten opened his mouth and let out a bay of laughter. Though they obviously had no idea what was so funny, the women who had been attending him began to laugh as well. "Mynheer Drake," he said, through a mouthful of the pie. "I am a seasoned tradesman. I make my home on Gallina. I have seen enough to know when someone is trying to make me raise my price with a plant. That fellow is no more a 'reputable tradesman' than I am a poet."

"That he is not," Nic assured the man. "I apologize. I was not aware there was a man of honor upon Gallina."

"There are a few. I am one. Four hundred and seventy-five kronen is a very good deal." Maarten plucked a small bone from the recesses of his gums, then directed it at Nic to drive home his point. "I have a caravel that would be specially suited for your purposes. It is worth five hundred kronen, but I will trade. Would you see it?"

"I would." Nic heaved an internal sigh of relief that their subterfuge had not ended in disaster, after all.

"Then have your people come to my shipyard at dawn," said the man, pushing back the bench and adjusting his waistcoat. "We'll have you back on the seas by breakfast."

Nic bowed low. "We shall see you there. Come," he said to Darcy and Maxl. Once his back was turned to Maarten, Maxl nodded, grinned, and gave Nic a thumbs-up sign. Nic sighed and motioned to Knave at the door. "You too."

Knave looked sheepish as he took his leave of the meal and the ladies. Aware that his comrades were all glaring at him after they left the room, he shrugged his shoulders. "I'm sorry. I froze! I didn't know my motivation. Ask Armand," he said to Nic. "He'll be the first to tell you I don't do well without a script."

Nic's response was little more than a growl. "That much is obvious."

18

---

*Actors, like vermin, produce nothing but filth and excrement.
Both eat anything in plain sight, fair or foul. The only
difference between an acting troupe and an infestation is that
I have had infinitely more entertaining evenings chasing lice.*

—THE PHILOSOPHER RACELL CLOUTIER,
IN PURGING SOCIETY AS A BASIS FOR CLEAN GOVERNMENT

I t's small." Nic's first reaction to the *Sea Butterfly* was
the same as it had been when he'd spied it. Nestled as it
was in the middle of Maarten's private docks, surrounded
by the hulls of so many larger craft, it somehow appeared
even tinier—like a child's play sailboat, set upon the canals
of Cassaforte with a string at one end.

"Aye, small but fleet." Maarten held up his lantern so
that it spread its light over the marvelous little craft. "A newly
built caravel. A mere ten years old. No damage. She can
easily carry fifteen sailors. Uses lateen sails for speed. You'll
be anywhere you care to be as quick as a wink in this little

beauty." He strode up the ramp from the dock and began to wander around the deck. "Sturdy, too," he commented, kicking the foremast.

"Speed is good," said Jacopo. He, along with the rest of the crew, stood upon the docks with Nic. After the debacle at Solange's, Maxl had sent Knave to summon the rest of Macaque's original crew with the cart containing the provisions, and to meet them at the town's far end, where they had all lodged the night in a barn. Maarten owned or leased a considerable amount of the waterfront docks there, and they were crammed full. It was difficult to conceive of so many ships abandoned by, or taken from, their owners, but here they were. Rowboats of all sizes and for all uses lay piled near the building Maarten used as his office. Small sailboats used for fishing or as pleasure craft were dry-docked closer to land. They were standing on a mazelike complex of piers that extended into the water and seemed to lead away in every direction. The purple dark of Gallina's harbor before sunrise sometimes made it difficult to see the details of every ship in their vicinity, but Maarten had provided lanterns to anyone who wanted, so there was light enough. "We need as much speed as possible," he reminded Nic.

"I know. I know." There was nothing wrong with it as far as he could see, and Maxl was already striding around the deck, leaning his blue face in to examine the ropes and riggings, his expression positive. He ordered several of the men to unfurl the squared sails so he could inspect their condition. Nic didn't even want to set foot onto the little caravel, though. It almost seemed to him that to stride aboard would be to claim it as his own, and he wasn't prepared for that, yet. "It's just so small."

"It's only a half-dozen spans shorter than the *Tears*," called out Infant Prodigy, who had already skimmed to the top of the rear mast, out of the lanterns' reach. Her voice was a pinpoint in the early morning sky.

"It is small," said the Signora. "I shudder to think of the lack of privacy below."

"But my dear," said her husband, reassuring all fears. "If we speedily make our way across the bonny waters, the inconvenience will be only short-lived."

"He speaks the truth, dama." Maarten stepped from the deck onto the ramp again to address her. His hand automatically ran over his smooth head, as if he still had hair to slick back. "You could reach the mountains of Tariq and the ocean in a matter of days if you so chose. Do you know," he said in an entirely different tone. It was as if he could no longer hold back the observation. "I've seen many a crew of…speedy shippers before, and I must say that yours is the most unusual upon which I've ever laid eyes." Nic felt dismayed at the man's words. He'd hoped to attract as little attention as possible. "It's not good or bad. Neither fish nor cheese, as we say in my land. But I will tell you. Any other crew of speedy shippers in the market for a little beauty like this wouldn't hesitate."

Nic sighed. He knew he should take the boat. Speed was of the essence, and he could tell from the many unspoken signs Maxl was giving him that so far there was nothing wrong with the caravel. Yet there was something he couldn't quite articulate that held him back from agreeing. It wasn't that his ego was struck a blow by having to command a craft shorter and stouter than the *Tears of Korfu*, for it had been no grand ship in the first place. It wasn't pride that held him back, nor fear. Something undefinable simply wasn't right about the *Sea Butterfly*, and for the life of him, Nic couldn't have told anyone what it was. "And there's nothing else available?"

"Not that would suit you. Not in your price range." Maarten seemed firm on that. "I am not cheating you, Drake. This little caravel could keep you afloat for many years to come."

Nic's lips curved into a Drake-like smile. "I appreciate your concern for the longevity of my career," he said, bowing. "Now please. Allow me to think it over."

"Certainly." Maarten withdrew with a little bow, and went back aboard to point out to Maxl the little ship's more compelling features.

Despite the early hour, Gallina's harbor was not completely dark. Reflected sun from Muro's face streaked across the bay, which was already spotted with countless little lamps and lanterns from the hundreds of craft that had set anchor overnight. It was as if someone had thrown a net into the sky, captured the stars, and let them settle onto the gently bobbing water. Nic walked so that he was out of reach of the lantern-lit stretches of pier, pretending to study the hulls of the neighboring boats.

Really what he wanted, though, was a chance to be

alone and to think. Not since the night on the deserted island had he enjoyed a moment to himself. Every moment of every day since, he'd been bluffing and scraping by, trying to find a way home. Now that he'd been handed the means to return to Cassaforte, he found himself balking. Why?

Was it the fear of returning to the city? Signor Arturo had promised an end to his work debt, so that couldn't be it. Was it that he feared being ordinary once again? There was something in that theory. Despite the fact that Nic could have lived quite happily never to witness violence or death again, he was able to admit to himself that part of him had enjoyed parts of the preceding week. He'd been respected. People had sought his opinion, and still did. They'd relied upon him, and not simply to bring their hot water or their breakfasts upon a tray. Maybe the old Nic could have returned to Cassaforte happy to start over as the stagehand for a minor and unnoticed theatrical troupe— or even as its young Hero—but at that moment, Nic still wanted something more. To hop aboard the *Sea Butterfly* and return home would set him free, but something within kept speaking to him to say that it wasn't right.

He saw the light from the solitary lantern, spilling an orange-white glow on the green-stained wood before he heard the voice speaking softly behind him. "Are you furious with me?"

"Darcy," he replied, shaking his head, "I can't stay furious with you for long." That didn't seem to be quite the answer she'd hoped for, but she nodded and stepped forward to join him. "One minute you're driving me absolutely insane, and then the next you're saving my life."

"If it's any consolation," she said, biting her lip as she stared out at the lights of the harbor, "my father has always said that I'm a handful." Nic laughed at that. Darcy took a deep breath and began speaking in a rush, as if she'd thought out what she'd planned to say, and meant to say it as quickly as possible. "I know this is all my fault. You'd never be in this mess if I hadn't dragged you in and appointed you our guide home. Oh, I certainly can talk about how my sex is as capable as yours. I'm bossy, true. Yet perhaps I'm not as competent as I thought, relying on you so much."

"Am I so terrible to rely upon?" Nic asked. He didn't dare face her.

"No! That's the crux of it, you see. We've put so much faith in you, and not once have you let us down. And what do I do, every time I open my fool mouth? Insult you, through my arrogance and rank. My father's rank, really. I've no privilege of my own to speak of." She cleared her throat, and over the lantern let her liquid blue eyes contemplate him. "Regardless of how I insulted you, I think—I think that we're all born with some kind of moral compass that we carry with us all our lives. Some people ignore them. You don't. Niccolo, I think you and I have our compasses pointing in the same direction." Her voice had grown soft, as if she were saying words she might regret later. "I'm very glad of it."

Nic's voice was gruff as he responded. "In what direction are they pointing?"

With her free hand, Darcy reached out for his. She

nodded out at the harbor, and the sea beyond it, and said simply, "Home."

It was strange, how many and unexpected were the sensations her fingers around his could create. His heart beat as if he were in danger, though he felt no fear. His skin prickled as if he stood in front of a fire, though there was none nearby. These feelings, at least, felt right. With these feelings he could have kindled more flames than burned on the waters that morning. They stood side by side, saying nothing more but clutching each other's hands as if afraid to let go.

While he regarded the silhouettes of Maarten's stock against the lightening eastern sky, Darcy asked a question. "Those girls at that woman's place. Solange's?"

"Hmm?" asked Nic, distracted. His attention had been diverted by the shadow of a large ship in the middle distance.

"They're not...I don't know why I'm asking you this. Is that the type of girl you like?" When Nic didn't immediately answer, Darcy's voice grew noticeably more nervous. "If it is, fine, that's the way it is, but I'm not..." She sighed. "You know, I *am* a girl. Despite what she said."

"Who said?" The longer he stared at the dark shadow, the more curious Nic felt. He took a step forward.

"Your Signora. She said I was basically a boy in a girl's costume. I'm not. Say. Are you even listening to me?"

By that point, Nic was not. "Do you see something strange?" he asked, pointing into the darkness. "There," he said. "That ship. The one over there. On the very edge of the docks."

"No, I don't. I can't even see—hey! I'm trying to talk to you."

In his curiosity, Nic yanked her forward. His feet sprinted as he searched for a connection to the next pier that ran parallel to his own. They ran past the *Sea Butterfly* once again, not noticing or caring that several of the crew, including Darcy's own father, witnessed them hand in hand. A narrower walkway connected to the second pier. They jogged down its length until at last Nic stood before the galleon he had noticed.

It loomed above them, tall and proud against the purple sky, its bowsprit jutting above the pier. Overhead, where once had been a figurehead of some sort were thick knots and gnarls, like the trunk of an old and twisted tree. Where the ship's name should have been painted was nothing at all. In fact, the longer Nic looked at the ship's hull, the more curious it seemed. When he dropped Darcy's hand and lifted the lantern to get a better look, the mystery deepened further still: the ship's hull was blackened, almost as if it had been charred and burnt beyond recognition. It wasn't painted, though, nor had it met with conflagration. "Odd," he murmured.

"It's awful," said Darcy. Her face was contorted with disgust as she craned back her head to take in as much of the galleon as she could. Its foremast disappeared into the sky, though Nic's eyes could make out the forestays running from its upper reaches to the bowsprit. The ropes seemed cobwebbed with age, or perhaps disuse.

"No," Nic breathed. This was a very old craft and, from

its general air of neglect, seemed to have been here for a long time. "It's magnificent. Doesn't it seem familiar to you?"

"Wait a moment. I was pouring out my heart to you, and you interrupted to look at a *boat?*" Darcy took a step back. "Men!"

"Come on," Nic said, jerking his head. He almost ran around to the narrower walkway leading down the ship's length. This dark ship, whatever its name, dwarfed the corsair bobbing next to it. At the farthest reaches of its stern a bay window jutted out where the captain's quarters would be. Its panes were inky and opaque. Three masts had the galleon, fore, main, and mizzen, each rigged with two squared sails. Though they had drooped and slumped with abandonment within their ties, Nic could guess that they were still whole. A ramp studded with crossbars ran from the pier to just behind the head rails. It was at a steep angle, so Nic held out his hand. "Let's look."

"Why?" Darcy appeared genuinely baffled at Nic's sudden obsession. "Nic, we should be helping the others on the *Sea Butterfly*. I should, anyway. You should be there overseeing."

"We are not going home in the *Sea Butterfly*." Nic sounded certain of that. His hand twitched, impatiently motioning Darcy to follow.

When she did, it was with reluctance. "We're not going home in this wreck," she said, following him up the plank. "It's horri…oh." She stopped when they neared the top. "Nic." Darcy had to let go of his hand. She clutched first her stomach, and then her head. "Stop. Really. Stop."

Nic had felt it the same moment as she. There was some force preventing them from stepping onto the deck. In the past, Nic had seen bits of metal magnetized by a lodestone sometimes attract each other, and yet sometimes repel. It was if some invisible and unseen hand pushed the pair away.

At least, that's what it felt like for him. Darcy apparently was having a more violent reaction. Struggling for breath, she sat down on the plank. "There's something evil here," she rasped out.

She was not far from the truth, Nic realized. Every surface of the ship seemed to seethe with a malevolent energy that, in the early dawn, was almost visible to the naked eye. Black and forbidding, it seemed to snake from the wood in coils, like moisture on the foggiest of days. "Something evil," Nic echoed.

"It's in my head. It's so loud—I can't…" Darcy was near tears. She began to slide down the ramp, crossbar by crossbar. "Nic, come away."

"Sssh," Nic said. He stepped down onto the deck, pushing past that gentle force warding him off. He trespassed, he knew, but some compulsion drew him onward.

Then he heard it. It came from a distance, but at the same time, from very close by. It might have even come from within himself, for all he could tell. "*Who are you?*" it asked.

"Do you hear that? That voice?"

Darcy shook her head, though whether she was answering his question or trying to rid herself of what plagued her, he could not tell. "Make it stop," she said, sounding tearful.

"*Who are you?*" Nic looked all around, trying to find the words' source. It sounded like a woman of deep and terrible voice, thrilling in the way Signora Arturo imagined herself during a climactic scene onstage; but it was like a little girl's inquiry, curious and without malice. At the same time, it sounded like a bell. Its echoing reverberated, growing louder and louder. He raised his hands to stop his head from buzzing, and maybe to keep it from falling off his shoulders.

"*Get away!*" Nic heard Darcy yell. "*Get out of my head!*"

"Darcy?" Nic could barely see now. The purple blackness coiling from the deck had clouded his vision. Across the boards he stumbled, hands to his ears, trying to prevent the voice from getting in. *Who are you?* it asked, over and over. *Who are you? Who are you?* "I'm coming back. Don't fret. I'm coming."

He had to let go of his ears to find the ramp by feel. He climbed atop a small crate and onto the slanted board, gripping for dear life as he let himself down. Darcy was back on the pier, trembling in a small ball. "It's all right," Nic assured her. He knelt down and put an arm around her shoulder. "Has the voice gone away?" She nodded, sniffling. "It has for me, too. What did it say to you? Did it ask who you were?"

"No, it..." She struggled for words. "I couldn't understand. It kept battering at me. It wanted to know something, but I didn't know what. It was just... not right."

Footsteps came pounding down the pier then, accompanied by points of bobbing light and the metallic sounds of the lanterns shaking on their grips. Maxl arrived first, his face full of concern. Nic nodded at him to answer his unspoken question. "She's all right." He watched Maxl as he looked first at the corsair as if expecting some sort of assailant to leap out from within, and then at how his face twisted with repugnance at the site of the black galleon.

"Th-Thorntongue?" said Jacopo, wrestling to produce his daughter's assumed name. He and the rest of the crew had caught up, drawn by the sound of Darcy's cries.

"I'm fine," she said. Darcy was not the sort of girl to weep in front of an audience, Nic knew. She wiped her face and struggled to her feet.

Trond Maarten pushed his way through the assembled people. "Good gods," he snapped in as impatient a tone as Nic had ever heard him use. "You didn't go aboard, did you?"

"Yes, signor." Nic stood as well, and drew himself up to his full height. "I did."

"You're a lunatic." Maarten swore under his breath. "Or you wish to be. Do you know how many men that ship has driven mad?"

"How in the world can a ship drive a man mad?" asked Signor Arturo.

Maarten laughed without amusement. "You spend five minutes aboard it, mynheer, and learn for yourself."

"*Don't!*" Darcy's voice was sharp as she reached out to prevent anyone from taking the man up on the offer. That, more than anything else, convinced Armand to step back.

"What is it?" Nic could not shake the ship from his mind, try as he might. He had to know.

The trader shrugged. "Maarten's Folly is what they call it. Named not, as you might imagine, after me, but after my father's grandfather, who started the business. As I was told the tale, this... this monstrosity... sailed into Gallina harbor during a storm and came to a rest."

"During a storm? Were there no survivors?" Nic asked.

"None. There were victims aboard, though, all deceased. Pirates. From a clan that operated off the shores of Ellada. All of them died in agony—not from the storm, mind you. But from the ship itself."

"Preposterous," said Jacopo.

"No, it's not." Darcy spoke up. "I would have been dead if I'd stayed aboard. It gets into your head. There's something wrong with it."

"Aye," agreed Maarten. He ran his hand over his skull, obviously concerned that the pair had so close a call. "So said my great-grandfather when he claimed it from the harbor, thinking he could resell it for a tidy profit. So said my grandfather, and his son, when it sat untouched for decades, and when they had to watch greedy men try to claim the ship as theirs go mad before their very eyes. So said I, the one and only time I set foot aboard its wicked deck. I'd offer three hundred kronen to any man who could remove its blight from my docks, but no one dares touch it. Maarten's Folly it will remain, during my life and that of my son. It's cursed."

The last word should have surprised Nic, but it didn't. Nothing else could have produced the malignancy that gripped Maarten's Folly. "Are you all right, Signor Drake?" asked Jacopo, extending a hand in his direction. "If so, let us return to the *Sea Butterfly* and be on our way, so that we trouble this good man no more." Maarten smiled and demurred, indicating that they had caused no inconvenience whatsoever.

"No." It was Nic who spoke, not any character he played. Yet his voice was as firm as the Drake's and as sure. "I'm sorry, Old Man," he said, shaking his head, and then at Darcy, intending the words for her as well. He jumped up onto the plank, causing several in the assembly, including Ingenue, to cry out in caution.

"Don't be a fool, boy!" Though Nic was only a few handspans from the ground, Trond Maarten cried out as if he were attempting some dangerous stunt from the heights of the ship's main mast.

"You heard the man, lad." Armand Arturo was so flustered that he accidentally trod on Urso's foot, but the large sailor caught him before he fell sideways.

The Signora produced a hanky from her bosom, into which she sniffled, "We couldn't bear to lose you, dear boy."

"This ship is from Cassaforte," Nic said, holding out his arms in its direction. He couldn't say why he was so certain, but it made sense. It had been the familiar curves of its hull, the graceful shapes of the windows and of even the masts themselves that had convinced him. Gnarled and blackened though it may have been, no other nation could have fashioned this craft.

"That may very well be," said Maarten. "I have heard it speculated before that only Cassaforte, with its strange magics, could have produced something so foul."

"She's not foul," said Nic. He made an appeal to the group. "She's one of us."

"It's a ship, boy. Not a woman." Knave's comment was met with a few uneasy chuckles, and at least one boo from Infant Prodigy.

"I've done much for you in the last few days." Nic looked around at the more than dozen people of whom he was in charge. He paused to allow those of the crew who could understand him to translate for those who could not. After he'd made the decision to abandon the *Tears of Korfu* and leave Macaque's unconscious body behind, he'd spoken to the entire company and given them the opportunity to leave, if they so chose. Gallina was a town where any of Macaque's five crewmen could find employment, legal or not. All had willingly chosen to follow him. He hoped they would listen now. "Allow me to do this for myself."

Darcy, however, looked the most distressed of all. "You won't be able to stand it," she warned him, coming to the plank's bottom but daring not to venture any further.

"A *zingari* woman once told my master I was cursed," Nic told her. "She said that only when I encountered one more cursed than myself would it be broken."

Her voice cracked with worry. "Since when have you listened to crazy *zingari* women?" she wanted to know. "You don't even listen to me!"

"Heed the girl," said Maarten, still pale. "She has your best interests in mind."

Yes, Nic realized. She did indeed. "I will return," he told her in a low voice. She nodded, then staggered back to her father. Nic tried to reassure her silently, but she refused to meet his gaze. To the rest of the company he gave a nod. The Arturos held each other for comfort. Maxl stood and gave his best salute in pure Charlemance style, with the palm faced out and the neck and back rigid. Maarten swore to himself once more and mopped his brow.

At the ramp's top, Nic paused, rebuffed again by the soft wall that seemed to stand in his way. Pushing through felt like passing from warm air into a pillow of cold. Scarcely had his foot touched the deck when the terrible ache behind his eyes began once more. The back of his throat tickled as it might before the worst of colds, then increased in intensity a hundredfold. He found it difficult to breathe. "*Who are you?*" he heard the woman's voice asking.

He stumbled to the galleon's center, foot over foot, barely able to stand. The pressure behind his eyes was so intense that, open or closed, all he could see were whorls of purple light. Nic's shoulder thudded against the main mast. It felt oily to the touch. "I'm Nic," he managed to mumble, though his lips felt as if they'd swollen and grown thick. Why had he thought that he, of all people, could break a curse? "I'm Niccolo. I'm nobody."

The voice wasn't satisfied. A vicious wind seemed to whip across its surface, stronger and more frigid than any storm the ship had ever weathered. He could feel its icy blast on his face as the anger of whatever inhabited this ship was unleashed in full force. "*Who are you? Who are you?*" The words battered away in his head, trying to break down every bastion of sanity it found there. Around him, Nic began to see the unearthly forms of men, pale as the blue summer sky and transparent as glass, mere wisps of forms writhing in pain. Perhaps they were the spirits of those who had died upon the galleon at sea, or the unfortunate crew from Ellada. Perhaps they were nothing more than the result of madness. Nic could feel the agony wracking every inch of their soundless frames. It made him grit his teeth, so intense was the rictus it caused. "I ... am ... Niccolo," he fought to gasp out. "I am ... Niccolo No-Name, the orphan. I am Niccolo the foundling, nobody's pride and joy."

"*Who are you?*"

He used the mast to straighten himself, still fighting against the cold and the stabbing betrayal of every muscle. If this entity wanted to know who he was, then fine, he thought to himself, stubborn to the end. He'd tell it who he was. He'd tell it every single person he'd ever been. "I am Niccolo the servant, the dung-slinger, the sewer rat. I am Niccolo the game skinner, the boot shiner, Niccolo the digger. I am Nic of the kitchens, Nic the rag-boy, Nic who tends to the mules. I am Niccolo who sleeps in the stables with the pack animals." With every word he felt stronger and more contrary. His voice had begun cracked and defeated, but now he spoke loudly against the zephyr's howl. "I am Niccolo Dattore. That is the name I chose for myself. I am Nic the dogsbody, the card-fetcher. I am Nic, to be wagered at taroccho. Niccolo, the stagehand."

The entity roared, but his cry was louder. "I am Nic the pirate-killer, the destroyer of ships. I am the Drake, feared and respected by all. I am Nic who wants to go home, and if

I am blessed, I will be Nic the lover. I am Niccolo Dattore, the cursed. And by the gods, this ship is meant to be mine!"

The world split in two. Later, when he remembered the massive noise, Nic could never be sure whether or not the sound was real, or whether it had been something he'd imagined. Certainly none of those on the pier could recall hearing the mighty cracking, nor seeing the brilliant flash of light that followed. In fact, none of them reported hearing Nic's cries against the invisible tempest at all. To Nic, though, the noise was both majestic and awe-inspiring. Never in any temple had he ever heard anything that moved him as much, nor would the sight of any king inspire him in quite the same way. Once the sound had receded into mere memory, he blinked, able to see once again.

The sun was rising. He stood upon the galleon still, alone and upright. Gulls cried overhead, arguing over their breakfasts, while in the distance he could hear the sounds of bells summoning crews to their duties. From the town was the same normal ruckus that might have been heard in Massina, or Côte Nazze, or Cassaforte itself. And as for the galleon—well, it was a ship. A mighty ship, yes, and one that had been neglected for far too long. Where before seething blackness had covered it like a mantle, now was merely a curious sort of crust. It was very like paint carelessly applied over a dirty surface, so that it cracked and peeled once dry. Nic knelt down and touched his hands to the deck. When he rubbed hard, the layer began to flake away, revealing the golden wood beneath.

His fingers ran over the smoothness under the grime.

The curse's voice, implacable and demanding, had vanished. In its place, he heard the sound of distant music, as must a fiddle player when he ran his fingers over his instrument's strings without bowing. Maarten's Folly sang beneath his fingers, its phantom strain a balm to his soul. Stronger now, he rose, though he itched to hear that song again.

Niccolo Dattore, owner of the galleon, leaned over its head rails to salute his astonished crew below. They gaped at him, scarcely able to trust their eyes. "What?" he cried out in a voice that was not the Drake's, but his own. His true own. "Am I that frightening a sight? Come aboard, all, and bring the provisions. Oh, and Maarten," he called out, planting his hands on his hips as he assumed a posture of sovereignty. "I'll be accepting those three hundred kronen, for taking your Folly off of your hands."

The tradesman blinked rapidly, unable to believe what he was hearing. "Certainly," he said at last. "Certainly, mynheer."

Nic watched him scurry away. Armand might have offered to buy him out of his indentures, but now Nic wouldn't have to rely upon anyone else to become a free man. He had done that himself.

19

Of all the wars I have seen waged, those upon the sea are the most brutal and the bloodiest. Upon land at least the earth may reclaim its own, but to be lost amidst a maelstrom of blood, wind, and water seems almost heartbreakingly sad.

—Captain John Smythe-Passelyon, in a private letter to his wife

Without challenge, Maarten's Folly had raised its sails and slid past the battalion of sixteen warships. The smallest of them had been easily twice the Folly's size, and the Folly was no tiny craft. By mid-morning, even the most vocal of those who had not wanted to leave Gallina aboard a cursed galleon—specifically, Ingenue and perhaps more surprisingly, the substantial Urso, who proved to be surprisingly superstitious—were somewhat mollified. They grudgingly had to admit that their new quarters were fairly spacious.

If one overlooked the black crust that adhered to the ship's every surface, they were even fairly luxurious. Though the original crew was used to the *Tears of Korfu*'s tight accommodations, the Arturos' troupe was not. Likewise, though the actors were accustomed to late-night gossips and the shambles of what they considered their backstage area, the original crew had been befuddled by the abundance of women's skirts and foundation garments spread around their quarters, the ever-present quantities of sewing as all the actors repurposed their old costumes for every possible piratical occasion, and most especially, the very notion of laundering. Maarten's Folly, on the other hand, had easily been constructed for a fifty-man crew and very likely could have billeted seventy-five. In the two levels of hold below, both the real pirates and their imitations could rattle about without finding a pin cushion or an unreasonably filthy stray garment occupying their personal space. The hatches allowed far more light and fresh air below than any of the seasoned sailors had ever experienced.

As for the crust, it began to vanish almost the moment the crew had stepped on board. Some areas, such as the thoroughfares on the deck that saw greater amounts of traffic, began to shine through immediately. Water and scrubbing seemed to help. Even those areas beyond reach of a human hand began to lose their burned and sooty appearance. By the second day of their voyage, where the ship's name ought to have been painted had begun to appear the traces of letters. *LY* were the only legible ones among them.

"*The Sailor's Ally*," Armand Arturo had suggested that morning, when they'd all leaned over the head rails to stare at the emerging wording.

"*The Lying Fool*," Knave said, after silently sounding out the spelling.

The Signora dreamily looked into the distance. "*Lena's Lyre*. That would be the most romantic."

They all peered at the lettering as if expecting the rest to reveal itself instantly. Stubbornly, it did not. Yet over the next two days they all noticed changes around the galleon. It seemed to be melting from one shape into another, like carved ice on a warm day. The skull-like projections to the sides of every wooden door that had seemed so forbidding, so sepulcher-like beneath the black scab, were revealed to be carved vines of grapes and gourds. The fireplace in the captain's quarters that had resembled a tortured face caught mid-scream broke loose from its black covering and proved itself an elaborate hearth of such intricacy that it had to have been carved by descendants of Caza Legnoli. It would have rivaled any hearth in the finest rooms of Cassaforte's cazas, or perhaps even the palace itself.

As for the ship's figurehead, which had the look of gnarled roots twisting from a thirsty tree to a river's edge, by the evening of the second day of the voyage, its face was visible from beneath the knobby morass. Smooth and feminine it was, with eyes that seemed to pierce the falling darkness to find the way home. Staring at her, Nic could almost imagine that the gilded wooden carving had been the source of that relentless questioning voice that still at times haunted his thoughts.

Maxl had assured them that, according to the maps he'd brought with him, Maarten's Folly should reach Cassaforte on the morning of their fourth day. It was on the night before that Darcy knocked upon the door of the captain's quarters and let herself in. "There is something very odd about this boat," she announced.

Nic cocked his head. He had been sitting at the captain's writing desk, which had been stocked full of paper. One of his boats, delicate and intricate in its folds, was still in his hands. "Please don't tell me you're just now noticing."

Darcy reconsidered her words. "Odder than ... what we're used to. Did you know that Maxl says it should take at least forty men to do the work that ten of us are doing?" Nic nodded. Maxl had repeated the same words to him many a time, usually with befuddlement in his voice. "Our anchor is enormous, Niccolo. You saw it. By all rights we should still be back in Gallina, still trying to shift it from the harbor bed. Ingenue and Infant Prodigy and I aren't exactly Ursos in size, you know. Yet it came up as if we'd been trying to winch nothing more than a bundle of wet wool." She began moving around the room, examining its rich mahogany paneling. Her fingers ran over the weathered table in its center. "When we do that thing with the sails to rein them in ..."

"When you trim them?" Nic automatically supplied the correct term. Not that he'd known, two weeks before.

"Yes, when we're trimming the sails, it's something that Infant Prodigy and I can do ourselves. Nic, that shouldn't be. It took twice as many to rein in those sails on the *Korfu*, and the winds are stronger here than they were in that part of the sea." She wasn't exaggerating. The waters closer to Cassaforte had been stormy and sometimes wild. "It's almost as if—Nic, what do you know about the blessings and signs? You know, what the Seven and Thirty do. It's what sets them apart from the rest of us. In return for their service to the country, the seven families of the cazas and Cassaforte's thirty noble families of craftsmen are trained in the appropriate prayers and signs of the gods to make."

"For their enchantments, yes." Nic didn't understand why Darcy was telling him things a child of two knew, in Cassaforte. "It's what made the Legnoli costume trunk different from any old chest. It held more because it had been blessed to enhance its natural purpose." Nic still felt a twinge of guilt whenever he thought of the present he'd left behind for Trond Maarten, in that trunk aboard the *Tears of Korfu*.

"But listen. When we had the fire at the nuncial house, last year, workers from Caza Portello came to Côte Nazze to oversee the repairs in the damaged rooms. Do you know how long it took? Less than a week." Nic shook his head. It was all mildly interesting, but he didn't see where Darcy was going with any of it. "Much of the damage they didn't have to repair," she told him. "They laid their hands on it. They made the signs and whispered the prayers. Niccolo, the wood slowly repaired itself. It was as if… I don't know, exactly. It was as if the blessings returned what was taken away by the flames. The tapestries, the windows all had to be replaced—they weren't Divetri windows—but everything that had been of Portello, the *structure*, seemed… healed." She waited to see if he drew any conclusions.

Nic thought about it. "And you think this ship is like that? Healing itself?"

"No. Not at all. I think you're right about the ship being of Cassaforte. That much is obvious. As you said, look at it. It was made by craftsmen." She gestured all about the room, indicating the ornate curved ceiling, the vault over the bay window with its wood-sculpted seat, and then the table itself, with its gryphon-shaped legs gazing fiercely in every direction. "I think the ship has been blessed. Perhaps I'll sound mad when I say this, but I think it knows who we are. I think it's trying to help us get home."

Nic was so startled that he stood up from the desk. He remembered the voice insistently demanding his identity. He'd even told it he'd wanted to return home. "No," he said, hushed. "I believe you. You're right."

"It makes sense. It's the only way it could be working so smoothly with only a skeleton crew. I think this ship could find its way home even if we were all simply sitting on the deck having a picnic and playing taroccho. It was built with the enchantments, and it's simply fulfilling its natural, primary purpose. It was built by Caza Piratimare, of the Seven."

Darcy's theory was so logical that Nic was astounded he hadn't thought of it before. No one had really spoken aloud about the galleon's strange way of correcting mistakes and making labor as easy as possible, perhaps out of a fear that drawing attention to it might cause it to cease. "I'm not of the Seven and Thirty," he said slowly. A chill spread up his spine, and dissipated right above his collar, making him shiver. "Nor have I ever had much to do with their enchanted objects. So I don't know what I think about that. It's spooky."

"It is a little spooky, but it shouldn't be. It's just what this ship was built to do, by the craftsmen of Piratimare. It's what it is."

"Why did you tell me about the nuncial house, though, if you don't think the ship's repairing itself?" Nic asked.

For the first time that voyage, Darcy looked at him with mingled pity and scorn. "The ship's not repairing itself," she sighed. "Don't you see? I think *you're* repairing it." Nic blinked, stunned. "Look around!" she said. "What parts of the ship have come back to life first?"

"The deck, I suppose," he said slowly, thinking about it. "The captain's quarters."

Her voice was like a stern school teacher's. "Correct. The quarterdeck, where you spend your days. The quarterdeck, where you stand at the ship's wheel and make adjustments to our course, and see that things are done. And the captain's quarters, where you sleep and eat. In other words, the two parts of the ship where you spend the most time."

As Darcy talked, Nic flexed his fingers. He remembered the way the deck's wood had seemed to sing beneath his fingertips, the first time he'd touched it. It still sang to him now, every time he took the wheel. "That can't be."

"What do you know of your mother? Your father?" Before Nic could speak, she supplied the answer. "Nothing. Who's to say that one of them wasn't of Caza Piratimare? Perhaps your mother was a disgraced cazarrina who left her insula because she was large with child? Or what if you were the bastard son of a cazarrino who never knew he'd gotten his lady love pregnant?"

A flush had crept into Nic's face the moment Darcy began talking of his parentage. "Every poor child dreams that his parents are princes and princesses. This is the sort of invention you might find in one of Signor Arturo's plays." To Nic's surprise, his throat sounded more choked than he would have supposed. He took a deep breath and tried to continue. "It is not my life."

"Oh, of course." Darcy stood upright and curtsied with mock formality. She crossed the room to the door, and let her hands rest on the latch. "Of course it's not your life. Your life is much more mundane. Shipwrecks. Pirates. Deserted islands. Curses on ships that only you among scores of men can dispel. Forgive me for assuming you are anything special, after so much normality." Noting that she'd left him speechless, Darcy opened the latch to let herself out. "Oh, Niccolo?" she asked, all innocence. "What is that in your hands, anyway?"

"Why ... just a paper boat."

"Oh, I see. A paper boat. Like every other paper boat you've built?" Her eyes traveled around the room, taking in the little paper sculptures that lay upon every flat surface. "Like the paper boats you've made ever since I've known you? How long have you been making those paper boats, Nic?"

"All ..." He gulped. "All my life."

"Interesting," she said, her voice level. "It comes so naturally to you. I wonder where you get the urge? Hmmm. Well. Good night."

She had made her point. Nic tossed the scrap of paper that was in his hands onto the table, as if it burned. That hadn't been fair. Building the little boats was simply something he did with his hands, to keep them from being idle when he was alone. It was harmless. It didn't mean anything. It only transformed unwanted scraps into something better. Something no one else ever imagined for them.

By the time Nic thought to follow Darcy, to contradict her, she had vanished from the deck and gone down below. He didn't make pursuit.

Darcy had been unfair, to set his heart aflutter like that. She'd been unwise to give him such hope. It would be marvelous to be of Piratimare blood. To have sprung from one of Cassaforte's famed Seven families would be an immense reversal of fortune. He wandered outdoors in the direction of the ship's prow, his hands idly tracing the railing as he walked. In his mind's eye he could see the scene as written into one of Signor Arturo's dramas. Hero would wander across the Caza Piratimare bridge in the humblest of his clothes, while the Piratimare family (played by Signor Arturo as Vecchio, and the Signora in her most resplendent and waist-cinching of dresses) waited with open arms and tear-stained faces at the bridge's end. Pulcinella, as the family's housemaid, would have prepared a feast that could have fed most of the city. Infant Prodigy would have the role of the younger sister, given to performing cartwheels around the massive table. Even the most hardened of men would be hard-pressed not to reach for his handkerchief, at the sight of so many sunny faces and so happy an ending as that.

A sudden break in the waves brought Nic back to reality. The galleon had run into choppy waters, throwing him off-balance. From the quarterdeck, illuminated by the stern lights, Maxl threw his captain a cheerful wave and began whistling. He pointed in a direction beyond Nic, then curled his fist and pointed his thumb to the heavens. Nic turned to see what Maxl had been so happy about. In the distance he finally spied lights. Small clusters of them, steady and unmoving, burning brightly against the dark. Cassaforte.

They were nearly home. Nic's heart pounded at the realization. That scene he'd imagined moments before could be a reality before the week's end. He could easily be that prodigal son returned to the Piratimare fold, loved and accepted, finally enfolded within the embrace of a family. A noble family at that. But to what end? The ship lurched uncertainly in the rough waters as he thought about it. The family he'd gain would all be strangers to him. Likely they would shut him up in some sort of insula to teach him the craft of shipbuilding, the moment he joined the clan—though wasn't there some kind of ritual selection process for that, and wasn't he too old for it? He knew so little about the Seven. Certainly he'd never have the opportunity to see the Arturos again, nor Maxl, nor even Renaldo and Michaelo if he'd been able to track them down once more.

Hadn't they been more family to him during the worst of times than any Piratimare?

What else? To Nic a roast fowl leg and a mug of hard cider was feast enough. The costume he wore now, with its high boots and white shirt, had suited him fine. And was it really his fantasy to vault from servant boy to commander of servants? He couldn't envision it, try as he might. He knew too well what it was like to endure the commands of those bent on satisfying their own pleasures, ever to have servants of his own. His captaincy had been different; he had been alongside the crew the entire time. The orders might have seemed to come from him, but he was working just as hard as they to achieve their common goal. No, if becoming one of the Seven meant accepting the ministrations of servants, he could never join their ranks.

The galleon heaved up and down as it sailed forward, bringing closer the lights of his home city. Cassaforte looked peaceful by night. Hundreds of lights dotted its shores, from boats at rest and, higher, from the cazas upon the seven islands surrounding the city. Even more shone from the city's center, setting the sky before him aglow. Nic grinned at the sight, so glad he was for it. He also laughed a little at himself, for allowing himself to be seduced with the vision of a life that would never—could never—be his own.

He ran his hands over the rails so he could feel the wood beneath his skin sing out at his touch. This galleon, wherever it had come from, needed him. For now, that was all he needed to know about who he was.

For several moments he watched the dancing lights

from the city and listened to Maxl's cheerful chanty, whistling in the background. Then he cocked his head, curious. Some of those lights should not have been dancing at all. "Maxl," he called, snapping his fingers. "Bring me the spyglass."

It was in his hand a moment later. "I am never being to Cassafort City before," Maxl announced, looking over Nic's shoulder. "I am hearing it is beautiful, for a city of savages and magicians."

Nic spent a moment adjusting the glass. The lights he'd seen shouldn't have been there. He swore an oath beneath his breath, but refused to panic. He'd been brought home for a reason, and already he'd found it. "Sound the bell," he commanded Maxl. "All hands on deck immediately. Cassaforte's on fire."

20

Soft living does not a brave man make.

—An old Cassafortean saying

I cannot believe it has come to this." Jacopo Colombo slumped against the rail, one hand pressed to his forehead. He looked as if he might be about to weep. "It is beyond all dreaming."

A stiff crosswind had sprung up to match the roiling waters. The galleon's crew went stumbling toward the aft as the ship pitched up. The main mast sails began flapping crazily as those who had been adjusting them lost hold of their ropes. "Trim those!" Nic barked out, a split second before Maxl could. "And stand ready. We don't know all that's happening yet." Signor Arturo, Knave, and Urso scrambled at his command.

"Pays d'Azur has besieged the city!" Jacopo protested. "We are too late!"

Nic paused only so that he could address Jacopo directly. "That is impossible. You know very well that Comte Dumond's warships could not have reached Cassaforte before us. Take a look." He thrust the spyglass into the old man's hands so that he could see for himself. Six of the city's magnificent naval vessels burned where they had been anchored. It was their sails and masts that flamed so brilliantly against the night sky. Great clouds of black smoke were beginning to billow to the heavens from their hulls, blackening the purple and brown silk banners flying from their masts.

Alight too was the southern port complex, and many of the boats docked there. Though the waves and wind obscured any sounds that might have been coming from shore, Nic could imagine the chaos. Smaller boats as yet untouched by the fires had been loosed from their moorings and drifted, unmanned, to collide and drift away from danger. Merchant ships desperately trying to escape the conflagrations pushed between them. Nic could only pity anyone caught in the confusion. "Good gods," muttered Jacopo.

Darcy happened to be running by with a coil of rope in her arms just then. "Every hand is needed now," she informed her father. She grabbed the spyglass from him and thrust it back at Nic as she passed. "Especially in a time like this."

"Go," Nic told them both. Then, to Jacopo, he said, "We'll get through this." The nuncio nodded, though he didn't seem convinced when he accompanied his daughter to the foremast.

Once again the ship pitched up in the water, then plunged down. This time, the crew was not caught off-guard. Nic was so attuned to the galleon's motions that he managed to stride to the quarterdeck without clutching at anything for support. He sprinted up the stairs, took hold of the ship's wheel, and adjusted the rudder. Maxl watched, then commented, "You are not wanting to go into the city?"

"Into that pandemonium? Not likely." Nic peered through the glass again, focusing on the outer edge of the upheaval.

"No huzzah, huzzah, whupping the Azurites? No paying the back?" Maxl sounded a little disappointed.

"Those aren't Azurites," Nic said. From time to time he could see little arcs of fire shooting from small craft to their targets. "I think they're pirates. I'm willing to wager that the *Tears of Korfu* was not the only band of buccaneers the comte approached to do his dirty work." Another small arc of twirling fire flew from a little cutter. The vessel had sliced its way through the waters to the side of one of the merchant vessels, where it had launched its deadly missile. Nic saw an explosion of flame aboard the merchant ship's deck. There was a flurry of motion as its crew scattered to escape. Several appeared to jump overboard. Nic lowered the glass and handed it to Maxl. "What manner of weapons are they using?"

It took Maxl a moment, but very soon he had an answer. "I am not knowing what to be calling it in your tongue. For us, we call it the Device Infernal," he said. "But it is a bottle, yes? Of glass? And it is filled with spirits? Pure spirits, very easy to catch on fire. The top is stuffed with a rag. The rag is set on fire, so when it is thrown the bottle is breaking and *sploosh*." Maxl made an exploding motion with his hands. "Very dirty fighting, it is being. No honor to it." He spat on the deck. "Pirates from Ellada, it is their invention."

Nic got the general idea of the infernal device. "Very dirty indeed," he agreed. He thought things over for a moment. "We'll go after them," he said at last. "It's clever of the comte, sending a fleet of scrubby pirates to do his dirty work for him. No offense intended."

"I am not taking any," Maxl agreed, amiably enough.

"He's taking out the naval boats, of course." Nic could map the strategy in his head, plain as anything. "A quick surprise strike. They might not be completely destroyed, but they'd be useless for several days, if not weeks. Then they're creating bedlam at the ports." It was too far to tell if Cassaforte's western shipyards were under attack as well, but Nic would have wagered his own freedom that they were. "In and out, unannounced, under cover of darkness, no one to see them coming or going. People will say to themselves, 'Oh, it was only pirates,' tote up the losses, and let their guards down. Then the real battle fleet from Pays d'Azur moves in, and Cassaforte is helpless against them. If we capture one of the pirate cutters, we can find out from its captain when they intend to attack." Maxl let out a huff of air through his nose. Another followed. Soon the man was laughing. "What?" asked Nic, irritated. "Do you think this is funny?"

"No. That is not what is funny. " Maxl gestured at the city's horizon. "All you are wanting, all this time, is this being home again. You bring the girl and her father as you promised. Your job is ended. You can drop them here, say bye-bye, then sail off again and keep yourself away from siege. So why, Master Nic? All this swashbuckling—you are not having to be doing any of it."

Maxl had been the last man he'd expected not to support him. The betrayal stung. Through clenched teeth, Nic replied, "I am not doing it because I have to. I am doing it because I can."

To Nic's surprise, Maxl laughed louder. "Good, good!" he cried. He clapped a hand on Nic's back, and nodded his blue face in approval. "You not thinking now like a boy. You thinking like captains are doing. This is what honor is being. Yes? That is why I am laughing, my friend. Come!" he said, indicating that Nic take the ship's wheel. "We are chasing pirates now."

It was with a flush of pride still animating his face that Nic stood at the fore of the quarterdeck a moment later to sound the ship's bell. He had never used the pattern before that indicated the crew to fall in and assemble. Macaque's men knew well enough what it meant, and the actors followed. Once they were in place, waiting and expectant, Nic looked at the faces below him. They were all silent, waiting for him to speak. He hoped that what he had to say would not disappoint. "My crew," he said. "My comrades." Nic paused while the pirates who had a grasp of Cassafortean translated for the others. "This journey we've taken together has been strange indeed." A few people nodded in agreement. "I...I must thank you for your remarkable service. We would not be here tonight were it not for each and every one of you."

"Hear hear!" shouted Signor Arturo, doffing his hat.

Thus far that night, Nic had not made any declamations as the Drake, or as anyone else. He was simply being Nic Dattore, captain of the galleon and leader of its crew, speaking from his heart. Not one of the men or women gave any indication that anything more was necessary. "This place—this city of Cassaforte—is my homeland. It is the homeland to many of you before me. I know that we pirates are men without country. We answer to no king, no comte, no counselor, save that of our own hearts and senses of honor." He looked around the assembly. By now, the faces were as familiar to him as his own. "What I am about to request of you is not anything Captain Xi would have asked. It is nothing that Macaque would have asked—had you been able to pull him away from his cards." A ripple of laughter sounded throughout Macaque's old crew at that joke. "No, what I am asking is much more dangerous.

"There are men out there, pirates under the pay of the Comte Dumond, who are setting afire this country's harbor using infernal devices. I believe they are trying to weaken the city so that it will be defenseless against the armada of warships we saw in Gallina's harbor." At the mention of the infernal devices, a number of Macaque's men shook their heads and made signs to warn off ill spirits. None of the Arturos' troupe knew what Nic meant, for such things were alien to Cassaforte. "Cassaforte's ships of battle are burning even now. They are unable to defend themselves against these ruffians. But we can help." Having to project so loudly in order to be heard over the water and wind was taking more energy than he knew. Suddenly Nic had a great deal of respect for the Arturos, who often had to struggle with noisy and unappreciative crowds. He paused and took a deep breath. "I know that asking pirates to come to a country's aid is not usual. It's unconventional, yes. But there is honor in it, and I cannot turn my back on my homeland. Anyone who chooses to help will receive my deepest gratitude. Any man—or woman—who wishes not to be a part of my plan may retire below deck. Neither I nor anyone else will think unkindly of it."

The whispered translations ceased seconds after Nic finished speaking. He indicated the hatch closest to where the crew stood, and gestured to it. Though heads turned to see if anyone would step away, no one did.

After a sufficient wait, Nic nodded. It was difficult not to smile, so at long last, he allowed himself to. "Thank you, friends."

From beside him, Maxl punched his fist into the air. "Are we being cowards?" Like a lion he roared, his long mane of hair tumbling as he shook his head in defiance. "Or are we being the kings of pirates?"

"We are pirates!" shouted the Arturos at the top of their considerable lungs. The second time, they were joined by Infant Prodigy, Ingenue, and the rest of the troupe. "We are pirates!" On the third cry, many others joined in. Nic, however, only had eyes for Darcy. Her tear-streaked face shone as she looked up from below. *"We are pirates!"* Over and over the crew shouted the three words as loudly as they could, joined in by even the men who did not speak the language. They appreciated the sentiment, well enough. *"We are pirates! We are pirates!"*

"First Mate Maxl," cried Nic, ringing the bell in the pattern that dismissed his crew back to their duties. "Bring the ship 'round."

Enough accounts were later told of that night to confuse any save those who were actually there. Ardent historians trying to make sense of the tales of sailors who witnessed the battle—stories told largely in taverns over increasingly large flagons of ale, it must be admitted—might have arrived at any number of baffling conclusions. Some said Maarten's Folly had swooped down upon the ships burning on the outskirts of Caza Buonochio, rescued those stranded in the waters there, then swung back around to the east in order the purge the southern ports of attacking freebooters. Others would have told of a galleon captain with a shining sword and a thirst for vengeance, who ferreted out the pirate cutters with an almost supernatural accuracy and sent them all to a watery grave. Some said that the captain's galleon swept from Caza Buonochio all the way to Caza Portello, leaving ship after pirate ship as nothing but splinters and driftwood in its wake. A few argued that the galleon set course around the entire city, from the Insula of the Penitents of Lena in the east all the way around to the Insula of the Children of Muro in the west, before coming to rest to an applauding and adoring crowd.

The real facts were these.

There were indeed many refugees stranded in the waters of the Azure Sea around Cassaforte. Some had jumped from the burning warships, but more had attempted to take their small fishing or merchant crafts away from the infernos and had been stranded or capsized in the heavy waves. They were difficult to rescue without stopping, but even more difficult to leave behind. It was the Colombos who hit upon the notion of employing a length of netting suspended from the port deck. To its perimeter had been woven a number of air-filled bladders that caused it to float, allowing strong swimmers to fling themselves into the net, cling on, and, despite the galleon's speed, climb up and onto the deck. Darcy and the Signora and Pulcinella saw to the bedraggled victims. Many were angry at their attackers, and experienced sailors at that; they immediately began pitching in with the sails and running down the hatch to fetch whatever Maxl ordered. Those with little experience aboard a sailing ship aided as best they could with helping other survivors to safety, so that their masses swelled aboard the Folly's deck.

It was perfectly true as well that the galleon destroyed a number of the pirate's vessels in one glorious fell swoop, though whether it was by sheer luck or some extramundane phenomenon, Nic could never say. Four of the tiny craft had pulled close together far to the south of Caza Buonochio so they could exchange more spirits and rags for the construction of infernal devices. Somehow they did not see the galleon's blackened hull moving in their direction, nor did they hear the cry of its captain as he called out to pull up the net and extend the sails to their fullest. Nic wrestled with the ship's wheel to bring the galleon around at a sharp angle, trusting on his instinct and the glorious singing of the ship beneath his feet to tell him how to proceed.

Only too late did the men in the boats see what was happening. "*Lyria! Lyria!*" Nic plainly heard them yelling, perhaps warning each other. Maarten's Folly slammed its nose into the grouped vessels, crashing through three of them as if they had been matchsticks. The fourth managed to evade the impact, but in his panic, its captain failed to steer completely out of the galleon's course. Its wide aft slammed against the little boat, sending all ten of its pirates overboard into the rough seas without taking on so much as a scratch.

The crew cheered at that maneuver, but the survivors that had been brought aboard the ship began to ask questions: who was this bold captain in the strange and unusual garb? Where had he come from? When they learned from the crew that he was known as the Drake and that he was a man of Cassaforte defending his city, their respect grew.

The galleon was not everywhere at once on that night, much as its captain wished it could be. It cut a path from Buonochio to the east, collecting more survivors close to the southern ports before sweeping past Caza Divetri. A lone pirate cutter there had pulled close to the Divetri docks at the island's lowest point. From his high vantage point, Nic could see that the pirates aboard the vessel had lit the wicks of two infernal devices and were preparing to hurl them onto the highly-flammable wooden piers. The sudden appearance of Maarten's Folly, however, caught the attention of at least one of the pirates. He pointed and yelled something at full volume, the only word of which Nic recognized was that word again: *"Lyria!"*

The roar of disapproval from the survivors caught the pirates off-guard. Several of those Darcy and Jacopo had rescued from the waters only minutes before dove from the sides of the ship to board the pirate cutters. Overwhelmed and totally unused to being attacked when they had always been the attackers, the pirates panicked. Some jumped. The two holding the infernal devices had the presence of mind to haul back and toss them with all their might. Twin balls of fire arced through the night onto the galleon. One hit the lower deck, crashing on impact. The spirits within caught on fire immediately, licking high into the air. A woman survivor clutching her infant son to her breast shrieked and ran, so close she had been to the explosion. The other burst near the mizzenmast, its contents roaring into a blaze that seemed to roast Nic's cheeks. One of the pirates let out a catcall of triumph. It was cut short when a survivor, a deep-chested fisherman who had lost the means of his livelihood that evening, punched him squarely in the face.

The twin infernos flared higher. The galleon's crew was

more than ready for them, though. Maxl had earlier set some of the survivors to fetching several of the heavy bags of sand used as ballast in the ship's depths, and given them spades. Wherever the flames licked, there the survivors scooped the sand. Infant Prodigy led the effort to douse the fires. When the blaze near the mizzenmast was gone within seconds, she swung from a rope over the quarterdeck rail, somersaulted across the deck, leapt to her feet, grabbed a free spade, and smothered the rest of the second blaze by herself.

Nic had kept an eye on the pirates as the galleon had approached. He knew which one had been shouting out orders while the others had followed commands. Over the deck rail, he pointed to the man in the water, recognizing him immediately by the pad of fabric covering one eye. "Give me that one," he told the survivors in the water. Instantly they swam to the man and overcame him. It was only a few moments later that his drenched and unconscious body was restrained and locked in the hold. "I always knew an eyepatch was a bad idea," Nic muttered to himself. He gave orders to those swimming below to guard the Divetri docks and not to let any of the pirates set foot in the city. The waterlogged pirates, for the most part, would rather face the wrath of the sea than that of the angry mob. They swam away into the night.

The galleon enacted a similar scene near Caza Portello's private docks, and then prevented the depleted crews of two cutters from scaling the rocks of Caza Cassamagi. By the time Maarten's Folly changed course once again and had swung back to the city's southern docks, the pirates were on the run. The mere sight of the galleon coursing across the waters set the remaining cutters scattering. They vanished as silently as they had come, back to the western seas. The renegade pirates had done the damage they had intended, anyway. There was nothing Nic could do about the navy's ships burning to ruin all around the city's perimeter, nor about the sorry state of the city's southern seaport.

It was at Piratimare's extensive private docks that the galleon finally came to rest, with no less than four disgruntled and dripping pirate captains in tow. Somehow the word had spread of how to douse the infernal devices, for everywhere Nic looked he could see little piles of sand. Members of the household, noble and servant alike, stood over them with shovels. Those who had caps waved them and cheered as Nic ordered the anchor dropped.

The confusion that followed on that fateful night was to Nic little more than a blur. There was a moment when he realized that he had done what he had set out to do. Instead of feeling glad for it, though, all he wanted was to make sure Darcy and the rest of his crew were all right—but especially Darcy. He found her wet from grappling with survivors. The long waves of her hair were matted with sand. Yet she was safe, and her eyes shone at the sight of him. That alone had been worth any risk he had taken. There were the Arturos, too, and the rest of the troupe, whole and unharmed and glowing as if they'd taken six curtain calls.

Macaque's men were cheering as loudly as anyone else

assembled on shore as the crew and the survivors swept Nic down a gangplank that the people of Piratimare had with all haste brought to the galleon. And what an assembly there was. It seemed as if the entire population of Cassaforte had squeezed onto the caza's grounds. At the sight of Nic and his crew stepping onto dry land, they all shouted and cheered. Nic was conscious of some of the survivors pointing him out to the crowd. The roar in his ears deafened him.

"It's all for you, lad," he heard Signor Arturo announce. When he turned to try to find the actor in the crowd around him, though, it seemed composed only of unfamiliar faces. No, there was Maxl, his blue face immediately distinguishable. Darcy was pushing her way to Nic's side, overwhelmed by the closeness and the noise. They clutched hands, feeling more lost and stranded than they ever had on that distant, deserted shore.

Several minutes of confusion and uproar followed. All Nic could do was gape at the sheer number of people who still were crowding into the caza to see the ship that had vanquished their attackers. He felt not so much the center of a successful production as the star attraction of a freak show. *Come see the pirate boy!* the broadsides would announce. *Gape at the blue-faced man and marvel at the fat lady! Toss lundri to the girl in boy's clothing!* It was not what he would have pictured at all, had he ever stopped to imagine this night. He and Darcy looked at each other with wide eyes and clung tight.

Some semblance of order was restored when, after what

seemed like an eternity, the crowd near the Piratimare lower bridge was parted in two, divided by a crimson arrow that shot in Nic's direction. It was a contingent of palace guards, moving swiftly in formation and coming to a stop in front of him. Despite the rigid postures of the uniformed men and women, they looked as weary as he. Many of their gold-trimmed tunics were dirty and covered with sand. To his surprise, the leader of the group saluted him. The crowd immediately hushed, anxious to hear what followed. "I am Captain Esparsa. Am I addressing the man known as the Drake?" asked the man.

"Indeed," Nic replied, automatically in character. He was surprised that the guard knew his name. Then again, there had been more than ample time for the survivors who had stayed behind on the Divetri and Portello docks to have spread the word. "I am, sir."

There were some spontaneous cheers. Captain Esparsa waited for them to die down before he asked his next question. "And are you the captain of this craft, the *Allyria?*"

"The...?" Surprised, Nic turned to regard the Folly. He heard Darcy gasp beside him. Vanished were the last tracks of blackness from its hull. The galleon seemed bathed in a golden light. The figurehead, previously obscured, stared out at him from beneath the bowsprit, her face serene, her eyes stern. Where before they had only been able to make out two letters, they now could see the ship's true name, spelt out in flowing script: *Allyria.* So that was what many of the pirates had been shouting, at their approach.

Still astonished, Nic returned his attention to Esparsa.

"Yes, Captain. I am. I have brought to you four of the pirate leaders responsible for the attack."

"Then the city owes you a debt of gratitude this evening." Nic grinned at the words. His pleasure was short-lived, for Esparsa made a gesture that sent two guards to Nic's side. They clasped his hands behind his back. He felt ropes digging into his wrists. "However, I regret to inform you that we have been searching for you for some time, Signor Drake," Esparsa continued. In a more assertive voice, loud enough to be heard over the restless crowd, he announced, "By the authority of King Alessandro the Wise, I hereby arrest you. The charges are as follows: the forgery of artwork; the dissemination of stolen materials; the scavenging of Caza Portello in the days after its fall three years prior; intimidation; failure to pay taxes..."

As the list of charges went on and on, a bewildered Nic found himself surrounded by crimson and being dragged away. Such was his hero's welcome.

21

It is said of the pirate Fireclops that he endured nine years in a Gallina prison without complaint. What is usually not noted is that he preferred his incarceration to having to face the two mistresses, three wives, five assassins, and countless creditors waiting outside the prison gates for his release.

—Alejandro Franco, A Life at Sea

To say that Nic suffered during his incarceration was something of an exaggeration. As far as prison cells went, his was most cozy. The bed was clean and its linens fresh. The compartment itself was at least as large as the captain's quarters aboard the *Tears of Korfu* had been, and the prospect of the Via Dioro was most pleasant. He had a writing desk equipped with a quill, powdered ink, and an abundance of smooth writing paper. The guards who brought him his breakfast had been personable. One of them had even stopped in the doorway, bowed, and thanked him for saving her uncle, who had lost his shrimping boat at sea the night before. Had this been his home, Nic could have done very well in the space. It was far more comfortable than any place he'd ever lived.

However, the prospect of spending months, if not years, within the room's four walls did not sit well with Nic. He spent a restless and mostly sleepless night pacing the room, listening to the rain and staring out of the window at the thunderheads over the sea. He didn't know where Darcy had been taken or what had happened to the crew. Separated from the people he knew, he could have been dressed in silks and housed in the most elaborate chambers of any of the cazas and he would have been as miserable.

Thus it was with much relief that sometime after his midday meal, Captain Esparsa himself unlocked Nic's cell, saluted, and told Nic that his presence had been requested. Where, and before whom, the man would not reveal. Nic found himself surrounded by a cohort of guards and escorted from the guards' headquarters across Palace Square in the direction of Cassaforte's single biggest structure. All he could do was gulp, stare up through the pouring rain at the massive dome crowning the royal house, and hope for the best.

He sat in a parlor of sorts for some minutes, watched by two guards at two of the room's three gilded doorways. The marble floors, the intricate windows of leaded glass covered with rain droplets, the rich carpets imported from Yemeni, the display case of Catarre curiosities that dated back four hundred years—it was all lost on Nic in his nervousness. For all he knew about Cassaforte and its laws, he might have been facing his sentence and execution that very day. After what seemed like a year of waiting, the unguarded double doors opened and a girl slipped out.

She was a very pretty young woman of perhaps eighteen or nineteen years, with fair skin and hair that had been gathered into a netlike reta cap that hung over her neck. Her dress was very plain. Judging by the work apron that covered her unadorned gown, Nic might have pegged her for a servant. When he noticed that she was looking at him, Nic struggled to his feet, as was the custom. "Good day," he said, a great deal of nervousness in his voice.

"Good day," she echoed. For a moment she leaned against the closed doors, frankly regarding him. Her eyes were still lively when she wrinkled her snubbed nose and remarked, "What a curious getup you have on. You're that Drake fellow, aren't you?"

"Yes. No." Immediately Nic felt self-conscious about the pirate costume he wore. It was fairly dirty from the night before and although he was relatively fresh according to the benchmarks of the sea, by the rarefied standards of any palace servant, he must have looked and smelled like the worst of beggars. "I pretended to be. I called myself the Drake, at sea. But I'm not the same Drake that the guards want for forgery and ... um." The young woman had a curious ability to make him quite uncomfortable. It felt as if her eyes pierced through him to see things that no one else could see. Some sort of energy shimmered around her when she moved in his direction, as if she crackled with invisible sparks after shuffling across a wool carpet on a very cold day.

Yet the day was warm, and she glided rather than shuffled to his side. "Your name is Niccolo Dattore," she announced. Nic was so surprised that he could barely nod. "Captain Esparsa means well. But even he eventually had to concede that you looked too young to have been involved in the trafficking of stolen art for well over a dozen years. Unless," she added, with a quirk of her lips that made her tilt-tipped nose appear quite charming, "you were an exceptionally talented infant."

Just then one of the double doors opened again. A man stepped out, shaking his head. "How frustrating," he said upon spying the girl. The robes he wore were expensive but not elaborate, Nic could tell. Signor Arturo would have given anything for his Hero to have worn them in the role of the ne'er-do-well son of a noble family, or as one of the many princes he played who were always disguising themselves as commoners. "They talk and talk and never decide upon anything."

"Precisely," replied the servant girl. She seemed glad to share the man's opinion. "Which is why I detest these meetings. Action over debate. That's what I advocate."

"Yes, and—oh. Hello." Only then did the nobleman appear to notice that Nic was in the room as well. He reached out and vigorously pumped Nic's hand.

"Cazarro." A mysterious smile danced across the girl's lips. "This is the young man you were discussing. You might have seen him last night upon your docks."

"Eh?"

"Cazarro Ianno Piratimare," said the girl, enunciating

each word as if the man were slightly deaf, or perhaps merely excited. "May I present to you the young man calling himself the Drake. His name is Niccolo Dattore. He is the clever captain of the *Allyria*, the ship that saved so many last night."

"Was." Nic had only just gotten over his fear of lifetime incarceration. Now he was so intimidated to be in the presence of the cazarro of Piratimare that he froze. The fellow's face was covered with care lines. His nose was large and red, and his eyes darted up and down Nic's narrow frame almost greedily, but he seemed like a kind man. Luckily, the cazarro seemed to be as speechless as he. "I was captain of the *Allyria*."

"Are," said the young woman firmly. Nic looked at her. For the first time since he had been arrested, he could feel a flicker of hope. Had she overheard something?

"But dear boy... oh my goodness, you are a boy, aren't you?" The cazarro gaped again. "Do you know what the *Allyria* is?"

"I am not certain that any of us know what the *Allyria* truly is," commented the girl. It struck Nic as an unusually intelligent observation.

"Well, no, of course not. You shouldn't have been able to... it's impossible for you to have... unless, of course, you..."

Nic could stand it no longer. "It was very pleasant to meet you," he said with a bow. As he hoped, the formality silenced the man. Cazarro he might have been, and Nic intended to pay him the respect his family was due. Yet Nic was not required by any law to listen to anything he or any other Piratimare might have had to say. Nor did he want to hear. Not now, and not for a long time to come.

Luckily, the doors opened once again. The head of a young man thrust out. Nic saw nothing of him beyond a shock of blond hair and clear green eyes. "Listen, are you coming back in?"

The girl crossed her arms. "You'd like that, wouldn't you?"

"In fact, I very much would," said the young man. He was much the girl's age, outstripping Nic by only a very few years. "I despise these meetings as much as you."

"Ah," said the girl. She kicked at the hem of her dress as she marched back over to the doors. "But it's your job, and not mine."

"I *could* order you ..."

"But you wouldn't." She leaned forward and gave the fellow an affectionate kiss on the lips. Nic wasn't sure where to look. Glancing at the servant couple seemed to violate their intimacy, while peeping at Ianno Piratimare seemed risky. The man was too liable to open his mouth and blurt out whatever he was thinking or suspecting. Nic merely cleared his throat and stared at the floor.

"No, I wouldn't." The blond-headed young man reached up a finger and chucked his sweetheart on the nose. "But I might if you don't get back in here." Without further ado, the head disappeared.

The girl sighed. "Good day, Ianno. I suppose I'm to be tortured some more," she said to the cazarro of Piratimare. To Nic's surprise, she lay both of her hands upon his own left arm and began escorting him to the double doors. "Spending my days under Ferrer's watchful eye isn't enough, apparently. Now I'm to be talked to death in high meetings of state as well. Come along," she added, as she pulled Nic from the parlor into the chamber beyond.

Whenever the Arturos had portrayed a scene set in a palace, or in the estate of the Seven and Thirty or some foreign noble, they had always relied upon little pieces of glass, cut small and applied thickly, to indicate jewels. Anyone seeing any of the Arturos' potboilers would have come away with the impression that every surface in a royal home was encrusted with jewels. The cups, the plates, the chairs, and the costumes all glittered after the Signora and Pulcinella had been at them with the pot of horse glue.

Absolutely nothing in the inner chamber into which Nic was pulled was covered with diamonds, rubies, or even semi-precious stones. He could tell, however, that the spare and impeccably dressed room was the most lavish outlay of wealth he'd ever seen. From the massive tapestries adorning the far wall, to the Buonochio paintings hanging high above, to the gold-lined mural of skies and stars upon the chamber's ceiling—it was almost too much for a single pair of eyes to appreciate. Several figures sat around the single longest table Nic had ever seen. Like the abandoned Legnoli costume trunk, the table obviously had been carved in one piece from a single mighty blackwood tree in the royal forest. Only the tree that had been felled for this purpose was far, far larger.

Nic was so amazed at the opulence that at first he utterly

failed to notice Darcy standing up from the table and making her way around it. She tripped over to meet him, and Nic wondered how he ever could have been dazzled by anything else. Her hair had been washed and brushed and shone more brilliantly than cut glass in the glare of the brightest footlight. Her blue eyes sparkled brighter than sapphires. Most impressively, the dress she wore suited her so well that Nic failed to remember that she had spent most of the last two weeks in boy's breeches. "By Muro's foal," he gasped, his hands stretching out to take hers. "You're ... *glamorous.*"

"Yes, I know." Maxl's voice was proud. He, too, had come around the table to meet Nic, though Nic's eyes had only been on Darcy. "The Colombos, they make Maxl clean up to see king. 'Maxl,' they say, 'you are stinking like seaweed. You cannot stink so much before the king.' I say, I am sorry, but how did I know I am stinking of seaweed? Everything on the sea is stinking of seaweed. Yes? So I had a bath," he said with pride. "It is making me glamorous indeed, no?"

Nic had to grin. The former pirate had cleaned up admirably. His long hair had been washed and braided so that it fell in a long rope down his back. Instead of the primary paint the color of a child's wooden toy, someone had found him blueing of a more subtle shade, like the deep morning sky. He had applied it only to the forehead, above the eyes, and to the cheeks. In the expensive clothing that someone had loaned him for the occasion, Maxl looked as if he belonged more among the damas and ritters of his own country than the crew of the *Allyria*. "Yes, Maxl. You look particularly glamorous today. That's indeed what I meant. You look all right," he added to Darcy, shrugging.

"And now you're the one stinking of seaweed," she joked back.

He probably did. Nic wasn't so overwhelmed by Darcy's sudden transformation that he completely neglected to hear what Maxl said. "And we're to see the king?"

In answer to his question, Darcy's eyes darted from their end of the table down its full length, to the room's other side. Nic heard a man clearing his throat. When he turned, he saw a tableau of people surrounding an oversized chair in which was seated an elderly man with long hair of the purest white. It flowed down the back and sides of his head and mingled with his snowy beard. Though he wore only the plainest of robes and Nic had never seen him in person before, it was perfectly obvious who he was. Wasn't his face on every luni and lundri that had passed through his hands? "Oh gods," he yelped as he fell instantly to one knee. The motion managed to make him vanish completely beneath the table's edge. "I beg your most humble pardon, Majesty. I am a stupid … stupid … clod."

"Oh, rise, rise," said the king in a jovial voice. He did not sound strong, nor give the impression of strength. Given that he had been on his deathbed a mere three years before, however, it was remarkable that King Alessandro was alive at all. "It pains every joint in my old carcass to see you contorted down there. Besides, who cares to look at an old man like me when there's a pretty girl about. Eh, Milo?"

When the king nudged the blond youth beside him knowingly, Nic's heart sank. It was the young man whose head he had seen only a few moments before. "That's Milo Sorranto," he murmured to Darcy.

"Yes," she said.

"Milo Sorranto, the named heir to the throne."

"Yes," she repeated. She had been around the titled all her life. She wouldn't understand his confusion. "Then that's..." The girl in the apron sat beside the heir. Their eyes met once more. Nic hazarded a fatal guess. "Risa Divetri?"

"Of course." Darcy inspected him closely and hissed, "What's the matter with you?"

He wanted to cover his burning face. "I thought they were servants," he explained, mortified when her eyes flew wide.

As was the custom in Cassaforte, the king could name anyone as successor to the Olive Crown and the Scepter of Thorn, ignoring his own offspring if he so chose. Milo Sorranto had been named heir to the throne mere weeks ago. The king's only son, Prince Berto, had been banished to the distant island of Portoneferro after his role in the kidnapping of the seven cazarri and the attempted coup against his father. He had died by his own hand only a month after his imprisonment. The coup had largely been stopped by Risa Divetri, who for a few days had valiantly assumed the title of Cazarra of Divetri and kept her household from ruin. Milo Sorranto had been instrumental in aiding her, as had his sister, Camilla. And there was Camilla to the rear of Alessandro, dressed in the crimson of the royal guards, her breast decorated with the medals that declared her the king's personal bodyguard. Her hair was as blond as her brother's, and her eyes the same shade of green. "Well, they're definitely not servants," Darcy whispered back, yanking him down toward the table's far end.

"I beg your pardon as well, signorina," Nic stammered as he approached. "I did not know you were Risa the Enchantress."

The Divetri girl's lips quirked. "Is that what they're calling me now?" she asked. "I suppose it could be worse. Risa the Snooty I shouldn't care for. Risa the Appalling, I'd like even less."

"How would you care for Risa of the Incredibly Loud Mouth?" Milo asked with a friendly jeer.

In reply, Risa stared at the heir for a moment. Her lips worked silently. Suddenly Milo's hair appeared to catch fire, blazing with a red-blue flame. Darcy and Maxl both startled and began to fly to the heir's side. Jacopo, who had been sitting close to the heir near the table's head, pushed back his chair to distance himself. Milo himself sighed, appearing unconcerned. "She's doing the fire illusion again, is she?" he asked, waving Maxl and Darcy away. "Really, Risa. It was amusing only the first dozen times."

The flames went out, leaving Milo unharmed. "Children," said the king reproachfully. "We do have serious matters before us."

"I'm very sorry." Risa crossed her arms and flounced into a chair. They seemed to have a great deal of familiarity between them, the king and Risa.

Jacopo seemed still shaken by the unexpected display of sorcery from the Divetri girl. He pulled his chair close to the table once more, pointed to a map of the Azure Sea that lay before the king, and spoke. "We have been telling King Alessandro of the threat that is Pays d'Azur, Niccolo. We have convinced them of the threat from their ships of war."

"Very grave, indeed." The king appeared wearied as he turned his attention once more to the situation at hand. Nic wondered if the banter between the heir and Risa Divetri might not have been for his benefit, a deliberate display to lighten his heart. Alessandro appeared very frail as he pulled the map closer. His hand trembled. "Never in my lifetime has Cassaforte faced a greater threat."

Nic noticed that Risa appeared to be staring at him. In front of the place where she sat to the king's left lay a square of mirrored glass. As the monarch talked, she had traced several signs over its surface. Now, hovering inches over its surface emerged an image, floating in the air like a rainbow. And like a rainbow, Nic had no doubt that if he attempted to touch it, it would prove as elusive. "That's them," he said, pointing to the oval-shaped illusion. In its center he could see the warships of Pays d'Azur, dark and ominous on the water. "You can see where they are?"

"Alas, no." Risa appeared disappointed in herself. "You can see them in your mind. I am only sharing that image with the others."

"This is a memory, then?" Nic asked, trying not to sound let down himself. It would have been useful to spy upon their enemies remotely.

"As best as we can estimate, the Comte Dumond and his forces could be anywhere between twelve hours to four days away." The king leaned back in his chair of command, and turned to his heir.

"We must assume the worst, and act upon it," Milo replied in answer to the unspoken question.

"Which is why we must immediately send envoys to Vereinigtelände." The man who spoke had heretofore been silent. He was a coarse-faced man with blunt features that seemed hewn out of stone. Somehow they managed to complement his uniform, which was a highly decorated variation of Camilla Sorranto's. He struck the table with the side of his fist. "Vereinigtelände would assist us in the event of a siege. They did so during the last Azurite Invasion. Had we settled matters an hour ago, I could have had a party on the road north by now. With a nuncio as esteemed as yourself at its head, to express our deep need," the man added, with a chair bow to Jacopo.

Jacopo replied in kind. "And I would be more than willing to serve, High Commander Fiernetto."

"I wouldn't," Darcy muttered darkly, beside Nic.

So this was Lorco Fiernetto, High Commander of the King's Guards. It was a well-known name in the city, as since the coup of three years before he had commanded not only the royal guards, but the naval guards and those of the remote posts as well. The king nodded, acknowledging the commander's point. "We have no objection to an envoy to Vereinigtelände, Lorco," said Milo, speaking for the monarch. "Where we differed was in our naval response."

"There is but one response." Fiernetto leaned over and thrust the map beneath Milo's nose, as if proximity might help him better understand. "We send our top naval personnel to Massina using what large craft we have available. Massina would also aid us. It is our only solution."

"What large craft are left?" Nic found himself asking. He reddened slightly at his boldness, but he knew better than anyone present what he had witnessed the night before. "I mean no presumption, Signor. But with my own eyes I saw six of Cassaforte's warships destroyed not twelve hours ago."

"They are all gone." The high commander refused to meet his eyes. He looked only at Milo and the king. "But there is the *Allyria*."

Nic felt as if he'd been knocked to the ground with a single blow. "My *Allyria*?"

Darcy's face looked pinched. Jacopo held up his hand before his mouth, disguising whatever expression hid behind. "After the devastation of last night, we are left with a city of gondolas and the tiniest of fishing craft. Any foreign merchant vessel that escaped the conflagration is long gone. The *Allyria* has been delivered to us for such a moment as this. It was made to be unsinkable. Loading it with the appropriate personnel and sending it to Massina is the only solution." Again, Fiernetto refused to look in Nic's direction.

"It was made to be what?" Nic sounded out of breath when he asked the question. He still felt as if he were staggering in the dark. He couldn't bear the thought of the *Allyria* being taken from him. Perhaps it was wrong of him to think so, but that galleon was his. It felt like it was his. The prospect of losing it affected him as deeply as if a physician had suggested removing one of his limbs.

Risa turned to Nic. The image floating above her mirror was a miniature view of the *Allyria* as Nic had seen it the previous night from the docks, golden and shining, its figurehead pointing at some greater destination in the distance. He found himself a little uncomfortable at how easily the enchantress could slip into his mind like that. "Ianno Piratimare was here to give us the history of the craft, as best he knew," she explained. "Do you know of Allyria Cassamagi?"

"Oh gods," muttered the high commander. "More history."

A shush from Milo silenced him. "I know of the Bridge of Allyria," Nic said. "And my ship."

Risa nodded. "Both were named after her. Allyria Cassamagi was an enchantress of exceeding skill. It was she who tied the Olive Crown and the Scepter of Thorn and the horns of Cassaforte together to establish a peaceful coexistence between the ruler and his subjects, among other marvels. Upon her death, many centuries ago, she left instructions to the Piratimare family of how to build a craft that would be unsinkable and virtually indestructible."

"An asset to the country, not a toy." For the first time, Lorco Fiernetto looked directly at Nic. "To be commandeered in times of dire need, such as this."

Risa continued, unperturbed. "The family lost these instructions and did not discover them until three hundred years ago. Though they thought it folly, at the advice of Caza Cassamagi they built the ship and it was put into service, only to be lost on its first voyage. The Piratimares assumed that Allyria's instructions had been faulty, or their execution of them, and that the boat had indeed sunk with its crew."

"Only it had not," said Milo. He looked at Nic. "We now think it must have been taken by pirates. And as Allyria intended, the ship became non-functional in their hands."

"Cursed," Nic whispered.

Milo nodded. "Ianno was very firm on the fact that only someone of pure Piratimare blood should have been able to reclaim the ship."

He seemed about to say more on the subject. Risa, who had witnessed Nic's discomfort in the presence of the cazarro earlier, smoothly broke in. "But somehow you managed anyway, Niccolo Dattore. And for that we are grateful."

Nic had pressed his lips together tightly while Milo spoke, but now he looked at the Divetri girl with appreciation. He cleared the lump that had gathered in his throat and said, "But Massina is in the opposite direction of where you want to go. The *Allyria* needs to go into battle. Not to retreat."

"I have thirty years of tactical experience in these matters," said Fiernetto. "What have you? Two weeks?"

Nic would not have been summoned to this roundtable of war if his opinion had not been wanted, he realized.

He found himself unafraid to give it. "I know that ship," he countered. "I know what she was made to do."

"Boy." The high commander sounded as angry as the rain without, beating against the chamber windows. "What good will one galleon do against sixteen or more ships of war? The *Allyria* has no cannonados."

Nic refused to be provoked by being addressed as *boy*. Instead, he turned his attention to Risa. "Isn't there some sorcery you could perform? Your powers are wondrous."

"You flatter me well, Captain," she replied. Nic was a little surprised she addressed him as such. "Like a sponge I have wrung dry my brain this morning, trying to think of some way that I can lend aid, but I am dry."

"Couldn't you ... I don't know. Repair the damaged vessels with your enchantments?" She shook her head. "Enchant what small craft we have to become mighty warships?"

For a moment, when she paused, he had hope. But then Risa demurred once more. "I have the knowledge to make something appear more of what it actually is than before." She wrinkled her nose. "It's all about the object's natural function and is difficult to explain. I could make a gondola appear to be a warship, but it would still only be a gondola. It would not hold more than two or three people, nor could it do the things a warship could do."

"That's still a good idea, though." Milo snapped his fingers. "Perhaps if we stationed some old gondolas around the city's perimeter and made them appear as warships, it would at least make the Comte Dumond think twice before attacking."

"Yes, we can do that. Thank you, Captain," said Risa, smiling at Nic.

"But it is not a solution," Fiernetto reminded them all. "One craft, no matter how ensorcelled, cannot meet an entire armada."

"In *The Admiral's Secret Daughter, or, The Mermaid's Revenge*, the entire fleet of Atlantia is poised to strike Hero's country, but he takes his fleet to meet them so that they minimize their chances of Atlantia gaining even a single foothold," said Darcy.

Nic was not the only one who gave her a baffled gaze, but when he remembered how much time Darcy had spent among the actors, listening to their gossip, he understood. "It's a drama in five acts," he explained. "The Arturos made very good receipts with it."

"The point," said Darcy, "is that the city would be at a disadvantage, should the armada reach us."

"And now we are taking strategic tips from minor dramatists," Lorco Fiernetto grunted with impatience. "Delightful."

"Actually, Commander, there's much to be learned from the stage," Nic said, leaping to Darcy's defense. "Cassaforte would be in far worse shape had I not spent many months learning from the Arturos. You should be thanking them, not spitting upon them." He drew a deep breath and declared, "I know it is better to take the enemy by surprise than to allow them to do the same. I know a bold gesture is better than a weak deed. And most of all, as the lady said, I know it is wiser to meet the enemy at sea than to wait until we are besieged." Nic remembered how the Drake would have kept his considerable cool in a similar situation, and drew upon it. "I have no doubt that Allyria Cassamagi would have wanted her countrymen to meet the threat head-on, rather than retreat like cowards."

No comment could have been more calculated to make an enemy of Lorco Fiernetto than that. The man lunged out of his chair, spittle flying from his mouth. "Take that back, boy! I'm no coward!"

The uproar that followed was so intense that Camilla Sorranto reached for her sword, ready to act if necessary. A single voice cut through the commotion. "Gentlemen. Ladies." The king sounded wearier than ever. He had endured the talk long enough. For a moment, as the dispute settled, he whispered into Milo's ear. Milo nodded, then replied back, his eyes glancing at Nic. The king leaned forward and spoke. "High Commander. Prepare your envoy to Vereinigtelände, with our nuncio as its head." Jacopo folded his hands and bowed, acquiescing to the king's command. "And Lorco. I will tell Caza Piratimare to grant access to their docks, where the *Allyria* still rests, beginning tomorrow at sunrise, so that you may send your people to Massina. That is our decision."

Nic felt deflated. The high commander rose from his chair with an expression of triumph, and passed from the room with a series of bows to everyone save Nic. It was hateful to think that he had won. From across the table, Darcy attempted to engage him with her sympathetic eyes. He found he couldn't meet them.

"Dattore," said Milo. "A word before you go."

Nic stood taller than the heir when he approached. He was so tall, in fact, that Milo had to pull him down to whisper in his ear, shaking his hand as he did so. "His Majesty has given that idiot Lorco access to the Piratimare docks tomorrow morning. It is his wish, however, that the *Allyria* remain with its true captain." When Milo let go of his hand, Nic found that he had left something hard and round behind. Nic's eyes widened as he uncurled his fingers and saw that Milo had given him a gold coin of sorts. No, it wasn't a coin, he realized, but a medallion, much like those worn by Milo's older sister, or the high commander himself. Only those acting on the king's behalf could bear such medals. Nic almost trembled from the honor.

Risa Divetri had assumed his other side. "There is a stone stair on the outside of the sea wall by the lower Piratimare bridge," she murmured into his ear. "Many of Piratimare's hired laborers find it faster to follow it to the bottom and take the path skirting around the island's edge, than to traipse through the caza grounds to the docks."

Were they really trusting him in this matter? Nic's eyes searched for the king. Camilla Sorranto was escorting him from the room but the ancient ruler turned long enough to smile in Nic's direction. "Thank you," was all he could say, so emotional he was. Milo nodded. Risa laid a hand on his shoulder.

Then they were gone, trailing after Alessandro and vanishing from the room. Once they had left, Darcy came to his side. "What did they give you?" she asked, wonder on her face.

Nic uncurled his fingers once more and showed her the medallion. "A second chance."

22

Often I hold my head in my hands upon hearing the youth in our tutelage discuss the so-called "proper" way to solve a problem. So consumed with propriety, these young people! It is a wonder that any of them ever understand that sometimes a conundrum requires the most improper and unlikely of solutions.

—Arnoldo Piratimare, Elder of the Insula of the Children of Muro, in a letter to Gina Catarre, Elder of the Insula of the Penitents of Lena

The armada from Pays d'Azur lay but five leagues south-west of Cassaforte—scarcely a two-and-a-half-hour sail. It was through a curtain of rain that Nic first saw the formation, silhouetted against the black sky by cascades of lightning. Blots on the horizon, they were, a dozen and more. All were pointed in the direction of Cassaforte. Nic rang the bell and shouted for the sails to be taken in. The storms that had roiled the waters since the night before showed no signs of stopping. Whether or not the _Allyria_ was unsinkable, the waters tossed it like a house cat with a toy. Nic, however, stood firm.

It had been the *Allyria* that had brought him here. It had been Nic at the ship's wheel, calling out orders, but he could no more have forecast where on the pitching waters of the Azure Sea the foreign warships would be, than he could have predicted where to find a pin in a roll of hay. No, it was as if the ship's feminine figurehead had led the way. The craft had known its purpose and winged him to this spot, speaking to him through the very wood beneath his feet and under his hand. Captain Delguardino's tricorne had been soaked through long before, but it kept enough of its shape so that he could see Risa Divetri watching him. She, too, would stop from time to time to place her hands on the quarterdeck rail, or upon the ship's wheel itself, not seeming to care that she was soaked.

"You feel it too," he had said, the very first time she put her hand on the wheel.

She had looked at him with surprise. "You can sense the energies?"

His response had been simple. "They sing to me."

She had barraged him with questions after that. What did they feel like for him? How did they sing? Did he feel energies in other objects, or just the *Allyria*? Although she seemed disappointed that he only felt the ship's pulses and no other, she was impressed that he could at least sense those. "They bear the pattern of Allyria Cassamagi's enchantments," she explained. "Very similar to the Olive Crown and the Scepter of Thorn. If only I could understand them better!" Since then he'd been extremely conscious of her scrutiny. Every time the *Allyria*'s song changed and he made adjustments to the course, she had pressed her hands to the deck and listened, with both glistening water and a faraway expression painting her face.

"Extinguish the stern lanterns!" he cried. One of the three large lamps was already dark, its flame drowned by the torrents descending from the sky. Qiandro rushed to douse the others. "Black out the captain's quarters! Ladies and gentlemen, from this moment on, I don't want to see a single spark of light visible aboard this vessel. Not a lit pipe, not a lantern, not a spark from a flint. Am I clear?"

"Aye!" shouted the crew.

That Risa Divetri should be aboard the *Allyria* was still something of a shock. Under cover of dark, Nic had taken the path along the sea wall that Risa had recommended. He was not surprised, upon reaching the pier where the Allyria had been docked, at finding the ship's crew there. He had dispatched Darcy earlier in the evening to assemble them, if they would go. All of Macaque's men had greeted him eagerly with thumps upon the back and Cassaforte-style handclasps. Maxl had changed into a looser-fitting outfit, but still boasted the dandified face-painting of that morning. With both hands, he bestowed upon Nic the *shivarsta* that the guards had confiscated from him the night before. Nic had gladly returned it to his side. It didn't sing, like the *Allyria*, but it had been with him the entire journey and he would not part with it now.

"Thank you, friend," said Nic.

Before he knew it, he'd found himself clasped in one of

Maxl's enthusiastic bear hugs, and kissed upon the cheeks. "We are all with you," he assured Nic.

"I'm glad to hear it!" Nic sputtered, trying to get away so he could breathe once again.

By "all," Maxl had included the Arturos and their troupe. That was no surprise, either. They had received the most rapturous applause in all their lives the night before, and to a person they hungered for more. Signor Arturo had hugged Nic as well, and the Signora had buried his face so deeply into her expansive bosom as she wrapped her arms around him that he thought he might never surface. No, what had left Nic stupefied was when three figures on the dock, almost indistinguishable from the night itself, removed the hoods from their heads and turned to greet him. "Cazarrina," Nic had said at the sight of Risa. "Highness," he had said to Milo.

The last of the three was bent and frail and tottered forth with a cane in his hand. To the king, Nic had said nothing until he fell to one knee. "Majesty," he had whispered, conscious that around him all his crew were doing the same. "It is good of you to come see us off."

"Oh, that's what I'm doing, is it?" King Alessandro had indicated for Nic to rise. "I rather thought I'd have a bit of a ride on this miraculous vessel." Using his hood to keep the rain from his head, he looked up at the *Allyria* and to himself, whispered her name. "Most miraculous indeed. Oh, rise, please rise," he had huffed. To Milo, he added, "It's the most annoying part of being king, all the bowing. You'll learn soon enough."

"I hope not," Milo had replied.

"But sir—" Nic had been aghast at the thought. "It won't be safe. We don't know what will happen…"

"Young man. Do you know what will happen if we stand here?" Nic thought it a philosophical question, and had shaken his head in reply. "I do. I'll catch a cold from this beastly rain. Trust me. You won't want to see how curmudgeonly I can be when I'm sneezing. Now, prove to me you're worthy of that medallion," he had said, poking at Nic's chest with his cane, "and show me to someplace dry."

Nic had complied with all possible speed, yet once they were in the his quarters, he still had objections. "But Majesty, I have no plans. No stratagems."

"You have yourself, Niccolo." Alessandro had eased himself into the captain's chair, sighing as his old bones protested. "And you have your crew. For now, that will be enough. Take me to the armada, so that I might see it for myself. Then we will think on what to do."

Now that they had reached their goal, Nic entered the pitch-black cabin, more lost than ever. He wondered exactly for how long he would be shut into that pleasant prison cell, if he failed to return to Cassaforte with its three most important political figures whole and intact. He should never have consented to allow the king and his heir onboard. Milo Sorranto was more than willing to lend a hand where needed, however, and Risa seemed hardened to the wind and weather. Maxl had much the same thought, as he dived in the door after Risa. Darcy and the Arturos followed, trailed by others of the crew who were not below.

"You women of Cassaforte," Maxl said, his teeth chattering. "You are much stronger than you look. There is hair upon your chest. Yes!"

"I should certainly hope not." Risa cupped her hands together and produced a glowing ball of deep red light that illuminated her face from beneath. She released it so that it sat on one end of the table, its surface spinning and writhing. Even when the boat rocked from side to side, however, it didn't shift—unlike Nic's paper boats, which fell from side to side on the mantels, desk, and tables, casting crazy shadows as they tumbled. She then moved to the table's other end. "It won't be visible from afar," she assured Nic. "We can't be knocking heads in here."

"And for that I am grateful, my dear." King Alessandro had long been dry, but he pulled himself closer to the orb of light that Risa set down, as if warming himself with it. He, too, shivered, making Nic wish they had brought some kind of coals for the cabin's fireplace. "Now this is what I call a council of war," he said, indicating that everyone should sit down, captain and pirates alike. Sparks of defiance twinkled in his eyes. "So much better without High Commander Fiernetto, don't you think?"

Milo shook his head. "Majesty, you've taught me too well for me to dismiss the opinions of a man who is only doing the job for which he has been appointed. Fiernetto means well. Though he is a bit of a ..."

"Pig head," Risa supplied. She sat down next to Alessandro, then put her arm around him and laid her head on his shoulder, as if he were her grandfather. She was trying to warm him, Nic realized.

"Yes," agreed Milo. "And not much of a creative thinker. Which is why we need you, Captain." He leaned back in his chair, expectant.

Before his crew, it was difficult for Nic to admit to his shortcomings. He spoke slowly, hoping that what he said wouldn't diminish him in their eyes. "I am not educated, like your high commander," he said. Outside, the storm seemed to roar louder, as if laughing at him. "I can barely read. I'm not learned in military strategy. I'm nothing but a poor brat who's bluffed his way from one end of the Azure Sea to the other."

"That poor brat thought of a strategy the high commander did not," Darcy asserted. Nic softened to hear her defend him so hotly. "You were the one who suggested Risa enchant the gondolas to look like warships. Not he."

"Signorina Colombo is correct," said Milo, nodding. "Your lack of training in traditional military strategy is an advantage, when it comes to outthinking those for whom it is hidebound instinct."

"Now is the time, if any, to decide upon what we are to do." The king coughed, prompting Risa to rub his shoulders with worry. "A stormy night. The might of an entire nation versus the valiance of a renegade few. It's very like one of your dramas, is it not, Signor Arturo?"

"Ah... well... yes... that is to say..." For once, Signor Arturo was speechless. He bobbed and fussed with his hands fruitlessly, while his clothes dripped a steady puddle onto the decking.

"That's a good one," the Signora was heard to whisper to him. "Make sure to use it when we get back."

"Poetic, really, when you think about it." Another round of coughs racked Alessandro's form, but he waved off both Darcy and Risa, when they reached out for him. "Cassaforte's old king, surrounded by the generation that will soon supplant him. So, Niccolo." King Alessandro leaned upon the table, only to be pushed back into his chair by a sudden lurch of the waves. "What say you?"

Although he had spent the last three hours commanding a ship through a storm like he'd never experienced, at the monarch's question, Nic's hands twitched with sudden nervous energy. He'd warned the man that he had no plan of action, and yet here he was, being asked to provide one. "Perhaps knowing where the armada is could be valuable enough," he said, trying desperately to make something good out of the situation. A few of the boats he'd folded from paper lay on their sides upon the table. He grabbed one and began to worry at it. "Do you have some sorcery that would allow you to tell someone, back in the city?"

Risa shook her head. "Had I thought about it before we left, perhaps. At the time I did not think it wise to advertise that we were going to sneak the king away from his guards and drag him out of the country. Your sister is going to kill us all, by the way," she added to Milo.

"She can't kill me," he assured her. "That would be treason."

"A little thing like that won't stop her."

"Create a weapon, then. One against which they would be powerless," said Darcy.

"There are limits to what even Allyria Cassamagi's enchantments could do." She looked as disappointed with herself as Nic had felt moments before.

Maxl stepped forward. "I think that we are steering to great big ships," he said, excitedly playing out the scenario with his hands. "And when we are getting close, poof! You turn everyone into frogs. On other boats. Not on this one."

Nic could have sworn he heard a suppressed snicker from a certain member of the Divetri family, but the storm had once again picked up, and he might have been mistaken. "Thank you for clarifying that for me, Signor Maxl," said Risa. "But no."

"Speak up, if you have ideas," said Nic to the crew. "Now is not the time to hold your tongue."

The ideas came slowly at first. The Signora thought of a massive net, real or ensorcelled, that might snare the armada and keep them from proceeding. Qiandro, once his thoughts were translated, was all for using the *Allyria* in the same way the pirates had used their cutters the night before, and tossing infernal devices aboard the ships. Risa rejected the first as impossible, and Nic had to turn down the latter for the lack of any materials with which to make the infernal devices. Then the ideas came faster. They could speed back to the city using Risa's powers, and then build a magic shield around the city. Risa could cause lightning to strike the Azurite ships and reduce them to rubble, or drown the sailors with rain, or cause hail to fall over their vessels and weigh them down so grievously that they sunk.

Risa had to reject every suggestion. "The enchantments of Allyria Cassamagi just don't work that way. I'm sorry. I wish I could do some of those things, but I have no concept of how to go about them. I'm learning, without a teacher. Your captain made a suggestion yesterday of enchanting gondolas around Cassaforte so that they looked like warships. He thought it might scare off the Comte Dumond, or at least delay them. That I can do, because the very nature of a boat is to be … boat-y. It wouldn't *be* a warship once I'd done it, but a simple change of appearance is within my limited powers." She looked around the assembly once more, looking very much like the young woman she was instead of the powerful enchantress she was supposed to be. "I'm sorry."

Nic was looking down at his hands. While Risa spoke, he felt electrified by possibility. "Do it now," he said suddenly. When he whipped up his head and met Risa's startled glance, his eyes were wide and alive. "Do it now."

The Infant Prodigy interrupted him. "Perhaps if we captured a squid, you could transform him to look like a *very big squid monster* and scare the Comte Dumond with it."

Risa held up a hand to arrest any more talk about that plan. "What do you mean?" she asked. "Niccolo, we left before we could set up any unused boats around Cassaforte's perimeter. Even if I had, I couldn't give them the appearance of Piratimare warships from this distance."

"Not there." Nic's brain could have outpaced the fast-

320

est gallop of any thoroughbred horse. "Right here. Right now."

Darcy didn't understand, either. "We didn't bring any gondolas with us, or even rowboats."

"Nic, unless you explain, I'm afraid I'm going to have to entertain the squid idea," said Risa.

"They're all around," he told Darcy.

Maxl also didn't follow. "The armada, yes, it is all around us."

"No." Nic thrust the folded object beneath Darcy's nose. "These." She stared at him for a moment. Then, in the glow of the red orbs, he watched her smile. It was like a ray of sunshine breaking through the gloom. To Risa he said, "Paper boats. There are a dozen and a half around this room alone. Where there's paper, I can make more." She seemed to be staring at him as if he were mad. He hastened to reassure her. "They're real boats. They can float, for a while."

King Alessandro smiled. "I believe, Captain, that you have arrived at another brilliant bluff. That makes two within the space of two days. I must insist my officers take more sea air." He settled back into his chair.

"It was all Darcy," Nic said, bathing in the girl's glance. "It's exactly as she told me once. I've been making these all my life. Now I know to what end."

"Inestimable girl," said the king. He looked fondly upon Darcy. "Keep her safe."

"This could actually work!" exclaimed Risa. Nic could tell her mind was racing as well. "I can retard the effect of the water upon them for a while."

Nic hadn't finished, though. "And remember what you did with the heir's head?"

Milo peered at Nic with an expression of long suffering. "Which time?"

Risa spoke. "I know exactly what he's talking about," she said with a wicked grin upon her face. "Let's get started."

Milo rose. "Will you take my arm, sir?" he asked the king.

Alessandro demurred. He seemed most weary from the weather and the late hour. "I shall hear of it when it is done," he assured his heir. To Risa, he added, "I will rest here a while. Bring me gladsome tidings, my dear. And Captain." Nic had already reached the cabin door, but he stopped to listen. "Thank you."

Though King Alessandro remained within, the entire crew raced to the deck armed with the paper fleet. Thankfully the rain had lessened in its intensity and had become a mere drizzle, though the *Allyria* still pitched to and fro from the wild seas. The lights of the armada, which was struggling against a stiff headwind, were no closer. Risa had taken one of the globes she'd created and perched it upon her shoulder. When everyone huddled around her, the glow upon their faces created a spooky effect. "Let's try," she said.

"Three at first," ordered Nic. He pointed. "Infant Prodigy. Maxl. Knave."

Cupping their hands in the way that penitents carried doves to the temple, the three crew members leaned over the ship's railing and tossed their little paper boats onto the waters. Risa stood nearby with both palms raised to the heavens. Whispered words fell from her lips. Her eyes drew back into her head so all that was visible were the whites.

Nic watched as the little specks of white grew more faint as they fell into the water below. A streak of lightning stretched from clouds to the sea. During that bright split-second, it seemed to Nic as if the scraps of paper stopped tumbling upon the wind. They gained weight, and mass, and motion. Then, where nothing had been before, three immense craft began sailing toward the comte's armada.

They were large warships from the Piratimare ship-yards, graceful and lithe, looking more as if they'd been sculpted by an artist than assembled from thousands of individual pieces of wood. Their sails, crested with brown and purple, were full and proud. Cannonados projected from ports beneath the deck. Their stern and cabin lights glowed brightly, and even cast reflections upon the water. Without anyone on board, however, and with the straight course they took across the water, they projected an eerie, almost ghostly effect, no matter how real they seemed.

Risa raised her hands higher. Without warning, the ships caught fire. Several members of the crew instinctively shielded their faces from the blazes, though they knew that it was only a mirage. Long tongues of flame licked from every porthole. All the decks were alight.

"Fireships," breathed Nic. His eyes gleamed.

"In my country we are calling them hellburners," said Maxl, with wonder. The wind was helping the illusion by forcing the flames in every direction. The ships sailed on in their collision course with the armada.

"Darcy. Signora. Urso." Once the first flank was on its way, Nic indicated that the next three boats be launched. Soon the number of blazing vessels had doubled, then tripled as another three joined them. Risa continued her whispered prayers. By the light of the ships, she seemed pale. Nic hoped she could hold out long enough to see this bluff through.

All aboard the *Allyria* seemed to hold their breath as the illusory battalion began to near its goal. At first it seemed as if no one aboard the Azurite craft had seen the burning boats bearing down upon them. Then Nic thought he could hear the sound of bells clanging and shouts being carried over the wind. From the lead ship in the formation he saw a spark of light against its hull, and then, seconds later, the roar of a cannonado. Its missile, a stone ball, passed harmlessly through one of the first three boats and splashed into the water. A massive plume of water rose into the air where it hit. Another followed, and then another, growing increasingly closer to the *Allyria*.

"Leave your paper boats with Thorntongue," Nic cried out. "And man your stations. We're bringing the ship around." To Darcy he added, "Keep them going. And watch out for Risa."

"I will," she promised. Already the crew was filling her arms with the boats that were left. "Good luck," she yelled as he ran for the quarterdeck.

By now the sound of the cannonados was growing. The

first of the burning Cassafortean hulls had made its way between the Azurite warships into the middle of the formation, and the ships were beginning to break course. Those on the outside had changed their orientation completely so they could bring their guns around to face their attackers; the head ships were heeling hard so the fireboats would not be behind them. A cheer went up from the crew, which sent Nic scurrying away from the ship's wheel to the rail to see what happened. He saw that the hull of one of the closer ships of the armada sported several gaping holes from the cannonados of its own fleet. When the ship keeled upright, the damage was below its water line. Almost immediately, it began to drag down into the sea.

"More," Nic yelled down at Darcy, so loudly that he felt his throat become raw. "More fireboats."

Her face was awed and scared when she looked up at him and nodded. Another folded paper boat flew from her hands into the water. It transformed into one of the hellburners and joined the seemingly unending stream of inferno ships confounding the enemy.

The cannonado fire was endless, now, as the armada's ships fired shot upon shot in an attempt to still the restless fireboats. One of the shots must have connected with the tiny paper boat hiding within the illusion. Nic saw it wink out, its flames immediately extinguished. Most of the stone projectiles went right through the illusions and into the Azurite warships. Nic watched as a mast split and tumbled, crashing onto the deck below. A boom sounded from another of the armada's vessels minutes later, when cannonado shots from a friendly ship connected with its supply of *yemeni alum*. The explosion let loose a belch of fire that rose like a scarlet ball into the air, splitting the ship into two.

The armada's captains were busy, for several minutes, trying to avoid the burning debris even as they continued to batter each other with the ceaseless fire of their weaponry. The number of ships dwindled from sixteen to fifteen, and then from fifteen to twelve to seven. By the time the last of the fireboats reached the scattered armada, only two boats remained. Both were mastless and broken and drifted without aim among the smoldering wreckage of what had been a once-mighty fleet.

They had won. The last lights of Nic's flotilla of illusions winked out, all at once. On the deck below, Nic heard a thump. He left the ship's wheel to find Milo with his arm around Risa Divetri. "It's all right," he was telling her in the most reassuring of voices. "It's over."

"Is it?" she asked. Her head lolled back to an upright position. She dropped her arms so heavily it seemed they might fall from their sockets. Then she began to sink to the ground.

With cries, Darcy and Nic both leapt to catch her. Milo had the situation well in hand. "She's unhurt," he assured them. "But worn."

"There are smelling salts in the captain's quarters," Nic told Darcy. She nodded and ran to get them.

Milo unloosened the clasp around Risa's neck. "Let's get you inside, dear one," he suggested. The heir had worn a mischievous expression on his face for most of the time Nic had known him. It had seemed almost painted on. Now, however, he was plainly worried.

"No," she said. With some remnant of energy, Risa pulled herself up to a sitting position so that she could lean backwards against the rail wall. "I need the cool air." She breathed heavily. "It's over?" she asked.

"Yes it is. You were brilliant." Milo kissed her forehead. "As always."

"Was I?" she asked, almost sleepily. A smile crossed her lips. "I think you may thank our captain for most of the brilliance."

Milo might have said something to that, but Nic had turned his head. His attention had been attracted by the smallest sound, that of a glass phial hitting the deck. It rolled with a rattle toward where he knelt. It was the smelling salts that he'd asked Darcy to fetch.

Eyebrows pulled together with bewilderment, he reached out to take the phial in his hand. "Darcy?" he asked, looking up.

She stood outside the cabin door, hands by her side. A man's arm choked her neck and pulled her close to his body. The man's other hand held a knife. "Niccolo?" she rasped out, frightened.

Despite the bedraggled appearance of the man's uniform and his smoke-smudged, bruised face, Nic recognized her assailant immediately. He bared his teeth and growled the name: "Comte Dumond."

23

We all grow old, my dear. It is nature's way of preparing us, ever so gently, for the reality that a younger generation will replace us in time's mad rush.

—KING NIVOLO OF CASSAFORTE, TO ALLYRIA CASSAMAGI,
IN A PRIVATE LETTER IN THE CASSAMAGI ARCHIVES

❧

Almost nothing remained of the comte's finery. The coat of blue velvet was a shredded mess, its trim torn or missing entirely. The stylish tricorne he once had boasted was nowhere to be seen, nor were his shiny boots. He stood before them in his stocking feet, snarling like a mad dog. His periwig was askew enough to reveal the speckled and bald head beneath. "Stand back," he warned Nic. "The girl should have died long before this. We all know it." At that moment, Maxl came running up from the *Allyria*'s fore, as did Urso and Qiandro. They scudded to a halt when the comte jerked Darcy around in their direction and pressed the knife's blade to her throat. They held up their hands. Urso dropped the sword he'd been holding.

"People don't live or die according to your timetable, Dumond." Nic rose slowly to his feet, hands out and plainly on display to keep the crazed man at ease.

"Oh, they do," the comte assured him. He was deranged, Nic realized. The certainty of his defeat had unhinged him. "I assure you, they do."

The motion he made with his shoulder and arm made everyone within distance shout out. Out of instinct, Milo Sorranto reached for his weapon. Darcy shrieked. Just at that moment, Knave wandered into the crowd, unaware of anything out of the ordinary happening. "Captain," he called out to Nic. "I just now found a curious rope hooked around the forward railing. When I looked down, there was a little boat floating…oh." He saw the comte and Darcy struggling close to the door of the captain's quarters, and stopped talking.

"Unsurprising, that you'd resort to your Cassafortean witchcraft rather than fighting a real battle," spat the comte. "Do you call that just?"

"Is it less just than hiring the lawless to do an army's work?" Nic wanted to know. "Is it less just than leading a sneak attack on a nation that has done nothing to you?"

It was no good reasoning with the comte. He was beyond reason. "Captain," said Milo, with warning in his voice, "a man with nothing else to lose is the most dangerous of all." Nic knew it, too, from hard experience.

"Yes, listen to your friend," hissed the comte. His eyes

were wide and wild. "You never know what a man with nothing to lose might do. Starting with the death of M'selle Colombo." His grip around Darcy's neck tightened. Her face was already red. The color began to deepen.

"Your grudge is against her father, the nuncio," Nic reminded him. His voice taunted the man. "He's not even here. He's on his way to Vereinigtelände. She's just his daughter. A nobody."

"She'll do."

"Let her go and we can talk about this." Nic took a step forward.

The comte, in turn, backed against the cabin door. "Talk with a pirate? What is the honor in that? I'd as soon talk to my hounds. I should have gutted you all in Gallina. Talk to me after I've cut her throat and we've both bathed in her blood."

"Look at you. All this talk of honor. Is it honorable, what you've done this night? How many young men and women perished tonight? How many of their mothers and fathers, sisters and brothers, are in their homes right now not knowing their loved ones' blood stains the waves?" Nic snarled. "If that is honor, I want none of it. For shame, sir." The rebuke seemed to have some kind of effect on the comte. He looked startled. Nic pressed it to his advantage. "What would the court say if they could see you now? Is this truly the Comte Dumond, the man the king hand-picked to lead his invasion?"

"Niccolo," growled Milo in warning.

Nic pouted, mocking the man. "Is this honor, Dumond? A grown man, picking on a helpless little girl?"

The comte opened his mouth to speak, but Darcy was one step ahead of them. Some of the redness had drained from her face and now she could breathe again. She inhaled deeply, and with a swift motion lifted her boot and slammed it down as hard as she could upon the top of the pirate's stockinged instep. The comte screamed in pain. Darcy took advantage of the moment to draw her arm forward, and then drive her elbow under his rib cage. The knife clattered to the ground.

"I am *far* from helpless," she snarled.

Nic should have run to retrieve her then, but he and everyone else were too shocked to respond. The comte reached out, grabbed Darcy by the hair, and before anyone could have stopped him, disappeared into the captain's quarters, slamming the door behind him.

It was then that Nic sprinted forward, hearing something being dragged on the floor within. He grasped the handle and yanked it down. The door wouldn't budge. "Open, damn you!" Nic shouted. He stood back several steps and lunged, nearly dislocating his shoulder when he collided with the wood. "Ow," he complained, tears in his eyes.

Milo rattled the latch. "He's jammed the door somehow."

From where she'd collapsed near the rail, Risa struggled to her feet. "The king—!"

Nic froze. He and everyone around him had the same

thing in mind. Comte Dumond was alone with the king. "Beat down the door!" Maxl called. "We are ramming it!"

"This ship is built to withstand that," Risa reminded them, panic in her voice. "It won't work."

Nic refused to stand down without a fight. "I need something," he said. The spyglass was still in his pocket. He ran to the little porthole window set next to the captain's door and began to attack the panes with it. The ship itself might have been built to resist assault, but the little window had not. It cracked, then burst with a shatter. The spyglass was ruined. Nic threw it down and pressed his face to the hole, smelling the familiar smoky aroma of his quarters. A shard remaining in its pane dug into the side of his face, drawing blood. He didn't care. "Darcy!" he called out.

She was kicking and grunting with pain as the comte dragged her toward the room's center. King Alessandro remained in Nic's chair. His eyes were closed. His head had settled gently to one side, and his hands were in his lap. He'd fallen asleep gently, as infants and the very old do. The comte saw the king at the same moment. Nic let out a strangled cry and pulled out his head and thrust his arm through the porthole, though what he grabbed for, he had no idea. By the time he had his face repositioned, the comte had stopped. "Sssh, sssh, little girl," he said, a finger to his lips. "Let us not waken the old man."

"Dumond!" Nic's voice was strangled and strange. He was conscious that to his left, the crew was still attempting to batter down the door.

"Sssh!" The comte let go of Darcy's thick hair. While she

struggled, he picked her up by the shoulders and shoved her brusquely against the fireplace, where she crumpled against the wall. He then crept around behind Alessandro, who still slumbered soundly. "We do not want to wake him. It would be frightening for a man of his age to rouse so suddenly."

"Stop!" Nic ordered the crew. Breathless, they stood back from the door. Nic pressed his face against the glass once more. "The old man is nobody, comte. Come out and surrender."

"Fool." The comte had completely lost his periwig in the struggle. With his hard eyes and shorn head, he looked serpent-like. Breathing heavily, he licked blood from his lips. "Fool to think I don't recognize the King of Cassaforte—Alessandro the Wise, bearer of the Olive Crown and the Scepter of whatever-it-is!"

"He's not," Nic said, bluffing wildly. "He looks like him. He's my uncle."

"Fool!" the comte repeated. "Or should I say, how very *prescient* of you to tell me to leave the girl alone. You were right, Captain. Killing her would have been of no honor. Killing *him*, though!"

"Leave him alone!" Milo shouted in Nic's ear. He had been struggling for a peep through the window the entire time.

"Oh, no … no, my pretty." Darcy had risen to her feet and clutched the back of the wood chair closest to her. Her face was hard and focused. Nic recognized that expression—she had worn it often enough, the first days they had met. The comte knelt beside the captain's seat and slipped his hands around the sleeping man's neck. "One step closer and he dies."

"All right," she said. Both Nic and the comte turned their attention from her back to the king. That was their mistake. Both of them failed to see, before it was too late, Darcy wrenching the chair into the air. With all her might, she swung it around and behind the comte. Wood met bone with a sickening crack, and the comte splayed forward, half onto the table, half off. After a moment, his body slumped down into an unconscious ball on the floor. "You can't kill a man who's already dead. Fool."

It took but a moment for Darcy to remove the high-backed bench with which the Comte Dumond had jammed the door. When she opened it at last, Risa and Milo were the first to rush in. Both ran to the king's side. Maxl was next, springing forward to check on the comte. "Is the cad alive?" Nic asked.

"I hope so," said Darcy. Her jaw was set and she swaggered with a victor's triumph, but Nic could tell that she was badly shaken. "I want to see him pay."

Maxl nodded. His fingers ran along the side of the comte's neck. "He is pulsing."

Darcy sniffled. A thin trickle of blood dribbled from her nose. She staunched it with her thumb. She faced both Maxl and Nic as if challenging them to defy her. "I trust that the bonking on the noggin was the best way to solve that particular problem?"

Maxl backed away. Urso and Knave had collected the comte from the floor and were taking him out the door, to be locked down below. "You are not getting the objection from me," he said, both hands in the air.

Darcy's eyebrows rose when she faced Nic. "Nor from me, Thorntongue," he swore. He couldn't stand it any longer. He had to hold her in his arms, to make sure that she was still whole. Fortunately, given Nic's natural reticence, she seemed to be feeling the same way. The pair clung to each other as they had never clung to anyone before, rocking back and forth as if afraid to let go. "Gods," Nic finally said. "I was so frightened."

"Because my father would have skinned you alive if you'd let anything happen to me?"

"That too," Nic murmured into her hair. "Don't ever make me worry again."

"Do you really think that's likely?" Darcy wanted to know.

"No," he said. "I don't."

Only when he turned his head did he remember the king. He pulled away from Darcy to see Milo leaning against the table, lifeless and seeming sick to his stomach. Risa had tears streaking her face. She stroked Alessandro's white locks as if he really were sleeping. "Oh, Dom," she sighed.

"Is he really … ?" Nic whispered to Darcy.

She nodded, and sniffed again. "I could tell, when he brought me in here. Nic—I think he *knew*. I think he died the way he wanted. At battle, not in bed."

Nic had to swallow several times before he found his voice. The last words he'd heard the man speak had been of thanks to him. "Clear the room," he said to his crew. "Allow the heir and the cazarrina their chance to mourn."

Darcy helped escort out the Arturos and the others, for now forestalling questions about her well-being. Once the door was latched and the cabin quiet, both he and Darcy approached. "Are you all right?" Darcy asked, touching Risa's arm.

"It's fine. It's not as if we didn't expect it," said Risa. With the ball of her thumb, she dabbed away the last of her tears. "He was a very old man."

"Still." Darcy held out her arms, offering comfort. Risa gratefully accepted.

Which left Nic to address Milo. The young man hadn't said a word since he had entered the room. "Do you need something?" he asked. He'd never seen anyone so pale. "A drink? Water, or something stronger?"

Milo smiled weakly, and waved off the suggestion. It seemed as if he was trying to will himself anywhere else but here. "Risa," he said at last, looking away from Alessandro. The old man still looked as if he was only taking the shallowest of slumbers, and might waken any moment. "I can't do this. I can't be king. I'm *not* a king."

"You're not king until the cazarri meet to give you the crown and scepter," she reminded him.

"Those people all like me. They're not going to refuse. They're going to do it and then I'll be king and—oh, gods." He gasped for air. "They'll expect me to be kingly. It's too much. It's just too much."

Nic was no stranger to stage fright. In the wings, he'd

seen many a young actor afflicted with it. His mind flashed back to a time when he himself stepped into the captain's quarters of a ship for the very first time, and how he seemed to freeze from the sheer ponderousness of it all. "Milo," he said, confidentially. "Can I call you that?" He crooked his arm around the heir's neck, and walked him across the cabin. "When I was much younger, a very wise man told me something that I've taken to heart ever since. Acting is something you do every day. You do it when you sit at a council of war and pretend to agree with someone when in reality you don't. You do it when you're frightened beyond all reckoning for the girl you care for, and don't want it to show. Sometimes *seeming* to be a thing is all your audience needs to get by. And if you seem to be a thing long enough . . ." He patted the heir on the back. "It won't matter that it's not who you once were."

They were close to the exit now. Through the broken porthole, Nic had spied all the crew assembled on the deck beyond, kneeling and facing the door. They waited for news. Nic knew that it would be best if it didn't come from him. "So what do I do?" asked Milo, listening intently. His eyes were still wide and scared.

Milo repeated the same words that had been given to him, long ago. "You take a deep breath. You stand straight. You become the person you want them to believe in."

"And then?"

"And then," said Nic, "you go on."

Milo thought about it for a moment. Then he nodded, thanks in his eyes. Nic heard him take a deep breath, and watched as he corrected his posture and thrust back his shoulders. He was still pale, but more composed. "I think I might be ready," he announced, nodding at the door.

"Then you are."

"But I don't know what to say. Those people outside will be looking to me, and I don't have any words for them."

With his hand on the heir's back, Nic opened the latch. Into the dawn's mist and fog they stepped together, side by side. "The lines will come," he assured Cassaforte's new king. "Believe me, they will come."

epilogue

Appearing tonight only, after their heroic feats upon the Azure Sea!
Arturo Armand's Theatre of Marvels, performing not one, but
both of the plays that have brought them international acclaim,
written by the lauded Armand Arturo himself: "Infernal Mysteries
of the Bloody Banquet: A Tale of Blood and Woe!" and "School for
Strategem: A Rollicking Comedy!"

—From a broadside pasted upon Cassafortean lampposts

Be nice to him. It won't cost you anything."

Darcy's fingers stung where they swatted him, causing Nic to rub at his shoulder. "I am nice to him," he protested, knowing the words were a lie.

"You flinch like a kicked puppy whenever he looks
your direction," Darcy chided. "He's trying to be kind in
the only ways he knows how."

"I know. But he's been kind all morning. Over and over
again." Nic had thought, after the last half-dozen spurts of
conversation, that Ianno Piratimare would be returning to
his work. As it was, the sounds of hundreds of hammers

against wood in every single one of Caza Piratimare's dry docks made it nearly impossible to talk. With all the repairs and rebuilding of the city's warships left to be done, Nic thought the man would have a better occupation than hovering. Now he was painfully aware that the cazarro had spun around at the bottom of the nearest ramp and was returning. "Oh, gods," he muttered, trying to force a friendly smile onto his lips.

"You, stop." Darcy had stored aboard the *Allyria* a trunkful of breeches and boys' shirts for later, though for the moment she wore one of her prettiest gowns. The breeches were more practical at sea, Nic had to concede, but he preferred her as she was now. Radiant, golden, and gleaming—much like the remarkable galleon behind them. "Cazarro," Darcy murmured as she gathered her skirt and curtseyed.

"Cazarro," said Nic for what felt like the dozenth time that morning. He bowed yet again.

"No, no, no need for such formalities among—yes. Well." Ianno Piratimare colored. "One more thing occurred to me..."

"If it's about the crew you've so generously provided, Cazarro, my first mate has already learned their names. They'll be well-taken care of," Nic assured him. From fear of what the man might have to say, Nic always felt compelled to take control of every conversation they had.

The cazarro blinked, as if that had been the furthest thing from his mind. "Oh. Naturally. Yes. Your... Maxl is a good man. A very good sailor. A shame he's so... blue. Yes. Well. And naturally, it will be an honor for them all, learning the workings of the marvelous craft my forefathers built. Yet what I wanted to say…"

Nic coughed. "And of course, the provisions you have provided will see us through quite handsomely."

Ianno Piratimare bit his lips, interrupted again. "I can't claim credit for all of that, my boy. All the merchants of Cassaforte want to be able to say the *Allyria* set sail with their donations aboard. No, what I've been meaning to tell you all morning, though I haven't really found the courage…"

Even at the height of the battle of the Azurite armada, Nic's heart had never pounded harder than it did whenever the cazarro of Piratimare seemed about to make some kind of confession. His heart in his throat, Nic stammered out, "You…you really have been too good to so common a fellow as I, signor. I can only thank you again, and hope that I am not intruding upon your pressing duties."

The cazarro, taken aback, looked up at the seagulls shrieking loudly in the sky. After a moment, he lowered his head again. Nic could have sworn that his eyes were swimming with tears, though it might have been from the sun. "Niccolo Dattore…" Ianno might have allowed Nic some leeway thus far, but he was one of the Seven. As such, he was no stranger to administering discipline, and it was in a stern voice that he continued. "You will hear me out on this matter. All I have wanted to tell you is that if ever in your life's journey you find yourself without a place to rest—if you have nowhere to go of your own, that is—well. You are always welcome at this caza, for as long as any Piratimare lives here. There it is, then. It's said."

"That is most handsome of you, Cazarro," said Nic. "Most handsome indeed." He was aware that his voice sounded choked. He sniffled, and immediately colored. "There's much sawdust in the air, this morning. I think it's making me a bit sneezy," he said, trying to sound casual about it.

"Yes," agreed Ianno. He seemed to be feeling the effects of the sawdust as well, and drew a handkerchief from his pocket so that he could blow into it. Once they both were composed again, he smiled. "Farewell, young man," he said, kissing the tips of his crossed fingers and raising them to the heavens. He then shook Nic's hand, and pressed his lips to the back of Darcy's knuckles. "I pray you both a swift and safe journey."

"We're only going to Orsina," laughed Darcy. "Not the ends of the world."

As if on cue, the members of Armand Arturo's Theatre of Marvels began parading down the ramp. Quite a spectacle they made as they approached, followed by a donkey-cart carrying their many trunks and set pieces. A number of the workers transporting armfuls of wood and other supplies to the building sites stopped to gawk at the carnival-like display of color and costume. "Why, a gracious good morning to you, Cazarro!" Armand Arturo, in a new liripipe hat of bright red and the deepest of purples, bowed so low that it appeared his forehead might scrape the wood beneath his feet. From somewhere he had appropriated a cape embroidered with gold and silver threads that made him look like royalty, and an ivory-handled cane. When both the cape and the liripipe's tail slid over the back of his head, he jumped upright and wrestled wildly to escape.

In fact, all the troupe had appeared to have gone on a shopping spree. Knave also sported a new cape, though it was far shorter and not as engulfing as the Signor's. His tights were of an eye-popping orange, and his shoes bore buckles of pure silver. Pulcinella's normally colorful gown had been exchanged for one of a diamond pattern in so many hues that it seemed as if she'd been eaten by a lacy patchwork quilt. Ingenue was dressed in the purest white, but her necklace flaunted a large pale blue jewel that matched the one pinned into her coiffed hair. Infant Prodigy seemed determined to wring out another two years of early adolescence before she turned thirty, and had found a dress so frilly and babyish that any normal girl would have scorned to wear such a juvenile thing.

The Signora, however, outshone them all. Her gown had so extreme and stiff a farthingale that her waist appeared to be mere inches wide, while her skirts and bust had expanded to larger proportions than ever before. Her hair had been curled and dyed a dark red. Rings glittered on every finger, and a large opal sat in the middle of her forehead. And from somewhere she had acquired two tiny twin dogs, which she clutched against her bosom. "Cazarro!" she trilled, stooping a bit in lieu of a curtsey. Then, in the same thrilling alto, she added, "Darling Signorina Colombo! Niccolo! Or should I say, Captain Niccolo?"

"Signora." Nic gasped slightly as he found his former mistress embracing him, smothering him with perfume and hair and puppies. "I see you've packed for the occasion. Had to hire people to carry all your new trunks, did you?"

Nic nodded at the men and women straggling behind, who grappled with the troupe's luggage. The Signora allowed Nic to breathe again. "Not at all!" she exclaimed, smiling at all and sundry. "They're our new actors."

Armand Arturo made the necessary introductions. "This is our new Vecchio," he said, throwing his arm around a young man gone prematurely gray. "And we have a Braggart! Think of the scenes I can write! And these two will be our Scholar and our Columbine. Every troupe could use a saucy servant character, eh?" he asked with a wink at the latter girl, which immediately he pretended was a mote in his eye for fear of being seen by his wife. Confidentially, he added, "We've added eight new players in the last week. We're the troupe to be seen, now. Most of them defected from Filippo Fianucci's Cavalcade of Comedy."

"I told you that Filippo swine would rue the day he called me a third-rate actress," said the Signora, not without some satisfaction.

"And you're still Hero, signor?" asked Nic, grinning.

The actor seemed sheepish. "Well. I still have a year or two left in me, lad. And naturally, the audiences in Orsina want to see Armand Arturo in the role that made him famous, don't they?"

"We may not have made our original engagement due to pirates and sieges and such," said the Signora, kissing both her puppies in turn, "but after all that, we're practically famous! They're itching for our international tour," she told the cazarro.

"Hurry now! Be coming!" called Maxl from the bottom of the gangplank, where he'd just planted his big boots. Now that he'd had a few good meals in him, he looked less skeletal and more handsome than ever. His blue face beamed as he regarded the troupe. "You!" he cried, pointing to Braggart. "You are looking strong. You are sent to be my new deck boy, yes? Swabbing all day? We tie rope to your waist and dunk you in sea, upside down, to catch fish for suppers. Yes?"

"Me?" squawked Braggart, appearing suddenly to regret having defected from the Cavalcade of Comedy.

"Yes, you, actor-boy. No, I am making the joke. You would make shark bait and be eaten in two bites. Hah! Hah!" Maxl paused as Ingenue reached his side.

"Hello, Maxl," she murmured, her eyelashes fluttering demurely. "It's good to see you again."

Now that she was substantially cleaner and dressed in finery, it was difficult for Maxl to ignore Ingenue's charms any longer. He gulped, then used his hands to smooth his hair and his long ponytail. "*Oola*, miss," he murmured.

"Suave," Nic pronounced, slapping him on the shoulder. Maxl looked affronted and made a face. "Very suave, my man. Have the crew help the Arturos with their things, would you? We've a port to make by week's end."

It only took a whistle for Maxl to summon some of the men and women Caza Piratimare had supplied. They swarmed down the gangplank and immediately began to tackle the Arturos' belongings. Ingenue stuck like horse glue to Maxl's side as he pitched in with the crew, until at last they were up and aboard the *Allyria*.

"Don't be long, Niccolo," cooed the Signora. "Armand has been working on my five-act drama about Zanna the Huntress and I want to run a few ideas past you. You've a head for these things. Cazarro." She tottered, turned, and dipped once more before Ianno Piratimare, who lingered. Nic had almost forgotten he was still there.

"Fantastical woman," said the cazarro, shaking his head as he watched her attempt to navigate her wide skirts up the gangplank. "You seem to have a talent, Niccolo, of surrounding yourself with the most improbable individuals."

If there had been one thing Nic could not have predicted the cazarro might say, it would have been that. He snorted. "It used to be a curse," he said. "But in the end, it might have turned out to be a blessing."

"Don't misunderstand me. They're all very nice people. Very engaging. But … odd."

To the cazarro, Darcy said, "Fret not. I'm neither nice nor engaging, signor. I count myself the lucky exception."

As Ianno began to splutter, gallantly ready to contradict her, Nic found himself agreeing. "No, she's not exactly nice. Bit of a temper."

Darcy screwed up her face and nodded. "I still haven't shown you how to throw a proper tantrum, have I?"

"And she has a little problem with that violent streak." Nic gazed at Darcy with fondness and reached for her hand.

"And the bonking on the head," she agreed, entwining her fingers in his. "Always with the bonking on the head."

Ianno Piratimare's eyes darted from one to the other, uncertain if they were teasing. "Yes. Well. I'll let you be on your way, Captain." He paused and thought to himself for a moment, then bowed. "A good voyage to you both."

Perhaps it was kindness that moved him, or perhaps it was purely the spirit of the moment, but on impulse, Nic reached out and grasped the cazarro in both arms. While Ianno seemed unable to decide what to do, Nic clutched the man tightly for a moment, and then thumped him between the shoulder blades. "Many thanks again for your generosity, cazarro," he said at last, releasing him. He took Darcy's hand once again. "I'll see you when I return."

The cazarro stumbled away, a happy man.

"Thank you," Darcy said, once they'd set foot on the Allyria. Below, several Piratimare workers danced up to remove the gangplank.

"For what?" asked Nic.

"For being nice to him."

"Ah." Nic nodded. "You were right. It didn't cost me anything."

"No, it didn't." Darcy watched as the workers shielded their eyes against the sun and waved at them. She waved back with her free hand. "You know, he told me the youngest of his six daughters ran away some years ago."

"Darcy." Nic yanked at her hand. "Enough."

"I'm just saying that he has a lot of fatherly affection he wasn't able to bestow! It's natural that he treats you like the son he never had." Nic shook his head, unwilling to speak on the subject. They stood by the rails and listened to the racket of the hammers, saying nothing for a few moments. "Are you going to miss it?"

"Miss what?" asked Nic, though he knew what she meant.

"Cassaforte. All of this. You just got home."

"I don't really have a home," Nic said. "I love this city, but I've had so many masters ..."

"And now you're your own." Darcy seemed to understand. "I barely know Cassaforte," she admitted. "And I can't go back to Pays d'Azur. I suppose I've no real home, myself."

Nic regarded her shining face and said exactly what was on his mind. "Then let this be our home," he said, gesturing to indicate the *Allyria*. "And here," he said, bringing their knit fingers up to their faces. He kissed her hand. "Wherever we can do this, together. That will be our home, too."

That morning, her hair was so golden it outshone the medallion Nic wore on his chest. Her eyes were bluer than any ocean. When she smiled, it was as if the gods had lit him his own personal sun, burning brightly over a private island they alone shared. "Yes," she breathed. "I'd like that very much, Captain."

From behind them, Nic heard someone clearing his throat. It was Armand Arturo, lingering on deck. "I hate to interrupt," he said, coughing awkwardly.

"You aren't." Nic let go of Darcy's hand. She winked at him and skipped off to change into her more comfortable boy's clothing. "I promise you, you aren't."

358

"Ah good." The actor watched Darcy depart, a knowing look in his eyes. "Lad, I have one question before we set sail," he said in a soft voice. He studied Nic carefully, as if it were particularly tricky in nature. "Niccolo. Son. You *will* get us to Orsina this time, won't you? No pirates? No shipwrecks? No skullduggery?"

So nervous did his old master sound that Nic couldn't help but chuckle. "That I will, signor," he assured him. "No harm will come to you under my command. You'll have the audiences eating out of your hands by week's end."

"Good lad. I'm glad. And I believe you. Thank you for saying so." Armand seemed relieved as he strode in the direction of the hatch. His step gained a little spring. He even whistled a bit before turning. "Of course, if something perchance did happen, not that I wish it would, of course..." The actor shrugged. "I'm certain it would be interesting."

Nic's chuckles turned to laughter. "I wager it would. Maxl!" he cried, excited to be off on his own. "Hoist anchor! We're off to Orsina!" The *Allyria's* bell rang, and its new crew began to assemble on deck.

"It would be most interesting, indeed." The actor laid a finger aside his nose and smiled to himself as he tossed the crook of his cane onto his wrist. "To say the least, lad. To say the least!"

About the Author

V. Briceland wanted to be an archaeologist when he grew up. Instead, he has worked as a soda jerk, a paper-flower maker in an amusement park, a pianist for a senior citizens' show-tunes choir, an English teacher, and a glass artist. He likes writing novels best of all. He lives in Royal Oak, Michigan, where there is a sad lack of ruins to be excavated. Visit his website at www.vbriceland.com.